ROBERT ADAMS

ALTERNATIVES

with
Pamela Crippen Adams

D0123686

BAEN
FANTASY

ALTERNATIVES

Copyright © 1989 by Robert Adams & Pamela Crippen Adams

A Baen Books Original

Baen Publishing Enterprises
260 Fifth Avenue
New York, N.Y. 10001

First printing, May 1989

ISBN: 0-671-69818-4

Cover art by Ken Kelly

Distributed by
SIMON & SCHUSTER
1230 Avenue of the Americas
New York, N.Y. 10020

Printed in the United States of America

CONTENTS

THE GOODWIFE OF ORLEANS

A tale of the time of
Henry the Great

Roland J. Green

Prologue

In the chateau of Vincennes, outside Paris, Henry V, King of England and heir to the throne of France, lay in a sleep that feigned death.

Or perhaps no longer feigned it. Two hours ago the doctors had said he could not hope to live above two hours. Likely enough, the King's soul was struggling free of his wasted body, or perhaps had already taken wing.

King Henry knew where he was, and it was neither Heaven nor Hell, neither France nor England. It was on a barren hillside under a hotter sun than either land ever knew, with a walled city upon another hill in the distance.

The city was under siege, with great bombards raising clouds of white smoke when they fired and clouds of dust when their stones struck the walls. Banners flew from the walls. Though they were too far to make out clearly, with a vision that was not of his mortal eyes the King knew they were the banners of the Mohammedans who held the Holy Land.

Now other banners passed before the King, close enough to make out even had he been waking. The storming parties were going forward, knights and soldiers and siege craftsmen all mingled, with a diversity of armor and weapons that passed belief.

Yet there were longbows in good number following those banners, the longbow that had won at Crecy, Poitiers, Agincourt, Orleans, and a score of

3

lesser battles. The longbow that had won back France for its rightful heirs, the Kings of England.

The banners streamed in the hot wind, easy to read. Many were Burgundian, others from lands under the Holy Roman Emperor. Still others told of cities and realms in Italy, Spain, and even such distant lands as those ruled by the King of the Swedes. It almost passed belief, but the King would have sworn that a few banners bore the misshapen cross of the Greeks of Constantinople!

Foremost among all the banners was one quartering lilies and leopards. These were the most ragged of all the banners, but behind them followed the greater part of the longbows.

As if flung forward by magic, the host closed with the walls. Christian and Mohammedan grappled in the breaches, and their false prophet gave the Mohammedans desperate courage.

That courage was not enough. The Christian banners vanished into the breaches, then rose on the walls. Cheers thundered, as loud as if the host was standing around the King and not miles off.

Now a man hard upon thirty stood before him, small of stature but not ill-made, with heavy features ending in the Valois nose the King knew so well. He wore armor with more plate—more cunningly-shaped plate—than the King remembered ever seeing, and had a dignity that made it seem he was the King and Henry his petitioner.

For the first time, the King knew himself to be speaking.

"See your kingdom, Louis of Valois. Your father gave me France. I give you Jerusalem."

"God gave both gifts," the man addressed as Louis of Valois replied. "I will pray for the wisdom to use His gift as well as you have."

The King wanted to speak again, but he could not form words on his lips or even in his mind. He felt himself as a fly in amber, trapped for eternity in a place that was neither Heaven nor Hell nor even Limbo.

He could not put his prayer into words, but somehow he understood what he was praying:

Lord, I have sinned. I have cast down where I must build, if I am to fulfill my vow, to build again the walls of Jerusalem.

"Grant me the wisdom to build."

King Henry heard these last words not only in his mind but in his ears. He felt rather than heard movement around him. Did others hear also?

Perhaps he would know, after he had slept.

Bertrand Duvant, Baron of Belmain in Herefordshire:

I doubt that anyone at Vincennes had done other than resign himself to King Henry's death. Even those who thought doctors were more wind than wisdom could not doubt the words of comrades who had seen too many dying of wounds or sickness.

So when the doctors and attendants came running out as if the chamber was on fire, crying that the King was alive and speaking—if the Archangel Michael himself had brought word, most would have doubted for a little while.

I doubted too, but I also had the wit to find a way into the chamber. With my own eyes I saw the King sitting up, taking a cup of some broth that looked like piss but past all doubt *alive* and in his right senses.

I came out of the chamber even faster than I went in and began contriving the means for a ride to Paris. I knew who should be told at once that King Henry lived, and I doubted that anyone else had thought of it save perhaps the King himself—and he had not put the thought into words.

The first step of the journey was to find Tom of Ramsford, the captain of my household. After that I could leave the rest to him, knowing that he would work as well as he would have for his father. Agincourt men are like that; we go gladly to Heaven or Hell alike for each other. I was a page and Tom was a full-fledged archer the day we won France, but we were both *there*.

Tom put everything in order as he usually did, except for my armor.

"Begging your pardon, my lord, but I've put everything but one helm and your tournament harness in the hands of the armorers. Otherwise in your next fight you'll be bare as a tavern trull."

"We can't have that. But I can't ride Grand Jeu to Paris in a hundred pounds of harness."

"I wasn't thinking of any such thing. I've the lads out and about for a jack that'll fit you."

"Wager you a cup of wine that it'll be next Michaelmas before they find one."

"Make it ale, if you can find any in Paris that's fit for a Christian to drink."

"Done."

Tom won the ale, I may say. He found a Burgundian crossbowman who was my size or nearly enough, and brought his jack to me. With a Milanese helm on my pate and a good horse under me and a good man with his bow beside me, I'd be well-enough provided against robbers.

"Please God these Frenchies never learn the longbow," Tom said as we crossed the courtyard to the gate. "Or that we're better friends with them than we are now when they do."

"Pray for the second, if you're going to pray," I told Tom. I hadn't had to wait until Michaelmas for the jack, but I'd waited long enough to hear a half-score men repeat and ponder the King's words. He might not have been in his right senses, but I thought then and I think now that God's wisdom came to him in what had been his death-sleep, and with that wisdom came the desire to live.

Henry of Monmouth had a way of grasping what he wanted and not letting it loose, whether it was a kingdom, a wife, or life itself.

Tom shot me an inquiring look as we mounted, but after that the road and the dark kept him quiet. It was only a middling road even dry by daylight, and now it was dark and the rain had left hock-deep mud.

We still made good enough time to reach Paris well ahead of the messenger someone finally thought to send. I told the guards at the Vincennes Gate that

I had word for Queen Katherine's ears only, and two of them recognized me and let me pass. With that beginning, I went on so swiftly that the mud on my boots was still wet when they brought me to the Queen's chamber.

Queen Katherine was small of stature, but very fair to look upon save for the Valois nose. She had somewhat marred her looks by weeping, which a saint could hardly have avoided at a time like this.

"My lord of Belmain, is it?"

"Yes, Your Grace."

"I remember you from that fair joust against the Burgundian—his name I forget."

She swallowed, and I understood she would be content to talk politely for some time, to put off the moment of learning that she was a widow.

Since that moment had not come (and never did), I saw no cause to delay.

"Your Grace, I come to tell you that the King has rallied. Against all the odds, he is alive. I have heard him speak sensible words and seen him take broth."

She quivered like a plucked bowstring and closed her eyes for a moment. "Will this— Is he spared?"

"The doctors fear to say one way or another."

"They said this?"

"Your Grace, do you expect a doctor to admit ignorance?" That made her smile, and it was a smile most pleasant to see. I wished King Henry to have the same pleasure once more.

"No. If they had such courage, my father—" The smile froze for a moment, at the thought of her wretched, mad father, Charles VI of France.

It was time to finish as boldly as I had begun, riding off without leave to bear word.

"Surely he will live long enough for you to come to his side. After that—it is in God's hands, but your presence may help God."

"I have not been summoned all these days of his sickness," she said fiercely. "Is he of another mind now?"

"It was never his command that you not be summoned," I said. *No one can call pleasing both King*

and Queen treason, and it may even be the truth.
"Those around him were waiting for his command, and it never came. I think he was not altogether in his right senses for somewhat longer than we believed."

"If I could hope that this was true—"

"Your Grace, you can do more than hope. If you will gather up suitable ladies, I have a good company of men less than an hour behind me. By the time you are ready to travel, they will be ready to guard you."

It was then that Katherine of France knelt on the floor, weeping like a child and thanking God at the same time. It might have seemed that she was kneeling at my feet, but I knew otherwise. Her heart and eyes alike were so full she knew not what she did.

Her ladies ran in, greatly alarmed. I think they were in more fear of me at first than I was of the French knights at Agincourt. Then I told them the news, and *they* started weeping and praying, at about the moment when Her Grace rallied and stood close enough to me to whisper.

"What did my lord husband say, if it was not a summons to me?"

I repeated the King's words, and now the Queen looked a trifle bemused. "He spoke of a Louis of Valois?"

"So it seemed to those who heard."

"My brother is dead."

"This seemed to be the son of your brother Charles."

"My brother Charles has no son named Louis or anything else!" Now her eyes had a spark in them. It struck me that when her King and lord was fit, he would hear something in plain French about his not summoning her to Vincennes.

"Perhaps it was only a part of his dream of taking Jerusalem. That has been much on his mind, I know."

"As do I," she said, then colored. I knelt, and she gave me leave to go. As I left, she was ordering her ladies to the work of preparing for the journey, as sharply as a captain with a band of fledgling archers.

Thomas of Ramsford, in Herefordshire:

Lord Belmain says a bit about the Queen and her ladies crying. When he came out of her chambers, I'd say his eyes weren't quite dry neither.

It was a right good thing he came out when he did. The real messenger was there by then. He must've run straight to the Queen's chambers, too. He didn't run fast enough though. The news was all over everywhere by the time he came.

He was some lord or other, I forget who but I think a Frenchie. He looked right unhappy when he heard the news was there afore him.

Then he looked even unhappier when he saw Lord Belmain sort of standing over him. He wasn't a little man, but most regular-sized men looked little when Lord Belmain stood by them.

"What's this?" was all he could ask.

"The Queen's Grace is preparing to travel to Vincennes, to greet her King and lord. I wished her to be prepared to depart as soon as my men arrived."

"Your—men?"

He sounded like a great big frog, who's just seen the spit being sharpened to roast him.

"Of course! Do you think I ride around the country by night with no one save a single archer for company?"

I pretty near spoiled Lord Belmain's act by laughing out loud. That made the messenger's men look at me. I looked back at them. So did Lord Belmain. Between us, I'd wager we'd been in more fights than all of them put together.

That's the way they wagered, too. So we didn't have to do anything like draw swords in the Queen's chambers. Queen Katherine, God rest her soul, might have been none too happy over that.

We stood kind of close to the door for a bit, until the Queen sent somebody to the stables for horses. The somebody came back with one of our people, who must have reckoned they'd best hurry if the messenger wasn't to snatch the hog's share of any glory going 'round.

That was our luck and I told our man so and Lord Belmain did the same. If our man hadn't come when he did, the messenger might have had some idea about calling us liars for saying the Queen should go to Vincennes. A right nasty mess, that would have been.

Now we had fifty men and the messenger had about ten, and that kind of settled matters. All we had to do was wait for the Queen to get dressed, and only God and maybe not even Him can hurry a woman along in that.

Once I'd posted our men, Lord Belmain took me aside and told me what the King had said. I listened, but I reckon I must have shown I didn't quite believe it. I reckon, too, that I must have said the first thing that came to my head.

"My lord. If the Frenchies think the King's really promising a Valois in Jerusalem—they might give up. Then who's there left to fight?"

"Wasn't that ransom from Agincourt enough, Tom?"

"You know I sold it before we got to Calais!" (That's what happened to most of the ransoms from Agincourt. We archers didn't kill nearly so many of the Frenchie prisoners as they say. We just sold them to some lord for things we needed right then and there, like shoes or bread or some herbs against the flux.)

"Better luck next time. There will be a next time, too. Even if we do go crusading, the Turks won't give up without a fight. They carry fine swords and build houses filled with beautiful women. They can have three or four wives, you know."

I didn't, but I was right curious, so Lord Belmain told me some more about the Turks. He hadn't read near as many books as he had later, after we went to Italy, but he seemed to know more'n a lot of priests or clerks.

Then he lowered his voice and said, "The Turks can wait. All the French won't give up, and then there's the Emperor. We may even have to hunt down a few Burgundians, and you know they wear cloth-of-gold under their armor!"

He was guying me and I said so, which he took like a man instead of a lord. But he'd made me wonder about who we'd be fighting next. By the time we and the Queen were riding back to Vincennes, I'd reckoned to stay in the wars a few more years. Twenty-six wasn't old enough to go back and never see anything except where one furrow ended and the next one began.

I

From *Battlefield and Council Chamber: The Life
of Bertrand Duvant, Duke of Chartres, Marshal of
England, Marshal of France, Baron Belmain* (Bruges:
Maison de Clio, 1987):

—wintered in Germany. No records exist of what
the Baron and his entourage did in Nuremburg and
Augsburg, except entertain extensively and purchase
new armor.

It has been suggested that the mission to Germany
was a pretext for taking leave of Cardinal Beaufort's
household in Rome. It is certain that the Baron's
distaste for the Cardinal's greed and intrigues was of
early origin. It is therefore possible that the Baron
wished to avoid a personal conflict that would have
embarrassed the Crown and in particular the Baron's
patron, the Duke of Bedford.

It is equally certain that the Baron was even at this
early date entrusted with diplomatic missions of a
highly confidential nature, for which no written records were allowed to exist. Since the free cities of
the Empire were a significant factor in the balance of
power among the Double Monarchy, the Duchy of
Burgundy, and the Empire, Nuremburg and Augsburg
would have been logical places for the Baron to have
more in hand than the purchasing of new armor and
the hiring of armorers.

On May 21, 1429, the Baron and his entourage
were approaching the borders of the Duchy of Lorraine . . .

Bertrand Duvant:

Making an early start, we reached the Meuse before the sun was well up. Our ford led us on to a low-lying island, which I judged to be used by the nearby towns and villages as a common pasturage for their cattle. The remains of rough shelters showed that it had also once been a refuge for the folk themselves in time of war, but it was good to see that the shelters were tumbling down.

We were halfway across the island when we startled a flock of sheep into movement. They scurried off every which way, bleating and bumping into trees and one another like the silly creatures they were.

The shepherdess stood her ground. She was a country lass, not yet twenty to look at her, dark and sturdy. Her gown was plain and much patched but clean, and her staff was dark and shiny with long use.

Indeed, there was nothing to set her apart from a thousand other village girls tending the flocks, save the way she stood and stared at us as we rode up. It had been some years since the French countryfolk fled the *goddamns* as if we were the devil's own spawn, but no young girl wisely mistakes any band of soldiers for God's angels.

Yet this was what she seemed to think of us. She stood as though God's hand was over her, to keep every man of us from so much as a carnal thought about her. As I reined in, I could not remember ever seeing such peace and joy on a living face.

I commanded the rest of the men to remain and rode forward, me and Tom of Ramsford alone. Seen closer, I put aside the idea that the girl was mazed in her wits. She was now looking me up and down with as much care as any tavern wench weighing a man's purse and prowess, yet there was nothing brazen in her regard.

At last she spoke. She had a light, very clear voice, with a deep Lorrainer accent but nothing that made her hard to understand.

"You are the giant *goddamn* I saw."

Now, the fact that I am well above the common

stature has followed me since I was ten years old. I do not complain overmuch, since I would not have survived Agincourt otherwise. The worst of it is having to spend most of my ransoms on horses fit to carry my weight.

"I am no giant, and I should like to know where you saw me before."

"God sent Holy Saint Michael and Blessed Saint Catherine to show you to me, as he sent them to show the danger you are in."

If she had said that before I saw her from close at hand, I would have dismissed her without further thought as an addlepate. I am sure that the men behind were wondering if I was addled, spending so much time talking to a country girl.

That was one reason I took Tom with me. He would keep his tongue between his teeth. By now he had also seen the girl from close at hand, and I saw that he understood the same as I.

"What danger? We are strong enough to fight off any bandits, and the river is not running high."

"Beyond the ford, in the woods, the danger waits."

"Damn you, girl, what danger?"

"God does not love cursing, but it is His will to protect you or I would not have seen you."

"Well, I do not love riddles. What kind of danger? Or we ride on, and may you and your—visions take much joy of each other."

I would have said something much more like a soldier, save that with those wide gray eyes fixed on me my tongue would not shape such words. It would have seemed like pissing before an altar.

The girl heard my change of words and smiled. Then she described a band of mounted crossbowmen with a few men-at-arms, waiting beyond the ford. She described this cunning trap as clearly as if she had seen such things every day of her life.

Or as if she had been set out here, to lure us into a real trap by warning of one that did not exist.

I said as much to Tom, and he nodded, then added, "We'd best learn if she's got a true tongue or not. It won't do, for the folk hereabouts to think they can play tricks on us just 'cause there's some words down on parchment sayin' peace."

"Indeed. Pick six more men to come with you and me. We'll see about crossing upstream of the ford on a raft. Eight is enough to spring any traps."

"If there be none?"

"We send the girl back to her family with a message, to birch such pranks out of her."

By this time some of the other men had ridden close enough to hear. One of them, Owain ap Hugh, grunted like a boar disturbed at feeding.

"I know a better cure for her than that. Give her to me for an hour."

Owain was the best archer of the troop after Tom, and also a great man for the women.

The girl stared at Owain, and I saw what I had never expected to see—Owain dropping his gaze before a woman. Then she shook her head sadly.

"You should not speak thus, good soldier. Not when you are so close to death."

Owain laughed so hard that he nearly fell out of his saddle. I felt no more wish to laugh than I had to curse, and Tom seemed to share my thoughts.

"Unpack the axes and start cutting trees for a raft," I commanded. "Anyone who has not broken his fast can do so while the raft is building. Girl—and what is your name, by the way?"

"Jehanne, my lord. Daughter to Jacques D'Arc, of Domremy."

That was the next village downstream of the ford. So she might well know the countryside as well as what she said hinted.

"Well, Jehanne, can you make us a fire? If you do, you can share what we have, little though it may be."

She made a graceful courtesy.

"Gladly, my lord. I did not think God would have commanded me to warn an evil man."

I was glad that most of the men were too busy dismounting and unpacking to watch my face.

Thomas of Ramsford:

It didn't take long to build the raft or sweat it into
the water. By then I'd picked the other six men. One
of them was Owain, and if he hadn't come of his own
will I'd have knocked him on the head.

I wasn't going to leave him on the same island
with Joan D'Arc, not with his ways. He might just
reckon that nobody much would care what happened
to a girl who didn't have all her wits about her. He'd
have been wrong, but that wouldn't have healed
Joan.

So maybe it's me that's to blame for what happened to Owain. We were on the raft, crossing to
the far bank of the Meuse, when Owain tumbled
over the side. He couldn't swim a stroke, and besides he hit his head on a floating log as he went in.
So he went straight down without a gurgle or a
bubble, and Joan turned out to be right about him.
Except that I don't reckon he saw God, who surely
hadn't told Joan about the half of Owain's sins—

But that's neither here nor there, as my Mam
would always say when I came in late with some long
tale about why I couldn't have come sooner. What's
more to the point, is that Joan was telling the plain
truth about the men waiting for us. If she hadn't told
us, Owain would have had a deal of company, that
day on the Lorraine border.

They were about thirty, so we didn't have anything to fear once we knew they were there. But in
his longheaded way, Lord Belmain got the notion of
taking prisoners.

"I should have suspected it from Jehanne's description," he said. "These men are too well-armed
and garbed to be common bandits. Somebody set
them here for a purpose, and no one but Jehanne
warned us."

"Reckon the Domremy folk are with them?"

"Either that, or they've put the folk in such fear
that no one dares tell us except Jehanne, who seems
to fear nothing except God."

Lord Belmain was always a one for seeing the best

in the Frenchies, even then. I won't say that time
didn't prove him right, but it was a bit of a trial back
then. "So we want prisoners, right, m'lord?"

"Do the French drink wine, Tom? We'll have to
send someone back to bring the others along. Then
we can turn these louts' own trap against them. With
luck, we'll have a good bag."

Something about Lord Belmain that I didn't mind,
he always saw a fight as just a bigger and better hunt
against more dangerous game. He didn't hate hardly
anybody he fought against, not even the Turks, unless they were treacherous or stupid enough to spoil
his sport.

Red Jack of Worcester was our best swimmer, so
he went back. We had plenty of time to find good
places for ourselves, before we heard a whistle at the
ford. That meant the others were across the river.

Lord Belmain guessed right about where the others would move, to hit our lads. We were twelve
archers ready to shoot, and we had such beautiful
shooting as I never dreamed of at a fair. We had half
of them down before the rest of our lads even put in
their spurs.

By the time they came up, we were in among
them, and knew they were Burgundians. Now, back
then they were supposed to be our friends, but it's a
damned unfriendly thing to lie in wait for a man and
we told them so with our swords and knives and
clubs. Lord Belmain had a mace, and if you don't
believe that a mace can spatter a man's brains even
through his helmet you never saw his lordship swinging one.

After a bit they couldn't be calling for quarter fast
enough. It wasn't the easiest thing to get the rest of
the lads to give it, because they knew they'd have
been dead meat without Jehanne's warning.

It helped that she came along, riding double with
Cornish Will, then got down and started praying
over the dying. That stopped most of the killing, and
Lord Belmain's orders stopped the rest. His voice
was as big as the rest of him, and they must have

heard him halfway to the Rhine. He also still had his mace, and nobody wanted to argue with that.

Finally we had all six live Burgundians trussed up like fowl for the pot, and Lord Belmain and I were sort of looking at each other. I reckon we were both thinking the same thing:

Here's a fine lot of people who haven't any right to be where we found them, doing what they were planning to do. We need to learn why they're here— and then tell somebody big enough to tell us what to do about it.

Jehanne of Domremy, daughter of Jacques D'Arc and Isabelle Romee, of Domremy:

When I came to the place where the Burgundians and the English had been fighting, the battle was over. Many of the Burgundians were dead. The Burgundian captives and some of the English were hurt.

I dismounted from Cornish Will's horse and went to the wounded of both sides. I heard their prayers and held their hands, as I might have done for my brothers if they needed it, which thank God and His Saints they never have. When the English needed help with the dressing of wounds or the splinting of broken limbs, I was also there to be a second pair of hands.

I heard some of the *goddamns* wondering aloud why I helped both sides. I knew that some of them were in fear of me, because of what happened to Owain the Archer.

I could not have done otherwise than I did, even had they threatened me with their swords. Since I first knew what pain was, I could not stand to see any live creature suffering, even a frog or a snake. That I would have told them, if they had asked me.

More than that, I do not know if I would have said. My voices were from God, and God had not made it His business to calm the fears of every band of English soldiers, even when he had set me about the business of warning them.

I do not know how long it was before there were
no more men in need of help. I went a little aside
from the battlefield and sat down upon a fallen tree.
I rested my hands on my knees and my chin on my
hands, and I think I closed my eyes and even slept
for a moment.

I awoke to find Thomas of Ramsford standing over
me. He was looking at me with curiosity, not with
desire, although he seemed a man who took much
joy in life. I thought that even then, but it also
seemed that he did not give himself over to the
Devil's temptations of loose women and drink. Certainly the English had no camp women with them,
which was another reason I was pleased to have
saved them.

"Hullo, Joanie," he said. He spoke fair French,
although he made a dreadful stew of my name.

"Godspeed, Thomas. Are you hurt?"

"No. Well, just a scrape or two. I've had worse
cutting wood. I thought you might be needing some
of this."

He gave me a skin of wine, and when he saw I was
uneasy with it, gave me water to wash it down. I
gave both back and felt as if I could sleep again, for I
was very weary.

"You did good work, both for us and for the
Burgundians."

"The Burgundians are God's children too. At least
they are when they stay where God put them and do
not trouble the peace He sent between France and
England, when He spoke to King Henry."

I saw that this surprised him and did not altogether
please him. But as before, I could not see my way to
speaking of my visions. I also knew that Guillaume
Fort, our priest in Domremy, would tell the English
as much or more than they wished to know about
everything I had done or said for many years.

"Loving the Burgundians is something I'll leave
to God. Right now, I just hope your work's kept
some of them alive long enough for the question.
I'm mightily curious what they're doing waylaying

English soldiers in Lorraine, or anywhere else for that matter."

He seemed to expect an answer to that, and when none came I could see he was disappointed, even angry. I did not fear his anger, for I saw that it was like that of my father or brothers, when I did something as my visions had bidden me. They did not understand, and they feared that I had confused my own will and God's, so that I would run into danger.

I knew as well as I knew that I was virgin as long as God willed it, that my counsel came from God. Nothing that came from God could put my soul in danger, and I did not fear for my body.

After a time Thomas rose and said farewell. After another, longer time Cornish Will rode up on his old bay mare, and asked me to mount. I did so, and we rode for Domremy.

II

Bertrand Duvant:

Long as the day was, the evening shadows still stretched far before us when we rode into Domremy. I had no wish to harm our wounded or kill off our Burgundian prisoners before their time. I also thought it prudent to send a small band of our best archers and woodsmen along each stretch of road before we entered it.

They found nothing and neither heard nor saw much that might have been a lurking enemy. It seemed that all the Burgundians in this part of the country had been in that one band.

Nor would this have been unwise, if we had not been warned. Striking without warning, thirty-odd men could have slain or taken the half of us at least. The seasoned men of our band knew that well, and they were not in charity with those who muttered about "being saved by a witch."

"Would you rather be picking quarrels out of your lights?" Cornish Will said to one such. "Me, I don't think the Devil's got it in him, to make virgins do his bidding. Leastways, that's what the priests always told me."

I noticed that Cornish Will hardly minded having Jehanne's arms around his waist, for all that he truly named her virgin. I had no fear of that, however, for Will was not Owain. A girl like Jehanne, with chastity written large upon her, was almost as safe with Will as she would have been in a convent. Safer, considering what had happened to some convents in the course of the war, and that few nuns are as deft with the quarterstaff as Will. (Few folk in all Creation, if the truth be known.)

So we rode into Domremy. It was good to see the people out in the streets, going about their affairs, instead of shuttering their houses and driving their flocks into the woods. Either they had no part in the matter of the Burgundians, or their part was hidden so deep they had no fear it would be discovered. As long as they kept the peace, I would be content with either.

I still took care to flourish our silver in plain sight. A few-score *livres tournoises* will buy a good deal of peace and rather more food for men and mounts. Even the English shilling was beginning to soothe the palms of Frenchmen.

I rode straight to Jacques D'Arc's house and found that he was in Vaucouleurs doing business for himself and others of the village. Jehanne's brother Pierre greeted me. He was rather what his sister might have been had she been a trifle taller, smaller in the bosom, and garbed like a man. I saw at once that he had been in fear for her.

"Your sister has taken no hurt," I said. "Indeed, she has done good work today. She saw a band of robbers that she feared might make off with her flocks. Instead of running, she stood her ground and warned us. With your sister's warning and God's help, we made an end of the robbers.

"At least I think we made an end to them. We are putting some of them to the question tonight, to learn if there are more and if so, where."

I could see on his face doubts about how much of this to believe. I decided against offering money until I had spoken with the village priest and Jacques D'Arc. If Pierre D'Arc doubted his sister's chastity, he was a fool, but I learned early in life that the world holds more fools than even the Devil could have contrived.

It was well after sunset before I sat down with the priest, Guillaume Fort. Tom had done his usual fine work finding proper quarters and food for men and horses alike. I rode out a mile in every direction from Domremy, learning the way the land ran and where the Burgundians' friends might lie in wait.

I found the overgrown ruins of a castle that must have been built under Charlemagne and abandoned about the time of Richard Coeur de Lion. I also twice saw men who seemed not to want to be noticed, but they were far off and made no hostile gestures.

I still thought it prudent to ride well-accompanied, and to return to Domremy before dark. When I did, my belly was reminding me that I had mounted without breaking my fast and been crossing the Meuse about dinnertime.

So it was very late when I called on Guillaume Fort, late enough that he was not only impatient but weary. I apologized for the weariness, but not for the impatience. Like many village priests, he thought himself of rather more consequence than he was.

Over watered wine, he asked how long my men would be staying in Domremy. I said, as long as needed to run these bandits thoroughly to earth. He asked, how long that would be. I said, God only knew, but it might help if I learned more of Jacques D'Arc's daughter Jehanne.

"I can tell you nothing of her, that you would not care to learn of your own sister."

"Cannot, or will not?"

Father Guillaume flushed. "I can only tell the truth."

"Even when it might mean danger for some in your parish?" He had the courage to glare. "No, hear me out, Father.

"I ask nothing told you under the seal of the confessional. By God, Saint George, and Saint Denis, I swear this." I silently prayed to the same that I would not be foresworn.

"But this concerns very nearly the peace of the Realm of France. There is danger to it, and to the village of Domremy, and all I learn from you will go to fend off this danger."

"Do you swear that also?"

I swore formidable oaths, until he seemed persuaded. Indeed, he finally laughed.

"You would have long since had Jehanne calling you to a halt. No one who has known her long dares swear in her presence, not even old soldiers. Her tongue is as chaste as the rest of her."

"Has she a vocation?"

"She has visited the hermitage at Notre Dame de Bermont to ask that same question. All the answer she says she had, was that God intended her to aid the Realm of France by keeping the peace between France and England."

"Well, she did good work in that cause today."

I told of what had happened, leaving out only that the enemy were Burgundians and Jehanne's voices.

Father Guillaume noticed both omissions. "Are these simple robbers, who sought the lives of sixty English soldiers?"

Oaths and prudence both suggested telling at least some of the truth. Father Guillaume might be no scholar, but he seemed to have a countryman's shrewdness.

"They seem to be Burgundians, in Burgundian pay, or at least disguised as Burgundians. Which, we hope to learn tonight."

A scream echoed through the streets. The learning was beginning. I hoped it would not take long, for the sake of everyone including the fool being questioned.

"I see. And—did Jehanne say that God had spoken to her, showing her the—Burgundians?"

"Yes."

"That makes—six times—since her first—dream."

"When was that?"

Father Guillaume told me, at greater length than I would have dared ask. Late as it was, he was a man fond of the sound of his own voice, but I was happy to listen.

Much of what he told me has long since passed from my memory. One thing has not. Jehanne had first heard her "voices" the very day that King Henry rallied in his chamber in Vincennes. Only God—or the Devil—could have sent knowledge of what happened near Paris all the way to Lorraine so swiftly.

If she was a virgin, the Devil could not be working through her. That left only God and His Saints—and I say truly, that even so I was not altogether happy at being in debt to such as Jehanne.

She might balk at much of what would have to be done, before the Burgundians and their friends were rooted out of their last burrow. If she spoke against us, I feared that the men and the villagers alike would give ear.

However, there was also much to which no one with their wits about them would object, and Jehanne certainly was that. (Nor was she alone, in my experience. I wonder if God sharpened the wits of the French countryfolk as he took away the wits of better-born Frenchmen.)

The first thing would be done tonight: to write a letter.

The second thing would be done in the morning: to send it to Vaucouleurs, there to be put in the hands of a messenger riding for Paris. God willing, in five days the matter would be in the hands of the Duke of Bedford, and better hands than that for such matters God never made.

My thoughts turned to finding parchment. My mouth was open to ask the priest for some, when another scream echoed through the streets of Domremy.

This one was beyond doubt a woman's scream. It came from the direction of the church, and shouts followed hard upon it. Then I heard the clatter of weapons and more shouts.

I closed my mouth and drew my sword.

"Father Guillaume, I think the robbers are in your church. Would you come with me? Some may need your presence before this is over."

Father Guillaume was pale, but he was also but one pace behind me as we hurried out the door.

Thomas of Ramsford:

It was God's own good fortune I didn't go with
Lord Belmain to the priest's. Otherwise I'd have
been drinking bad wine (never met a priest yet who
kept good wine) and listening to a lot of talk 'bout
Joanie, telling me things I learned for myself from
her.

As for Joanie—but that's me, getting ahead of things
again. Old soldiers don't have to tell every story
sideways.

I was tired, but I didn't want to sleep yet. I ate a
bite or two of real old mutton, washed it down with a
cup of fair wine, and listened to the lads chatter.
Some of them were wagering on how soon Lord
Belmain would try to buy Joanie from her father to
warm his bed.

I don't say he wouldn't have been doing that, with
another kind of girl. He'd have paid a good price and
treated her decent, too, and sent her back home
with a fine fat dowry. Lord Belmain was fond enough
of the women, and it says a lot for that little Welsh
spitfire who got to be his Duchess that after he wed
her he never shared any bed but hers.

I made the rounds, to see that all the lads who
were supposed to watch were watching and sober
enough to know what they saw. I also had an eye
out, to see that no one was with any woman who
didn't want to be where she was. (We're Harry's
soldiers, and not being God, he couldn't make us
into monks. But we do try not to send all the decent
women running for the hills.)

I forget just how I came to be there, but I ended
up in sight of the D'Arc house. It wasn't much, but I
remembered how it looked, and there was something by the back door that hadn't been there. I got a
little closer, and there was enough moonlight to show
it was somebody in a smock and boots, with a big hat
that pretty much hid his head.

Now, I wasn't surprised to see one of the villagers
out and about when they might be up to no good. It
surprised me to see one of Joanie's kin there, and it

hurt, too. Like the beginning of a toothache, that you just know's going to be fierce in a few days.

Anyway, I followed the man down the street to the church, and saw him go in. That didn't surprise me either. Half the Frenchies' plots have a priest in them somewhere. If we tried to load all of the ones we've caught in a single ship, we'd need one bigger'n the *Royal Henry*, and she carried eight hundred folk back from Jerusalem.

The man was heading for a right good surprise, I thought, because his priest was hosting Lord Belmain. I decided I'd better go on in and keep watch, in case the man had friends. Lord Belmain was good as any three men, but a stab in the back can do for the best.

The church had just a couple of good candles for the altar and otherwise a rush taper here and there. I saw the man go right down to kneel in front of the altar, without taking off his hat.

That bothered me. Either the man was really scared of being recognized, or it wasn't a man at all. I've known a good few women to dress up as men for one reason or another. Some of them were reasons for being here tonight.

I didn't have much time to waste guessing. Right to the left of the altar were two pillars set close together. I saw something moving between them, out into the open, toward the man.

I reckoned the man's friends were coming out of hiding, like rats.

Then I saw a knife in the "friend's" hand, all raised to strike.

Maybe I made a sound. Maybe the killer made a sound. Or maybe God had something to do with it. Anyways, the man jumped up and turned so fast his hat fell off. Long dark hair fell down, and I recognized the face.

"Joanie!"

That was when she screamed—the one time I ever heard her scream.

Jehanne D'Arc:

I was listening for God, when I heard footsteps
behind me. They did not frighten me, until I heard a
voice I knew.

"Whore!"

Both the word and the voice put me in fear. I
jumped up, so that my hat fell off. I turned to see
the man I expected. Gerard de Sionne had married
Hauviette Delay, a gossip of mine since we were no
more than twelve.

In was then that I screamed, for it seemed that
Gerard could not be doing this unless God had turned
away from me. That did put me very much in fear.

I know that Thomas of Ramsford shouted about
then, but I did not hear him. For a short space of
time, I could hear only the voice of my fear.

Then Thomas leaped upon Gerard and they grappled together upon the floor, rolling backward and
forward. They shouted and cursed and sought each
other's lives with steel and with their bare hands.
They were so intent upon each other that they did
not see a second man step out from between the
pillars.

I did not scream this time, because I was no
longer in fear for myself. If God had abandoned me,
nothing I did or left undone would make any difference to me. If God was still with me, I would know
in His good time, my soul was safe, and my body was
at His service.

Either way, I could not abandon Thomas. The
second man was drawing a sword. I gripped my staff
and stepped forward. I truly do not know whether it
was me who made him hesitate, or fear of striking a
friend.

Certainly he hesitated long enough for the church
door to open and Lord Belmain to enter. His guards
were with him, some three or four, and our priest
Guillaume Fort after them.

The second man struck at me. He was unskilled
with his sword, or else God guided my hands in
raising the staff. The sword struck the wood, cutting

into it, but bouncing so that the swordtip cut my head on the left side.

Then I flung myself to the ground, because I saw the lord's guards raising their bows. I knew that they would wish to shoot with no fear of hitting friends. They did this, and the second man fell, pierced by three arrows.

The men on the floor rolled over so close to me that I knew I could grasp Gerard's foot. I did not know what God wanted of me, but I knew what I owed Thomas.

I fell upon Gerard's feet. He kicked fiercely, striking me in the breast so that I felt a sharp pain. He did not kick himself free, and Thomas fell upon him and beat his head upon the floor until Gerard was senseless.

I lay upon the floor as if I had swooned, because I feared I would swoon if I stood up. I heard Lord Belmain speak sharply.

"Surround the church, turn out all our men, and let none of the village folk leave their houses until I give them leave."

"I am sure—" Father Guillaume began.

"I am sure of nothing, save that anyone outside their house until I give them leave may be taken for a—robber."

"It shall be as you wish."

"It had damned well better be, by the splendor of God!"

Father Guillaume coughed. "And what of—Gerard and his—friend?"

"A poor friend, to spin webs to catch one who might have been honest if he had not been tempted. Like the serpent in Eden, he is gone to his master the Devil.

"As for Gerard, he will answer some questions, willingly or not. I want healing for him. If anyone in this plaguey village knows a well man from a hurt one, bring them. Otherwise my men will do their best, and you can watch to see we do him no more harm."

I learned afterward that Lord Belmain must have

been greatly angered, to speak so harshly of Domremy. It was his custom to show more honor to all among the French, which was one of the many ways in which he served peace and France.

"I am here," I said. "There is no need to wake anyone."

Lord Belmain smiled at me, as though I were not less than a merchant's wife.

"If anyone's still asleep after this brawl, they may need burying rather than healing. You're in no state to help others, Jehanne. Tom, I leave her to you."

"Well, my lord—" he said, looking down at Gerard.

"Tom, do you think even that witling's head is harder than a stone floor? Or do you think he is some champion of a romance, able to best five men barehanded?"

"Well, my lord, putting it that way—"

"I do. I also put Jehanne in your care. See that she has all she needs, including a return to her father's house."

I had no fear that Thomas needed any such warning. Indeed, I had almost more fear of my father than of a man's lust. Gerard de Sionne's father had been a boyhood friend of mine, and my father would not thank me for my part in bringing Gerard to his death.

I was able to stand unaided, but when I put a hand to my head it came away bloody. Thomas took my hand gently, as he would have held a newborn puppy.

"Come, Joanie. I'll have to be trimming your hair to get at the bleeding, but I'm not so bad a barber. Then it's home and to bed with you, if your father and I have to lock you in your room!"

"My father—" Old doubts and new silenced me.

"Joanie," he said softly. The guards were picking up Gerard and the dead man, and the others had withdrawn a little distance. We might have been alone.

"Thomas, I came here to pray. To pray to know, what I should say of those in Domremy who might be—who may think they are saving France when they are really fighting the peace God sent."

He put his arms around me even more gently than he had held my hand. He seemed to fear that I would weep, but that was far from my thoughts. I felt empty of tears and much else.

"Well, Joanie. Maybe you got yourself an answer. Maybe it was God sending me around tonight, to see you and follow you here. I know I don't look much like an angel, and I surely don't feel much like one, but who knows?"

I shivered, but not from cold or fear. When he denied that he was an angel, his voice was so like St. Michael's that I had to look to see that it was only an English captain of archers in travel-soiled leather.

He went on holding me, until the shivering passed. He had healing hands, Thomas did, and I hoped that it was God's will that I be healed.

For now, I saw no harm in being alive to pray for the knowledge I lacked.

III

Bertrand Duvant:

The folk of Domremy kept the peace that night, after the brawl in their church. This most assuredly both pleased and surprised me.

I could not be sure that our enemies both within the town and without it were not biding their time, seeking a better moment to strike. I could be sure that their best moment would be that night, before my men could make use of any free gifts of time.

We were beyond the village at dawn, Jehanne astride one of the baggage mules. With Thomas and most of the men, I repaired to that ruined castle and set about putting it into a fit state for defense. The walls were half-crumbled, but the keep still had a roof and the well held water fit to drink. There was enough and to spare of timber for making a palisade fit to stand against anything save artillery.

Of that, we could be sure our foes had none. What else they might have or lack, only they and God knew. So I sent my message to His Grace of Bedford well-escorted, with twenty men under Cornish Will, and also Gerard de Sionne and the other prisoners, straitly bound. At Vaucouleurs would be royal messengers, ready to ride, and also the Sieur Robert de Baudricourt, who held the right of high justice under both the King of France and the Duke of Lorraine.

To which one he would give ear if they sent different advice, I knew not. I did expect that he would hold the prisoners safe and close, so that they would neither flee nor perish in a way that could rouse the country against us.

I was certain that my men could do all that sixty-four Englishmen could do, but sixty-four of God's angels led by Saint Michael himself would have lively work against a countryside in arms.

Will and his men were back on the evening of the second day. By then one could tell the gate from the walls of our stronghold. With half again as many hands and no few fresh tools Will had "found" (he told me) on the way, the work went forward swiftly.

It was as well this was so. Our stronghold served us for ten days, and twice saved our mounts from "robbers." Once at least they were truly robbers, with no aim but a few quick and easy *livres tournoises*. Instead, they found a quick and easy road to their master the Devil, once I was satisfied they knew nothing of any "Burgundians."

The second time, when it may well have been the Burgundians, we had warning from Domremy itself. Actually from the nearby village of Greux, but a trustworthy man nonetheless, a farmer named Jean Colin.

I asked Jehanne to look at him privily before I spoke to him, and had the answer I had expected:

"Do you wish that I denounce him? For before God and by Saint Michael and all the other saints in glory, I will do no such thing unless I am commanded by God."

I wasted no time being angry with her, although I confess I would have been hard put to do the same over such an admonition from the Pope himself.

"I will not command what God does not allow, Jehanne. I also will not forgive being taken for a fool. I only wish to know if he is indeed the farmer Jean Colin as he says he is, and if he has the repute of being a trustworthy man."

She peered through an arrow slit and nodded. "That is truly Jean Colin," and she described his family and how she had helped him with his stock at greater length than I care to set down here. She concluded, "I know him to be a good Christian and honest in all that I have seen him do."

Which was about as much as I could in reason expect from the girl, so I went down to speak to Jean Colin well-enough satisfied.

Thomas of Ramsford:

This Jean Colin was a sturdy fellow of twenty-five or thereabouts, who'd had Joanie helping with his stock a good many times. Not just when they had to be driven to someplace they hoped would be safe, but day in day out.

He also didn't seem much in fear of his lordship, which would have been his bad luck with some other lords. With Belmain, being a baron and everything else he got to be was part of him, much like his hair.

"I come to warn you of talk in the village, my lord," he said.

"Talk can't harm a sparrow, let alone armed Englishmen," Lord Belmain said.

"Burgundians can, if they strike when you are foraging," Colin replied. He grinned. "Or at least the men some of us think ought to be called Burgundians."

"I suppose you won't tell me who those men are?"

"Maybe a time will come when you can know who we are."

"And God will send an angel to tell you when that time is?"

I swear to God, Colin looked at Lord Belmain like his lordship had been caught lifting a sheep.

"Jehanne's voices are not a jesting matter for some of us, my lord."

Then he had the decency to look a mite frightened, as if he'd finally said too much. "Forgive me, my lord," he kind of stammered. "I didn't mean—"

"You mean well toward us and I suppose toward Jehanne. I'll forgive more than a frank tongue if that's so."

"Thank you, my lord. I've brought—a message— for Jehanne—and more for your men."

More men than Jean Colin must have had a hand in bringing what came into the stronghold a bit later. There was a sucking pig and five goats and a barrel of fair wine and another of really good cider. Except for Jean, all the men kept sacks or scarves around their faces. I wondered if they thought we had Burgundian spies in our ranks, or some such foolishness.

Oh yes. Jean gave his lordship a couple of bundles for Joanie, and his lordship handed them over to me to give to her. One was from her father, the other from her brother Pierre.

The one from her father was gowns and shifts and shoes and suchlike, all women's stuff. She held it up to make sure that it all fitted, then put it down.

"God has commanded me to remain virgin as long as this serves Him. How can this be, one woman among soldiers? Yet I was certainly allowed to ride away with you, as though my soul would be in danger in the village."

I saw she was after thinking of God's abandoning her again, and I didn't want to see her hurting from that. I also didn't know what to say that would help her. Saying I'd protect her would be fine with some other woman, but Joanie wasn't some other woman. She was—what she was.

"Well, if you need men's clothes, there's some of the lads as have a spare shirt or two." Then I didn't exactly hear voices, but I did make a shrewder guess than I usually did off the battlefield. "Open that parcel from your brother, before you fret yourself."

She did, and it was a couple of changes of men's clothing from the skin out. She looked at them like they might be a chest of gold, then went down on her knees. I turned away, because I didn't think I ought to look at her face when it was like that.

I stayed turned away until she stopped thanking God for her brother's wisdom and asking Him to protect Pierre. Then I turned back, and nearly tripped over the clothes she'd had on.

She'd stripped them off right then and there and was pulling on the new ones. When I saw her, she didn't have a stitch on above the waist and not a whole lot below. It didn't seem to make any difference to her, either.

I looked at her breasts, which were a fine fair sight, I won't deny. Then I understood why she wouldn't have fretted herself about being seen bare as Eve before she listened to the snake. I just didn't feel what a man feels when he sees a fine woman mostly bare.

It didn't worry me, either. I somehow knew that with any other woman, I'd feel what a man ought to and do what a man could if the woman was willing. Joanie was a little apart from other women, and even wondering if she might be willing seemed not quite right.

I still thought I owed her a warning.

"I hope you're not planning on doing this every time your clothes get too dirty."

She poked a bare toe into what she'd taken off. "No, only when they have a life of their own. I'd ask that these be washed, but they might bedevil the water. The campfire is the only place for them."

I reckoned that the stink might drive us all out of the gates into the hands of the Burgundians, but promised to do as she asked. As I went out, she'd pulled a little brass mirror from her father's pack and was working the snarls out of her hair. Even when she dressed as a man, she didn't like to look like she'd spent the last fortnight lying in a ditch.

Jehanne D'Arc:

I was ashamed of my mistake before Thomas of Ramsford. Not at being seen unclothed, for I knew God would not let him make any mistake about this. He would know that I was only eager for clean clothes, and that I trusted him.

But it was not something to be proud of, to put such an honorable man where God had to protect me from him. It seemed to me, that for asking too much of Him God might leave me without His protection for either my body or my soul.

Then I would be in great peril indeed. So when I had garbed myself in seemly fashion, I prayed to know if God's favor was still with me. I also prayed that if I was at the mercy of men, I might find someone such as Thomas of Ramsford. For him, mercy was more than a word.

IV

Bertrand Duvant:

How much trouble Jean Colin's warning saved us, only God knows. (Perhaps the Devil, if some of those we sent to their Master told him.) Certainly we made our foraging parties as strong and well-armed as we could. We also furnished them with good coin, to pay for as much as we could of what was needed.

That was less than I had dared hope. From Greux and Domremy and other villages along the Meuse, we had as much as they could spare, perhaps more, certainly all we needed and a trifle left over in case of a siege. I was certain that the fine harvest of the year before and several years' peace had much to do with this generosity. I was equally certain that if the "Burgundians" really had the hearts of the countryside, we would have had little or nothing.

At first I had some fear of poisoned wine, but Jehanne offered to drink some from each new barrel.

"In battle, I am the least useful among you," she said. "So my death will do less harm to the peace God has commanded for France and England then the death of any other here."

I nearly choked on a bit of mutton then, not because it was poisoned but because of what I was hearing. This country girl was offering to throw herself into the breach to spare seasoned fighting men danger!

As did most who heard Jehanne, I thought: *If God were to place that girl at the head of an army, the army would sweep all before it.*

I also thanked God and the Saints (especially Saints Michael, Margaret, and Catherine) that Jehanne saw the Double Monarchy as the wellspring of peace for France. If she had seen the *goddamns* as a scourge to be cast out of her land—to this day I thank God and those same saints that I never had to fight such a battle!

As the days passed, we were somewhat disquieted that no message came from Vaucouleurs. When the time reached ten days, I was preparing to send another message to de Baudricourt. I was also preparing to take it myself, trusting that Tom, Will, Jehanne, and such goodwill as we had in the country were enough protection for our stronghold.

We were actually packing for the sortie on the eleventh evening when I heard the sentry hail riders at the gate. I did not hear the reply, but I did hear the stamping and neighing of a good twoscore horses. Whoever had come, they were in some strength.

I reached the gate as the captain outside raised an angry shout. I peered through the twilight at the man's shield, saw the arms of Orleans with the bend sinister upon them, and knew who had come.

"Jean! Jean the Bastard! What brings you here?"

"Bertrand, *compère!* I bring much that you may find useful, when we have had a chance to unload it. I hear that you have wine enough to be hospitable?"

"We do," I said, and summoned the gatekeepers to open. Whatever Jean had brought or left at home, he was here, and of few men could it be so truly said that he was "a host in himself."

I had a lighter heart as I ordered my squire to prepare to greet the Bastard of Orleans.

Thomas of Ramsford:

The Sieur Jean and Lord Belmain were pretty far into the wine before they thought to invite me. I didn't mind. Two men who'd faced each other in battle three or four times—they'd have a lot to say that wasn't for anyone else's ears. When you add that it was Lord Belmain who'd unhorsed and captured the Bastard at Orleans, then refused more'n a token ransom—well, God send me someone to be that close to me, is all I can say.

Come to think on it, He did, but that's getting ahead of my story.

I had enough wine, because the Bastard had brought forty, fifty men, and they were kind enough to make it worth my while to find them dry corners and firewood. They even had a little gun with them, and a gunner who called himself Dietrich of Antwerp, which I'm sure as I stand here wasn't his baptized name but no matter, he knew his art.

A little more time, I took up telling those lads who didn't know about the Bastard, why his coming was good news for us and bad news for anybody we were going to fight.

He was the bastard son of Louis of Orleans, the one who was Queen Isabeau's lover and got himself killed for it in 1408. That made him half-brother to Charles of Orleans, the present duke. He'd been a soldier almost from when he could pull on armor and fought us hard until the peace. After that he must have reckoned that King Harry and the *goddamns* were in France to stay, and it were better if they had some Frenchies around that they had to listen to.

Also, I reckon he believed in King Harry's promise about the Crusade, and was too good a soldier to want to miss out on that. He put his money on the right dog; he never saw Jerusalem but nobody did more to open the way there.

There you go again, Tom, running ahead of your tale.

After I'd settled everybody in as best I could, I didn't have long to wait before Lord Belmain called me up. He and the Bastard had their feet propped up on a chest and a jug of wine on the chest itself.

"Jean, meet Thomas of Ramsford. He is next to me among the English. If we both fall, your men can do no better than to follow him."

Dunois put his feet on the floor and pushed the jug toward me. "If Bertrand says you know war, I'll take his word."

I thought I ought to bow; he was cousin to the Valois, even if the lefthanded kind.

"I'm grateful. Not that I'm going to be saying much if you both fall, except maybe 'Every man for himself,' and rally at the Domremy church.' But it won't hurt if I'm obeyed."

"I doubt it very much," Lord Belmain said. "Tom's been in about as many battles as the two of us put together. But let's see what we can do to make sure we can toast victory with the rest of this wine."

"I brought only one barrel, Bertrand. Sorry, but I was in some haste. Orders from His Grace of Bedford are best obeyed before his messenger leaves you!"

"Tell me what I do not know, such as how deep our friend de Baudricourt is, in his intrigues with the Burgundians."

What with the wine and old battles, I reckon they'd forgot that I'd just come in and this was like being tossed out the schoolroom window into a snowdrift. Lord Belmain raised his cup and let the Bastard tell me.

It seemed that the heart of the plot was the Royal Governor in Vaucouleurs, the Sieur Robert de Baudricourt. The Burgundians were really sent by Philip, but de Baudricourt had armed and mounted them after they came into France. His idea was for them to make enough of a rumpus so that he could call out his men from Vaucouleurs, maybe with royal help. Then he'd turn his coat and raise the country for Philip the Good.

"His Grace of Burgundy is being less openhanded than usual, I'd judge," Lord Belmain said. "If de Baudricourt fails, there's no harm done. He's been paid little and he can always be disowned.

"If he sets the country alight, on the other hand, half of Philip's work will be done for him. What little remains to be done, he may hope the Emperor or the Duke of Lorraine will do."

"But I thought the Duke of Lorraine had sworn to King Henry both as friend and vassal!" I muttered.

"The Lorrainer's sworn so much to so many that I doubt anyone save God knows what he'll do," the

Bastard said. "I'll wager my best mount that he doesn't."

All of which made me glad that God didn't make me a nobleman, who had to worry about that sort of thing even between fights. Where I spent my wars, a friend was somebody who wasn't shooting or hacking at you and an enemy was somebody who did.

All of which also made me a little thoughtful about what we were going to do about de Baudricourt and the Burgundians. I began to think maybe that what the Frenchies call a *Sauve qui peut* (which means in English, "Save yourself if you can") was a mite closer than I wanted it.

I was pretty sure of it when Dunois and Lord Belmain started talking about what we were going to do. It seemed they had the idea of just marching right up to the Burgundians' stronghold and cleaning it out. That, they reckoned, should tempt de Baudricourt to come out into the open to help his friends.

Now, don't mistake me. I don't say they were the kind of nobles the Frenchies had at Agincourt, who couldn't think of anything but going straight at the enemy and trust to God. Both Lord Belmain and the Bastard would have given the Devil a good chance at their souls for another way.

Trouble was, there wasn't any other way. Leastways, I couldn't see one, and I allow that I wasn't much if any wiser in war than either of them. So I didn't fuss. I just wanted to know the odds, not being that Frenchie paladin, Roland or whoever, who thought worrying about the odds was cowardly.

"We won't be facing more than a hundred men in their stronghold," the Bastard said. "The gun's big enough to knock in any gate they can have built. De Baudricourt can lead at most three hundred men out of Vaucouleurs. If he can bring half of them through the forest to his friends' help, it'll be a miracle bigger than Agincourt."

That still meant two to one odds, but Englishmen and picked Frenchies were either of them worth twice their weight in Burgundians and traitors. A fair fight didn't worry me.

Although one thing did—

"My lord Bastard, you're sure of all this? I don't reckon we have much to spare for surprises."

"His Grace of Bedford had a few suspicions of his own and told me where to look," the Bastard said. "Also, we kept our ears open when we were on the trail of Gerard de Sionne—"

"What?" I shouted. "That bloody—"

"De Baudricourt says he 'escaped,'" the Bastard said. "I'd not wager a half-cup of English beer that de Sionne's still above ground. But we had to pretend to believe de Baudricourt, and it turned out as well that we did. Some of his men talked a trifle freely, with a little help from the wine—that's why I only have one barrel left—"

"Jean, you always did tell a tale arse-end foremost," Lord Belmain growled. He held up his empty cup. "I suppose if I'd held you to a proper ransom, I wouldn't have even this much."

"Very surely," the Bastard said. "You'd have spent it all, and then had to borrow from the Jews to pay me back when the English foreswore their ransoms under the peace treaty."

What Lord Belmain said, I didn't hear. I was bowing my way out, to see about putting the lads to rights, any of them who needed it.

Talking to Joanie too. She didn't need any putting to rights, not her. What I prayed as I went downstairs was that she'd have the sense to stay behind, even if it wasn't Saint Michael telling her!

Jehanne D'Arc:

I could see that Thomas bore a burden on his soul from the moment he entered the chamber. So could the other English present. They almost ran from the chamber.

"Joanie," he said, more harshly than I had ever heard him speak in battle. "We're riding out pretty soon, to fight the Burgundians and any who come to help them."

"God grant that we strike a great blow for—"

"Joanie, that 'we.' You thinking after going?"

"Thomas, that is the first time I have ever heard you speak foolishly. I have been called to the same work as you do. How could I hold back?"

"Joanie, did God ever show you what happens on a battlefield? Or what happens to the women when they can't run?"

"The peace came too late for a good score of folk I knew," I said. It seemed that not only would he speak foolishly, he would take me for a fool. This brought both anger and grief, as I had thought better of him.

"There was fighting enough in Lorraine and Champagne," I added. "I learned the wisdom of wearing men's clothing, driving cattle to safety."

"Pity you didn't learn the wisdom of staying out of danger you don't have to face!"

"This is not such a danger. God did not show me how to do otherwise than ride with you. If He does, I will gladly don a skirt and wave farewell, then pray that I may wave a greeting."

That surprised Thomas. He seemed to think I spoke of him alone. He had not thought to have such regard from me.

In truth, I wished to see all those who rode out to fight for God's peace returning. I also knew that I must be among them.

"Thomas," I said, "you cannot take me back to my father's house. Not if you fear I have enemies in Domremy. They would seek to strike down both my father and me.

"If I remain alone in the stronghold, the enemies will surely come. Then you will lose me, whatever that may mean to you, and your stronghold as well.

"The safest place for me is with you."

Thomas looked about him at the walls of the chamber, as if they could give the answer that his wits could not find. I prayed that God would give him a wise head to match his good heart.

My prayer was answered, although after so long that I heard men in the courtyard shouting for Thomas. It was also long enough for me to think of boxing his ears. God had commanded me not to shed blood, but I did not know His wish in the matter of bringing sense to witlings.

"Joanie, I don't ever want to fight an army with you leading it. If you'd led at Agincourt, it might be Duke Charles who's calling himself King of England and not our Harry of Monmouth King of France."

The last of my anger blew away like smoke. "Thank you, Thomas."

"You won't have much to thank me for if I don't find you a helmet and some armor. Do you want to send a letter to your father?"

"Thomas, I know not A from B."

"I didn't reckon you did. I can read a mite and put down my name. I'll ask around among the Bastard's men. There's bound to be some kind of scholar with them."

He held both my hands as he would have held his sister's, then departed. I knelt, then rose again. I had prayed for so much and been granted so much of what I prayed for that any more seemed beyond reason.

I knew that I rode to the peril of my body, but if I rode at God's command, my soul was safe. More than that, I think no man or woman can ask.

V

Bertrand Duvant:

We rode out from the stronghold before cockcrow. I trusted the folk of Domremy to warn us of any plots they knew of. I did not trust them to learn of every skulking foeman.

Beyond the forest around the stronghold, we kept to the roads for greater haste. Dunois rode with the vanward battle, I rode with the rearward. About the time we heard the bells sounding matins, I spurred forward, leaving Tom Ramsford to ride in my place. I had the notion of a few words with the Bastard, and of giving Tom a chance for a few with Jehanne.

Whether he said them and what they were, I do not know. I know I have not yet forgot what the Bastard said.

"Good day and Godspeed, *compère*. All is well with your men?"

I almost said, "They are of the breed of Agincourt and Orleans," but there were within hearing Frenchmen not so easy with those memories as the Bastard. Instead I nodded.

"Good. We wager our lives and theirs. The game is worth the stakes, though. Or so I pray."

I had the reputation of a longheaded man, but in truth Jean the Bastard of Orleans was always a thought or several ahead of me.

"I will pray the same, but might I ask why?"

"Consider. What His Grace of Burgundy hopes to gain by this cannot be casting the English out of

France. He has not staked enough to be hoping for
such a prize.

"But if he finds that he can trouble the peace of
both realms for pennies—pennies to his bulging cof-
fers, at least . . ."

"He may send more and more such Burgundians,
to wear down his 'friends' like dogs worrying a bear."
At least I had the wits to follow where Jean led.

He nodded, his sharp features seeming to grow
sharper. "He can pay for more such disturbances
than either realm can endure. France is exhausted
by being conquered, England hardly less so by con-
quering. In a battle of the purses, Burgundy is a
match for both realms together."

"We are not challenging the Burgundians and their
hirelings to such a contest," I said. "We are going to
grapple them before they can draw their purses!"

The Bastard laughed. "Indeed. If the day is ours,
it will tell Philip that England and France can join
hands against his tricks. It will also tell him that even
our small bands can strike down twice their number
of his hirelings."

The not altogether knightly thought came to me,
to ask what it would tell Philip if we lost. I set that
aside swiftly and with an easy mind. I did not wish to
even think myself less bold than Jehanne.

Also, the truth of the matter was that I did not fear
our suffering any defeat that would encourage His
Grace of Burgundy. We might be overwhelmed by
numbers, but such a "victory" would leave de
Baudricourt a proven traitor with only a handful of
men at his command. The work we had begun, the
Duke of Bedford or one sent by him would finish.

The knowledge that we rode to the traitors' deaths,
whether or not we rode to our own, lifted my spirits.
They rose further when Jehanne began to sing—some
ditty from her childhood, but one that caught the
men's ears.

She sang one song after another until we were well
into the hills.

Thomas of Ramsford:

When we got into the hills, Joanie stopped singing. I thought she was tired, so I dropped back and
offered her some wine.

She only rinsed her mouth out with it, then spit it
out and drank water. When she had wiped her mouth,
she shook her head.

"I am weary, but elsewhere I could go on singing.
Here in the woods—I feel apart from God."

"I thought you knew these woods, Joanie."

"I have seldom gone beyond the fairy tree."

"The what?"

"A huge oak, not far from the village. The girls
would go there on the saints' days, to dance and
hang wreaths."

I don't mind admitting I was glad, hearing about
the saints. The thought that Joanie might have been
up to some serious witcheries wasn't a good one to
take into battle.

She was right about the woods, too. They were
thick and dark and pretty near uninhabited, except
for woodcutters' huts with maybe enough land cleared
around them for a kitchen garden.

We camped by one of those huts the first night.
Some of the lads stood guard to make sure the wood-
cutter didn't go off and wag his tongue at people he
shouldn't.

We could have gone straight on to where the
Bastard said the Burgundians had camped, because
it wasn't that far. Neither he nor Belmain had any
such notion, though. They reckoned the Burgundians
had time to set deadfalls and suchlike around their
camp, easier to spy out by day than by night.

I also reckoned that Lord Belmain had something
else on his mind, maybe something he hadn't even
spoke of to the Bastard. If we came up by day and
found the camp weakly guarded, we could try rush-
ing it by what the Frenchies call a *coup de main*.

I wouldn't have wagered the two shortest hairs on
Joanie's head for our doing that, but Lord Belmain
was always one for doing things faster than the next

man. He always said that if the enemy had to worry
'bout what you were going to do to him instead of
the other way 'round, it was as good as having a
hundred more longbows on your side.

Well, we barely had a hundred men altogether,
and only sixty of them longbowmen. I hoped His
Lordship was right, and put out about twice the
sentries I would have usually. We'd seen aplenty of
signs that the trails hereabouts had been used recently, and by shod horses and booted men.

We spent a cold night, because His Lordship didn't
want any fires, but we had food and water. I offered
Joanie a share of my cloak, but she wrapped herself
up in her own and slept a little ways apart. I reckon
she wasn't offended, and I know I wasn't. I did reach
out and touch her hair a couple times, just to be sure
she was really there.

We also spent a quiet night, which is to say that
nobody attacked us. Off in the woods, we heard
enough noise to be sure we were on the right road to
the enemy's camp, or at least to somebody's.

We kept things quiet in the morning, just snatch-
ing a mouthful of bread and cheese, those of us who
had any appetite at all. Joanie didn't take wine,
again, but she did polish off a good piece of bread
with cheese toasted on it, which is more appetite
than I could pretend on the mornings of my first
three battles. (I won't say much about Agincourt,
where I had the flux so bad I didn't dare think about
food!)

The sun was just above the treetops when we got
sight of the enemy's camp. That was later than you
might think, because the trees were up on hills and
both trees and hills grew pretty tall around there.
But I reckoned and so did Lord Belmain, that we
had a fair chance of finishing matters today.

With that thought, we drew up just outside bow-
shot of the camp and put Master Dietrich to work
setting up his gun.

Jehanne D'Arc:

I had eased the men about having me among them with my songs. This eased me also. I could again be as certain as anyone could be, that I was about God's work and in His hands.

I dismounted to spare my horse, but did not disarm save for taking off my helmet. I was not going to be storming the Burgundian stronghold, I knew. I had small skill in arms, and my voices had bade me not to shed blood.

I had also heard Thomas and others wise in war wondering aloud if our foes were all in the stronghold. There might be fighting elsewhere than upon its walls.

Also, my voices had said nothing about this first battle being my last. If it was not, I would do well to learn to bear the weight of armor. By God's mercy, I was strong and well-knit, as fit to do this as a good part of the men.

I tethered my horse and walked to where Master Dietrich was at work upon his gun. It was a small one, in two pieces, each carried slung between two stout mules. Other mules carried the gunpowder and so many tools that one might have thought a smith was setting up a forge in the woods.

As I approached, I saw where the gun would lie. A heavy log was being shaped with an adze, to bear the gun. I also saw that Master Dietrich had not chosen the place well.

"My lord gunner," I called.

"No lord, but a busy man," Dietrich replied. He was as large, although not so well-made, as Lord Belmain. "But for you, I can find time."

"God will reward you, Master Dietrich." I pointed at the weeds around the log. "Here, those mean wet ground. Will your gun do as well on wet ground as on dry?"

Master Dietrich looked at me, then at his apprentices. I think it was their not meeting his eyes that made him suspicious. He walked over to the log, picked up a stick, and thrust it deep into the ground.

Thrice it sank in deeply. Now his look at his apprentices was fierce. They almost fell over one another, moving the log.

"My thanks, Jehanne," Master Dietrich said. "If you were a man, I'd take you on as an apprentice. Although I'd wager I'd have to fight Tom Ramsford for you!"

"God made me a woman, Master Dietrich. He also allowed sadly many battles in Lorraine and Champagne before the peace. I saw and heard some of what happened in those battles. I also listened to those who had fought in the war elsewhere."

"And got your ears well boxed for it, I'd wager?"

"My father was never unjust, Master Dietrich. If he ever did such a thing, it was out of fear that I would commit some folly. By His mercy, God put that beyond me."

"I don't know as even God can cure people of folly," Dietrich said. That seemed blasphemous, yet certainly God allows much folly. Is this to teach those who can learn?

Master Dietrich now had returned to his work of placing the gun on dry ground. It seemed only a moment before he had the afterpiece between his knees and was ladling powder into it. Yet from the sun I knew that it must be close upon noon. I felt no hunger, but knew that I would be weak if I ate nothing, and also knew somehow that I should not be weak.

As I ate bread and salt meat, I saw the men of both bands building rams and shields. Some of the shields were so large, I wondered what they were for. Thomas had a moment to tell me that they would be held over the heads of the men, to fend off arrows and stones.

"If Master Dietrich shoots half as well as he talks, the gate's no great matter," Thomas said. "But we'll still be wiser to send a couple more parties in other ways. Bad luck to one won't wreck everything."

At this moment someone shouted the challenge in the rear. Someone else shouted back, foul words. I did not need to see the other men grasping weapons to put my helmet back on. As I ran toward my horse, the first arrows fell into the camp, and the first longbows began to reply.

I saw Thomas in the middle of the archers, shouting orders in between his own shots. Some of his speech was as foul as that of the enemies, but I knew that this was only his tongue, not his heart. From the shouting on both sides, I knew that the attackers were a band of de Baudricourt's men, who had come upon us in a way such as to surprise both sides.

It seemed to me that our men were less hurt by the surprise than the enemy. It also seemed to me that it was God's favor, the enemy coming to us instead of our having to chase them over hills and down valleys.

Certainly the English archers were doing well. Many of the enemy's crossbowmen had already fallen. The Bastard's men also had crossbows, which they used with skill. Both shot often and well at the enemy's horse.

While the footmen did their work, our horse were mounting. I saw Lord Belmain wheel his horse, and his standard bearer do the same. Watching them while I prayed for God's favor for them, I turned toward the Burgundian stronghold.

As I did, the Burgundians swarmed like rats from a burning barn, out through the gate and even over their half-tumbled walls. I had no doubt that they wished to take us in the rear while we faced de Baudricourt. I also knew somehow that there were far more of them than we had expected.

I ran toward them, as swiftly as I had ever run in the girls' footraces. Truly, it seemed that my feet did not touch the ground. I heard shouts, from only God knew where, and arrows and quarrels began to fall around me.

None struck me, but not all struck the earth. Lord Belmain's standard bearer brought his horse around in a great circle and shouted a warcry. As he did, he was struck from his saddle. The standard plunged down, but by God's grace the butt end of the staff sank deep into the ground.

It was wavering but had not yet fallen when I gripped the shaft.

As my hands closed on it, I heard my voices without seeing anything, neither God's angels nor the enemies. All seemed a pale blue mixed with gold. The battle sounds gave way to the tolling of mighty bells.

Dear Child of God, bear this test and pass on to a place of great joy.

I could not doubt that this was the time and place of my death, but that Heaven awaited me after my last battle for God's peace.

So I gripped the staff of the standard, as the hail of arrows and quarrels eased. I saw that this was because the Burgundians were close upon me, and those upon the walls feared hitting their friends.

There was no one within hearing for my confession, save God, so I made it silently as the enemy rushed upon me.

VI

Bertrand Duvant:

I do not know who led the band of de Baudricourt's men that struck us from the rear as we faced the stronghold. I do know that he went to Hell with a good many lives on his conscience, if indeed he had one.

Had he kept better watch, he would have seen the traces of our coming and not been surprised to encounter us. Had he kept his wits about him as well, he might have privily sent a messenger into the stronghold, which we had by no means surrounded.

Then the Burgundians in the stronghold might have sortied against us at the same moment their allies were striking our rear. We would have been caught between two fires, and hard put indeed not to be burned.

As it was, by the time the Burgundians came against us, we were holding their allies, even forcing them to give ground. Both my men and the Bastard's were fighting as if they were not merely of one land but born of one womb, with neither French nor English among them, only men facing a common enemy.

I was too much engaged with the enemy to turn and face the sortie, but my standard bearer was otherwise situated. He was free to turn and charge. I saw him do so, I saw him fall, and I saw my standard of the Golden Hand raised almost in the moment of its fall.

As if I had been beside her, I knew that it was Jehanne who raised the standard again.

"Rally! Rally by the Golden Hand!" I shouted. Then I was once again too busy with foes pressing close to think on what might be happening behind me.

I did not see how the Burgundian sortie faltered and its men strung themselves out in a long line across our rear. Others told me about it afterward.

"It was like Joan was a line of Swiss pikes," Cornish Will said. "Or maybe it was God's own hand put down between them and us. Maybe He loves her even more'n she thinks, enough to save anybody she fights for."

Fear or God or simply the need to array their line better, it surely halted the Burgundians. Then the Bastard of Orleans rode into their left flank.

Tales are told, that Jean the Bastard was so careful to array his men properly that he left himself no chance to display knightly prowess. (No one ever questioned his courage.) This was never so that I saw. When he was within reach of a foe, that man did well to commend himself to God.

Tales are also told of this battle, that Jean charged at the gallop, with his lance couched. Knights seldom gallop, and never on such uncertain ground with so little space to gain speed. Nor is the lance so handy a weapon at close reach.

Jean struck the Burgundians with sword in hand, laying about him like a man possessed and cleaving heads and arms to either side. At last his sword stuck in a Burgundian skull thicker than its fellows, and he unhooked his mace and went to work with it.

The entire Burgundian left dissolved. The center showed signs of rallying, but about that time Master Dietrich had his gun ready and touched it off.

I thought that it would make mostly smoke and noise, like most guns of such modest size. Somehow, though, Master Dietrich had contrived to fill it with a hatful of small stones. These sprayed the Burgundian center like arrows plunging down on a field of sitting birds.

That center became a rabble of men screaming, writhing, or fleeing, as mixed as the meats in a pasty. By then I was free of foes ready to hand, and could lead the five or six men still mounted toward the remaining Burgundians.

I was riding up to my standard when a sudden uproar of shouts and clashing weapons broke out behind de Baudricourt's men. I reined in, since this had to concern me, and saw that they also were now having to fight in two directions. In the shadows of the forest I could not make out who had come in such timely fashion.

I only hoped that it was a true friend, and not a case of more of de Baudricourt's men being mistaken for an attack. If so, we were still in no small peril. I could see no one standing around the standard, nor around the gun.

I eased my horse in among the fallen around the standard, plucked it from the ground, and held it high.

"For God and the Realms of France and England— forward!"

I thought I heard echoes of that cry behind me, but no one but a fool looks behind him when charging a foe.

Thomas of Ramsford:

Lord Belmain didn't know who was ramping up and down in the rear of de Baudricourt's men. I was a mite closer, so I could make them out.

It was the folk of Domremy and Greux, with Jean Colin and Pierre D'Arc right up to the front. They mostly had pikes and clubs and flails, but a few of them had old swords or maces. They were coming on every whichway, and I could see that the best part of them wished they could be somewhere else.

But they were where they were, and doing a right proper job on de Baudricourt's rear. They weren't for the most part what you would call seasoned fighters, but they had numbers and determination. Their opponents weren't any more seasoned, and they weren't near as determined.

I saw a good few of de Baudricourt's folk stand gawping, not knowing which way to turn. Most of them didn't stand or gawp long, 'cause our archers had the range down to a finger and no wind to spoil their aim.

I did order a few of the lads to turn around and give Lord Belmain and the Bastard a little help.

"Just tickle our friends from Burgundy a mite," I said. "Keep them running, but not too fast for the knights to catch up."

The way it turned out, the Burgundians ran so fast that their friends couldn't close the gate behind them in time. Lord Belmain was up with the last Burgundians and rode right in through the gate on their heels.

Now, I don't want to take anything away from the Bastard of Orleans. But I always think Lord Belmain gave him a little more than his due, and himself a little less. His lordship went straight into that stronghold without knowing if the Devil himself might be waiting, the other side of that gate. He went straight in, and that frightened the Burgundians out of the last of their wits.

In about the time it takes to drink a cup of good ale, the stronghold had yielded. The Burgundians outside who could still run mostly did so, into the forest. De Baudricourt's men would have liked to do the same, cutting their way through our Frenchie allies on the way. My archers had to drop a few of them, to put the rest in the right mind for yielding when the Bastard rode up.

About the time they did, I started fretting about not seeing Joanie up and about. There was a whole pile of bodies around the gun and where the standard had been. I recognized Master Dietrich, who'd certainly died game.

I knew Joanie would have done the same, but it pretty much curdled my bowels, to think that she'd died at all.

Jehanne D'Arc:

The standard felt like armor sent by God, to protect me against the Burgundian enemies of His peace. I had no fear of anything while I held it.

Whatever it did against my enemies, it did not do against my friends. Master Dietrich, God rest his soul, did not look before he shot off his gun. One of the stones it flung struck the side of my helmet, opposite where Gerard de Sionne had cut me.

It did not make me senseless, but I could not keep my feet. I thrust the staff of the standard a forearm's length into the ground, then fell face down beside it.

The battle around and above me seemed to pass very swiftly. Not knowing who held the ground I lay on, it seemed best to pretend death. Twice I was trodden on, by friend or foe I know not. I saw Lord Belmain pass close enough to touch, to seize his standard and raise it.

When he had passed on, I thought it safe enough to rise and seek the safety of friendly ranks. As I did, a quarrel from a crossbow struck me on the right thigh, well toward the rear. It did not go deep, but the blow knocked me down again.

I felt the blood flowing, and thought it best not to move until it stopped. Also, I was of no mind to be hurt a *third* time by friends.

This did not save me, for when Thomas of Ramsford ran up he came so fast that he trod on my hand. It seemed beyond reason to endure this in silence.

"By my staff, Thomas! I have been shot twice today, and now must I be trampled?"

"Joanie!"

Thomas was not so large a man as he seemed at first, but he found the strength to lift me as if I was a child, so that my feet were free of the ground. He was holding me thus when I saw over his shoulder my brother Pierre coming toward us.

"Jehanne! Are you well?"

"If this *goddamn* archer will put me on my feet—"

"Sorry, Joanie."

He set me on my feet. I promptly learned that

they would still not quite hold me up. I had to grip Thomas's arm and lean my head against his shoulder for a moment, before I could stand alone.

Pierre was watching this with doubt written large on his face. "Jehanne—what have you been doing among these soldiers?"

"She's been as safe as the Blessed Virgin might have been," Thomas shouted. "You'd better believe it, you poxy little—!"

"That's ill repayment for our helping you—" Pierre began. He looked ready to draw his sword, and where matters would have ended had he done so, only God knows.

I stepped away from Thomas and spoke more harshly than I had ever spoken to my family since they ceased to doubt my voices.

"Pierre, I swear by Holy Saint Michael, Saint Catherine, and Saint Margaret, I am as virgin as I came from my mother's womb. I have received neither violence nor insult at the hands of any man in this company. Whatever they owe you, you owe them a temperate tongue."

Pierre sighed. "Sister mine, I believe you. I will pray that you can persuade our father."

"If he balks—" Thomas began, but I found courage enough to put a hand over his lips.

"Hush, Thomas. I must fight this battle myself. Now, good brother, can you tell us how you came to be here in arms? That needs more explaining than what I have been doing among the soldiers."

"Our father can answer that better than I. I do not know how he gained pledges from some threescore men in Domremy and elsewhere, to come join the attack on the stronghold. I only know that at least that many came with us. I doubt if all of them were happy to be pitched straight into a battle, but few of them ran off."

"Well, I take back everything I said against you, Goodman D'Arc," Thomas said. "I'll even add a mite of praise and thanks. We've still to run the leader of the wolf pack to ground, but we've done for most of the cubs.

"Now, do any of you know a mite of leechcraft? Joanie's hurt enough so I don't want to just leave her be."

"If Robert Suigar's whole, he can do well enough," Pierre said. Then he embraced me. "Jehanne, I don't know where your voices will take you next. But if you need a friend—there's worse for that office than a brother."

"If I need such friendship and our father consents, I will not say no," I said. But it seemed to me that if it was my fate now to leave Domremy, I might have other friends as well.

Or more than friends, if it was God's will.

I knew I needed time to myself, to pray to know what that might be.

VII

Bertrand Duvant:

We had put an end to de Baudricourt's whore-
mongering for the Burgundians that day before the
stronghold, although we did not know it at the time.

Our prisoners included a round dozen of men of
gentle birth, chief among them one Franquet d'Arras.
Them we held for the royal justice; the rest we
disarmed, stripped of all but sufficient garments for
decency, and turned loose. We lacked the men to
guard a host of prisoners, unless we asked the countryfolk for aid in that matter.

Neither the Bastard nor I would have this. We
trusted and honored the countryfolk, but would not
put them in the path of great temptation. Not until
we had sufficient men to fight them, if they had
second thoughts about aiding us.

The countryfolk were never put to the test. De
Baudricourt's own strayed sheep turned on him when
their friends and kin drifted back, next to naked and
with word of a hostile country around them. I never
learned all that I would have wished to know about
the fight in Vaucouleurs, but we had no doubts about
its ending.

Whether he jumped, fell, or was thrown, the Sieur
Robert de Baudricourt was found dead at the foot of
the west wall of Vaucouleurs, some six days after the
fight at the stronghold. A few other townsfolk were
not seen again, either, at least in this world.

We had peace once more on the borders of the

Realm of France, until the next time Philip the Good chose to foment rebellion and treason. It was King Henry's decision, to execute only the Sieur Franquet. The others were heavily fined, stripped of any honors, and offered a free passage to Burgundy if they chose to take it. About half did.

There were also honors to be distributed, as well as taken away. I cannot say what came to the Bastard and myself without sounding vain, but those who had helped us were also rewarded generously. Taxes were largely remitted and gifts made to the maimed and the kin of the dead.

That came from the Crown. There was also a respectable sum of silver found in the stronghold, that was ours to distribute as we wished. Philip the Good had not been a tightpurse with his hirelings, so that after we had rewarded all of our own men there was still a good knight's estate left.

Neither of us had nay doubt where it should go. The doubt was, where she would go with it.

"If she has a vocation, she will do better than most in a convent," the Bastard said. "What say you?"

Certainly Jehanne would do better with a proper dowry than most peasant girls sent to convents, who had small chance of a decent life. Yet I could not see even the most moderate of abbesses enduring a novice who talked to angels. It would be ill reward for Jehanne, to end up being expelled from a convent or even sent before the Inquisition.

I had hopes that King Henry would see that the Pope needed him more than he needed the Pope. There was small need for the Double Monarchy to buy the favor of His Holiness, by letting the Inquisition's spies roam the lands like mad wolves. However, I also had doubts that His Grace would change his mind soon enough, when Jehanne could surely talk herself into a charge of heresy within a fortnight if she set her mind to it!

"I say that a convent is no place for her," I replied.

"Then what is?" Jean asked, rather peevishly. "I do not see her staying peacefully at home and being the staff of her aged parents. Not without most of that dowry going into her brothers' hands and from there God knows where."

"I have no quarrel with that. If it didn't happen at once, it would surely happen once her mother died. There's the real head of that family."

"Then why not give her that dowry to marry some fit man?"

I reminded Jean of Owain's water fate.

"She said she would be a virgin as long as it was God's will," Jean reminded me. "Perhaps we should let her decide what is God's will in the matter. If she decides that she is now free to wed, we certainly have not far to seek the man."

"No. Tom of Ramsford has had an eye for her ever since we came to the stronghold. He'll be down on his knees thanking God and everybody else."

"He'd better get up off his knees sooner or later," the Bastard said, refilling our cups. It was about the last wine in Domremy, and I reminded myself to seek more, if we were going to celebrate a betrothal. No couple was ever properly blessed in such near-kin to vinegar.

"Well, there are things a man can do in such a position," I began.

"None of your Italian ways, Bertrand," Jean said, grinning. "I'm for leaving matters to God's will and Tom's manhood."

I raised my cup to that as well, but with the unspoken thought that Jehanne's will had more to say in the matter than anybody else save God.

Thomas of Ramsford:

I had enough work those last days in Domremy to keep two men busy. So I had little time to think about Joanie and precious little to talk to her.

Lord Belmain did speak of the gift that was coming to her, from the Burgundian silver. Also, I did talk to her brother Pierre once or twice, and he seemed fretful. What about, I still can't be sure. I imagine it was either Jacques D'Arc fussing about what might have happened to Joanie among the soldiers, or

Pierre's wanting to get his long fingers on his sister's dowry.

Pierre D'Arc was a brave man and no fool, but I didn't get the feeling that a penny ever came into his hands without coming out again pretty well squeezed. I hoped Lord Belmain would reckon on the trouble this might give Joanie, and take proper care.

What I didn't dare hope for, was that I'd be seeing Joanie again. Domremy's a fair ways off the roads I'd mostly be traveling for the next few years. I'd most likely come back to find her wed to Jean Colin or some such, with a babe or few of her own. (I reckoned that if she wanted to keep her dowry, she'd best marry someone who could hit her brothers a smart rap on the knuckles if they reached for it.)

I hoped that would be the way of it for her, because Joanie was just too full of juice to be shut up in a convent. Not that she wouldn't make her way there, or anyplace else between Heaven and Hell. But waste not, want not.

All of which is taking this tale from Paris to Rouen by way of Bourges, and making my throat dry. But I really can't believe that I didn't see what was right there just for reaching out my hand to it. I reckon it was being a soldier too long, and thinking I was no fit match for a girl who probably wanted a home.

I also reckon it was God's own gift of good sense to Joanie, enough for about six women, that put everything to rights.

It was five days after we had word of the death sentence on Franquet d'Arras. We'd built ourselves a good few huts in and around our stronghold, and I was keeping enough state to have one all to myself. Not that I couldn't touch the roof without standing on my toes, but I didn't have to listen to anybody's snores or nightmares.

It was one of those days when I'd had enough work for three men, not just two. I'd blown out the candle and crawled under the fleeces before I noticed there was something else in the straw.

No, *someone* else. I felt it, and knew it was a woman and alive, which wasn't an unpleasant surprise.

It wasn't unpleasant, either, to find that she didn't have so much as a kerchief between her and me.

Since I had no more on myself, I reckoned we could have ourselves a bit of fun if she was awake. I'm not one for tumbling a woman without her being at least awake enough to say yes or no.

I was ready enough, too, because we weren't bringing camp women around out of respect for Joanie. Between that and all the work I really had lived like a monk for the best part of a month. If you can call that living . . .

Anyway, I put a hand on the woman's shoulder, and all of a sudden I heard a voice I knew say:

"I hope that is you, Thomas."

If I'd put my hand on a red-hot iron, I couldn't have jerked it back faster.

"Joanie?"

"Who were you expecting?"

"By my hope of Heaven, nobody. I'd planned to sleep alone tonight."

I could hear her swallowing. Then:

"Thomas—can you change your mind about that? I—if it is God's will that I go to a convent, then I will obey. But if it is God's will that you want me for your wife—I will obey more gladly."

If I'd been in a battle, I'd have been dead five times over before I got my wits back. When I did, I found that I'd put my bow into the bed between us.

She touched it, touching me at the same time. I really wished she hadn't touched me. I'd taken my hand off her, but that hadn't helped much with other parts of me. *They* were reckoning Joanie as a woman here to be well and truly tumbled, whatever my wits said. My shaft had never in all my days been so ready to fly!

"Thomas, why do you have your bow in the bed?"

"Well, in the tales the traveling singers told when I was a lad, if a man wanted to sleep chaste with a lady, he put a sword in the bed between them. I couldn't find my sword, and anyway, the bow's my true weapon."

"Is that your only weapon?"

I almost asked her to find out for herself, but I wasn't rightly sure how she would take it. I also was very sure how I'd take it, and what might happen afterward, and how much it would turn what we had between us sour.

"I'm pretty well armed, for some kinds of battle. But—Joanie, are you sure you want to fight that kind?"

For answer, she grabbed the bow and threw it out of the bed. It thumped on the floor, and I knew that I really wasn't myself when I didn't worry about its being broken. Any other woman who used my bow that way, she'd have been eating standing for a day or two.

Or maybe there was good reason for my not thinking about my bow. The moon was out from behind the clouds now, and enough light came through the chinks to show Joanie pretty well.

I've already said as much as proper or maybe a bit more, about what a handsome girl Joanie was. Now I wanted to look away for the same reason I didn't want her to touch me. After a bit I really got my head turned away.

Then Joanie started to cry.

Not real loud crying, but something worse. Somebody trying to pretend they're not crying. It hurts to be that way, and it hurts to hear it.

I reckoned it didn't matter what else happened or didn't happen, if I could stop Joanie crying. So I took her in my arms, me like Adam and she like Eve, and held her until she stopped crying.

"Thomas—" she began.

"I'm not your husband, so this isn't a command. Just friendly advice. Call me Tom."

"Very well, Tom. Do you—find me—undesirable?"

If I hadn't nearly strangled not laughing, I'd have waked everybody in the stronghold. I decided that if Joanie knew something about the ways of men, she could answer that for herself. If she didn't know, it was time she learned.

So I put her hand where she could tell just how

undesirable I didn't find her, and left it there. I also prayed that whatever happened would be the right thing, the first and last time I prayed at a time like this.

After a bit she laughed.

"Thank God!"

I knew there was more to come, so I just stroked her hair and waited.

"Tom. God guarded me from men's desire, so long as I was doing His work for the peace of France. It was right and proper that this happen, so that I could be a virgin as long as needed."

"Now it's not needed?"

"I would pray not to be guarded from the desire of the man I want to marry."

Anybody who wonders why I wasn't thunderstruck at a girl so forward—well, they never knew Joanie. What she wanted, she made plain as the nose on her face, which was a pretty plain thing even if you didn't notice it after you saw those gray eyes—

But there I am, passing wind when there's a story to finish.

"Do you think you are?"

"By my staff, I should say not!"

"By your staff or by my staff?"

She laughed. "I think neither of us will be foresworn."

Then I took her in my arms, not afraid of anything because I knew what I wasn't going to do. She cuddled in there nice and comfortable, but I could feel she—not exactly wanted more, but wanted to know why she still had her maidenhead.

"Joanie, we're not even betrothed. You don't come virgin at least to the betrothal, somebody's sure to tell your father. Then he'll think worse of you and the worst of us. You're pretty longheaded, fighting for peace for France. Fight for peace in your own family for a bit."

She sighed. "I never thought to find myself offering my maidenhead to a man wiser than myself."

"Modest, aren't you?"

"If you know more about my father than I do myself, is that not wisdom?"

I had the feeling that this was only the first of a whole lot of times Joanie was going to flatter me into seeing things her way. But I was too tired and too happy and still a little too full of desire to care.

Also, I had the feeling that there were worse ways to see things, than Joanie's way.

So I kissed her and put my arms around her good and proper, and that's the way we fell alseep.

Jehanne D'Arc:

So the place where I was to find joy was somewhat this side of Paradise.

Not that Tom and I found only joy in our years together. That was not and could not be God's will. But we seldom lost understanding of each other, so the joy was never as far away as it was for men and women not so blessed.

Epilogue

From *Orleans: Guide to Historic Sites* (New Bristol: The Traveler's Library, 1953):

76 Rue Saint Loup. Not architecturally remarkable, but an exceptionally well-preserved example of late-thirteenth century French domestic architecture. From 1442 through 1478, home of Sir Thomas Ramsford and his wife Jehanne.

They were the parents of Sir Jean-Bertrand Ramsford, Captain of the Royal Archers of France in the Burgundian War, 1473-77. The Lady Jehanne is also commonly believed to be the author of *The Book of the Goodwife of Orleans* (dual-language edition, Van Eyck and Sadler, 1902).

*   *   *

Historical Note

In our own history, King Henry V of England died in 1422, without ever being crowned King of France.

Charles the Dauphin succeeded his father as Charles VII and was in turn succeeded by his son Louis XI.

Jehanne, the daughter of Jacques D'Arc of Domremy, heard voices and saw angels commanding her to crown the Dauphin as King of France and drive the English from the land. She embarked on her quest in 1429, with the aid of Robert de Baudricourt. Her first victory was relieving the English siege of Orleans, in which the French army was commanded by Jean, Count of Dunois, the Bastard of Orleans.

She then had the Dauphin crowned at Reims, but in 1430 she was captured by the Burgundians. They sold her to English, who tried her on a trumped-up charge of heresy, and in 1431 burned her at the stake.

She was rehabilitated in 1445, became a popular heroine in France over the next four centuries, and in 1920 was canonized as Saint Joan.

THE SPIRIT OF EXMAS SIDEWAYS

L. Neil Smith

Introduction

A Brief History of the North American Confederacy

Nine score and fifteen years ago, with the ink only just sanded on the United States Constitution, President George Washington and Treasury Secretary Alexander Hamilton decided it was time to try out their shiny brand new powers of taxation.

Their first victims would be certain western Pennsylvania agricultural types long accustomed to converting their crops into a less perishable, more profitable, high-octane liquid form. Unfortunately, for the President and the Secretary, many of these rustics, especially near the frontier municipality of Pittsburgh, placed a slightly different emphasis than high school teachers do today on the Revolutionary slogan regarding "Taxation without representation." In their view, they'd fought the British in 1776 to *abolish* taxes and they weren't interested in having representation imposed on them by that gaggle of fops in Philadelphia, the nation's capital. They made this manifestly clear by tarring-and-feathering tax collectors, burning their homes to the ground, and filling the stills of those who willingly paid the hated tribute with large-caliber bullet holes.

Feeling their authority challenged, George and Alex dispatched westward a body of armed conscripts equal of half the population of America's largest city (Philadelphia, once again, later famous for air-dropping explosives on miscreants charged with disturbing the peace). Four hundred whiskey rebels, duly impressed by this army of fifteen thousand, subsided. The miraculous process by which the private act of thievery is transubstantiated into public virtue was firmly established in history. The results—chronic poverty and unemployment, endless foreign wars, and reruns on television—are with us even today.

Meanwhile, in another western Pennsylvania far, far away, one Albert Gallatin, Swiss immigrant, Harvard scholar, and gentlemen farmer changed his mind about talking his neighbors out of an uprising that might get them all killed. Instead, he decided to organize and lead them, inspired by a single word in the Declaration of Independence, which doesn't appear in our version of that august document.*

A highly erudite and persuasive fellow (in our universe he invented the field now known as ethnology and became Hamilton's replacement in Jefferson's Cabinet), he shamed the fifteen thousand *federals* into marching with him against the City of Botherly Love. Washington was shown a suitable backstop and shot for his transgressions. The Constitution was replaced by the revised Articles of Confederation it was supposed to have been in the first place. And the government, deprived forever of its looting privileges grew smaller every year thereafter, guaranteeing the survival of individual liberty and giving rise to unprecedented peace, prosperity, and progress.

Albert Gallatin became the second President of what would some day be the North American Confederacy.

*See *The Probability Broach* by L. Neil Smith

FRI 23 DEC 212 A.L.
20:00 O'CLOCK

"He's dead."

'Twas the night before the night before Exmas, and the first she'd spoken to me for two hours. It wasn't necessary. I'd seen it when the call came; the old guy's face, the entire front half of his skull, blown off with the exit of some soft, heavy, high-velocity projectile.

"How long?" I asked as if we'd been speaking to each other that evening. Our breath made empty word-balloons in the air before our faces.

"At least two hours."

As a Certified Healer, Clarissa made a pretty fair medical examiner. Two hours—the same two hours it had been snowing down here on the plains. The same two hours she'd sat beside me in the Neova HoverSport, arctic silence at three hundred miles per hour, with the wireless playing "White Christmas," over and over again. An old Bing Crosby standard in the states, it was a recent import to the Confederacy. Two hours. As a detective, I'd learned to mistrust coincidence. Right now I just resented it.

We'd been returning from what you might call a less-than-successful mountain holiday—I'd call it less than successful—Edward William Bear, though I settle for "Win," and his erstwhile sweetheart, blond, bronze-eyed, and I believe the word is "buxom," Clarissa MacDougall Olson. We'd received the call on the car 'com. After a year of waiting for the goddamned thing to ring at home while Clarissa went on paying the bills, all of a sudden I was wanted at the scene of somebody's violent demise.

But Win, if she'd been speaking to me, Clarissa might have expressed resentment of her own as I hung the dashboard pickup back on its hook, staring, with the autopilot set on GEORGE, at snowflakes sand-blasting the windscreen, *we're supposed to be in town in time for Exmas with Mother. We've still got shopping.* She didn't have to say it. She didn't bother, just as she didn't say, *You're forty-nine years old, Win, can't you go back to playing private eye* after *the holidays?* She was right. About the shopping, anyway. I hadn't even found her a present yet. I had other worries. I wasn't sure she'd still be around to open it on Exmas morning, and I didn't care for giving people gifts I'd paid for with their money.

So, instead of letting the Neova follow its chromium nose to Genet Place, to the warm familiar garage it might have called home (if it had been speaking to me) in the metropolis of Greater Laporte, where a thousand miles of prairie pile up against the Rockies between rivers I'd been calling Cache La Poudre and Big Thompson most of my life, I wrestled the wheel toward the east side, the old Caesar Rodney subdivision, reeking of ancient affluence even by local standards. Maybe the fancy plastic business cards I'd ordered hadn't been a waste, after all. Maybe I wasn't quite as foolish as I looked to myself in the ad I'd recorded on Channel 1572. Maybe the three pounds of Springfield mass under my left armpit weren't gradually deforming my spine for nothing.

By the time, some fifteen minutes later, I backed off on the ducted fans, lowered the soft, fat tires, rolled to the address on the interactive map, and negotiated the sinuosities of the private drive, the wireless had given up on the Groaner and switched to "Silver Bells." I climbed out through the Neova's gull-wing, extracted an *El Pungentissimo* from my tunic pocket, and lit it, out of reflex, with a hand-sheltered wooden match, although the fringe of my *serape* hung limp in the frost-bitten silence.

Snow sifted down like the soapflakes in Charles Foster Kane's crystal ball, courtesy of Cheyenne Ridge Power & Light, who control the weather to any extent it can be controlled. The other side of the ridge (we'd passed through the road-cut coming down from Laramie) a blizzard raged over the landscape, reducing visibility to Angstroms, forcing me to trust the road company's subsurface guidance. Between Owl Canyon and what would have been Wyoming, there must be a hundred onscreen warnings about mule deer crossing the greenway. But, as Clarissa sat as far at the other side of the car as she could, her expression funereal, her arms folded across her picturesque chest, I'd been worried about broadsiding mastodons migrating back for the glaciation.

At the scene, an urban tract in the twenty-acre neighborhood, the body, zapped at contact range in the back of the head with a typical Confederate hand-cannon, had been identified by elderly Alberta Mott, co-owner of the property on which it had been found. The other co-owner, her brother Seaton (pronounced "shotten," and he sure as hell had been), was cooling off on the frozen ground with his face distributed over several dozen square feet in an eighth-inch crimson layer beneath a discreet covering of fresh-fallen snow.

FRI 23 DEC 212 A.L.
20:00 O'CLOCK

"Okay, let's back up once more."

I lit the evening's third cigar, eyebrowing the stiff, getting stiffer every minute under a lacework of ice-crystals sparkling in the Neova's headlights like a display in the window of De Sade's Drygoods. The stuff was still falling, threatening to become an inconvenience. We might have gone to the house, ablaze with warmth, a hundred yards away. Clarissa, her arms folded tighter than ever, shifted from one foot to the other beside the car. I was feeling blue

about the lips myself. My toes in the ends of my
hand-tooled stovepipes might have been Tootsie Rolls
for all the feeling they had. Still, I'd found a degree
of discomfort—twenty degrees in this case—works
wonders getting the truth out of witnesses.

Four of same, starting with the sister: white-haired,
rail-thin even under a hooded cloak, Alberta Mott
had never been anybody's vision of delight no matter
how many decades you peeled off; business bigwig
Freeman K. Bertram, discovering his taste for kilt-
wearing didn't fit the climate, I'd known since Day
One in the Confederacy; I also knew Ham Charles of
NeverSleep Security—during the year I'd struggled
getting established, I'd ingratiated myself with his
profession as a matter of course.

None had seen the actual killing, or I wouldn't
have been called. The sister had been in the house
all day, getting ready for cocktails. Bertram and Merse
Littleshin, the fourth at this Waterloo Bridge party,
working late in anticipation of time lost to the holidays, had been on the 'com with one another about
the time of the murder, the former from his penthouse atop the mile-tall pyramid that houses Laporte
Paratronics, Ltd., the latter from his office on the
campus, halfway across town. Bertram and Miss Mott
had bundled up and come down after I'd arrived.
The closest thing to a real witness was Littleshin,
whom I recognized from our recent conversation on
the 'com.

Preserving evidence, I'd used the Neova's 'com
pad, an electronic clipboard half an inch thick, linked
to the vast tangle of communication, entertainment,
information storage and retrieval on which Confederate civilization depends. Pulling the walnut-sized
pickup from a socket at the pad top, I'd stretched the
retractable cable to its limit, scanned it over the area
where the body lay. Even at this distance, twenty-
five or thirty feet, I'd be able to zoom in later and
count nose-hairs.

"Tell me again how you found it."

"Please, Detective!" Littleshin blinked and gulped
at the same time, fighting some kind of eruption.

You never know what it'll be until it happens. He was big, impressive-looking, six feet, a hundred ninety. Oglala Sioux at a guess, mocassins, gloves, high-collared doeskin jacket, long, thick braids done up in fancy silver bands. Handsome bastard, stoic as hell most of the time, I'd bet, but it wasn't helping him right now. "He was my dear friend and colleague," Littleshin lifted a broad hand, indicating the object of our conversation, then let it drop to his waist, shoving a thumb into his semi-formal pistol belt. "Seaton Mott, Chairman of the Board of Trustees of Laporte University, grew each year in wisdom and lived to see a hundred seven summers. Even in death, one does not refer to such a man as 'it'!"

"This one does." I shook my head. I'm Ute, myself, both sides of the family, five-eight, two twenty-nine. Not so much overweight, I like to think, as undertall. "You will, too, if you want to feel better sooner. Your friend's gone, Mr. Littleshin, the part you cared about. What he left behind can help us figure out who did this, but only if we skip the sentiment. Killings have a short shelf life, the longer one remains unsolved—"

"*Win.*" Clarissa didn't finish. She thought I was being hard on him. Maybe I was, but I was right, and she knew that, too.

He blinked and gulped again. "Quite correct. As I said, following long custom, I'd gathered, with other members of the Board of Trustees," this time he lifted the hand at Bertram and the guest of honor's sister, "for a holiday drink with my . . . my old friend the evening before Exmas Eve." I thought he was going to lose it on "old friend," but he went on. "Arriving somewhat earlier than the others, I was told that Seaton was strolling alone, enjoying the gentle snow-fall. Such walks are—were—a habit with him. I'd often accompanied him. Sometimes we'd walk here, sometimes in a wooded park adjacent to my office, discussing this and that as old friends will. I'd thought to do so again. I searched his favorite spots, and found . . ."

"Steady, now."

". . . *it,* and called you on my pocket telecom."

In the snow, his mocassins had left the second of two sets of footprints, a quarter hour old when we'd arrived. The others were friend Seaton's, harder to make out given their hundred minutes' seniority, but unmistakable. Both led to an evergreen-surrounded clearing, seventy or eighty yards from the driveway, where the body had been lying, according to Clarissa, an hour and forty-five minutes when discovered. Littleshin had managed to stay put beside the left-overs, as instructed by telecom, without throwing up or otherwise spoiling any evidence, until I got there to make permanent records.

I'd let the pickup linger over those prints, tracing both sets back to the house. At the rate snow was falling, anyone stomping around here the last two hours should have left traces. Mott had. Littleshin had. So should the creep responsible for the small, circular hole at the back of Mott's head, ringed with a dusting of used pistol propellant ("powder burns" as the media love calling them, militantly mistaken as they are about everything else), which told me the wound had been inflicted from a distance of mere inches.

But by whom, Santa's eight tiny flying reindeer?

"Okay, Mr. Littleshin," we'd been over it all a dozen times by now, "one more question. Why did you pick *me* to call?" Maybe my one big moment, eighteen months ago, still had some advertising value.

He reddened, a neat trick, given the cold and his ethnic background. "I, er, asked Directory Assistance for the investigator most experienced with crimes of extreme violence."

"Right." The Confederacy is nothing if not a land of contrasts. I'd had this teddibly British wimpier-than-thou routine constantly from individuals who considered themselves more civilized than United Statesians, ever since I'd come here. I turned. "Ham, how's the family?"

Mine weren't the only headlights illuminating the scene. Despite *his* ethnic background—simian as any orangutan can be—Ham Charles seemed to enjoy the cold. A head shorter than me, draped in urban cammies, the red-bearded security specialist was as wide as he was tall. I noticed, in a professional way, that he was wearing his old service pistol, a .476 Esquimaux issued to certain volunteer regiments during the War Against the Czar in 1957 (referred to locally as 181 A.L.). He'd been busy with his own evidence-collecting. Now he waddled across the snow (the kind that squeaks underfoot) humming "We Wish You a Merry Exmas." He was on overtime. I'd never cared much for the embroidery on his uniform. Too many bad associations. Overhead, a small dirigible with the same NeverSleep Eye-in-the-Pyramid logo emblazoned on its fuselage, had maneuvered floodlamps into position, adding to the confusion of light and shadow below.

"Little woman's fatter every day," Charles grinned. "Kid'll grow up to be a gunsmith, we let him live. Win, this never woulda happened, they'd let us set up perimeters like I wanted. Customer's always right." He snorted the sarcasm. "Any idea who's paying you?"

He had a point: he patrolled on contract, I'd been called and come running. I wasn't sanguine about perimeter alarms, however. Confederate crime is rare (one reason for Littleshin's snotty attitude about the States) and it wouldn't have been worth it. What really griped Charles was the job of keeping the newsies out. Their lights and their demented gabble were perceptible at the property line, even from where we stood. I expected gunfire any minute—or maybe it was wishful thinking.

Being a doorknob rattler by profession, Ham's natural assumption was that the killer was some evil-minded outsider he'd failed to *keep* outside. I was working on a different assumption: who said the killer wasn't one of the insiders I was dealing with? Except in my late homeland, where, until Bernie Goetz became a hero, slaughtering strangers was a national sport (Bernie would have been an ordinary citizen here, with only his odd preference for underpowered weapons to distinguish him), a murderer needs reasons for selecting his victim, reasons someone he already knows is likeliest to offer.

"Pardon me, Detective." Littleshin again. "I couldn't help overhear. I believe I may speak for the University Trustees, horrified as we all are at what's been done to our Chairman."

From the Neova's direction, out of one corner of my ear, I heard a 'com shrill. Clarissa reached to get it. I dismissed it from my mind.

Littleshin went on. "I'm not certain how one does this, but we wish to hire you to expose Seaton's murderer. I suggest, no, *demand*—" For emphasis he drew his own gun, a stylish .39 caliber SEK III, matte black with bright metallic highlights glinting along the sighting rib in the lamplight "—that you begin with Dora Jayne Thorens, the one person who could have done this, or would have wanted to."

"Nonsense!"

I'd opened my mouth, was interrupted before I got a word out, and shut it to avoid frozen tonsils. Miss Mott trudged from where she huddled beside Bertram. "Merse Littleshin, you haven't any right to speak for the Trustees."

He shrugged. "I concede that any decision will have to be confirmed—"

"Mrs. Grundy's having a crisis." Clarissa came close, lowering her voice. "I have to go see whether there's anything to it." In the last stages of rejuvenation, she was always having a crisis. Or somebody was. Now that I thought about it, I was surprised Clarissa hadn't been called away earlier. Miss Mott was waiting, not listening to whatever Littleshin had to add.

I turned to Clarissa, a familiar sour expression settling itself on my face. "Okay," I told her under my breath. "But what happened to 'We've got shopping to do in time for Exmas with Mother'?"

Clarissa gave me a look; I remembered she hadn't said that. "I have to go. I'll send for a hovercab." Her tone was impatient, her thoughts already somewhere else. "If you wish, I'll perform the autopsy myself."

"Young man." Miss Mott hadn't heard our exchange. For a moment I wished she'd shut up and let me finish one thing at a time. Charles gave me a look of professional sympathy—or maybe one married sapient to another.

I let out a disgusted breath. "I'd appreciate that," I told Clarissa, referring to the meatcutting. "Take the Neova, though, and let me call a cab."

"I have to pick up the van and my equipment," she explained, exasperation in her voice. "Anyway, you're the one who uses the car as an office."

I'd been trying to say something nice—look what it gets you. "Okay, call a cab, then. Ham, here, will tell his men to let it pass." The orangutan nodded. "See you when I'm through here."

She shook her head. "Not tonight, Win. I really ought to do my rounds, now that we're back in town. And Mrs. Grundy needs me."

I didn't ask *What if I need you?* Instead, I directed my attention to Miss Mott. "I'm sorry, you were saying?"

"I said I lived with my brother many years, he a bachelor, I remaining unmarried to take care of him. It's true Mr. Littleshin was Seaton's friend. I've never had much liking for the man and never attempted to conceal it. For the University to hire you would require unanimous consent of the Trustees. One of them, Jennifer Smythe, is on vacation and cannot be reached."

"The President of the Confederacy?" I'd known she was visiting a low-gee Lunar health resort, we'd gotten a postcast from her last week. What I hadn't realized was that she was a University Trustee.

"Being a Trustee myself," Miss Mott continued, "I'd vote against hiring you, although for no reason you may imagine. Seaton and I are the last of our line, young man, brought up to take care of our own. If you're willing, however, I'll engage you privately to discover who murdered my brother."

It suited me. I still had to find a gift for Clarissa (her mother, too, although to tell the truth, I'd always preferred Ebenezer Scrooge *before* he was intimidated into a state of altruistic perfection). Now I knew how I was going to pay for it. During twenty-seven years as a Stateside cop, I'd never worried about things like advertising, bookkeeping, billing. I'd had the City & County of Denver taking care of that. I collected a check every month, whether the paying customers liked what I was doing or not. Life is hard in a free country, don't let anybody tell you otherwise.

I turned to look, but Clarissa was gone.

"Okay," I told them, "let's go over it one more time."

SAT 24 DEC 212 A.L.
02:15 O'CLOCK

"Come in, Win. Even in these circumstances it's splendid seeing you."

Like Littleshin, my own first thought had been of Deejay Thorens, a girl physicist at Laporte U., Ltd. The universe, I'm told, contains an infinite number of sub-universes, places where the Kennedy of your choice escaped assassination, the Russians got to the moon first, or Johnson pulled it off in Vietnam. The U.S. of A. where I was born in 1939, the North American Confederacy where I wound up in 1987, represent only two such alternatives.

In the Confederacy, when Alexander Hamilton had first tried collecting whiskey taxes under a brand-new Federal Constitution, he'd set off a rebellion, just like at home. Here, the rebels had enlisted the fifteen thousand conscripts sent to suppress them and marched on the capital. No more Constitution, no more Hamilton. *Sans* revenue, government grew smaller every year, all but disappearing in the end. Folks here are wealthier, enjoy a more advanced technology, live longer.

I'd been caught in an interdimensional wringer when a cabal of latter-day Confederate Hamilton admirers had tried importing tactical nukes—something never invented here despite the advanced technology—from the Land of the Fee. In an America wracked by depression and oppressive government, I'd been a Denver dick, investigating the homicide of another scientist, which turned out to involve Federal agents allied across the borders of reality with the Hamiltonians. During a large-caliber difference of opinion in this guy's lab, Deejay's "probability broach" had sucked me into the Confederacy.

In theory you can travel backward in time to what was, forward to what will be, or sideways to what might have been. The first two are still theory as far as I know, but Deejay's broach represented an artificial moth-hole in the fabric of what's what, through which I'd fallen from one world to another. Generated by high-energy machinery at one end, the other could show up anywhere, a doorway where there wasn't any wall. Such a doorway, I reasoned, might account for the way Mott had been murdered without leaving footprints.

Revving the Neova, I'd trundled down the long, Lombardian drive, having called ahead, despite the hour, to Deejay's campus quarters. Like Las Vegas or L.A., Laporte's a twenty-four hour municipality, geared for those of us who run on Transylvanian Standard Time. Maybe somewhere along the way, before or after seeing Deejay, I could get in a little moonlight Exmas shopping.

"Thanks, Fraülein Doktor Professor."

I wasn't sure what kind of name Thorens was, but Deejay had Icelandic genes somewhere. Outside, it was twelve degrees below freezing. Inside her apartment, it was fewer degrees than that below blood temperature, like I was being invited into a blast furnace. Shrugging out of my snow-damp *serape*, I handed it to her, along with my battered gray felt, gave my boots a swipe, and raised my eyebrows. Deejay was fair, blond, maybe an inch taller than me—so is Clarissa, though I've never been fussy about it—slender, with accretions of non-slender in all the most decorative places. Her eyes were the shade of blue you see peeking out between black storm-clouds on one of those Rocky Mountain summer afternoons when it rains and shines at the same time. I'd always thought she looked more like a showgirl than a scientist.

"You may not think it's so splendid after we're through talking. Like I asked on the 'com, can you prove where you were from seventeen to nineteen last night?"

She wore a one-piece satiny athletic outfit in a criminal shade of flesh-colored beige that fit her like a coat of baby oil, and a metallic pistol belt across her hips supporting a short, lightweight .375 automatic. Shoving my hands in my pockets, I followed her into a room full of white tile and light-colored laminated hardwood, centered on a blue-green amoeba-shaped pool. As always, I had trouble watching those hips sway in front of me, not to mention various parts south, without imagining what it would be like to . . .

She gestured, we sat on a low couch. She didn't wait for me to ask if I could smoke, but offered me a handworked box matching the decor, let me make my selection, then picked out a cigarillo for herself, lighting both from a laser on the coffee table. Water filled the room with pleasant lapping noises, reflected light.

"You mean the time of the murder?" she answered, getting her cheroot going. "I was in my lab from twelve hundred yesterday until just before you called. Fourteen hours straight."

She didn't look it. "I hope you can prove that." I exhaled smoke. It evaporated six inches from my face, a gridwork in the table's surface generating negative ions. Leave it to a physicist. "I know a man determined to hang what happened on you, or have me do it."

I described the circumstances. Her eyes widened, then gathered annoyed wrinkles. "Littleshin." She took a furious drag. "That rat, it couldn't be anybody else! He's saying I used the broach to kill from a distance, isn't he? Well, it can't be done, although the reasons for it are technical. Aside from that, I can't offer any—the word is 'alibi,' isn't it?—except corroboration from a graduate assistant who just left on vacation."

"Good timing." I leaned back against a cushion, enjoying the mild flavor of the cigar (mine taste like smoldering cardboard) along with the scenery. "Better find your assistant, make sure he has an alibi. You're dead right about Littleshin, pardon the expression. What were you doing in your lab last night? And why does Littleshin have it in for you?"

"Two questions," she replied, "with the same answer. We've been working overtime for several weeks specifically on account of Littleshin and Mott. They intend—intended in Mott's case—to stop my research for political reasons. They're opposed by Jenny Smythe—Jenny's a Trustee—and Freeman Bertram. We don't know where Mott's sister stands. I wanted to get in as much practical work as possible before the next Board meeting."

The Board ran by unanimous consent like all Confederate organizations. They couldn't touch Deejay's work, but they could make decisions difficult, appropriations impossible. "I didn't know Jenny was a Trustee before tonight. Guess she has to be something besides figurehead President of North America, can't be any money in that."

She shook her head. "None at all, but—"

"What 'practical work' were you doing?" I sat forward, dropping a gray ash into a tray. "Dragging more unsuspecting victims away from friends and family in their native continua?"

She colored. "I thought you didn't have any family in the States."

"Not many friends, either." I sat back again. "What are you up to that Mott wants—wanted—to stop?"

She turned, looking straight at me. "I meant to explain that. Thanks to you, Win"—she smiled—"Jenny has a practical use for the probability broach."

I raised my hands, palms outward. "Leave me out of it. There's that word 'practical' again."

"She wants to infiltrate the States." She nodded. "Support groups working against its government, and free its people from centuries of oppression."

I blinked. "That's practical?"

"With the right backing. Mott and Littleshin claim we're being sponsored by commercial interests, simply to open my new markets. And, as far as that goes, they're right. Revolution at a profit, that's the practical aspect. We even expect competition in the long run, from Interworld, if nobody else. They—Mott and Littleshin, I mean—say it's immoral to interfere with another culture, even to save lives or salvage the future of an entire world."

My world. I was reminded of a similar reluctance to interfere, abetted by a handful of Marxist Congressmen, which had lost us Central America, Mexico, Canada. I was also reminded, watching Deejay, listening to her, that I'd always felt uneasy in her presence. It wasn't any different this time. In addition to her qualities as a scientist, which I was qualified to judge only in terms of the interdimensional slapstick she'd involved me in, she was a bright, attractive young woman. I'm a sucker for bright, attractive young women. Most of my life I'd felt invisible to them. Deejay, however, seemed to like me, and that led to involuntary speculations which weren't just unprofessional and without redeeming social value, but which left me even more uneasy than before.

Feeling sweaty (Deejay did keep her apartment like a sauna), I reached up to shove a finger into my necktie and loosen it, only to realize I hadn't worn one in months. Just because Clarissa and I were having trouble living together after a year, didn't mean . . . I recalled that, looking forward to seeing Deejay for the first time in a long while, I'd forgotten to stop for that Exmas present. Some husband (or whatever) I was. Some detective.

Get hold of yourself, I told me. This was nothing particularly new or threatening. Given my current domestic dissatisfactions, I was finding myself tempted by beauty and brains. It had happened to billions of men before. It would happen to billions more before the sun burnt out. In the States, fifty percent of all marriages ended—

I stopped. This wasn't a train of thought I'd meant to climb aboard. With difficulty, I refocused on what Deejay was saying, instead of the soft, full, moist, warm lips she was saying it with. Something further about "revolution at a profit."

". . . commercial interests at the meeting. Jenny and I, because we were only after results at that point, and worried about potential competition, made the mistake of saying we failed to see anything wrong with that."

"It does seem consistent with Confederate tradition," I observed, inhaling smoke, nodding as if I'd been following her all along.

"Besides," she agreed, "it was our impression, Jenny's, mine, that Mott would oppose anything new, simply because it was new."

"I guess a person could get set in his ways"—I grinned—"after a hundred and seven years."

Stubbing her cigar, she shook her head: "I don't think it had anything to do with that, Win. There are natural-born neophiles, who seek the new because it is new, and their opposites, natural-born neophobes. Maybe there's no logical reason to value one over the other, but I have personal, aesthetic preferences. They include making sure my mistakes aren't just repetitions of somebody else's. Anyway, it wasn't age with Mott. All he and Littleshin saw in the broach was instantaneous transport, a sort of matter transmitter. I tried explaining why that wasn't sensible, how it would take two sets of apparatus, since the broach only operates between alternate worlds—and the power it would consume—but they called me an 'obstructionist.' "

" 'Don't mess up my beautiful theory with facts,' " I quoted. "That's how San Francisco wound up with a subway system more expensive than buying a car for everybody in the Bay Area. What else was Mott against?"

"Well, he was on record, in his youth, as being against Confederation—he wanted to keep the Old United States separate from Mexico and Canada—as well as recognition of the rights of sapient non-humans."

"Chimpanzees," I supplied, "gorillas, porpoises, killer whales." I still had trouble getting used to it, though some of my best friends were simians or cetaceans. "Orangutans, gibbons, maybe even yetis."

She sat back against the cushions at her corner of the couch and folded her hands in her lap. "He was a more recent opponent of what he called the 'unnatural' process of biological rejuvenation."

"Hmph. A Renaissance man, our Mr. Mott. You'd think somebody with one foot in the grave and the other on a produce-counter cliche—"

"You'd think so. I'd think so, too. I have nightmares, Win, about getting old and dying. But Mott—"

"Could have been a judge of his own life and unwilling to prolong the agony. If so, he was unusual. I think most Confederates are neophobes. Even without rejuvenation they live twice as long as people in the States and usually die by violence—they slip in the bathtub or get chewed up and spit out by a hovercraft—because it's the one thing left that can kill them."

"Or perhaps because, from a neophile's viewpoint"—she smiled, shuddering at the same time—"a quick, violent death is preferable to the alternative."

I grunted. "I always thought so."

We sat a while, Deejay contemplating her nightmares, me feeling guilty over thoughts I'd been thinking about her. Of course there weren't any laws against thinking. There weren't any laws at all, which seemed, oddly enough, to be the source of problems between Clarissa and me. Nothing in the Confederacy is illegal. The closest thing to law, in any formal sense, is the Covenant of Unanimous Consent, quilled by Albert Gallatin, second President of the Old United States, following successful overthrow and execution of the first President, George Washington. The one punishable violation is initiating force against another sapient, and even that doesn't put it right. Swap "punishable" for "interruptible," the idea's clearer. With no government to bestow its mixed and dubious benefits, and being in the habit of carrying personal weapons all the time, Confederates solve their own problems, at the moment and location they arise. Any honest mugger, rapist, or B&E man will tell you this is a deterrent that works.

"Confederate crime is rare," I found myself repeating aloud. Along with a tall drink, Deejay had offered me a copper for my thoughts, asking after Clarissa. I was dog-tired, hadn't eaten in hours (I forget when I'm working), and there was nobody else to talk to. "And Confederate criminals an endangered species. That makes this a swell place to live, my fine feathered physicist, but a hell of a place for a detective to earn a decent living, short of discovering where Uncle Ethelbert absently misplaced the family hovercraft, or finding strayed cats for teary-eyed little girls." Deejay raised her eyebrows, but didn't say anything. I took a swallow of my second drink, noticing it was halfway gone already. "I admit I've been desperate enough to take a couple of cases like that. Maybe a couple of dozen."

She nodded. "And Clarissa?"

"Clarissa, otherhandwise, is in on the ground floor of a brand-new growth industry: 'the unnatural process of biological rejuvenation.' You know, I had a partner in the States once, another cop named James J. James. The J. stood for— But never mind that. He claimed that success in a capitalist society, in any society, consists of thinking up something you can make for a nickel, sell for a buck, and everybody has to have one, twice a day, or die."

Deejay laughed. I liked the way her eyes looked when she did that.

"Rejuvenation," I continued, "doesn't fit the criteria as well as, say this Pennsylvania paint-remover we're drinking, but it works about the same."

She tipped her glass. "How's that?"

"In the first place, considering it amounts to a kind of immortality, it's dirt cheap, I've seen bowling alleys that charged more for a season pass. Medicine is a competitive business in the Confederacy, not the first step to canonization it represents in a galaxy far, far away. Just to give you an idea, Clarissa MacDougall Olson, H.D., makes *housecalls*."

"So does my Healer." Deejay shrugged. "So what?"

"I'll tell you: for anyone under the age of forty still unfortunate enough to be living in the States, housecalls are a quaint prehistoric custom where the doctor came to you, instead of your bundling up, trudging out into the cold to add pneumonia to whatever ails you, then risking chicken pox or cancer virus during hours in the waiting room spent thumbing through a dog-eared stack of last year's *Reactionary Digest*."

"More to the point," Deejay suggested in a kind, sisterly tone I found myself resenting, "Clarissa's very busy, isn't she, meaning you two have less time together than is good for your relationship?"

I tossed back the rest of my bourbon, set the glass on the table. "Old age," I informed her, "as I'm sure you know, isn't a natural process, like growing up or going male-pattern bald, it's a disease."

"Several diseases." She sipped at her own drink. "Cheerfully cooperating to ruin your whole life. You didn't answer my question, did you?"

"I'm the detective. I'll do the questioning. Where was I? Oh yeah. Depending on the customer's condition, rejuvenation can use up weeks or months, be a gradual, part-time project, or require full-time therapy. In either case it's a complicated, individual proposition. Clarissa tries to make up her overhead on volume. She succeeds."

"Which makes—" Deejay said, reaching out, sisterly again, to pat my hand, "all things being unequal, for quite a difference in your respective incomes."

"It's damned hard on an old flatfoot's pride," I told her.

I wasn't just talking about Clarissa.

SAT 24 DEC 212 A.L.
04:17 O'CLOCK

The snow had stopped. The sky was clear and bright with stars. Toward Kansas, it was beginning to glow with the coming dawn, still hours away, as I endured the mortal shock of emerging from Deejay's hot, humid digs into the bone-biting cold of Rocky Mountain winter and crunched across the freeze-dried lawn to the Neova, gasping and shivering. When I'd unstuck my fingers from the handle, climbed inside, and slammed the door, a familiar voice was issuing from the dash. "*—ward William Bear, consulting detective. I'm not in my car right now, but if you'll wait for the beep, then leave your name, number, and the time you called, I'll get back to you— beeeeep!*"

"Win—"

On the little screen, Clarissa's gaze was averted, as if she were reading from notes. I grabbed the pickup, fumbling with the keyboard to shortstop the answering program. "Clarissa, I just got back. Listen, baby, I'm sorry about the way things happened tonight. I—"

"I'm between stops and haven't much time." She didn't look up. The tone she cut me off with was wasted on a human being, I might as well have let the machine handle it. "Here are preliminary autopsy results. The subject was shot with what my references call a 'jell-tip': thin nylon jacket, jellied liquid teflon core, self-destructive and forensically untraceable. Caliber could be anything from thirty-five to fifty-five. I have to cut this short. I double-booked two patients by mistake, but can get to both if I run."

"All right, sweetheart, take care of—" She rang off, ending what only a hermit who hadn't heard a human voice in decades would call a conversation. I was left in the bitter cold and failing darkness with a blinking light that told me I had other messages.

"*Freeman Bertram here, MENcken 7–8504.*" In velvet smoking jacket and matching kilt, he reclined in overstuffed luxury. "*It's a little before three hundred, December 24th. I was curious how things are proceeding, having a personal interest in the beauteous and unjustly accused Professor Thorens. Call me when you have time. I don't mean to jog your elbow.*" It was hard to believe Bertram had once been a Hamiltonian, and harder not to believe, considering he'd once absorbed a laser-blast intended for me. But Bertram and Deejay? Never in a hundred years. The machine clicked and gabbled.

"*It's—how I detest these machines—it's past three in the morning, young man. I should like to have a progress report from you.*" No image displayed itself; instead, I got a tourist brochure view of the Mott estate, taken in summer. To get even, I imagined her in a cheap print robe, face-grease, and hair curlers. "*In future, I would prefer that you call me*

*at intervals, rather than my having to call you. I
believe you have my number."*

Screw her. It hadn't been my habit to make progress reports when I was with the City & County. Not until the job was over and I could report that. I waited for the next message, watching my breath deposit surrealistic frozen patterns on the windscreen, shimmering and multicolored where the streetlights shone through. God, I hate winter.

"Detective? Merse Littleshin." The background was a room no more than a block away. He looked exactly as he had hours ago, sitting against a backdrop of snow-covered pines just outside his office window. *"I'm calling to discover what effort you've been making. How soon can I expect to hear that Dora Jayne Thorens has been confined where she can no longer threaten anyone?"*

That was it, messagewise. I'd probably had media calls—murder isn't simply rare in these parts, it's a sensation—but I've got a program to filter them out by key-word, dumping them where the little dot goes when you turn off the TV. Bertram I'd catch later. Miss Mott, for all that she was a client, was also a suspect. I'd grill her on the pretext of reporting as she wanted. She probably wore fuzzy slippers, too. As for Littleshin, screw him *and* his pet llama. I had shopping to do. I punched a 'com number Deejay had given me. Instead of a sapient visage, my screen filled with a big round yellow face, two black dots and a curved line for a mouth. Another recent import from the States.

"Life," it asserted, *"is an intelligence test—beeeep!"* I told the machine I'd appreciate a call from its owner, Deejay's laboratory assistant. Then, since I was already there, I decided my next stop would be Littleshin's office, where I found he'd been doing some investigating of his own.

SAT 24 DEC 212 A.L.
04:25 O'CLOCK

"Detective! It appears we've both been fusing the midnight nucleus."

This time I held onto my coat. Where Deejay was Icelandic at heart (or at least at thermostat), this guy was British and kept his office like a meat locker. Smoke issued from my mouth and nostrils, although I hadn't lit a cigar for an hour. Lights were off in the anteroom he'd let me into. A single fluorescent in the inner office flooded his blotter with sickly greenish light. He sat behind his desk, I sat on a chair colder than my car's upholstery. In spite of the hour, he hadn't opaqued the window behind his desk. The self-cleaning non-glare glass was almost invisible. Over his shoulder, I looked into the little wooded park he'd mentioned earlier, snow-covered and picturesque under the starlight.

"Yeah," I answered, "I was in the neighborhood—"

He beamed: "Detecting! Perhaps I can assist! From the University physical plant manager, I've learned of an enormous power draw accountable to Thorens's laboratory the moment Seaton was killed. Wouldn't you say it's time you placed her in custody?"

I cleared my throat. "Arrests are a touchy business, Mr. Littleshin."

Not, I thought, like home, where individual rights are the original legal fiction. Here it's more like persuading someone to check into a luxury hotel. The arrestee pays for the temporary accommodation of his choice, posting bond, not to guarantee he'll stay put, but to demonstrate willingness and ability to make restitution to his alleged victim.

"And woe unto the guy," I wiggled a preacher's finger, "who picks an innocent individual to arrest. It's the former, not the latter, who'll wind up paying restitution for the remainder of his life."

Littleshin leaned back in his chair, steepling his fingers under his chin. "I've never seen anyone arrested, or known anyone it happened to. Are you saying Thorens could sue the University?"

"I'm saying she could sue you." I took my hat off and ran my fingers through my dandruff. It was *cold* in here. "Or, more importantly, me. They say you can't get blood out of a turnip, but I'll bet a lot of turnips got squashed, finding that out."

He took a deep breath. "Tell me what I can do to help, then."

I shrugged. "Get off my back. I'm working for Miss Mott, but I won't put up even with her nagging me. Answer a few questions about Seaton Mott and his past associations."

For an instant, I thought he was going to climb on his dignity. So did he. Then, spreading his hands, letting the motion travel up his arms until it turned into a shrug, he agreed to tell me whatever I wanted. In the end, it didn't come to much: school gossip, Board politics. Without prompting, he gave me the same story Deejay had about Jenny's subversive application of broach physics. Except that he and Mott were the goodguys.

SAT 24 DEC 212 A.L.
05:01 O'CLOCK

I exited Littleshin's office annoyed and worried, climbed into the Neova (which I'd left idling for warmth) and tried the graduate assistant again—*"Life is an intelligence test—beeeep!"*—without success. Somewhat soberer than when I'd left Deejay's apartment, I recalled something she'd said about potential competition in the probability broach business.

"Directory, please."

The screen resolved into the image of a cartoon porpoise bobbing at the edge of a transparent tank. "General Directory," it replied in its whistly cetacean voice, "for the Greater Laporte area. May I help?" Something else I'd never quite gotten used to was dealing with the animated personae of interactive computers.

"Do you have a listing for Interworld, Limited?" That, I'd gathered, was the other outfit working on broach technology.

The pseudo-cetacean closed its big brown eyes in thought. "Let me see— They may be reached at ERIs 2–2323, or, during their present construction phase, in temporary quarters beneath the intersection of Pearson and Shaw. Will that be all?"

It was enough. The Neova rose on its skirts, blew snow from under its tires, and headed south on Confederation. I like the way Laporte handles street crossings, no minor matter when hovercraft traffic blurs by at a hundred MPH. To avoid splattering pedestrians on windshields like grasshoppers on a biker's teeth, out of desire not to create ill-lit mugging-grounds, and from a lack of Other People's Money gathered at *official* gunpoint, to pay for storm drains and traffic signals—not to mention a dearth of legislation against turning a profit—a string of subsurface malls has evolved. You can simply ride the horizontilator from one corner to the next, or stop at emporia ranging from newsstands and fast-fooders to department stores and sitdown eateries requiring reservations. In the end—James Burke please take note —connecting these burrows one by one with laser-bored, shop-lined tunnels paralleling the streets top-side, they wound up with a city beneath the city, like the old Gene Autry serial.

Upstairs acreage is for residence. Seen from the air, this metropolis of two million resembles the Amazon basin or the Argentine pampas more than it does Fort Collins, Colorado, which occupies the same spot in the universe next door. Nobody planned it that way. You can earn a degree in "spontaneous order" at the local think-factory, but any mention of building codes or zoning laws invariably evokes stares of horror and incomprehension.

SAT 24 DEC 212 A.L.
05:20 O'CLOCK

Despite the many shops I visited in the subterranean consumatorium at the corner of Pearson and Shaw, fortified for the Exmassacre to come later today, I couldn't find a thing I liked. I'd gotten a bite to eat—squid-burger and kelp fries at Delphinus Deli (don't knock it till you've tried it)—which elevated my outlook a while. A cannabist had a glittering display of silver, gold, or platinum roach clips and cocaine spoons, your name engraved no extra charge, but Clarissa wasn't into drugs, a quality I'm sure her surgical patients appreciated. I tried a couple of weapons shops, but the girl in my life had a gun, .11 caliber Webley Electric, and she was a one-gun girl. I wished, on my own account, for more time to drool on the transparent countertops at Thanatek, Ltd.

Interworld, Ltd. turned out to be a hole in the wall suffering delusions of a future. The Chief Engineer was a Carl Sagan impersonator and forty-year-old technokid with a thousand light-year stare and mad-scientist hair blown straight back by sheer force of intellect. He talked like my old class notes from high school.

"The university?" He sat on a corner of a beat-up desk beneath naked titanium ceiling joists separating unfinished walls of the fused silica which substitutes in the Confederacy for concrete. The light was dim, the air inside the little storefront laden with the incense of hot circuit board material. In the back I saw silhouettes of all too familiar-looking equipment. "Invented the technology—rather their two best workers, P'wheet and Thorens. Constipated fossils running the place couldn't invent a healthy urge to go to the toilet. Ahead of everybody in the field. Doesn't mean they're going to stay that way. Where are they going with it? Transport too expensive to be economical? More research? Interworld has a better idea. Making money. Tons. Once our machinery's operational . . ."

"Revolution at a profit?" Now he had me doing it.

"Tourism! Immigration—not much traffic the other way— Imports! Exports! Just wait until we're up and running!"

I watched through Interworld's unwashed windows as meager early-morning traffic moved through the underground mall. "Which you aren't. So you couldn't have been between seventeen and nineteen last night, when there was a broach-sized power draw?"

"Hmm. Noticed that. Wondered. Thorens must have been—"

"Fusing the midnight nucleus? All right," I nodded, "one more item and I'll let you get back to work. Explain this double-broach matter-transport thing. Sounds like a good idea to me. I want to understand the drawbacks."

He frowned. "Broaches eat power. Man-sized holes to other continua need 1.21 gigawatts minimum. To get from somewhere in this continuum to another in same—say Laporte to Chicago—requires two broaches, one here at Pearson and Shaw, opened on the equivalent point in the United States—"

"That would be about Eisenhower and Taft," I estimated, "in the town of Loveland, south of Fort Collins."

"Yes, and another in Confederate Chicago—a 'dirigible' broach, still experimental and even more expensive—aimed at the same point in the United States. Step from here to the States, cross the gap between apertures, and step back into the Confederacy in Chicago."

"I see," I told him. "For a total expenditure exceeding 2.42 gigawatts."

He shook his head. "Exceeding? Squared and cubed! Technical problems—phase interference, remote operation, other things—make the relationship geometric, not additive. More like five gigawatts, if everything is working perfectly, which it won't be."

"Hmm. And that's economically prohibitive?" I wasn't sure, in a fusion-powered civilization.

"Someday, maybe not. The technology will get better, more efficient. Power will get cheaper. Until then . . ."

"I think I get you. In the meantime, can I borrow your 'com?" I didn't intend accepting his claims without some confirmation. I figured the people to provide it, considering how expensive broach machinery is to run, would be Cheyenne Ridge Power & Light. Nobody had a monopoly, "natural" or otherwise, on the production of electricity, but, with their lines and grids and so on, power companies must operate a lot like banks. They had to talk to one another about things like surges or peak loads. Which exhausted my entire knowledge of power companies.

"Sure," the Sagan impersonator replied, "must be

around here somewhere." He found a 'com pad in a wastebasket beside the desk, handed it to me, and wandered off into the back. I let my fingers do the wandering.

"Confidential, young man," the elderly manager of CRP&L informed me. One thing about the Confederacy, at least for me at the tender age of almost-fifty, was the number of people in a position to call me young man. "Against company policy to hand it out to just anyone who wants it."

"May I point out," I asked, "that I'm investigating a murder?"

"How in tarnation'll violating our rights make up for someone violating somebody else's? Answer me that—but on your own time. We're calibrating tonight. You do your job, whatever that may be, let me get on with mine. I'm tired of being bothered about this."

Thanks a lot, Littleshin, I thought. I replied, "Look, I don't even know *why* this murder was committed, let alone who committed it. Suppose the killer's going after ill-mannered centenarian bosses of various major Laporte institutions? In other words, suppose the next victim on his list is *you?*"

There was a long pause. "All right, gimme a minute." He took five, but came back with the bacon. "I can't find any other major power draw at the right time, except for that at Laporte University."

"Okay, let me ask you about something else. What can you tell me about the storm you whipped up last night?"

A sour look: "You're aware that Cheyenne Ridge Power & Light controls the weather merely as a by-product of its power-generating operation?"

I was. Cheyenne Ridge, the geological feature, not the company, stood between Laporte and prevailing weather-bearing winds from the northwest, just as its counterpart in my world afforded a degree of natural protection for Fort Collins. Weather smacked into the upwind slope, vaulted over Larimer County, settled back to Earth in the neighborhood of bedroom communities north of Denver. Often, when the capital (represented here by the villages of Saint Charles and Auraria) was up to its elastic marks in fixings for street slush, Fort Collins was a veritable Gobi. Here, the power & light folks enhanced the effect with fusion-powered updrafts from giant heat-exchangers at the ridge-crest. If weather came from another direction, both Laporte and Fort Collins suffered, and there wasn't a thing CRP&L, or geology, could do about it.

"Then you're aware that we don't 'whip up' storms or charge anybody a tenth-ounce for moderating the climate. It's advertising, a gesture of goodwill, public relations. What's more, sooner or later we must permit the same amount of moisture to pass as nature would, or goodwill turns into a flock of suits for brown lawns, dying crops, and flooding further south. We restrict precipitation to the midnight hours, distribute it more evenly than nature would, but we look forward to a chance to relax and let things happen the way they're inclined to."

I thought about the blizzard howling between here and Laramie. "You're saying yesterday's snowfall was scheduled, using the holidays as an excuse?"

"I'm saying I might choose different words another time, but tonight I'm tired. We needed a little downtime for calibration and maintenance."

"And that began at eighteen hundred hours yesterday evening?"

"Should it come to lawyers, that's what the record will indicate."

That's what the evidence indicated. Snow had begun falling just before Mott was shot. I rang off and slogged back to my car. Lights were blinking. Two messages, one from Miss Mott, one from Littleshin, repeating their respective demands. My visit to the latter hadn't done any good.

SAT 24 DEC 212 A.L.
05:40 O'CLOCK

I tried calling Clarissa, but the 'com at home stuttered and produced a pleasant-looking young woman with blue-gray eyes and dark brown curly hair.

"Raukerk, may I help?" She looked familiar. It annoyed me not knowing why. From the circled cross on one tunic shoulder, insignia Clarissa wore on most of her own clothing, she was a Healer. She must have been on housecall, her image had that jiggly quality associated with hand-held 'coms.

"May I ask why you're answering Clarissa Olson's calls?"

She reached in a pocket and held up a card that told me she was *Loranna Kay Raukerk, H.D.* I recalled meeting her at a dinner gathering of Greater Laporte Healers Clarissa had conscripted me into. "Clarissa didn't tell you? She's cancelled her appointments for the next several days. I'm taking new business for her. And before you ask, I don't know where she can be reached."

I don't know why I felt embarrassed not knowing where Clarissa was. "You may not remember me, Healer," I told her, displaying one of my own cards, "but we've met. I'm Win Bear, a detective, um, associated with Clarissa. When she calls for her messages, tell her I'm looking for her, will you?"

"You bet, Win."

As she rang off, I watched the answer-light blinking again. Someone had called while I was on the 'com with Loranna Raukerk. Certain it had to be Clarissa, I punched buttons. Trouble was, I was wrong. What I got was an anonymous, synthetic voice, the kind used to sell insurance policies: *"You don't need the grief fooling around in other people's business will get you. Give up this investigation now, while you still have a choice in the matter."*

Whoever it was, they knew I didn't have any other jobs at the moment. Pounding panic back wherever I store it, I reminded myself, from Stateside experience, that only one call like this in every ten ever turns out serious.

Worried about Clarissa, I spent the next half hour checking everywhere she might be. I talked to Mrs. Grundy, rather, she talked at me. Desperate, I even called Clarissa's mother. She was gleefully unwilling to tell me anything of her daughter's whereabouts. She'd been instructed not to talk to anybody, and put a lot more emphasis on the word "anybody" than I suspected Clarissa had. In a way, that sounded like good news, more like Clarissa was sore than that she'd come to any harm. I had no choice but to continue the investigation I'd committed myself to, nursing the forlorn, stupid hope that her disappearance only meant she'd decided to end our relationship. I was willing to settle for that, provided she was otherwise okay.

SAT 24 DEC 212 A.L.
06:10 O'CLOCK

On the way to see my client, I stopped at the address listed for Deejay's assistant, about what I'd expected for a guy working his way through college, being paid in education and lab space. Imagine the home of a moderately successful Beverly Hills plastic surgeon and you'll get an idea of what passes, in Laporte, for the low-rent district. Back home, most land west of the Mississippi belongs to federal, state, county, or municipal governments, horribly inflating the price of what little's left. No such artificial scarcity prevails here. Every square inch is private and untaxed. I left the Neova in the drive (it's foolish to park any vehicle along a hundred-mile-per-hour street) and followed ankle-lamps along a self-defrosting walk. A pushed button got me a happy face display and the same *"Life is an intelligence test—beeeeep!"* which had been funny the first time on the 'com.

Onward and Mottward: imagine the home of a moderately successful Roman emperor and you'll get an idea of the door which was answered by the lady of the house, at the home my client had shared with her former brother. If I'd left my car on that street, I'd still be crossing the lawn to get there.

"Come in, young man, may I take your wrap? My, it's cold out, would you care for something warming to drink?"

I doffed the felt. "No thanks on both counts, Miss

Mott. I need to ask a few more questions, if you don't mind."

Halfway across her entrance hall, I was wishing for one of those moving sidewalks they install beneath intersections. It had been a long night. She ushered me into a room that would have looked well-furnished in Astroturf and goal-posts. "Ask whether I mind or not. Isn't that what a detective does?"

I grinned, seating myself on a sofa-edge. It occurred to me that one way to tell rich people from the rest of us is that they put their furniture in the middle of the room. "Right you are. I'd like to confirm some information I've gathered. Then I'll have a better idea what to do next." Seated across from me, she nodded. I told her, not attributing what I'd learned of her brother's dislike for innovation, citing Confederation, rejuvenation, non-human sapience, political uses of the broach. His attitude might not be crucial, but it was odd enough to warrant attention.

"He wasn't above changing his mind," she told me with an unhappy look on what had been a prunish face to begin with, "given sufficient motivation. For example, he had recently reversed himself on the issue of rejuvenation."

My eyebrows went up by themselves. "Did he offer any reason?"

She pursed her lips. "He planned to undergo the process as a sacrifice to necessity, pursuing his dispute with Professor Thorens and the President."

Don't ask how I knew, years of experience, maybe. She was lying.

SAT 24 DEC 212 A.L.
06:55 O'CLOCK

"Dear Lysander, of course she was lying!" the Laporte Paratronics chairman was living up to his title, leaning back in the same impressive recliner I'd seen on the 'com hours ago. Maybe he slept in it. Clamped to one arm was a tray with a teacup and a bowl for the dead bag. Mine was in there, too. In a similar chair, I sat, simultaneously warm and dry for the first time since last night, struggling not to fall asleep after twenty-plus hours on my metaphorical feet. This was the penthouse atop the mile-high pyramid, Aztec Modern decor, located at the north edge of Greater Laporte I'd visited before. Montezuma and the Egyptians would have died of envy, if they hadn't already been dead. TransAmerica might have joined them.

I raised an eyebrow. "But not about her brother's rejuvenation."

"Nor his determination where the probability broach was concerned." He set his cup aside, drew a cigarette holder from the pocket of his smoking jacket. "But I assure you, Seaton Mott had another reason besides politics, one his sister was all too well aware of, for wanting to be young again."

"Something—" I accepted a cigarette; you can only smoke so many cigars in one night. "—feminine." En route to this place, I'd checked on Clarissa again without reaching her. To my annoyance, there'd been another nag from Littleshin, which I ignored. I'd stopped at the graduate assistant's humble abode a second time, inquiring with the few neighbors conscious at that hour. In a transient student neighborhood, they'd proven unable to help. Now I was paying a visit on my old friend and former enemy, Freeman K. Bertram.

"For the first time in years, I gather"—he screwed a cigarette into his holder, lit mine, then his own—"he was seeing a young woman."

I inhaled and exhaled. "Anybody I'd know?"

Outside, through a window half the size of my living room, the winter sun blasted up over the prairie horizon without so much as a contrail in the aching blue sky. I knew that meant it would be colder today than last night. I'd be spending all my time afoot, taking tiny little Oriental steps to avoid falling on my big fat Amerindian ass. People who "Think Snow" are perverts.

He shook his head. "Watanabe was the name I recall, Violet Watanabe. Something to do with the University faculty, I think. A 'fortune-hunting bit of fluff' in Alberta's estimate—those were Seaton's words. Our political differences on the Board, his and mine, weren't personal, and he talked to me. I suspect that Alberta, who doted on him, was the slightest bit jealous of the plans her brother was making after his coming rejuvenation."

I grinned. "No pun intended. You and Littleshin were conversing about the time Mott was killed. Mind telling me about it?"

"I did most of the talking the first time. He wondered whether he'd taken the right tack with Deejay. He wanted to understand everything about the issue, perhaps to modify his position. I told him all I knew of the physics, its history and potential. It must have taken half an hour or so."

I frowned. "What do you mean 'the first time'?"

"Only that our conversation was interrupted."

"I see." I nodded. "About how long between halves?"

He considered. "Not more than minutes. Merse said he had a visitor or a call on another line, I forget. I suspect he wanted to use the bathroom. He called me back almost immediately. We continued for another half hour."

"Any witnesses to this conversation?"

"None at his end, I think. It was after hours. His secretary had gone for the day. Plenty at this end, though. I work in what amounts to my home. Several of my staff live in the building and are in and out of this apartment pretty much around the clock. More than one came in while I was talking to Merse. I was using, as I often do, a wall-screen, so he'd appear life-size, sitting against that big office window of his with the trees outside."

"Think there was enough time to get in his car, go kill Mott, then come back and finish with you? Mott's place isn't that far from the university."

He shook his head. "What you describe would take at least fifteen minutes. I don't think the interruption lasted more than two or three."

"Hmmm. Was sister Alberta jealous enough to serve brother Seaton a high-velocity jell-tip bullet, right in the old cerebellum?"

He looked startled. "How's that?"

"Thin nylon shell outside," I explained, "jellied liquid teflon inside. Melts in your brian, not in your gun." He paled, offering no reply. Living with a Healer had encouraged bad habits I'd acquired during years on Homicide. For most people, it was way too early in the morning for terminal ballistics.

"Change of subject: your company helped the University develop the broach in the first place. You're on the Board of Trustees. You also make no secret that you're fond of Deejay. Yet you say your differences with Mott weren't personal. How did you feel about his other plans for after his rejuvenation, which included cutting Deejay off from her work?"

"Great Albert's ghost, I'm a suspect!" He flicked ashes into the teabag bowl. "I suppose I ought to be flattered. As to what you ask, it's difficult to explain. My difference with Seaton wasn't personal, yet I felt personally about the difference itself, if you take my meaning. In any event, it isn't so much how I feel as what I plan to do. I'll continue funding Deejay, offer her working space here, if need be, regardless of what the Board does."

"She'll be glad to hear that—or has she already?"

"She has," Bertram replied. "Regardless of what Merse says, that ought to remove her from suspicion once and for all, don't you think?"

My own suspicions of Deejay had been minimal to begin with. I couldn't help it that I knew the woman. It was ludicrous to imagine she'd murder anybody for the reason suggested. Violet Watanabe, however, might turn out to be a hot lead. Thanking Bertram for the tea and sympathy, I departed from the pyramid, which is more than any dead Egyptian ever managed on his own.

SAT 24 DEC 212 A.L.
07:28 O'CLOCK

The same damned light was blinking when I climbed in the Neova. A quick call told me Clarissa was still out of touch. I watched the light, hoping one of the messages which had come while I was cutting up touches with Bertram was from the love of my life. No luck. Two were Littleshin. Sandwiched in between was another anonymous threat. Directory Assistance (this time a Rocky Mountain bighorn in a tuxedo) gave me an address for Violet Watanabe. She was a neighbor of Deejay's, as I expected, a professor of history in Laporte University's Department of Praxeology. I was there in five minutes.

"Odd," I said to the woman who greeted me at the door, "you don't look a history professor. We've got to stop meeting like this. Clarissa will get suspicious. Speaking of Clarissa, have you heard anything from her lately?"

"I'm just a smidge busy at the moment," Loranna Raukerk replied, not inviting me in. "Is there something I can do for you, Win?"

"It's possible. I didn't mention it before, but I'm investigating a murder. I'd like to have a few words with Violet Watanabe."

She shook her head. "I'm afraid Violet isn't seeing anyone today. May I give her a message?"

I shook mine right back at her. "I'm up to here with messages, giving and taking. I need to see Miss Watanabe as soon as possible."

She paused, thoughtful. "Come in a minute. I'll show you why Violet isn't receiving."

I followed her down the hall to a bedroom, where a young woman who did look like a history professor, from the bridge of her cute little nose to the top of her bright-colored comforter, lay with a sleep inducer taped over her eyes. The comforter was cheerful where sunlight streamed in from a nearby window.

"Shocked," the Healer told me in a whisper, "inconsolable with grief. She's been this way since she heard about Seaton Mott. That's why I've got her under sedation. Isn't it the saddest thing you ever saw?"

"Saddest thing I ever saw," I told her, "was a guy, flat broke, who sat two hours with his head in an oven before he realized they'd turned the gas off." I didn't say I couldn't imagine anyone being so inconsolable over my demise they'd require this kind of care. I don't know what the old goat had, but I was ordering a double.

Interviewing an unconscious subject didn't strike me as productive. I admit I walked around and peeked in the window, making sure Violet didn't hop out of bed to congratulate her accomplice on the fast one they'd pulled. That was what things had come to. At that, things might have been worse, I told myself. Violet might have had a second floor apartment. For that matter, this might have been a hit and run case. I might even have found a smoking gun at the murder scene, or a fired cartridge case. One man's evidence is another man's *non sequitur:* nobody collects fingerprints in the Confederacy, and they think license plates are something you put food on at an orgy.

With that thought, something Bertram had implied switched on a small, dim bulb over my head. Another five minutes got me back to the Caesar Rodney subdivision for the third time in twelve hours.

SAT 24 DEC 212 A.L.
07:45 O'CLOCK

"You said 'ask,' Miss Mott, so here goes: what was the exact nature of your relationship with the deceased?"

We were in what I'd begun thinking of as the AlbertaDome. Afraid I'd nod off on a couch, I'd taken one of those spindly parlor chairs that never look like they're meant to sit on. On a nearby sofa, Miss Mott was holding up well, if my guess was right. I wondered what sedation she was taking.

"Why," my client told me, apparently puzzled, "he was my brother."

"And maybe a little something else, besides?" I took a deep breath, ready to kiss off the first decent fee I'd had a crack at. "Who was it said incest is fine game as long as you keep it in the family?"

She sat up, stiff. "How dare you sully my brother's memory by jumping to such wild, irresponsible conclusions!" She trembled. I kept an eye on the little pistol, a .444 Willis, she wore crossdraw at her waist. I shrugged. "Look, when you won't tell me the truth, I can't be held responsible for my conclusions. It wouldn't be the first time my client turned out to be a killer." It would, in fact, unless you count the habitual killer I'd drawn paychecks from for twenty-seven years, but I never overlook the value of a well-placed lie. I must have said something right, despite the fact I'd all but accused her of being a murderer; she started relaxing.

"Listen," I continued. "Where I grew up, every second breath you take is against one law or another. But even when I earned a living enforcing those laws, I figured—and it damn near got me fired more than once—that a person's private life is his own business. Her own business. I'm not here to do anything except find out who killed your brother. Believe me, I don't give a rat's ass how you two entertained each other unless it's relevant."

It was her turn for one of those deep-down kamikaze breaths. "I've often heard it said, young man—Win—that custom's a thousand times more powerful than any law. I loved my brother more than eighty years, in the manner—which is to say the degree of intimacy—you suggest. You're the first, as far as I know, even to suspect. I suppose that means I hired a competent detective. I was a girl of fifteen when it began. Custom can also be stronger than the absence of law: neither Seaton nor I ever felt particularly proud of what we were doing."

"And along came Violet. Were you angry it was over after eighty years?"

"Eighty-eight years. I was, although I limited my vindictiveness to supporting Professor Thorens's position on the Board of Trustees."

Despite myself, I laughed. "I hate to ask, but, as you say, I'm a competent detective. I try to be, anyway. Tell me again where you were, what you were doing, when your brother . . ."

"As a matter of fact, I can. There is some advantage, after all, to being my age and the sort of person I am. I don't rattle. It occurred to me, when Seaton was killed, that someone would be asking me that before too long. I was preparing the house for a social gathering. Between servants and guests, I was never alone the entire time Seaton went for his walk until I heard his body had been discovered."

I'm hopeless: a detective should be more suspicious of people than I ever manage to be. I'm always the one most surprised when I discover that the soft-spoken shoe-salesman is the culprit who chainsawed his mother-in-law into chunks and mailed her to starving Ethiopians. I was impressed with Miss Mott and found myself wondering what she'd be like after rejuvenation.

SAT 24 DEC 212 A.L.
08:39 O'CLOCK

I pushed the button the third time that day. "*Life is—*" Happyface vanished, replaced by a fogbound chimp. "Who is it?"

I shook my head. "A surprised Win Bear. Curley Koman, I presume?"

"Guilty," came the reply, half-drowned by the hissing of a shower. I was surprised. Most chimps hate water and prefer aerosol pelt shampoos. "Come in and make yourself comfortable. I'll join you in a minute."

There came a click. I followed the door into a room cluttered with tools and gutted paratronics. The wall opposite, a floor-to-ceiling 'com screen, appeared covered with glossy photos, all of one subject, a public library, sometimes tax-supported, sometimes profit-making, which seemed to have counterparts in many versions of Laporte/Fort Collins. In some photos windows were missing, sandstone blackened by fireblast. In some the place looked like a candle left under a sunlamp, soft at the edges, puddled at the foundation. In a few the building was fine, but every leaf and blade of grass was gone, leaving bare earth. Others showed nothing but a rubble-strewn lot.

"You're looking at the graveyards of a hundred billion people." The bathrobed proprietor of this gruesome gallery emerged from another room toweling his head. "I've been out of touch with the world, sleeping sixteen hours. Working overtime nine weeks straight does things to my metabolism. I woke up earlier to messages from you, Deejay, some Healer, and one of the Trustees, all about Seaton Mott's achieving open-mindedness the hard way."

I turned. The Healer would be Loranna Raukerk, gathering background on her inconsolable client. "Which Trustee?" As if I didn't know.

He tossed the damp towel onto a chair arm, lit a cigarette, and sat. "You've got me. I make a point never to remember the name of anyone who introduces himself by title. We could find out, but a long Exmas message from my mother recorded over it while I was sleeping in."

I sighed with a need for sleep myself. "You've heard about Mott, you know why I'm here." I refused his offer of a chair. "What were you and Deejay up to around eighteen last night?"

"That's easy, testing Laumer's Hypothesis." He indicated the photos. "That's where all this came from: fiberoptic probes made through a minibroach while the machinery autocycled from one continuum to the next."

"Laumer's Hypothesis?"

"Out of an infinity of possibilities," he quoted, "a majority of Earths will have been destroyed by biological or thermonuclear warfare."

I nodded, understanding. "I always thought surviving civilizations would be rare, myself." The chimpanzee nodded back. "One reason," I went on, "that the President and Deejay were anxious to salvage the United States I grew up in. It may not be much, but it's all it's got."

"You said it, not me. I guess the judge is still out on Laumer, but, as you can see for yourself, Mr. Bear, we've had some mighty powerful testimony in favor of the S.C.U.M. Syndrome."

This time I didn't ask, just raised my eyebrows.

"A poor thing," he shrugged, "but mine own: 'Selective Cultivation of Unfit Mentalities,' a corollary to Wilson's S.N.A.F.U. principle. In any hierarchy, nobody has any reason to promote the interests of anyone more honest, capable, or intelligent than they are. Ergo, the higher you look on the organizational ladder, the less honest, capable, and intelligent any individual is likely to be. Scum floats to the top, and, in cultures with governments, the scum have their fingers on the thermonuclear trig—"

BRAAAPSH! That's the closest I can get to it. Koman had been cut off by a hailstorm of projectiles smashing through his front window, ripping stitches in the door. He went down levering a pistol from his bathrobe pocket. My S&W Model 58 materialized in my hand. I pointed it at a maroon 211 Varga riding across the lawn on its inflated skirt as it spewed slugs into the house. The .41 Magnum bellowed, leapt, bruised the web of my thumb as it splashed wind-shield fragments into the driver's compartment. Koman got in half a dozen semi-automatic comments before he dropped his gun and collapsed. The Varga spun, righted itself, and vanished down the block.

I yelled "Healer!" at the apartment's emergency programming, then made a call of my own, asking a single question. The answer was "no."

By this time, Koman had lost consciousness. Breathing and pulse were okay. Help was coming. Some things were the same here as in the States: the hovercraft would turn out to be stolen. I'd failed to bag the assassin. Nonetheless, I felt proud of myself for the first time in a long while. The call had been to Ham Charles. His people had been watching Dee-jay's place around the clock. She hadn't set a toe outside; probably on downtime like her assistant. Others were being watched, as well. Some apparently knew how to shake a tail—no particular talent was needed for that in a culture where shadowing a suspect was an unperfected art—they'd lost track of Littleshin and Bertram both. It didn't matter. I still couldn't *prove* who'd pulled the trigger on Mott, but I was certain I had the problem damn near solved.

SAT 24 DEC 212 A.L.
12:00 O'CLOCK

The Healer—Raukerk again, who seemed to be the only Healer in Laporte not on vacation—had departed, leaving Koman safe in his bed. The media had crawled back under their rocks. I was in my car around the corner, unblessed by their attention, playing with the 'com again. I'd put out a bulletin on the Varga to NeverSleep, Securitech, and every other outfit I could think of, including Griswold's, the ones so tough they burn *before* they loot. *Brrr.*

Still no trace of Clarissa, but I'd had another anonymous call: *"Now you know we mean business. If you want to see your girl alive again, book a ticket to the Kingdom of Hawaii and forget the Mott case."*

I couldn't think. Hours without sleep and not much food had zombified me. I wasn't doing Clarissa or myself any good. I went home to Genet Place and blacked the windows for an hour of sleep in a cold, lonely house.

SAT 24 DEC 212 A.L.
20:00 O'CLOCK

I was awakened, it seemed almost the second I dozed off, by a call from Littleshin. "Detective, you're ignoring—you're in bed!" Sitting behind his desk, he looked like he'd been up all night.

I peered at my Seiko. I hadn't set the alarm, or I'd slept through it. Eight hours had passed. I propped myself on an elbow. "That's a hell of a deduction. Ever think about the detective biz?"

"I warn you, don't make me angrier. I have influence, and friends with a long reach. You'll be looking for a new line of endeavor anyway, once it's understood that, through your negligence—"

"Not letting you breathe down my neck every five minutes?"

He ignored me. "—Dora Jayne Thorens has fled unpunished."

"What the hell are you talking about?" If he was right, why hadn't I heard from NeverSleep? Getting rid of him, I tried to contact the physicist at her apartment. Not even an answering program. She wasn't at her lab. Disturbing Koman—his wounds were less serious than I'd first believed, and Confederate medicine works fast—I found the recuperating chimp didn't know where Deejay was, either. That made two missing women, Clarissa, and— In the darkened room, I tensed, feeling a hand on my naked shoulder.

"Win?"

"*Ghaaa*—Clarissa, *never* do that to somebody with a full bladder." Ordering the lights on, I rolled over. Missing Woman Number One lay beside me in our bed, frowning against the light.

"I'm trying to sleep," she groaned. "I thought I turned the alarm off. Do you have any idea what time it is?"

"Do you have any idea how you worried me, disappearing like that? Some freak's out there with a machinegun and your mother said . . . I mean I thought you'd decided—"

"I didn't disappear, I simply referred my appointments to a colleague to help you with this investigation. You didn't think I'd desert you?"

"Of course not," I lied, wrapping my arms around her. A considerable amount of time passed before I asked, "How did you have in mind to help me?"

She grinned. "I've already begun. Based on my experience as a Healer, I thought the women you'd talked to might tell me things, woman to woman, they'd never tell you, no matter how good a detective you are. For instance, did you know that Alberta Mott and her brother—"

"Sorry, I know that already. Try again."

She raised eyebrows. "I *am* impressed. If Miss Mott were half a century younger, I'd even be jealous. Well, how about the fact that Littleshin offered last month to intercede with the Trustees on Deejay's behalf?"

I sat up. "That I didn't know. From Deejay? I wonder if it has anything to do with Littleshin's talk with Freeman—no, that was only last night." I pulled covers aside and put my feet on the floor. "I'll need a

Coke or coffee or something if we're going on with this. Want anything?"

"Coffee. I'll even get up and watch you make it." She rose, without a robe—one advantage to efficient central heating—and followed me to the kitchen. "It didn't have anything to do with anything, except that, in return, he informed her, she need only submit to him sexually."

Dumping grounds in the sink, I began a ritual with the coffee maker that my hands knew better than my brain. "And Deejay, angry and embarrassed at a kind of blackmail rare in the Confederacy, refused."

Clarissa nodded. "I helped her disappear for her own safety. For most of last night, after you left her place, I hid her in my medical van and didn't answer the 'com. Now she's staying at Mother's."

"Meaning Ham sat all night watching an empty apartment. That oughta look great on the bill I send Miss Mott." I paused, trying to remember what came next, stopped thinking, and let my well-trained body go for the paper filters. "Your mother, hmm? Deejay might have been safer with Littleshin."

"There never was any love lost between you and Mother, was there?"

"Can't lose anything," I muttered, "that wasn't there to begin with."

Somewhere between losing count of the number of coffee scoops I'd ladled into the basket and slopping water over the countertop from a carafe designed by the fun-loving folks that gave us the dribble-glass, I realized I now had all the facts I needed to do something final about this case. The next step would be to make several telecom calls. Some things never change.

SAT 24 DEC 212 A.L.
23:50 O'CLOCK

It was corny, but I couldn't think of a better way. Deejay met Clarissa and me at her lab, along with Miss Mott, Littleshin, Bertram, Charles, bundled up against the cold, and Koman, with his arm in a sling.

The scientists had their instructions and went straight to the machinery, which resembled, more than anything, a scale model oil refinery draped in several thousand yards of copper macrame. There wasn't enough room to realize there wasn't enough room. And I still hadn't found an Exmas present for Clarissa.

"Deejay and Curley are warming the broach," I told the invited guests. I'd informed Littleshin I was about to nail Deejay, Bertram I was going to exonerate her, and Miss Mott that her secret would remain safe only if she showed up. Ham came on what's known in the trade as General RJ&F. "They're holding it to a small aperture, less than half an inch, using fiberoptics and this 'com display to show us what's on the other side."

"Young man," Miss Mott protested, "is all this nonsense necessary?" We were back to young man again. Clarissa could stop being jealous. We all stood elbow to elbow around a three-foot screen. Five or six paces behind us, the largest stretch of open floor in the room, the actual aperture glowed between a pair of six-foot coils that looked like they'd been invented by Nikola Tesla in partnership with M.C. Escher. Between us and the tiny, brilliant circle of blue light representing the edge of the aperture was a tangle of 'com equipment. The screen swirled with the beginnings of an image: howling wind, the blinding glare of an Arctic-style blizzard. The Siberian Express had arrived on the high plains of Colorado.

"Dorothy Gale was right," I continued, ignoring Miss Mott. "There's no place like home—thank heavens. We're looking at the exact spot we're standing, as it exists in another world. In the absence of CRP&L, the storm's moved down from Laramie, as you can see. The uncontrolled snow in Fort Collins is much deeper, and the streets completely deserted." It was true. Along Confederation Boulevard, known as Shields Street in the world we observed, and Guy Fawkes Esplanade, West Elizabeth Avenue, coextant with the southeast corner of the University, not a creature was stirring in the gray morning light, not even a snowshoe rabbit. Cars stranded along the street were reduced to amorphous humps by a yard-deep covering of yech.

"This," Freeman Bertram asked with a shiver, "is where you're from, Win?"

"All that's necessary," I replied, turning, "for me to step from this world into that one, is to spin that dial"—I indicated a control at the base of the central apparatus— "widening the broach."

Littleshin spoke. "Demonstrating what I've maintained all along, that only Thorens and her accomplice could have shot Seaton the way it was done, opening the broach, firing through the aperture, and closing it afterward."

"On the contrary," I told him, "I'm here to show, beyond the shadow of a doubt, that Mott was not killed through a broach, as first appeared."

That brought a satisfactory volume of gasps and murmurs, so I went on. "A broach can only reach from one world into another, just as you see here. It would take two broaches to reach back into this world, and, at the moment, there aren't two broaches operational in the whole Confederacy. The killer is an individual who should have known that, which is why I suspected him right from the beginning, although I couldn't prove it until now." I drew my revolver. "Mott was murdered from a distance, all right, but from a distance of no more than seventy-five yards, from the private drive of his estate, with an ordinary telescopically-sighted pistol."

I saw Ham Charles nodding to himself. He'd gotten it.

"But," Miss Mott complained, "what about—"

"The powder marks?" I finished. "After your brother was shot, his body lay cooling in the freshly-falling snow. The murderer went away and came back two hours later, neatly erasing the first tracks he'd made with the fan-blast of his hovercraft. Only then did he walk up, deposit powder 'burns' on the back of his victim's head, using a blank cartridge from which he'd removed the wadding, and telecom for help in order to divert suspicion from himself. Of all the detectives in Laporte he might have called, he chose me because he was sure an American, personally—but not technically—familiar with broach technology, would jump to the desired conclusion."

Littleshin began turning an interesting shade of purple halfway through my little speech. Now he erupted. "This is an outrage! Do you have any idea how long you'll be paying restitution for slandering my reputation?"

I grinned at him. "Might as well make it libel, too, because I'm going to hand Miss Mott a written report. You'll be interested to know I suspected you, Littleshin, even before you mentioned broaches and tried to implicate Deejay. I saw bare metal glinting on the receiver of your pistol, where the scope mounting hardware had scraped the black finish before being removed."

Bertram shook his head. "That's a terribly small clue, Win, on which to base the supposition of murder."

"Great oaks from little acorns. Besides, I'm an American. I'm used to looking for a particular motive that wouldn't make sense to the average Confederate. Everybody told me Seaton Mott was as reactionary about rejuvenation as he was about everything else. That meant his days—or at least his remaining years—were numbered. Littleshin, here, had always expected to inherit chairmanship of the Board of Trustees from him."

"But," Miss Mott objected, "to murder an old friend for a mere—"

"I know. It never fails to amaze me, either, how people do the most selling out for the smallest dabs of power. I've watched lifelong friends tear each other to figurative shreds and never speak to each other again, over the presidency of the local PTA. It's a disease. Learning that Mott had changed his mind and planned to undertake rejuvenation, Littleshin decided to remove him. He'd been disappointed once already by Deejay. He knew his desire for her was futile, so he selected a manner of dealing with his old friend which would place the blame on her, killing two birds with one stone."

Bertram frowned with concentration. "But how

could he have been at the estate killing Seaton while he was in his office, talking to me?"

I shook my head. "He talked to you from the estate, on his pocket 'com, probably mounted on a photo tripod to remove the characteristic shakiness. You assumed he was in his office because you saw trees behind him. It wasn't a view through his window, but from the driveway where he waited to kill Mott. For what it's worth, I have castings of deep tripod marks which his and other hovercraft failed to obliterate entirely."

SAT 24 DEC 212 A.L.
23:57 O'CLOCK

A glance at Littleshin told me he was almost soup, so I turned up the heat. "If that doesn't satisfy anybody, what do you say we take his gloves off and turn down his collar? He's got to have some cuts and scrapes from all the glass we dumped on him when he attacked Curley and me. How about it, Merse, old boy, show us your owie?"

That was it. Suddenly, Littleshin leaped toward the broach, slapping at the aperture knob. The brilliant blue-white circle expanded. A savage gust of unmoderated winter swept into the lab with a few short-lived snowflakes. Littleshin plunged through the broach. Bertram, Miss Mott, and Ham drew their weapons, attempting to stop him. I took a quick step into their line of fire and let off a shot of my own, over his head, to speed him on his way. The room thundered with the magnum report.

"Close it, Deejay, now!" I watched the aperture diminish even before I'd finished shouting. The silence which followed was long, as bitter as the cold the other side of the broach. I discovered I was still thinking, somewhere in the back of my mind, about finding an Exmas present for Clarissa.

"Young man," Miss Mott began at last, her tone indignant, "one would gather, from what you have said, that your United States is an unpleasant place, compared to the Confederacy . . ."

I refrained from answering, not even giving her a nod, fed up with Confederate sanctimony, unwilling to acknowledge that the place I'd come from, where I'd been born, was all that bad. I knew it was, but that was different.

"You permitted," she went on, "encouraged Littleshin to escape to that place. However unpleasant, it seems a trivial punishment, considering what he did. I want to know why—before you send me your bill."

"Miss Mott, I don't know whether it'll make you feel better, it depends on how much you value revenge. Before you got here, Deejay opened that broach, not onto my home world, but onto a place where humanity was recently destroyed by biological warfare. The buildings and so on are still intact."

"The chosen world"—Ham Charles grinned—"had to be one where a blizzard was raging, accounting for the deserted streets." I nodded. Ham hadn't been in on the deception, but he caught on fast.

"Arrests in the Confederacy are a touchy business," I repeated. "I didn't have enough evidence against Littleshin to convict him of jaywalking."

"But . . ." Bertram goggled and spluttered, not a pretty sight.

"What about the tripod marks in the snow I mentioned?"

He added head-bobbing to the goggling and spluttering, making it worse.

"I lied."

Ham Charles laughed out loud.

"However, given enough metaphorical rope," I went on, "Littleshin convicted and sentenced himself: to an extremely brief lifetime, marooned in a deadly environment. Life, as Curley's answering machine informs us, is an intelligence test—which Littleshin failed—Beeeep!"

That seemed to satisfy them, to the point they were all talking at once, Bertram and Charles slapping me on the back. Taking Clarissa by the hand, I ignored everyone's congratulations to look into her eyes.

"I was afraid, Win," she started before I could.

"You attract violence. I didn't want you dying in some fight necessitated by your profession."

"I thought it was my lack of gainful employment," I told her. "I'll look for something else day after tomorrow. That'll be my Exmas present to you. I was afraid I'd lost you altogether. I never want to feel that way again."

"Drat! I'm not making myself clear, Win. I don't want you to quit detecting. Worse than any risk, I hated the way you were losing your . . . your direction. Your self-esteem. The determination and vigor I see in you now is more than enough present for me. You've regained your identity, your . . ."

I grinned. "My manhood?"

Not liking the way I put it, but unable to deny the truth, she nodded. "I, er, I haven't had time to find you an Exmas present, either, darling. But someone else was thinking of us. I told my mother, a little prematurely, that we were making up our differences. She left for Luna in a huff—by invitation—using a ticket provided by the President of the Confederacy. I confided in Jenny, Win. I was so afraid that, sooner or later, feeling the way you did, you'd fall victim to some self-inflicted misfortune—"

"Like Littleshin did?" I looked at my watch. Three minutes after midnight. Exmas had sneaked up on us while we weren't looking. She nodded.

"Well, Goldilocks," I told her, nuzzling blond curls, "that's the way it happens, sometimes. As you'll discover as soon as I get you home and back to bed, sometimes you eat the Bear, and sometimes the Bear eats you."

COUNT OF THE SAXON SHORE

Susan Shwartz

Introduction

Even when I have known and loved a story for most of my life, there always comes a time as I reread it when I think that maybe, just this once, things will turn out differently. Hamlet will escape the trap set for him; Alexander will not die of fever; or, as in "The Count of the Saxon Shore," Arthur will survive the battle of Camlann.

In case you don't remember your Malory, your Geoffrey of Monmouth, or even your Mary Stewart or T.H. White, the battle of Camlann was fought because of a tragic mistake. Arthur's forces and Mordred's were drawn up in ranks while the king and his son discussed terms; it was understood that, if anyone drew a weapon, fighting would break out. But even as an agreement—such as it was—was reached between the old king and his renegade son, fate intervened. An adder stung a man-at-arms in the foot, and he drew his sword to slay it . . . thereby precipitating the last battle in which Mordred was slain and Arthur fatally wounded, compelled to retire to Avalon for the healing of his wounds.

But what if Arthur had survived that day? What would he do, his country in ruins about him, his troops slain, his enemies in his lands?

That—an alternative ending to one of Western culture's greatest legends—was the question that I asked myself when I wrote this story. To say more about it is to give away the tale itself: suffice it to say only that the choices I made in writing it involve the reasons why the story of Arthur is particularly dear to me—good lordship, faith kept, and survival despite the odds.

123

No, nothing is wrong with me; nothing at all, save the old knock I took on my skull years ago at Camlann. It pains me now and then, is all, and I see double—nothing more, I warrant you, than we all have done the morrow after one of the old king's feasts. The old king . . .

Aye, it will be strange to get used to hailing Prince Uther as King and young Constantine as Regent. No, Cornwall's Duke is not young, not young as you would call it. (And have you even puked yet after fleshing your sword in your first battle? You have? I held the shieldwall there last summer. A fine fight, indeed; and I beg your pardon, sir.)

Still, to those of us who have served Artos all these years, Constantine will always be young, the heir, (which should make Prince Uther look to himself if his Regent were anyone else); and Artos the King. The old King. After all, he was not young when I entered his service. That was after Camlann, or half-way through the battle, I should say.

The dizziness? Thanks for your arm; the fit will pass shortly. Thor's balls . . . I mean, by the White Christ, I promise you: it is nothing; it will pass. There. I'm in a muck sweat, but that's better. Some ale, maybe; but that's right. Today is a fast day, and, if I call for ale, the priests will carp, and I have heard enough wailing and scolding the past week to last me for another lifetime.

Still, it goes hard with an old warhorse to take help, but be a good lad and help me get away from the churchyard. Tell your friends . . . what shall you tell them? That old Beorhtwold has spent his whole life out of doors, and hates being shut up when the weather is fine. King Artos didn't make me Count of the Saxon Shore to sit in courts . . . or churches either, for that matter. I know that's an old title, but it was the one the good King gave me. It's been good enough for twenty years of service, and it'll be good enough to carve on my tombstone. I'm too old and too hardheaded, the King always said (it was a joke between us), to change much.

The sun's seldom this fine down here in Glaestingeburh, and, soon enough, I shall be locked away from it in the black ground's bed. Should not surprise you, I think, that, being Saxon-born, I use the Saxon name for the place and not its old, flowery name, Avallon, though the appleblossoms are sweet and the memory of my mother teaching me the words of the homeland she was snatched away from is sweeter yet. I think about her somewhat these days. Would have liked my Mairedd, who has the same soft voice; would have been glad that her son earned land in Britain.

You fight all your life, at the end of it, you've earned the right to sit and dream of the past. If you last so long, you'll know what I mean. And you've got a good chance of it, I think. Artos saw to that. We may even have peace this summer. The very thought feels stranger than this buzzing in my brain.

Na, I tell you there is no need for some gossip to disrupt the requiem and bring out my Mairedd; she has a right to mourn the old King, God knows, and she must stay to serve the Queen. Besides, all we need is the women out here, fussing and crying and dragging out the priests with their incense and their prayers and their everlasting reproaches that, even after all these years, I am not yet baptized. I attend services; couldn't very well not, given my title and all. What's more, my children are Christian, for so their mother would have it. Still, I have not yet allowed the priests to douse me with the water, which, they claim, washes away all sins. I tell them

I'm not sure that I've finished all my sinning yet. And laugh then to see them purse their lips.

Does that shock you? Ah, it is a new generation of fighters and a strict one. It never shocked my old King.

"The wisest man who ever served me wore the Raven's brand until he up and vanished into the Hills," he used to say. "I'd be glad to stand godfather to you, Beorhtwold. Just say the word and set the day. I'll even intercede with the good fathers to make it short." That, I can tell you, lured me closer to the altar than all the rants of that Gildas fellow. When he isn't scribbling, he's preaching, as gloomy as Jeremiah. Now there's a prophet whose words bite almost as deep as a real bard's satires! Friend Gildas had better not have aught bad to say about Artos today; a King should be spared hellfire and sermons at his funeral, don't you think? Especially such a King as this. I tell you; we'll never see his like again, unless he rises from his coffin and comes back to us. But I've seen death, and I saw Artos once the women laid him out. Dead is dead.

Well, sooner or later, I may let some priest—but not Gildas!—baptize me, so, when the time comes, they'll let me be buried in holy ground. Mairedd has a right to rest there, and, after twenty years, I don't want to sleep apart from her.

It's too fine a day to talk of death and burials, but we must, now that, finally, King Artos has gone to his long home. If we were in my birthland, we'd build him a proper barrow and send him off with his armor, his horse, and enough treasure to blind the eye of a court in the Hereafter. Then, after dark, we'd build a bonfire, and twelve of us would ride around it, singing his deeds. Or maybe we'd do it the oldest way of all—lay him and his gold in a high-prowed boat, nail down its sail, and let him fare forward over the swanroad.

You call me a taleteller? Hardly that, my friend. Few scops and skalds sing the old songs now. The ones that the bards don't laugh out of hall the priests get. It has been long and long since I heard lines of verse rise and clash one against the other like sword on lindenshield. I am no *scop*, as I said, but I well remember how the songs used to go.

Sit under the appletrees and swap tales until *"Ite, missa est"* and they all come out for the feast? You're a thoughtful lad, I mean, man. Yes, thanks, I *will* take your arm, so long as no one's around to see me do it. That's right; I can walk a bit faster, though I'm walking as if I've found my sea legs here on land.

There! If only we had something to drink—ale, mead—you say that the water in the well has been blessed? Can't hurt me to try it. Your health then, young sir, and long life to you!

Well, where do I begin? How I became King Artos' man: is that the tale you want?

The old *scops* would cry *"Hwaet!"* and give you a fine flourish on the harp, tell you the history of each man, then, finally, crack the bones of the history and suck out the marrow of the story, making you laugh and weep all the while. I can't do that, of course. Some of it, you ought to know. Today, we bury Artos son of Uther. Birth and the battle of Badon Hill made him Britain's King; Camlann created him King thereafter of the Saxons, Jutes, and Angles, who now dwell here. Me and my kinsmen, who longed for land, vowed to have it; by gift if we could, by sword if we must.

We were starving on the seacoasts. Ever see the lowlands? The soil's sick, and not much grows there. Just to keep our children from crying at nights, we used to sail out and raid. Now, mind you, I'm not saying some of us didn't enjoy the fighting and looting. That sort of thing gets into a man's blood. God knows, it was in mine; my mother was a captive stolen from Gwynedd by my father, who was sacking a farm and liked the flash of her ankle as she fled. Yes, she was Christian, and she told me of her home. You can see, not many of her lessons found fertile soil, though.

As I was saying, when you're that poor, after awhile you get angry at it. You stare over the water, and you think: "Those islanders have green fields and fat flocks and more land than they can till, but will they share it? Not they, damn them!" Yes, I say "we." Why should I be ashamed of my father's and my grandfather's people? They were brave men who wanted land and food for their families.

So, when Hengist and Horsa whispered in their ears of the land that Vortigern promised if they and their hearth-companions would but assist him, they fell in with the plan as easily as a maid at midsummer falls into the arms of some man with a slick story. Well, you know what happened. Vortigern married Hengist's daughter, and all looked very promising; but the British revolted. Sweet God, can you British fight when your blood's up and your land's at stake! You're mean enemies, but faithful friends.

Those of our fathers and uncles who struggled back in the few ships they could save holed up and licked their wounds. We have long memories, we of the shore, for injuries and the fair British lands we had lost. Already, even people in Britain were calling those lands the Saxon Shore. What could stop us from biding our time, packing our ships, and taking them back?

That same Artos and his wizard who had driven us out, that's what! After Badon Hill, though we tried again and again, the very name of Artos was as good as a shieldwall itself. That name-shield continued strong for twenty years, long enough for me to grow up and restless, more than long enough for the King's eldest son, Medrawt, to grow up and even more restless. Like Vortigern, he sent his spies and messengers across the cold surges of the gannet's bath, promising rich rewards and, sweeter than silver, finer than gold, green land. Now, King Chelric was my lord. And, as my father had been his sister's son, I was one of his *heorthwerod*—you translate that as "house troop," something like the Companions whom Artos himself kept about him—I sailed with him.

Now, I see that I have really shocked you this time. How do I dare, here, on holy ground in Glaestingeburh, on the very day of my dear lord's funeral, to sit here and admit that, years ago, I was his enemy? I was, though. Even after these twenty years of serving as his loyal man, and, God knows, when a Saxon says he is loyal, it means he will die for his lord, I remember that too. Would have slain him if I could, and basked in the glory, aye, and my sons thereafter.

Only then, I had no sons, no land; not much of anything but strength, guts, my father's old sword, my mother's blessing, and a damned hard head.

And good greeting to you too, sirs. Your friend Cynan has been kind enough to keep me company here in the sun. By all the— I mean, because an old man leaves the church to sit outside does not mean that he is faint. Sit and join us, if you would, and talk at whiles. I have begun to tell my lord Cynan here about the Battle of Camlann, which we fought in a May much like this, some twenty years ago.

As I was saying, when I was your ages, I had a damned hard head. And that's all that saved me at Camlann, that and the boar-figures welded onto my helmet. Ah, you British youths laugh at the way some of us old men still cling to the old way of armor and our helmets with their boar-guards, but I tell you, if those good old *hildeswin* hadn't been on that helmet to take the force of that swordstroke, I'd have left my blood and brains on the field like so many braver and better men. My own old lord Chelric, for example.

But I didn't know that at the time. All I knew was that my lord Chelric had ordered me to stand and hold, and I was damned well going to do it. I wasn't happy about things, though. After all, Chelric was a King, my King; and who was this Medrawt? Some bastard turned traitor, as I saw it. But he promised us land; and, lads, that was a chance we had to take.

Besides, sitting with us and drinking, he seemed to know the difference between his sword and his shield (if not his ass and his elbow), so we listened to him. He marched us along the River Camel as far as the place you call Slaughter Bridge. Believe me, that was the day it earned its name. There, on the water-meadow, he drew us up in battle order. There were about sixty thousand of us, and we were in seven divisions, one of which he commanded. We were in fine fettle. From time to time, we amused ourselves by shouting insults at the Britons, mostly about how Artos wore horns, not a crown, and that a king who could not hold his wife should not expect to hold his kingdom.

Looking back now that I've led a dozen or so campaigns of my own, I understand why Medrawt issued the orders he did. He was a rebel—which means that he started off on the wrong foot; he was fighting against a King some people likened to Caesar or Alexander; and he had suffered a couple of disastrous retreats. In short, he was desperate. Even the scurrile about Artos' queen was so much bluff; true enough, she had left Artos, but whether or not Medrawt had actually possessed her was anyone's guess—and almost anyone did guess. In any case, Medrawt had told us that we were to hold until we broke Artos' army and his heart, life and light together—or until we died on the bloody field with the eagles and ravens circling overhead, eager for slaughter, as the *scops* always say. They were certainly out in force that May.

All day long that battle tore back and forth across the field until the river flowed red, and the tide turned twice as salt from all the blood. Finally, they broke through our shieldwall (which hadn't the pikes to stand up against cavalry), and we were all on our own. I was fine for a time, dodging from fight to fight, screaming something brave and probably stupid about *Ic will nat fleon fotes trym, ac sceal further gan*. I will not flee the space of a foot, but shall fight on further; that's what it means. I told you, I was young and carried away with the chance to play the part of a hero such as I had always heard of. And besides, better to play at a hero's deeds than piss yourself with fright.

Then along came this monster of a Briton in front of me. Most of you are little fellows, but I tell you,

he was huge, big as Grendel; and he was swinging a
sword that was keen enough to have been forged by
Weland himself. I was no green youth, and I had my
full growth; but that man shattered my shield with
one blow and damned near broke my arm with a
second. I stepped back to get some fighting room,
for all the good that it did me. My foot tangled in
some poor sod's guts, and I stumbled, just as the
man swung. I took the swordcut on the side of the
head. It sheared those faithful, blessed boars off my
helmet, cut through the helmet, and shaved my hair,
and a good bit of skin. As I think back on it, I don't
know why it didn't smash right through my skull, too.

It damned well felt like it at the time. I felt like I'd
been hit by a glacier *and* a burning meadhall at
once—but not for long.

That's why I have double vision and blinding headaches from time to time. You can't live through a
blow like that and expect nothing to have been hurt.
Aye, it'll probably be the death of me one of these
days; but I can still hope that I die like a man, not
frothing and thrashing in a fit. Never mind that. It's
the churchbells. They make me gloomy, fey-feeling;
but that's another story.

Let me get my drift. I was talking about how I got
the knock on the head that makes me go all woozy at
the worst possible moments. Like today. To return
to the battle, when I woke, it was sunset. At first, I
couldn't see. Then I realized my mouth was full of
blood and mud from where I'd been lying, and some
of the muck had probably caked my eyes shut. I
wiped most of it away and tried to drag myself over
to a little stand of hazel bushes right by a bluff and a
little pond of clear water, and I puked till there was
nothing left in my belly. I drank some of the water,
puked that up too, and tried again. This time it
stayed down.

After the shakes stopped, I decided that I was
probably going to have to live. That was when the
trouble started. I set out to look for King Chelric,
and found him, sure enough. Dead; and three of my
cousins lying before him, guarding him in death as in

life—as I had failed to do. You may not know that, for us Saxons, it's a disgrace to leave a battle in which your lord has fallen. You did know that? Good: the races are mingling in Britain; we've done our work well, Artos and his men.

I didn't think that way at Camlann, though. All I knew was that I had not saved my King; worse luck, I had not died with him. By our—my old customs, that is, I could expect nothing more than the life of a wanderer, longing for honor and mercy, unless, of course, I could find Medrawt, who (you have to understand, I was pretty wobbly about the head and knees about this time) would stand in the place of my dead King.

So there I went, stumbling about the battlefield, over people and into things that even now make me sick to think of. Found Medrawt, too, all right.

There he was, one against three; only two of the three were in worse shape than I, and the third looked old and tired. Not winded, however. If I shut my eyes, I can remember it now. The stinks blowing away on the night wind, salt and free; me, standing there, ready to fall down in a faint; and the tall figures in their bloody chainmail.

Just as if he planned to challenge *eorl* Medrawt to a holmgang, the old warrior strode forward and shouted, "Now, give me my spear, for over there stands the traitor who has brought all this upon us!"

The other two knew what they were about, though. "Sir, let him be," one of them said, and he had to spit out blood and teeth to do it. "For he is wretched. And if you survive this miserable day, you will be avenged right enough."

The old man wasn't having any. The wind blew the clouds away, and I could see something gleam around his helmet as he advanced, his warriors trying to persuade him out of it, shouting something about a dream, something about a vision of his sister's son, and something about no one of Medrawt's men being left alive to help him. I knew then who I was watching.

Artos. My enemy.

"That isn't true!" I tried to yell, but I moved too

fast, and I fell. Strange: I was more caught up in the battle that I watched than in my own aches and pains.

"Leave now!" the man shouted, and his voice cracked. "If you stop now, this wicked day of destiny will be passed!"

Odd, I thought, for a Christian to talk of *wyrd*. If it were the old man's wyrd to fight, then fight he would. If it were his wyrd to die, then he would die—though, as I had always heard, fate will spare the unstained lord, if his will holds firm. Personally, I expected to see Medrawt spit him. He was younger and in better shape than his father, who looked ready to die of pure pigheadedness if nothing else.

His two men tried to grab him, but Artos broke free. "Now tide me death, tide me life," he screamed. "Now that I see him alone, he shall never escape my hands, for I shall never have him at a better time."

"God speed," one wished him, and they stood back while the old king ran toward the Lord Medrawt. It was mad, terrible, and wonderful at once. Here was Medrawt with sword and shield; here was Artos, holding a spear in both hands and shouting, "Traitor, now your death day has come!"

If anyone had any question about whether Medrawt truly was Artos' son, Medrawt's reaction would have set him straight. Rather than wait for the old man's temper to get the best of him, Medrawt immediately drew and ran at the King. That gave him a chance to pick his moment and his blow. He got under what little guard Medrawt had bothered with and struck him beneath the shield, a very crafty blow. It would have done your heart good to see it; all those years of practice and a natural gift paying off at the last. About a fathom of it went into him, and blood gushed from his mouth and nostrils.

You've probably seen it. When a man is gutstruck, he's dead. He just doesn't fall till you pull the spear out. Just so with Medrawt. He knew he had taken his death-wound. He *had* to know, because only a dying man would have had the mad strength to do what he did next. He threw himself forward onto the spear, till it stuck out dripping behind him, and swung his sword, two-handed, at his father's head, a wound much like my own.

And then they both fell down, and so did I. This time, I was sure that I was dead.

The moon was high in the sky when I woke up again. I was hot and cold at once, and I thought (if you can call thinking what was more like the instincts of a wounded bear) that I ought to make for what looked like a barn by the shore. I started off, and as I got closer, I saw that it was a chapel, built low to the ground, with wattle and daub patching botched stonework. It looked remarkably like a barrow, and I had this terrible feeling that I was walking toward my own tomb. Despite what my mother had told me about Christians, despite the fact that I too was half-British, there would be priests in such a chapel; they'd most likely be British, and, as I well know, Britons can fight. Not that I was any match for even a five-year-old girl, by then.

Well, by that time, I was pretty close to raving, so I forgot all that fast, and kept going toward it anyhow. I had all but forgotten my name, and I had certainly forgotten anyone else's, or much beyond the moment when I'd been hit.

Then this old man comes weaving toward me. I brought up my sword, and, believe me, it shook in my hands. Then I see that the old man is unarmed, though he's wearing mail, and he's wobbling as bad as I am. *How much harm can an old man do?* I think. Then I get what I think is a really fine idea. I'll bring this Briton to the priest in that chapel, who will be so glad that he's got his sick old countryman back that he'll look after me too.

So I stagger up to him, and we grab each other— like this!—about the shoulders; we're holding each other up; and the old man asks me, "Have you seen the brothers, Lords Lucan and Bedwyr?"

At the time, I could barely understand your language, gentlemen; some of you younger men are kind enough to say that I still don't know it all that well. But, when you're barely able to understand British *and* you've had a clout on the head *and* the man who's mumbling at you has taken a worse one . . . by the time I understood what he was getting at, the old man realized that I wasn't one of his, and he switched to Saxon.

When he saw that he'd damned near surprised what little life I still had out of me, he grinned. "Learned it from Myrddin," he said. "Now, have you seen Lucan and Bedwyr?"

Then he shook his head. "No, that's right. Lucan . . . he and his brother were bringing me to the chapel when Lucan stumbled. He had been holding one hand to his side, and when he fell, we saw why. He had been holding his guts in. So Lucan's gone, rest his soul." He signed himself with a gorestained hand.

"My sword, Caliburn . . . what?" He was coming back to himself quickly, too damned quickly, I thought. Gods, I had never seen anything like the way that old man recovered. He was remembering, remembering who he was and what had happened to him. And I was remembering too. What had happened to him . . . now he wore no helm. Still, the blood-crusted bandages about his head could pass for a crown; and I knew who he was, remembered, too, the fury of his battle with his bastard son. The Angles and Danes have a term—*berserkrgang*—for the way he had been. Now, your northerners are all madmen (it comes from the cold and the long, long nights), but even they don't like to get close to men who fight like that; and this one had his arms about me!

Soon he'd remember that I was an enemy, and, the way he was going, he would probably take my sword away from me and kill me.

"What did you do with your sword?" I asked, to keep him busy.

The King shook his head, thought better of it too late, and retched. I eased him to his knees and held his head, carefully, on account of the bandages. "I could feel myself dying," he admitted and looked up at me. The pupil of one eye was twice the size of the other: a bad sign. "You know what I mean," he

added. That was not a question. Thank God, enough of
my brains still sloshed around in my skull so I remembered not to nod my head and stir things up worse.

"My sword Caliburn," he repeated. "It's an old
sword, a fine one. The King's sword. If I were going
to die, I couldn't let anyone get hold of it, maybe use
it against Britain the way Medrawt used my second-
best blade, Clarent, on me. Bedwyr . . . I thought I
could trust him with my life; and so I could. Not
with my sword. I gave it to him and told him, 'Go to
the river; throw it in the water; and come back and
tell me what you see.'"

"Waste of a good sword," I said, owlishly, and
yawned.

King Artos rose from his knees, dashed his knuckles across split lips, and gestured. "You're supposed
to walk, not sleep, after head injuries. Let's keep
moving."

All that night, we walked the field, circled the
chapel, and—would you believe it?—never once
came anyone, man, woman, or woodwose—to stop
us. And there were enough of each roving the field,
looking for their wounded or their dead, or stripping
the poor bodies. All that night, we walked, and, as
we walked, Artos mumbled out his story.

"Bedwyr took the sword and went off. When he
came back, I asked him, 'What did you see?' He
answered, 'Sir, I saw nothing but wind on the water.'
So I called him a damned liar, and sent him to take
the sword out of whatever hiding-place he'd found
for it, and throw it in the water! When he came
back, I asked him again."

I can still hear how Artos' voice changed as he
repeated what this Bedwyr had said to him, taking
on the accents of the hills, like music, almost beautiful, even though the man who spoke them was hoarse
and almost mad. "Sir, I saw nothing but the waves
flicker and the waters grow dark."

"You traitor!" Artos turned on his eldest follower.
"You have betrayed me twice! Who would have believed that you, who have been so dear to me, you,

who have been called so noble a lord, would betray me for the riches of my sword. Damn you, go again right now, because your delay has made my wounds chill and put me in peril of my life."

Even as he spoke, the King grew angry, almost to frenzy, and I tried to calm him. But he broke free of me, just as he had broken free of Bedwyr and Lucan to slay his son: "Except if you do as I bid, if ever I see you again, I shall kill you with my own hands for wanting me dead because of the riches of my sword!"

Now, lads, here is a wonder. This King is my enemy; he is responsible for my lord Chelric's death; he has killed the man who I had hoped would take me in; he's just threatened my life—and here I am, trying to restrain him, tenderly, as if he were my own father, urging him to be calm, to rest easy, that Bedwyr is loyal to him, would never slay him, let alone for a pretty swordhilt . . .

You may say that my mind wandered. I prefer to say that, in that moment, as I clutched the King to prevent him, in his anger, from doing himself a mischief, my mind came home and knew the place for the first time.

All of a sudden, Artos sagged in my arms. One hand—a big, strong, callused hand that bore a huge ruby ring—patted my shoulder. "You're right, lad," he sighed. "Bedwyr would never hurt me. I know that now."

"What happened to the sword?" I had to ask.

"The damnedest thing," Artos confided. "Just as Myrddin prophesied. Bedwyr took Caliburn out of hiding, bound its hangers about the hilt, and threw it, as far out over the water as he could."

I could see it—can't you, men?—glistening in the cold moonlight, streaking down toward the water.

"And then," Artos' voice dropped to a whisper that I strained to hear, "an arm rose above the water, caught the sword, shook it, and brandished it three times, as if in salute. Then it vanished with the sword into the water."

I reached to touch the Thor's hammer that I carried and found it missing. So, it seemed, I not only didn't have a lord; I had no gods either. The fog was rising, so thick that I could barely see the man with me. I could well believe that even gods could get lost in fog like this. They were gone, but the man who spoke to me was warm and solid, for all his wounds. I would trust him and not some amulet.

"Now what?" I asked the king.

"I think I dreamed or raved. I commanded Bedwyr to get me to the shore; the poor bastard had to lift me onto his back to do it, and I thought his guts would burst out like his brother's. Once I was there, I lay panting and—I swear to you by the Grail itself—I saw a black barge sailing toward me. There were ladies in it, all hooded in black, all weeping. I think that one of them was a Queen. I ordered Bedwyr to put me into that barge, and let me lay my head in the Queen's lap. She wept that I had waited so long and let my wounds take cold; if you know *my* sister, you know how impossible that is. I had to be seeing things; had a summer fever once, and you wouldn't believe some of the dreams I had. But this beat them all."

I didn't know his sister, yet, were she the lady who had enticed her brother into lying with her, then turned the child born of that union into a weapon against the king, I could well believe that Artos had been raving.

"The ladies rowed away." Artos' voice was distant, dreamlike. "All I can remember now is Sir Bedwyr crying after me, " 'My king, what shall become of me, now that you go from me and leave me alone among my enemies?' "

I bent over the king, gentle as if he were a sick child. *"Hlaford min,"* I hailed him as my own lord for the first time, and the words comforted my ears. "What did you tell Bedwyr?"

"Comfort yourself, and do as well as you may, for in me there is no trust for you to trust in. For I must go into the vale of Avallon to heal me of my grievous wound. And if you hear of me nevermore, pray for my soul."

As King Artos said that, I found myself weeping,

as even now I do, my brothers, and you with me. "It is not true!" I told him, willing life into him.

"No?" asked the King.

"No!" I said firmly, and, staggering one against the other, holding each other up, we trudged back and forth. At times, he would fall, or I would fall, and demand to sleep that sleep from which there is no waking (head wounds are treacherous, you know). Then he would pummel me back into wakefulness, or I would shake him. Then we'd curse one another and slog on, talking though our throats went hoarse, and we coughed as much as we spoke.

I think he told me about his mother, the Lady Igraine, about his father, Uther, and his shadowy birth; I know I told him about my family. "Half-British, are you?" he mused. "That could work well."

All the while, I tried to convince him that his statement, "In me there is no trust in which to trust," was a lie—perhaps his first lie. After all, I trusted him, trusted him enough, at least, to stay with him.

Finally, Artos sighed. "I thought that it might be. For, as I lay there, life pulsed through my veins; and, for the first time in months, I thought that I might *want* to live. That is, if there were a reason for me to live."

"There's Britain," said I. "You have land and lives that look to you. How can you abandon them, especially now, when they cry out to you? I am landless, lordless now, and therefore an exile, yet it seems to me that the lord who allows himself to skin out of a tough spot by dying is every bit as much a traitor as the armsman who flees the battlefield."

The King bristled; he was Artos of Britain, and I had all but called him a coward and traitor. But he *was* Artos, and, after a moment, he chuckled. "Listen to me—what did you say your name was?"

I hadn't said; but now I gave him my name and parentage. "Beorhtwold," he rolled it about in his mouth. Unlike most Britons, he got it right. "Names have meaning. Yours . . . you could say, 'Bright power,' or 'power of light.' Or you could twist it, and call it 'ruler of Britons,' couldn't you?"

"You could, lord," I admitted. It is always better to humor great men when they muse; and this one was the greatest lord I had . . . have . . . ever met.

"Listen to me," said Artos. "And after you listen, give me your word, and I swear to you that never again will you call yourself landless and lordless. I am not letting this kill me. And I am not letting Britain die, not now; not ever! I propose . . ."

He pushed away from me and stood upright . . . "to resume my titles and my crown, to go on living, and to take this shattered, maimed land of mine, heal its fields and set about its shores a shieldwall so strong that the other three corners of the world might hurl themselves against it and break asunder like rusted swords. And this land shall have no Picts nor Scots nor Saxons nor Jutes; but all who say 'aye, Artos, I shall join you in this fight,' shall be British merely and shall share in this land. What say you, Beorhtwold, former enemy of mine? Shall you choose an end to hate and exile?"

I fell to my knees, but not from weakness, and reached up my hands for his to clasp round them for the oath. To have a lord again, and lands, and the promise of a lifelong fight that would be worth the struggle! I laid my face against our joined hands, and . . . no, though you men are as old as I when I swore to King Artos, you are young enough to feel yourselves unmanned by tears. I tell you, I was not ashamed of how I wept.

He had stripped an armlet from beneath his mail to give me in token that he was now my ring-giver when Bedwyr, leading a troop of men at arms, found us. He damned near spitted me, and, as I told him later on, when we all were thinking straighter, I don't blame him, and never did. What would you do if you saw your lord bleeding from a head wound, unsteady on his feet, and with his hands clutched by a bloodstained man in Saxon mail? On top of everything else, Artos had to explain who I was and what I was doing there; and that took some doing, even for

Artos. On pain of death, he bade his faithful men bear me up along with him and tend me as gently as if I had been reared in his household.

We were ill—my King and I—for weeks. But when I was healed, he summoned me and, before the remnants of his court, named me one of his Companions. And I knelt to receive a buffet on my shoulder, a belt, and a sword.

There! That is only half the story—how a landless, lordless Saxon joined the *heorthwerod* of his mortal enemy. The other half—how I rose to become Count of the Saxon Shore—that must wait.

Can you hear the churchbells, my boys? They're coming out now. Wipe your faces, and aid me to my feet. Quickly now, I would have no one—least of all my wife Mairedd—see me in need of help. It is proper for the old Count of the Saxon Shore to bow before the Queen, speak the empty words that will not heal her loss as they do not ease mine, and assure her that it will be my privilege to escort her back to her convent after she has seen her son crowned. Because that much of it, at least, is true. I have been her thane since I first saw her, ice-cold with rage. I do not want Mairedd to think that I am ill and beg her to choose another guard. The Queen— once she returns to Amesburh, none of us will ever see her again. Granted, it is but thirty miles away from here, but it might as well be thirty seas away. She will be lost to us in holiness.

You would hear the tale of how I became lord of the Saxon Shore? Tonight, at the feast, let us go aside, and, if you have naught better to do, I shall unlock my wordhoard again, though I am afraid it holds only pennies, and those of poor metal.

God bless your Majesty!

A fine feast, wasn't it, young Cynan? Ah, Artos would have liked it, but he might have called it tame. Nothing happened. Usually . . . *things* happened at his feasts; it got so that he wouldn't let us sit down to eat unless something weird—and I don't mean fated—showed up and demanded something or other. Well, maybe that he's gone; that's the strange part. Never mind: my mind's wandering these days right into a second childhood.

It's kind of you men to seek me out, even though the Queen—the old Queen, that is—agreed that all the ladies should come to the feast. I know that some of you are pledged, and others of you . . . nah, do not think I mock you; I remember how few the times seemed that I could find to speak to Mairedd before she'd agree to have me. She retired with the Queen, and that freed me up to slip away here.

Queen Gwenhwyfar—she's the old Queen now. Hard to think of her as the most famous woman in the world, the most beautiful, and, some thought, the most wicked. I don't know how much they tell you these days. You've heard—let me hear what?

That's right. When King Artos rode off to fight the Romans, he left his sister's son, Medrawt, behind as regent. Now, had I been Gwenhwyfar, I don't know how I'd have felt about that—or maybe I do. After all, everyone knew that Medrawt was Artos' son as well as his sister's: a bad seed, if ever was one. Adding insult to injury, the Queen herself was barren. So she hadn't given the king his heir and she wasn't asked to serve as regent herself: yes, friends, as a married man, I can tell you, I'd wager she gave her husband a cold send-off.

Now, remember, I wasn't there at the time. What I'm telling you is no more than what I heard, and maybe less than what you've heard. Some say that the Queen . . . let me put it another way. Some say that Medrawt wasn't content with his father's lands, but that he had to have his father's wife—and that this wouldn't have been the first time that the Queen had put horns on her husband's crown. Hard to believe, you say, and so do I: but these folk point to two children (safe now in an Abbey, I think) and call them her bastards by Medrawt.

Now, I ask you, how could that be true? Artos wasn't gone all that long—he wintered across the water, and was planning to push toward Rome itself when the news came that Medrawt was calling himself King. Not long enough, surely, to get one child, let alone two. Besides, Queens always have ladies with them, and where there are women, there are babes. I do believe, though, that Medrawt wanted her. She'd been a beauty and was a fine woman still; and I think that the *eorl* hated his father enough and was jealous enough of him that he'd take and wreck anything that Artos had.

But he wasn't counting on the Queen, who has every bit the strength of the women back home. She went up to Londinium with her own guard, who were loyal to her, took over the Tower of London, and told Medrawt . . . yes, I'd have given fine gold if she'd actually used words like that. I warrant, she knows them. He could have thrown everything he had at the Tower and not wrecked it; after all, it's one of the *eald enta geweorc*, the old work of giants like Caesar. But he was a good enough warleader to know he had to save his troops to fight his father; and so he did.

If she was innocent, why'd she retreat to the convent at Amesburh? Lad, lad, lad, how do you hope to marry if you know so little about women? Whether things were true or not true, she'd been *accused*, lad; and that kind of accusation sticks to a woman like horsedung. It's got to hurt, too. And the very idea that Artos and his Companions might have believed that she was an adulteress and traitor: my guess is that she wasn't just scared; she was furious. And maybe she had other reasons too . . .

So there she was, with the Sisters at Amesburh; and there she stayed all the while Artos gained strength. Couldn't have been easy for her, not to go to him and tend him; I know what my Mairedd is like when I've taken even a scratch, though she ought to be used to it by now. I wager she heard all the rumors, as a canny Queen must, and that she used all that time to try to plan out what was best to do.

Artos beat her to it, though. Once he was able to walk without falling over or read without getting blinding headaches, he called his Companions together, those who'd survived, and began to stitch his Britain together again. You've seen the ladies do fine sewing; well, I tell you, that needlework was nothing to the way Artos pieced the kingdom back. He named some new Companions, and I wasn't the only Saxon among them, either; what's more, he *made the old ones* like *the idea!*

So, the year was circling around toward winter again, when Artos called us all together. The harvest was in, what there was of it—it had been hard work with so many men slain who'd otherwise have brought in the crops. We had lords and women working out in the fields, there, at the end. But we were pretty well set for winter, or so we thought; and more than a few of us looked round the circle of Companions and thought, "We've done good work." Already, there had been a few marriages, and one or two of the new brides couldn't keep their food down: I was courting my Mairedd, and it promised to be a snug winter altogether.

Then Artos looked us over. "My lords and Companions," he called us; and we all half-bowed, half-nodded. Then he shook his head and dropped the high language of the court. "Lads," he told us, "it isn't quite working out. Something is missing."

There were a *lot* of somethings missing—or some-ones. All of his nephews, chief among them Gwalchmei of the Orkneyinga; his allies, Odbriht of Norway and Aeschil of the Mark of the Danes: those gaps in the Companions and allies hurt worse than a rotten tooth. Artos looked round and nodded. "Aye, I miss them too," he said, and rose and drank to their memory.

"But that isn't who is missing now."

He waited until we were all quiet, even the dogs gnawing their bones in the hall. The loudest thing there was the way the torches crackled when the fire hit a drop of sap.

"We need the Queen. *I* need the Queen."

If we all hadn't have been so shocked, all hell would have broken loose. Whatever else Britons and

Saxons don't agree on, we all stand together when it comes to giving a King a good argument. I saw one of the oldest companions rise.

"King, are you saying you'll order her back?" he asked.

Artos shook his head and smiled. "Order Gwenhwyfar? Since when has that been the best way to handle her? Not even when she was a girl and we were first wed. No. I am going to send a troop, an escort fit for a Queen, to her convent, and I am going to *ask* her to return. I will send my youngest Companions with my messages. Surely, she will see—" Artos grinned, but there was no mirth in it, and his eyes glistened "—how much they need the gentle leadership of their Queen."

You are all proven men of arms, so you know how that forms a bond among men who've lived through the same battle. Some of you have wooed; it strikes me that it's much the same thing. Ever since Camlann, King Artos had liked to keep me close by, not just to plan about how best to deal with the Saxons, but sometimes to talk over old times. By then, I was following Mairedd about like a motherless pup, though her family wasn't taking kindly to the idea of letting her pledge to me. If it hadn't been for the King, I might have given up. Given his favor and my persistence (plus my vow to let our children be baptized and brought up Christian), her father finally agreed. So I wasn't surprised when the king summoned me.

First, he congratulated me on my choice of a wife and had his man pour mead for both of us. Then, he sent the man away, and I started to wonder. Sure enough, he wanted me to lead the escort to fetch Queen Gwenhwyfar.

"She doesn't know me, lord King," I protested. "How can I ask her to put herself into my care?"

"With this," Artos pulled off his ring and spun it, pulsing hotter than blood, onto the polished table between us. "There's reasons for sending you. You don't know her: just so. You know nothing bad of her, only that your lord has set you the task of fetching her. And you've just been betrothed to a maiden, so you know how to coax. I'll vow, she'll need more coaxing than a virgin girl; whatever's happened to her, she's been hurt, friend."

Bless his soul, lads. He's dead, and it can't hurt to tell his secret, so I'll say to you that he gulped his wine fast, as if his throat was too dry to force out the words. "I don't *care* what they say. I don't care what she did, or what she felt she had to do. For twenty years, I have been bound to that woman, and I *know her!* She is loyal, if not to me, then to Britain; and I need her here, just the way a necklace needs a clasp. If she asks you, tell her that. And bring her back safe."

I knew a dismissal when I heard it, so I rose to go, tucking the ring into my pouch.

But "Wait," called the King, and he went over to a chest, opened it, and took out a necklace. Its woven gold gleamed like a peaceweaver's braids, and the gem in its clasp glowed purple, carved with the face of a long-dead lady: remnant of Rome; sign of a King's favor. "For your bride," he told me. "I hope that she will serve my lady when she returns as well as you serve me."

For once, when we rode out toward Amesburh, the weather held good: cold, dry, but sweet, like apples stored for the winter. The frost had hardened the old straight tracks, and, for part of the way, at least, I planned that we'd take the Roman roads, which are good even in the foulest weather. Of all the old works of giants in Britain, I count those roads the noblest. Forget about standing stones! What use are they, now the old gods have vanished?

In any case, I was in a high good humor. I had a promised wife; I was high in my lord's favor; the weather was good; I rode with friends and, what really pleased me, I could manage a day in the saddle now without aching like a gaffer or developing saddle galls that nigh made me squeak like a maidservant. So, the night before we reached Amesburh, when I took my turn at guard, I walked round the camp humming and singing to myself. Helped me keep awake, and made my companions laugh, warning me I'd find little to sing about once I was wed.

What was I singing? Something sad from home; sad songs go well in the winter. You may have heard the one about the exile: it's all about how a lonely man longs for pity, his lord's mercy, how he sails the frost-cold sea and dreams of his friends and his dead lord, and thinks that he's going crazy . . . I tell you, I was in a fine mood.

What do I sing when I'm in a bad mood? I don't.

So you know that much Saxon, do you, Cynan? You've got the fine voice of the West Country men; let's hear the part where the singer really opens up . . . I'll start it for you. *"Hwaer cwom mearg? Hwaer cwom mago?"* What has become of the horse? What has befallen the rider? Aye, that takes me back . . . we used to sing that one and damned near weep for the pity of it, by our warm fires.

All of a sudden, I hear the next lines of the song coming out at me like an echo out of the forest. "Where is the treasure giver? Where is the feast that was set forth? Where are the joys of the hall?"

I tell you, if I hadn't known we were in trouble, I'd have dropped my sword. Instead, I lifted my shield and crept on a pace. I wasn't singing any more, that let me assure you.

Someone was calling my name and speaking to me in Saxon from the underbrush. "You still croak like a pond full of frogs, Beorhtwold, you know that?"

So help me, I recognized the voice too, hoarse and tired as it was. "Waldhere!" I hissed. "Is that you? I thought you must have died at . . ."

"Camlann? When King Chelric fell and we should have died too? No such wyrd for me, but I see you're looking fine, fat and fit. And I hear more. Got a new lord, you do too, the old cuckold."

That got my temper up, as it was meant to; but I knew enough not to go charging off into the woods.

I'd sat next to Waldhere on the meadbenches too many times not to know that he never hunted or fought alone if he could help it; he was no fool.

"Come on out and say that!" I ordered. To my surprise, Waldhere did. He looked bad. Ever since Camlann, I suppose he'd been living rough—off the land, when he could; stealing, if he couldn't. He was thin, on the edge, and when they get that way, you can expect damned near anything.

"I hear you're off to the Sisters to fetch back the woman who caused all the trouble," said he. I didn't answer. I hadn't liked the way he had talked about my lord, and I didn't like what I thought he was leading up to. "Why not save us all some trouble, friend, and carry her off? By now, she must be used to that. And we could get a pretty ransom for her and safe passage back across the sea."

"I don't want to hear it," I told him, and held up my sword, careful-like, hoping that maybe a few of the men back in the camp might have heard me stop marching about and humming. "I've got a better plan. King Artos is a man I'm proud to have as a ring-giver. He swears that he'll give good land to any man who will pledge to live out his life here and treat it as his own country—Britain, not a welter of feuds and tribes. Come in with me; I'll speak for you, stand up for you . . ."

I was so carried away by the dream that Waldhere's nasty laugh brought me back to earth with a thump. I should have known then what I know now, what Artos knew lifelong: that there are builders and there are wreckers. And my friend, my old comrade-in-arms Waldhere had turned wrecker after Camlann. Still, I had to try.

"Is it gold you want?" I asked. "Safe conduct and passage home?" I didn't want to lower my shield to fumble at my belt for my pouch, but if he gave me his word, I'd have given him all the gold I owned, even what I was saving up as a morning gift. I owed him that, I figured.

"You've gone soft," he all but sang to me, "and

you've turned traitor. Now, call your fine Welsh friends and let them gut me, why don't you?"

I snorted. Maybe he'd been able to take me at practice two times out of three, but he was thin, sick, most likely; and I was in better shape than I'd been in since before Camlann. "Got a better idea," I told him. "I'll do it myself."

"Fine! Let's go!"

If this were home, we could have found ourselves a boat, rowed out to an isle, and had it out. Then whoever won would row back. My blood was up, and I was set to charge him then. But I remembered. I wasn't just on guard; I was leader here. Much as I might have enjoyed turning this into a private feud, I didn't have the right.

I'm afraid I knew how Waldhere felt. To his way of thinking, I'd betrayed King Chelric once by surviving the battle; and twice, by taking service with his enemy. Now, I was going to betray everything we'd ever prized for my new lord, even after I said I'd settle him quiet-like myself. Which, given the men who had lain down to sleep, trusting me, was the one thing I couldn't do.

Even if it cost me my life, I had to warn them.

What did I do? Let out a yell and charged blind into the woods. I cut Waldhere's legs out from under him, but three of his men circled me. When I could hear aught beside my own blood pounding in my skull, I heard shouts from the camp. Would they track me by the noise of the fight and come, or would they think I had tricked them and gone back with my Saxon kin? I didn't know. All I knew was that I had promised Artos, and I had the king's ring in my pouch.

My shield splintered, and I grasped my sword two-handed, trying to get my back to a tree. I know I took a couple shrewd cuts that bled like a pig for pudding, because I was weaving back and forth, blinking at the sky by the time my men came.

I'm pretty sure they thought I'd been elfshot, moon-struck, or some such, because I heard them laugh and say that the "big Saxon" was probably the only man in Britain to find trolls where never a bridge existed. Still, they had sworn to follow me, and follow they did. I almost wept from gladness to see them come crashing in on the bandits who circled me, but I couldn't. Instead, I spitted one of them—more luck than skill, then sat down in a hurry while the boys took out the rest of the bandits. Next thing I knew, I was propped against the tree, drinking something strong while they bound up my arm.

"May as well bury them," I told my men. "No one's going back to sleep tonight anyhow."

"Friends of yours?" I was asked.

Friends and brothers-in-arms once, but they'd stayed reivers, and I? Like my king, I had a country to protect.

"Not any more." They must have seen my face go grim, because no one asked me any more questions till morning.

I sat there while the British warriors buried the Saxons who would have cut me down like a sick dog. Then I ordered them to tie me on my horse. I had a Queen to fetch. For the first time, I realized that bringing Gwenhwyfar back to Artos was not a simple matter of obeying my lord and taking a ride with friends in the winter.

At least, my cuts did not fester. But I was still wobbling in the saddle when we rode into Amesburh and rang the convent bell. I sat a-horse expecting, God knows what: a troop of sturdy monks perhaps.

"Get *down!*" my second in command, Dafydd, his name was, mouthed at me. So I dismounted, not as easy as all that at the best of times, which this wasn't. By the time they opened the gates, I was sweating. The Sisters filed out in two lines; I've seen shieldwalls that weren't as well ordered as those women. Between those two lines of black robes stood the Queen, and she was as different from the nuns as a pearl is from a pebble. Oh, she wore the dark robes too, covered up from toe to chin. But in the pale winter noonlight, her braids were ruddy, almost as bright as the circlet that bound them or the cross that she wore. Against the black robes that she wore as proudly as if they were the finest of court garb, her skin was white as sea foam, even as it is now, though all I could see of it was her face and—I had to blink before I could believe it—her long, fine hands, one bearing the King's marriage-ring, folded upon the swell of her womb.

She carried a child, then. Was this why she had fled?

At that, I met the Queen's eyes, and I knew that if I valued my life, I dared not ask. Even more than Artos, she had the Roman presence, the gift to strike fear with but a glance. Those eyes were very bleak, but fire glowed somewhere beneath.

She had to have had her spies out, had to have known why we had come and even what we had met along the way. After all, she had the Roman schooling before her marriage to the King who had been a good deal older than she, a legend on earth; after her marriage, she learned statecraft from him.

Even though it was hardly my place to speak before I was spoken to, she waited . . . outwaited any craft or will of mine.

"Lady," I began in my feeble British and corrected myself. "Majesty, Artos the King bade me come before you and invite you . . . request you to return to your place at his side."

She raised a brow, a gesture sharp as the slash of a blade.

"In token whereof," I faltered as I reached for the ring and letter that Artos had given me, "I bring you these."

She motioned with one hand, and a little nun came forward to take them and bring them to her mistress, who spared them a glance, nodded, then waved them away as if they smelled foul.

"The King summons me," she said, and her voice rang out the way the ice cracks on a pond in spring. "How if I answer no?"

Now the fire truly smoldered in her eyes. Whatever else she was—traitor, adulteress, fugitive—she felt herself wronged; and a woman wronged is a woman angered beyond reason. Yet Gwenhwyfar was Queen as well as woman, so I hoped . . .

"Not summoned, Majesty," I forced out. "Requested. Entreated."

She laughed and reached out for ring and letter, sweeping them up in a movement as sudden as the rest of her was still. "So?" she asked. "Camelodunum just isn't the same without me, is it? He misses me, does he, and would have me back? For what?"

I could not withstand Mairedd when she frowned and stamped her foot; how could I face an enraged Queen and, in a tongue not my own, shape the courtly phrases that would persuade her to return to her husband? I would fail my ring-giver in the first task of any size that he had set me. Better by far that Waldhere had cut me down. Fire ran up my arm where his sword had hit me.

"For what, lady?" I answered with the truth. "For Britain. My ring-giver says that you are like the clasp upon a necklace. Britain cannot be healed without you. Nor"—to the end of my life, I will not know where the next words came—"will he."

"Your ring-giver." She considered my words and appeared to unbend only a bit. Like Artos himself, she switched then to my birthspeech, and its rough sounds, as she spoke them, had never been so fair. "Aye, I had heard that Saxons now serve him too. So, he sends me one of his tamed outlanders, does he?"

Even then, I knew that her anger was not for me. I bowed. "I am Beorhtwold son of Beorhtric, lady." So well did she speak my tongue that, if I shut my eyes, I could almost believe that I bowed before a lady of my own race, blunt, blond-braided, and likely, were she angered, to smack on the head the fool who had displeased her. Gwenhwyfar was nothing like such a one.

"Then he would have me back," mused the Queen. "And what will he say to this?" She held her hands away from the child-to-be. "Expose it at birth, as the pagans do; foster it out; or bring it up for the Church? A princess or prince, as the case may be."

Damn! You Britons are always so quick of speech. But would you believe that, of all the men, all the Britons who had ridden out with me, who had joined me in the fight against Waldhere and his looters, not one would aid me in this war of words? I stammered, stepped forward, then blurted out all that I could think of.

"A child follows its mother, lady."

"But what of its father?" the Queen hissed, bending forward. "If it is a girl, Constantine will inherit, no doubt. Britain needs fighters and claims that women are none such. But what if my babe be a boy?"

"He will not be the first son whose birth is doubtful," I said. "Think of his father."

She glared at me, and I repeated my words.

"Think of his father." Artos or Medrawt, rumor had attended them as surely as midwives had attended their mothers.

"He will not be the first babe to be whispered about. And, if he grows up strong and loyal, who shall care? Certainly not those of us who serve the King."

Certainly not Artos, who had been prepared, before the treason, to declare Medrawt his heir. And Constantine was twice loyal, despite his father's reasons to distrust Artos and his whole line.

How long Gwenhwyfar might have fenced with me, I do not know. Suddenly, I was bathed in a cold sweat, my sight was double, and I felt myself slipping to one side. Like a girl a third her age, she darted forward and caught me before I could fall. For all its fineness, her hand was as strong as that of any woman of my tribe.

She eased me down and pillowed my head on her knees and called for a basin and water, while I tried to protest and blinked. Her eyes were gull-grey, but cold as hail. When I tried to move, she held me down; and her hand was just as firm as those of the women in my homeland.

"Quiet, you," she ordered, and smiled to take out the sting of it.

I knew it; I had made an ass of myself and could

only hope to die of shame, though not of loss of blood, not from scratches like that, in the next moment. She had not even read my ring-giver's letter.

Expert as any army leech, she stripped the crusted, soiled bandages from my arm, slit my sleeve, and washed out the wound, glaring at my men and demanding to know who, clearly, among them was cut out for life as a butcher, not a healer. The men shifted from foot to foot and retreated somewhat, as she intended. I have heard drillmasters who were not half so skilled with their tongues.

"Who gave you this?" she asked, solicitous as the peaceweaver who poured out ale at my old lord's, my dead lord's feasts.

"His name," I found myself unable to deceive her, "was Waldhere, and he wandered Britain as an outlaw."

"Outlaws have no names," she told me. "But you knew his. What else was he?"

"Once, a kinsman; perhaps, a friend, across the water, when old king Chelric lived. Now, though, he was an outlaw, who sought to bring down the King and land I have sworn to protect."

"So you killed your own kin, your own friend, to protect him . . ."

"Protect Artos the King, lady? My lord can protect himself, should my life fail to ward him. I slew to protect Britain!"

"So his old dream yet lives, does it?" Gwenhwyfar sighed, and, to my surprise, the red heat in her eyes began to cool. She paused, as if unsure of how to say what she wished next to say.

She bent over me. "Now," she whispered. "Tell me. Does he look well?"

I blinked, too muzzy and slow to follow her. Mine is the skill of hands, not words, and ever has been. "Who?"

"Artos! How fares my husband? I heard that he was wounded, not expected to live."

I was young and newly betrothed; what did I know of the years of living together that forge a bond—

whether of hatred or love—between husband and
wife? She might leave him, betray him, curse his
name; but she would not cease to care—nor would he.

"Lady, I met him at Camlann. Ran into him, to
tell you the truth. We both had head wounds, and
we held each other up all through that dreadful
night. He heals . . . well."

"But says he needs me, eh?" Her breath was sweet
and her hands were very sure. I could drift forever,
listening to her, even though her questions came so
sharp and fast. I wished I were hale again, that she
had some great task that I might claim.

"We all need you. Britain is not Britain without
the queen to lead the women as the king guides the
men."

"And so he sends me a guileless young man who
can scarce speak our tongue, a man from whom, he
knows, I can learn whatever I want—or more than I
want. And the young man is wounded, and needs
me, too." Abruptly, her eyes went wet with tears,
and she dashed them away. Her hand was bloody
and left a smear on her face, but she never minded
that. "Do you know, Beorhtwold, how terrible it is
when you are not needed? When all runs well, and it
does not matter if you stay or go?"

I tried to say something, anything, that would not
earn me her scorn, but she laughed at me, and held
two fingers to my lips, silencing me.

"A night's rest for you, sir," she told me, and
snapped her fingers at my men.

"Then, tomorrow, assuming that you have no fever, if you have brought me a horse, I shall ride with
you."

"A litter . . ." my tongue was thick with relief and
faintness.

She grimaced. "You would do better in it than I.
Still, if your ring-giver and you insist on making an
old lady of me, I shall enter your litter and return
with you . . . to my husband."

The churchbells rang out, in tune with the ringing
in my ears, as my Companions picked me up, and, as

Gwenhwyfar commanded, bore me—"Gently, now! he's not a sheaf of grain!"—to guest quarters, I let myself rest.

I slept that day and the next. And when I was fit to ride, the Queen, as she had pledged, climbed meekly into her litter, and we headed back for Camelodunum. The story of my fight with my former kin had preceded me there, and it was then—and I praise your patience for listening so long to an old man—that Artos the King honored me with the ancient Roman title of Count of the Saxon Shore.

Prince—now soon to be King—Uther was born several months thereafter, a fine, healthy boy who looks like he will continue to do us proud. No one whispers about the Queen *or* her son where I can hear it, which suits me well.

Mairedd held the baby when the Queen was churched and claims that Her Majesty says that it was pity I was pagan and thus could not stand up beside her as sponsor. What else the Queen said on that subject Mairedd served up to me with supper for weeks and weeks. (Still does, when the mood takes her.)

What the Queen said to Artos I never knew, nor cared to. But, once again, a Queen sat beside her King at feasts and smiled at the Companions, weaving peace among them; and the ache in the hall seemed to fade into memory.

After all, it was years before a breath of scandal touched her, sunlit years, scented, they tell me, with apple blossoms. And the past twenty years since Camlann have been years just like those early ones, haven't they? More peaceful, you've heard from your grandsires? Thank them for that; thank the old men, and prepare to take over their watches from them. It grows very late.

And a fine night to you, too! That is, what is left of it. By all means, Cynan, walk back with me toward my quarters. Steady there, son! When you're as old as I am, you learn to hold your drink, or drink less. And I'm the one's been talking, too. Grant you, it's thirsty work, but I was busy and had less chance than the rest of you. Listen to them sing! Keep it down, lads! This was supposed to be a solemn feast! Heaven help them, a minute more and a little louder, and the priests will be down on them so fast . . . !

No, no need to worry about my lady wife. "Out tomcatting again, were you, old man?" she'll ask me. But as long as there's a twinkle in her eye, I know things are fine. She knows my mind.

You think *what?* Steady there, man; you've shocked me sober.

What makes you think that that's not all of the story?

What's that shadow? No shadow at all; that's my eldest sons, Aelfraed and Aelfric. You've seen them before, probably watched them practice. Aelfric's the man who teaches axe.

It's all right, sons; Lord Cynan here is a friend. At least, I think he is. (Tell them you're a friend; at their ages, they're not very patient, and their mother tells them they have to look after me.)

So, then. You think that there's more to the story, something that would explain why the old Count, who King Artos trusted with his life and his wife, would be wandering about the night before his King's burial.

I know the men from the West Country, sons. You can trust their words, especially the hillmen. And I know this one. Christian, aren't you, Cynan? Well enough. Boys, take him inside the church and swear him to silence, will you?

Well, that was quick enough. You don't go in for long prayers, do you? Just as well; we have a lot of work to do tonight. Have we got everything? Torches, spades, the . . . the replacement.

Replacement for what? For my King, man. Damn you to hell, I'll have your oath to me too, or I'll have your head!

Heads. That's it. You know the truth; you just don't know that you know it. Think, man, to your bards. No, I'm not touched in the head, not this time.

Aren't there whole batches of songs they call triads? That's right. Name me some.

Good. Your bards call them the three fortunate concealments of the Island of Britain. What were they? You can stop there, with the head of Bran the Blessed, son of the seagod Llyr, which was concealed in the White Hill in London with its face toward Gaul. And while it was in that position, no Saxon oppression ever came to this Island.

Do you see what I'm getting at now? Let's look at another triad. The Three Unfortunate Disclosures. It was before I came here with the other Saxons, too; or, maybe, we'd not have been able to make it over here. Artos disclosed the head of Bran the Blessed from the White Hill, because he did not desire that this Island should be guarded by anyone's strength but his own.

The day before he died, King Artos called me in to say farewell. He could barely speak above a whisper, and his sight was all but gone. But he knew me, and he told me to sit down. I remember every word he said to me. Here they are: "Beorhtwold, after a lifetime of listening to the bards, I have got to believe that things come in threes in Britain. God knows, in a lifetime of sin and blunders, I've made three bad mistakes. I begot Medrawt; well, I took back that life, at what cost you well know. I mishandled my match with Gwenhwyfar, and you helped me repair that error.

"But the third blunder is one that I knew I couldn't repair as long as I lived. I dug up Bran the Blessed's head from the White Hill after Badon. I was young and stupid and so stupidly proud that I thought Britain needed no other defender but me. Thought I was immortal in those days. Ha! We all learn better, don't we, friend?

"I can't see much, but I can tell light from shadow. I know when surgeons shake their heads, and there's nothing wrong, at least not all that much, with my ears yet. The last battle I fight is likely to be a battle to last till dawn, the way we did at Camlann. Remember that?

"Good man! We forged quite a bond that night. Now, by our old friendship, I want you to do one more thing for me.

"Sweet Christ, Beorhtwold, no! You can't really think that I'm asking you to cut my head off and bury it in the White Hill? It's not like I'm a pagan . . . your pardon, friend, not a pagan, but a savage, who believes that a man's soul lives in his head. Beorhtwold, when I'm gone, before they bury me, I want you to take my body and bury it by the shore at Camlann; you know the place. That's right, the bluff by the hazel bushes.

"Bury me with my face turned toward the sea so I can look out over the water and protect Britain just as Bran once did. That will make amends. And then, I think, I can sleep. It will be good to rest, aye, will it! But I swear, should anything come at my Britain, should anything break that shieldwall you've spent the past twenty years building for us here, I'll wake, and I'll rise, and I'll drive it back into the water. Are you with me?

"You're the one I'd choose in any case, but there's another reason. You're still pagan; the priests don't scare you. I know that if you swear your oath to me, you'll keep it. I have told Gwenhwyfar what I intend; she understands, too. All the same, try not to get caught.

"Stop grizzling, man! I don't want your tears; I want your oath on it, yours and your family's. For the last time, then, your hands between mine . . . there. That's done. I can go with the tide now. You can call the priests or the surgeons when you go, whichever you think will do most good. Farewell, and whatever gods you wish go with you."

You're damned right I'm going to honor my oath to him. He took me up, gave me heart and hearth, life where I thought only to die. He gave me a homeland and a family—and I am going to protect them from now until Doomsday, as my lord laid on me. I have labored lifelong to build him a shieldwall. Now his body will shield the wall we built.

So now you know the whole tale. The coffin lies in

the chapel, and we've got the body of an old man hidden, dressed in robes as much like those of the king as Mairedd and my girls could stitch. An old tramp, with no friends, no family. If Artos hadn't put his hand on me, I might once have been such a man, if I'd lived that long. This one, though, will sleep like a king till the last trump. And my youngest son guards the place now. No one will stop us; no one had better.

I tell you, this has nothing to do with King Uther! Besides, among my folk, a lord is King when he's acclaimed. Here in Britain, you need a mass and a crown and a parade of great ones to hallow a prince into a King. That won't be for days yet. When the time comes, you young men will serve your young King. For now, though, for now, you are still King Artos' men and do his bidding.

Don't shake, lad. Think of it this way; you're still serving the King. And this was the last, maybe most important, thing he ever asked of us. So, for your pains and tears, you'll be one of the last to get to say good-bye to him. And we can use the help. Now, come on. Aelfraed, hand our friend here one of the shovels. You go on before; your night sight's keener. No need to start at shadows or shiver. If anyone asks, you're walking home with the Count of the Saxon Shore and his sons.

Nay, I'm fine! It was just a long ride. I'm an old man; I'm worn out. Never fear, I'll sleep well enough once this is done. Listen to the waves! The water by Camlann is clear tonight. It was red and muddy during the battle, and you couldn't tell day from night for weakness and the mists.

You can light the torches now. Two of them, I think. That's right, over there! The hazel bushes have overgrown—careful, there's a bluff down there! How would I explain it if you fell and broke your fool neck? Here is where I dragged myself after I woke, that accursed day.

Or was it a blessed day, the day I met Artos? You dig, lads, while I try to puzzle it out. Dig deep; we don't want the king disturbed, you know, by anything less than red war.

Easy there. Watch your hands; those branches will cut right through them. Don't let them scratch his dear face. Here: wrap his cloak around him; he can have mine for a shroud too, and we'll add the Dragon banner. There you are, King. Rest easy now. Your last mistake is healed, your kingdom guarded.

Cover him up, boys! We can't let the torches burn out at his head and feet. Throw them out into the water. Aye, whirl them first: once, twice, thrice! How the flames leap, like blood running off a bright blade. It isn't the proper barrow and the song he deserves, but it's what he asked for—and the best we can . . .

The songs will come later.

Get me to the wagon; let me lie down. I'm not dying here; I'm not dying yet, either. I have to get back to Glaestingeburh and guard the Queen on her way back to her convent. You come home with us, Cynan lad. We'll feed you, put you up. After all, you've no family here to speak of. No father left, no brothers at all? That's hard, but, after this night's work, you can count on several.

Did I hear you say you were not yet betrothed? My eldest maid Tangwen is a fine cook; she has her mother's eyes and sweet temper. Maybe the two of you will like each other. If you do, frankly, I'd be proud to call you son. Not to rush you or aught; but think about it. After this night's work, we are bound forever, and old Beorhtwold looks after his own. Learned it from my lord.

We can settle that later. Just help me get home and rested enough to watch the young king crowned and guide his lady mother to Amesburh. Then, finally, I shall do what Mairedd has wanted all these years. With her beside me, I will walk meekly to the church and submit myself for baptism. The priest will sprinkle the holy water on my head and take my sins away. Though I do not believe what we have done tonight to be a sin, when the priest sprinkles the holy water on my head, even that breath of worry will be gone.

Pagan, people have called me, though for years I've been a catechumen, at least most of the time. Savage, I've heard a few whisper, though not when I could catch them at it. But I'm nobody's fool. Why should I be baptized till I was certain I had outworn my time of sinning? That time has come now, and so has mine.

A few months, perhaps years, more, and it will be time for the old Count of the Saxon Shore to step aside from his shieldwall. I leave strong sons to take my place. It may be that they will not need to disturb the King. But he will be guarding them. Should he need to rise, I shall beg the White Christ to wake me to serve him as shieldman on that day. He cannot refuse to hear his sinless thane.

Let the King rest, and the young King prosper. I can sleep now.

AND THE TRUTH SHALL
SET YOU FREE

Sharon Green

Introduction

This story is set about seventy-five years in our future, or at least what I'd like to *think* will be our future. In our current attempt to be fair to those who are accused of crimes, we bend over backwards for those who are guilty and completely ignore the victims of the crimes. Without changing anything at all, I could have projected a future where people are executed if they're so unwise as to be the victims of a crime. Since I happen to believe that more and more people are getting fed up, I've chosen to see a different future, one that won't simply set the stage for the innocent to be convicted of any crime people care to charge them with. Only the guilty will be convicted, a lot more easily and cheaply than it's done right now, and a lot more surely. If we'd only take the trouble to look around ourselves and *think*, we could make this world a lot more pleasant place to live in. And the beautiful part about it is we could have this right now—if we really wanted it.

Waking up was very strange, and at first I didn't really want to. I'm one of those who don't simply sleep, I *enjoy* sleeping, and the only kind of waking up that matches the enjoyment is the slow, I've-had-enough-of-this-now sort. I tried to resist when—something—began pulling or pushing at me, joggling me out of comfort, but it wasn't something like my mother, you know, something you learn to ignore. Whatever-it-was refused to be ignored, so I cursed under my breath and began coming out of it.

I had to take a deep breath to start it, but once I did it all began coming at once. My ears heard the soft thrum of machinery working smoothly, my nose smelled that more-than-clean smell you find in hospitals that don't get overwhelmed by the dying, and my body felt warm and relaxed and comfortable. I could also hear the sound of water gurgling slowly out of something, so I pulled my eyes open to see if I could figure out what was going on. I couldn't seem to remember where I'd gone to sleep, so I was curious about where I was waking up.

My first look at the room told me it was no place I'd ever seen before, and it sure didn't have much in the way of possibilities. It was only about twelve by twelve, had light peach-colored walls and ceiling—strips of ceiling, really; all the rest of it was light panels—and two closed doors. Furniture-wise it had whatever I was lying on, and two molded plastic chairs in white. The floor was light peach tiles, not even carpeting, and looked as clean as the walls.

While I was looking around the machinery hum was dying down, and suddenly it went off completely. One of the two people in the room besides me, the woman, made a sound of satisfaction, and the man looked up from a metal chart-book he'd been studying. When he saw my eyes on him he smiled, put the chart-thing down on one of the chairs, then came over to stand next to me.

"Well, congratulations, Angie, you made it," he said, sounding like he was trying to sell me a new car. "And not only *just* made it; you're probably the most successful one so far. In a little while we'll be checking you over very thoroughly, but I don't expect we'll be finding anything much at all."

I opened my mouth to ask him who he was and what he was talking about, but all that came out were these rough croaking noises in place of the words I'd wanted. Surprises like that tend to bother me a little, but the man shook his head and put a hand on my arm.

"Don't worry about rusty pipes, all they need is a little oiling," he told me with a smile, then turned to take a glass of something pale yellowish from the woman. "We've learned that this does the job better than what was recommended, so let's get it into you. No, don't try to sit up alone yet, you aren't strong enough. Take your time and let me help you."

He put an arm around my shoulders and raised me up a little, just enough to let me drink from the glass he held. The yellowish stuff in it had a fizzy-but-still-flat taste that really wasn't a taste, but since I was thirstier than I thought I drank it anyway. The glass wasn't glass but very smooth plastic, and the drink it held was warmer than it was.

When the glass was empty the man eased me down again, and I found there were things I was only just noticing. The two people I didn't know were dressed in thinnish one-piece outfits of the same light peach color, and I couldn't be sure but it looked like there were thin shoe-boots attached at the bottom of the outfits. I, on the other hand, wasn't wearing anything at all, and that really made me curious.

"If you two are into kinky shit, we're gonna have to dicker first," I said with a slur, but at least this time it came out as words. They didn't come out as strong as I'd wanted, but at least I was over the croaks.

"Angie, I'm going to have to ask you to speak Standard English," the man said, giving me another of those smiles. "Slang changes so fast even a computer would have trouble keeping up with it, and I've never been very good at it anyway. Your file tells me you're both literate and fluent, so will you do me that favor?"

"Sure, if you'll tell *me* what in hell is going on," I answered, starting to be more annoyed than curious. "I don't know you two and I never saw this place before, so let's have it. What are we supposed to be doing?"

"We're supposed to be waking you up, which we *did* do," he answered, then held up a hand. "Now, don't get upset because you can't remember what happened before you were put to sleep, it was arranged to be that way. The subconscious controls everything, you know, and they didn't want your subconscious to be frightened. You volunteered for an experiment and the experiment was a success, so now you can start remembering. Think back, Angie, and you *will* remember."

As he said the words I realized I *hadn't* been trying to remember, and since that didn't make any sense I changed it fast. I thought back to before I'd gone to sleep, back—back—and then I had it. The experiment, and my volunteering for it—and everything that had happened before it. I also remembered something that was supposed to have been part of the deal, a part I might be able to check out right then and there.

"I volunteered for a cold-sleep experiment, but they couldn't tell me how long it would last," I said, looking at him with what should have been the right amount of concern. "How long *did* it last?"

"Seventy-five years," he answered at once, his smile growing wider with relief. "The technique used on you was one of the most successful of the series, almost identical, in fact, with what's used as standard today. The volunteers in your group are being awakened every five years, to see if we can anticipate an upper limit to the cryonic suspension, but so far we haven't found one. Once you've gone through physical therapy and are on your feet again, you'll be welcomed into our present-day society. You should find it rather easy to adjust to."

"Easy," I echoed, letting him see just a little worry. "After seventy-five years, what am *I* going to be able to do? I won't know which end is up."

"There haven't been so many basic changes you won't be able to learn them fairly quickly," he assured me, the smile still firmly there. "Most of them were already being speculated on in 1993, the year you started from. Coming from a high-tech society as you do, a slightly higher-tech society won't be any problem. And don't forget—there's always a place in any society for a brave, selfless young woman like yourself."

He patted my shoulder before turning to the woman to ask her a question, and then the two of them began discussing the arrangements for moving me elsewhere. I kept my face straight while I listened to them, but inside me I was laughing like hell. All that bad luck I'd run into just before I "volunteered"— seventy-five years had been long enough to cure it, and now I was set to ride high again. They'd said if the experiment ran twenty-five years, my records would be sealed and not reopened without cause; if it ran fifty years, the records would be removed and destroyed. I hadn't really trusted them to do that, but it looked like the damned fools had kept their word. There couldn't be many people left alive who knew me, and my records were destroyed—which meant my new friends had no idea their brave and selfless volunteer had put her neck on the line to get out of having to spend thirty years in prison.

I was moved to a pale tan room with a hospital bed in it, and the bed looked sleek and simple compared to the ones I was used to, but otherwise not much different. Once in the bed I expected to be out of it again in no time, but that's not the way it went. I was so weak at first I couldn't sit up or even hold a glass to drink from, and that despite all the massaging the machine I'd slept in had done. I needed constant help—and a lot of sleep.

When I wasn't sleeping or having my body worked over, I was trying to remember how to eat. Swallowing liquids was all I was up to at first, and not much of those. For a couple of days I had to stay with some light brown stuff like the yellowish drink the man had given me, and then they started adding broth and thin ice cream fizzes. By the time they got up to real food I was able to sit up and hold a fork on my own, but they never did bring by anything worthwhile. No pizza or burritos, no greasy fries, and nothing like beer. Even their cheeseburgers tasted sanitary.

For the times there weren't people fussing over me I had television to watch, but not on the kind of set I was used to. They didn't make sets any more, only these silverish discs twice the size of silver dollars, and wherever you put the disc down a picture formed in the air above it. The real guts of the thing were built into one of the walls, and you worked it with a plastic remote-control handset. It was no big deal to learn how to use it, and most of the programs were just as stupid as the ones from my own time. More stupid, maybe, since they were all so mealy-mouthed bouncy and happy.

Or most of them were. At night I would settle down to flip channels, and most of the majors had programs that were banded in red. Red, I found out, meant somebody in the program would curse, or strip down to the buff, or screw somebody else, or beat up on somebody. One of the techs told me I could lock down the red button on the handset, and then none of the red-banded programs would come through no matter how much flipping I did. That left the blue and yellow and green and orange and purple bands, which the tech thought ought to be enough for anybody.

Like hell. The blue band was all goody-goody all

the time, not a word out of place, not an inch of underwear showing. Stand-up comics on that band were so clean they squeaked, which means I don't understand how some of them came off funny. The yellow band was all little-kid stuff, learning programs and groups doing things, and the green band was all game shows. Day and night, hour after hour, game shows without end. The orange band was all sports for the same amount of time, and the purple was educational—on every subject you could name, plus an extra dozen or two. I didn't know why they had so much, and especially didn't know why it was all separated.

"It's a matter of being free to choose what *you* want to watch," one of the male nurses told me, one who had heard what the therapy tech had said before he left. "That guy would love to push for flatting the red band, but he's bright enough to know if he did that, *I* could push for flatting the blue band. My opinion carries just as much weight as his does, and as long as he has what to watch and isn't forced to use the red band, it's none of his business that I *do* want to watch it. We're starting to learn to live our own lives, instead of trying to live everybody else's."

I'd listened to what the nurse said the way I listened to everything around there, nodding quietly as though I was trying hard to remember what I was told so I could think about it. Well, I was thinking about it, all right, but not the way *they* thought. I'd found right from the first that they were all so easy to con it was almost boring, but it wasn't the time or the place to make a move. Once I was out of that hospital I could start a real operation, and the marks would go down like pins run over by a bowling ball.

And there still were honest-to-god marks, worse than the jerks who believed everything I said. Back in my own time I'd had to work at making people believe me, not hard, mind you, but I'd still had to make the effort. It became a matter of, "Young woman, what do you have to say for yourself about the way you broke the law?" "Gee, judge, I didn't know what I was doing, I thought it was okay. I'll never do it again, I swear it." "Well, you'd better remember that, and not let me see you in my court again. Suspended sentence."

As I said, it hadn't been hard, especially if you cried a little and mentioned that your father had run out on your mother when you were too small to even remember him. That part everybody was ready to believe, even social workers who could have found out differently if they'd bothered checking. But they didn't check, most of them, because they were happier believing the line. And happiest yet if you didn't speak gutter. I'd learned young that if you spoke as well as the person who caught you, it didn't take long before they forgot all about what you'd done. English was the only class I'd never cut in school, and it had paid off more times than I could count.

But those marks—they were still around for the same reason they'd been around in my day. The woman who came in to clean the bathroom was one, and I'd known it even before she opened her mouth. She was the kind who was old on the inside, which had nothing to do with how many wrinkles she might have had on her face. Even without wrinkles she would be old, old and scared and a long-time loser. She reminded me of Teddi's mother, but since they didn't look anything alike I didn't know why—until she stopped once on her way out to talk to me.

"You're all alone today," she observed, giving me one of those smiles that tell you the words are just an opening toward something else. "Usually there's at least a nurse here."

"I'm doing well enough so that I don't need constant watching any more," I answered, trying to figure her angle. A reporter, maybe, trying to grab the story before anyone else could get it?

"Your getting better is something to be thankful for," she said, smiling that smile again. "I've read a lot about your time, so I don't think I have to tell you who you should be thanking for getting better. People in your time *knew*, and those who disagreed weren't allowed to spread their lies as easily as the truth was spread. Would you like someone here to help you do that thanking?"

"I—don't really understand," I said slowly, something of an understatement. The woman was middle-aged or less, sounded fairly well educated, and tended to keep her head up higher than should have been comfortable. Under her two-piece work suit of light yellow she was stocky, definitely leaning toward a spread around the middle, and I didn't know where she was coming from.

"We all need help in giving proper thanks to the One Who blesses us with His smile," she said, and right then I could hear the capital letters in her tone. "But there's no sense in doing it unless we do it right, and doing it right is really easy. You tell the people in charge of you that you want that help, and they *have* to provide it. If you like, I can even give you a name to mention. That way you'll get *him* and nobody else."

"A pastor or a priest, you mean," I said, finally getting what she'd been tiptoeing around. "You think I need somebody religious."

"Everyone does, even if they use today's laws to say they don't," she answered, this time giving me a really warm, very sincere smile. "The people here think they're doing you and the rest a favor by not letting men of the cloth come by unless someone specifically asks for one, but that's the kind of favor the devil will do you. If you show them you know what's right, they have to give in and let you do it."

"But the choice is mine," I said, feeling strange for a minute as I remembered what that nurse had said about the red band on television. "No one has the right to tell me what to do, not if I don't want to."

"That's exactly right," she said, her smile widening as she misinterpreted what I meant. "No one can tell you not to do what's best for your immortal soul, not even if they don't agree. Would you like me to write that name down for you, so you won't have to remember it?"

"Yes, why don't you," I agreed, then took the piece of paper and watched her leave with that big smile on her face. I ran a finger over the paper as I held it, enjoying the way the ink looked wet even though it wasn't, juggling in my mind all the possibilities of what could be done with that bit of evidence. By then I knew she was exactly like Teddi's mother, but unlike Teddi's mother, I didn't have to worry about what I did to her. All I'd ever done with my best friend's mother was argue, but even though it got to her it never did her any real harm.

"No, Teddi, you're not going to the beach Sunday morning with Angie and those other ruffians you hang out with," she used to say, too busy cleaning their apartment to even look at the person she was talking to. "You're going to church with me the way you're supposed to."

"But, Ma, the summer's almost over," Teddi would answer, just short of being up to here with that crap. "We only have a little while left before it gets too cold to go, and I don't see why I have to miss it."

"You know why you have to miss it," her mother had answered, scrubbing away at a sink that was probably whiter than it had been when it had been new. "Sacrifice and hard work are the only things that are worthwhile in this life, and it's about time you learned that. You won't find that out at the beach, so you won't be going. You'll be going to church."

"To make sure she doesn't find out the truth instead," I'd commented before Teddi could scream in frustration. "Lots of times it's easier not knowing the truth, isn't it, Mrs. B.?"

"That happens to be the whole point, Angie," Teddi's mother had said, her shoulders stiffening the way they usually did when she had to talk to me. "The only place you do find out the truth is in church, and once you understand that, everything gets easier."

"Hey, Teddi, you see that?" I'd enthused, turning my head to grin at my closest friend. "And you thought your mother would never get it. I told you she couldn't be that blind."

"What are you talking about, Angie?" her mother had asked the way I'd known she would, finally turning to look at us. "What is it that you think I 'get'?"

"Why, the fact that if you open your eyes in church, you really do see the truth," I'd answered, letting the innocence simply pour out of me. "Those people have the biggest con ever going, and most of the suckers fall for it. They don't know what God wants any more than I do, but they sure as hell know what *they* want. They want the suckers to give them money without their having to work for it, and that's just what happens."

"Angie, you haven't the faintest idea of what you're saying," she'd come back, her expression insisting she wasn't interested in nonsense. "Those are loving, dedicated people you're talking about, giving up everything their own lives could give them in order to help people save their souls. They have nothing of their own, absolutely nothing, and for the help they give they ask nothing more than a little of what *we* earn, just so they can keep going. If they're running a con, it doesn't seem to be working very well."

"Oh, sure, I know they don't *own* anything," I said, still bright and friendly. "All they get to do is *use* things, most of the time for their whole lives. Like houses, and cars, and housekeepers, and sometimes jewelry. The only difference between owning something and getting to use stuff other people own, is that you don't have to save up before you get it. And if you get to use it your whole life, why worry about whether or not you own it?"

Mrs. B. had opened her mouth, trying to think of something to say, but nothing came out. I gave her half a minute to show I was being polite, and then I went on.

"And I don't understand why it should cost money to save your soul," I said, pretending I didn't see her squirming on the hook. "My mom and dad have to pay a whole chunk of cash to the church, otherwise they can't go. And they don't even get to say how much they pay, the church *tells* them how much. I looked in the Bible to find where it said you have to pay to be saved, but all it said was you can't be rich or you won't get into heaven. If money is so evil, how come the church wants so much of it?"

"The church uses that money to help the needy, girl," she came back at once, finally on familiar ground. "They do wonderful charitable work, all over the world. Not everyone lives as well as you girls do, so you should be thankful for what you have. And thankful for being allowed to help others. Those who give charity are blessed many times over."

"Then why doesn't the church sell everything it has and give it *all* to charity?" I countered, putting on more pressure. "They come up with all kinds of reasons why they can't and shouldn't, but bottom line is they still keep what they have. And every year they take even more. They treat the bunch of you like slaves, telling you what to do, who to marry, what to eat, and where to go on Sunday, and you just lap it up because you like being conned. If you go along with the con, you don't have to live scared. If you go along with it, you don't have to be afraid of dying."

"You're not afraid of dying, Angie?" she'd asked then, a strange look in her eyes. "The young often feel that way, usually because they think they have it figured out. Do you have it all figured out?"

"Sure, Mrs. B.," I'd said with a smile, enjoying the way I'd gotten to her. "When I die I'll just make a deal with God, and then I'll be all set. After all, if He lets the church get away with *their* con—and all the other churches and things, too, since most of them disagree—then He's open to making deals. If He wasn't, He wouldn't let all those suckers get taken—and then blame it on the devil. Sure God's somebody I can deal with, and I'll get a hell of a lot more out of it than I would dealing with those con artists who claim to be working in His name. It's the suckers who never get a good deal, and I'm not a sucker."

"I wish I knew what you are instead," she'd muttered, still staring at me, and then she'd left the room. The next day Teddi had told me she wasn't allowed to hang with me anymore, and we'd both laughed. Her mother was a sucker who wanted to stay a sucker, but that didn't mean we had to do the same.

The truth is a great weapon, you see, something

people like Teddi's mother don't know. If you tell
enough of it those like Teddi, who need someone to
do their thinking for them, will believe everything
else you say, too. Teddi's mother tried to sound as if
she was telling the truth, but I was better at it and I
wasn't telling someone else's version that had holes
in it I couldn't cover. I told my own version, and that
made it just as true as anyone else's, better than
most.

Which meant Teddi's mother lost out all the way
around. I was happy for Teddi when she took off
with that good-looking hunk, leaving all her mother's
nagging behind. Nobody needs that kind of garbage,
even if they don't live any longer than Teddi did . . .

I moved around in my sleek-looking hospital bed,
considering the piece of paper I held with a man's
name on it, and then I let the piece of paper float out
of my fingers and down to the floor. When the duty
nurse came in to check on me, she noticed the paper
on the floor even faster than I expected her to. She
was one who couldn't stand having the room look
messy, and when she picked it up she spotted the
name on it.

Once I was asked where the paper and name had
come from, I couldn't do anything but tell the truth,
could I? While at the same time hesitantly mention-
ing how pushy the cleaning woman had been? The
nurse listened grimly while I commented with a sigh
that we'd probably always have that sort with us, and
then she'd marched back out of the room. A day or
so later I heard in a roundabout way that the cleaning woman had been fired.

I spent what seemed like forever in that hospital,
but the day finally came when they said I could
leave. I shed a few tears while saying goodbye and
pretended I'd miss everyone in that god-awful boring
place and, unsurprisingly, most of them seemed to
believe me. It had taken two trials back in my own
time to find enough people who *didn't* believe me,
and that despite the two witnesses who had seen
what I'd done. Those old people dying had been the
worst luck I'd ever had, but it hadn't all been my

fault. The first jury had understood that no one had warned me that might happen, and my lawyer had made it clear no one could hold me responsible for not knowing something like that. After all, if people *give* you the money they should be spending on food and medical care, is it really your fault if they die? No matter what story you told them to make them give you that money?

For a while I'd thought when they finally did let me out of the hospital I'd be on my own, but someone obviously didn't trust me or didn't believe I could take care of myself. Elaine Rider showed up to "help" me.

"You'll call me Elaine and I'll call you Angie, and that way we'll be friends right from the start," the woman said with one of those open, trusting smiles. She must have been somewhere in her thirties with dark hair and eyes like mine, but that's as far as any similarity went. She was a few inches taller and definitely on the pudgy side, her face included, and the clothes she wore looked like they'd been bought for someone else.

"I'm here to help you get settled into a normal life, Angie," she said, beginning to open the first of the boxes she'd brought with her. "The people running the experiment you volunteered for set up a trust fund for their subjects, to be used when the time came for them to reenter society. They didn't want any of you to be charity cases, and you certainly won't be. You'll have enough money to live on for a year, and if you decide on a career that takes longer than that to be trained for, provisions have been made to extend your financing as long as your grades and progress are satisfactorily maintained. To start it off I bought you some clothes, and once you're out of here you can begin building a wardrobe to your own taste."

She gave me that smile again, and it wasn't easy for me to return it. They were going to pay my way for one lousy year, and I was supposed to be grateful? After everything they'd gotten out of using me? I had more than that due me, a lot more, and since they wouldn't be giving it I'd just have to take it. They'd find out soon enough who they were trying to sucker.

"What kind of material are these clothes made of?" I asked Elaine, mainly to keep from asking what kind of a geek she was. She'd brought a loose pants outfit in tan and white with white sneaks, also underwear in a shade that made it look faded. The only good thing about the stuff was the material, which was very lightweight and looked pretty expensive.

"Oh, that's one of the last batch of polys," she said, this time with a small laugh. "They come out with a half a dozen new ones every year, and expect everybody to rush right out and buy them. A lot of people do, which is why the used clothing business is going so well. In certain jobs you *have* to be right up to date, which means a new wardrobe every couple of months. Even if you have the money you won't have the room for so much clothing, so you sell the previous batch after buying the new one. People who don't have to be quite that up buy from the used outlets, which makes more sense than buying new. After all, once a few months have gone by, it doesn't matter if you bought it new. It's still considered out. If you'll get dressed now, I'll give you a short tour on the way to your apartment."

If I hadn't wanted out of that hospital so badly, I probably would have taken that stuff and thrown it right in her face. Used clothes! If anyone had a right to new clothes *I* did, and once I got things set up the way I wanted them, that's what I'd have.

There were papers to sign from and by seven different people, but when they all finally stepped out of the way I was able to follow Elaine out to the street. The first thing I noticed was that the air smelled strange, and the second was the way things looked. Only third did I notice the traffic going by, but it was the first thing I mentioned.

"Those cars are so weird!" I said, staring at the mixture of dark colors and pastels. "Except for the bigger ones their shapes are all the same, and they're not making any noise. I also don't see or smell any exhaust."

"Oh, they finally got rid of the last of the growling monsters about fifteen years ago," Elaine said, sounding faintly amused. "If you don't have an internal combustion engine you don't get noise and smell, and these engines do more than the old ones could. They also make the air more attractive to breathe, not to mention being easier on the ears. But don't let any of the car manufacturers hear you say they all look alike. You're supposed to see how individual each of their versions of the basic sexy look is—even if they do all look alike."

She grinned at me as though we were sharing a joke, then continued walking along the street. Along the very clean street. I couldn't remember ever seeing a sidewalk quite that clean, and especially not in a city. There were litter baskets all over the place, but not with the usual signs on them. It seemed as if they expected people to use them without being advertised into it, which was sure as hell a weird thing to expect.

Elaine pointed out various things along the way, including a place she called an automart. It looked like nothing more than a really big supermarket, but I didn't see any checkout counters. What it did have was a wide-doored side entrance leading onto a parking lot, and people were wheeling out bags of groceries in wide, flat carts, or carrying out single bags. Inside the glass windows I could see people filling up carts with already-packed bags, and a board where three people without bags stood pushing buttons. One of the three left the board and went over to a place where a small bag was slid through a door onto a counter, picked up the bag, then left the store.

"Most people do their shopping at home through their computer, then come down and pick up their orders," Elaine said, obviously following my gaze. "By the time they get here it's all packed and ready, and all *they* have to do is get it to their cars. If they want to have the stuff delivered that can be done too, but they have to pay for the service. Those people over at the drop-in board are probably doing bread-and-milk-on-the-way-home, or you-won't-believe-what-I-forgot."

"The store owners must hate this kind of thing," I said, watching as one woman pushed a button on an empty cart and the cart went trundling back to the store on its own. "People spend a lot of money on impulse buying and on sale items, but if they're not there with the things they won't buy them."

"No, as a matter of fact the owners like it better this way," she said, moving really slowly to let me look as long as I wanted to. "Shoplifting isn't possible, so they don't lose a good chunk of their inventory on a regular basis. And when people shop by computer, they don't miss *anything* in the store. Sale items blink, specials glow, and you can tag certain things as maybes, to be decided on once you see what the total hole comes to. If it isn't ruin you can add the maybes, and don't have to bother trying to remember what they were. You can see what they were, just the way you can see all the rest of it, because computer screens are now just like television pictures. After the picture show is over, you also pay by computer. Saves the bother of having to drag around cards, checks or cash."

"I'll bet those owners like the idea of no shoplifting better than all the rest of it," I said, personally hating the idea. "They don't care if people have to go hungry, just as long as *their* stuff isn't touched."

"They most like the idea of not having to charge the rest of us for what others walk off with," she said, looking at me curiously. "And why would people have to go hungry? If someone has a temporary problem, there are agencies which give out short-term, no-interest loans. If the problem is more than temporary, there are other agencies to help you get straight. As long as your problem isn't that you don't want to work. A problem like that is *your* problem, and if you don't solve it fast you end up very uncomfortable."

"Uncomfortable in what way?" I asked, moving a little faster to match her now-increasing pace. "Some people have things wrong with them so they *can't* work, and there's nothing they can do about it. You're into giving people like that a hard time?"

"People who are really incapable of working are certified as such and taken care of," she said with a headshake, one hand gesturing a dismissal of what I'd said. "If it truly isn't their fault, the only thing they're kept from doing is having children. No one is silly enough anymore to simply *claim* they can't work, but there are still a few who have talked themselves into believing they can't or shouldn't have to. If one of that kind surfaces and a little therapy doesn't turn them around, they get sent out to one of the wilderness communities. Out there it's either pull your weight or go under, and most of them don't go under. With no charity or sympathy available, they get down to the real in a jump and a half."

That didn't sound any too promising, but it wasn't the time to ask for more details. Welfare cases were easy to tap, most of them so far into booze or shit that they didn't know they were being taken, and there had to be some of that kind around somewhere. No city got away with not having their share, it would only be a matter of finding out where they were kept.

A thought that made me look around again at the neighborhood we were walking through. Despite being clean it was obviously not one of your better areas, the age and condition of many of the buildings proving that. The worst ones of the lot were being worked on, some by professional crews, some by groups of people who looked like they'd just walked in off the street, but something was definitely missing.

"Street loafers," I said without realizing I was talking out loud, but the questioning look I got from Elaine gave me the message. "I mean, there's nobody hanging around on the streets. There are old people and kids walking around looking like they're always out this way, and nobody's bothering them. Did they do something in this neighborhood to get rid of the gangs?"

"They did something in all the neighborhoods everywhere," she answered, finally nodding in understanding. "Street gangs were declared uncontrolled packs of wild animals, and were taken into custody.

One by one they were questioned and tested, and those who weren't total losses were sent where they could be trained to do useful jobs. A lot of those kids had joined gangs in the first place only to survive, not because they enjoyed making trouble. They were sent a long way from their original cities, and weren't allowed to go home until after they'd established themselves as productive human beings.

"That left a lot of younger kids in the various neighborhoods, and they were the next to be examined and tested. Again the worst of the various lots were separated out and the rest were sent home, but not to be left to go back to their old ways. They were all made members of *new* gangs, but this time with responsible people leading them. The new leaders were just as hard on anyone who didn't obey the rules as the old leaders would have been, but it was necessary for the sake of the children. It takes time to learn how to accept kindness."

"What happened to the worst ones?" I asked, having a feeling I already knew the answer. "Did they put them in the slammer, or just out of their misery?"

"Neither," she said, turning her head to look at me. "They didn't have the right to simply kill them, not when a good part of the reason they were like that was society's fault. If they'd been taught better the first time they stepped out of line, most of them wouldn't have done it a second time. They were made the first residents of the brand-new wilderness communities."

"That's the second time you mentioned that," I said, returning her look. "What are wilderness communities?"

"They're an alternative to maximum security prisons," she answered, for some reason seeming very satisfied. "Prisons like that are a waste of money and effort, their sole purpose being to keep incorrigibles away from the rest of the populace. Someone finally got the idea that there was a better way of doing it, namely checking around in this country's wilderness areas. There are acres and acres of unused land out there, unused because they aren't accessible in any way but by air. They set up temporary shelters and brought in supplies, got crops growing and small herds of meat animals on graze, wrote out clear instructions on what to do next to survive, then delivered the incorrigibles to the areas and left them there."

"But that's horrible!" I blurted, more upset, for some reason, than I would have thought I'd be. "They were city kids, not farmers! It would have been kinder to kill them!"

"Aside from the fact that they didn't merit much kindness, they still deserved to be given a chance to survive," she countered. "If, in spite of everything, they were able to keep themselves alive, they had the right to be left that way. Not taken back into the rest of society after a certain number of years, you understand; that particular right they'd forfeited many times over. All they had left was to be allowed to live by the sweat of their own brows, if they could do it. Some of the communities had to be repopulated two or three times, but eventually they all had a core group of tough, determined survivors. The only thing they haven't yet earned the right to have is children."

"What do children have to do with it?" I asked, almost automatically. I was trying very hard to handle what I'd just been told, but for some reason was having trouble with it.

"Having children is no longer considered something anyone with the proper equipment can do if they're in the mood," she said. "If you want to mess up your own life that's your business, but you have no right doing the same to innocent children. Those in the wilderness communities would have taken their rage out on any children they'd had, or they would have raised them with an obsession for revenge. What they've developed instead is a complex adoption system involving newcomers, which will probably continue even if the law gets changed. The government has been debating the point of keeping them childless for years now, but so far they haven't agreed on any changes."

She rattled on about how each side of the argument

saw the idea, but I really wasn't listening any longer. I was too busy laughing at myself, for getting so worked up over what had been done to a bunch of losers. Those street gangs had been too stupid to survive, so they hadn't. I'd never been dim enough to run with one, which proved how much better I was. I was smart and I was special, and all I would get was what was due me.

We walked no more than about four short blocks, and then Elaine turned into a place that didn't look much like an apartment building. For one thing it was only three stories high, and with its front steps leading up to a single door it looked more like a brownstone than anything else. It was too wide for a brownstone, though, something I found out as soon as we walked inside. To the left was a really big room with couches and chairs and tables of various sizes, and to the right was an equally large room with one single table surrounded by chairs. The second room was clearly a dining room, but rather than being as fresh as that size table usually calls for, it was no more than neat and clean. There were also stairways to either side of the small hall we were in, both of them leading up.

A door opened in the far wall beyond the two stairways, and a woman came out. For an instant I thought I knew her, but then I realized why she looked so familiar. Even though she had brown hair and light eyes, her pudginess and expression were almost an exact match to Elaine's. She came toward us with the same kind of smile on her face, her attention mostly on me.

"Well, I'm glad to see you two finally made it," she said in one of those easy voices, stopping not far from us. "I've been looking forward to meeting Angie since I first heard she was coming."

"And now you *can* meet her," Elaine said with a chuckle, as though appreciating a joke. "Angie, this is Nancy Arrison, one of the two heads of this A & A project location. If you have any problems and I can't be reached, just talk to Nancy and she'll do everything she can to help you."

"And if you find you'd *rather* talk to me than to Elaine, she won't be insulted," the woman Nancy said with a chuckle of her own. "We're all here to help, not to force you into associating with people you're uncomfortable with. It won't be long before you make real friends, and then you'll want to talk to them instead of to me. When that happens, I won't mind either."

"What's an A & A project?" I asked, not only because I wanted to know. I also wanted to change the subject before I told them how tired maudlin makes me.

"Aid and Assistance project," Elaine said, sounding faintly apologetic. "I'm glad to see you aren't hesitating when it comes to asking about things you aren't familiar with. Even though we're trying to watch ourselves, we'll be making a lot of slips like that."

"This location provides a place for young people who need help with fitting into society," Nancy said, possibly seeing how little I'd gotten from what Elaine had come up with. "Some of them can't get along with their families, some are bewildered about what to do with their lives, some have never been taught to make decisions and be independent, responsible people. We provide apartments for them to live in, help them get jobs or apply for advanced training, and give them someone to talk to and ask for advice. Once they get their lives straightened out, they move out to apartments of their own."

"You must have a lot of these places," I commented, looking around again with no enthusiasm. "Most of the people I knew couldn't get along with their families, and even the ones who could didn't think much of becoming part of the rat race."

"The rat race," Elaine said with a small, mirthless laugh. "That's what civilized society was in your day, Angie, but we've progressed beyond that. There's a place for people who want to fight and claw their way to the top, but there are also places for people who want no part of that sort of competition. We try to make sure that the choice is never taken away from the individual, and that's the path to true satisfaction. If what you do is your unpressured choice alone, you find it much easier to live with."

"As long as it doesn't affect other people," Nancy added, but she wasn't really disagreeing. "If I remember my history correctly, Angie, your time had something they called the sexual revolution. Everyone decided it was their right to have sex with anyone they pleased, but they forgot about the responsibility side of that coin. These days you really can have sex with anyone you please—as long as you have your infertility certificate. The rest of us don't want to be buried under a flood of accidental and unwanted babies, not when it's so safe and easy to prevent. If you have sex without first going for temporary infertilization and end up pregnant because of it, you either assume full responsibility for the child, or you're infertilized whether you want to be or not. You're entitled to make your own choices in life, but that doesn't include being a burden to others."

"Well, I have to be going now," Elaine said in her usual up and happy way. "There are some things I have to take care of, and most of it involves you, Angie. You need credit arranged, a compufone installed, maps of the city, placement tests scheduled—name it, and it still has to be done. If you need to talk to me before I get back, Nancy will help you reach me. See you later."

I stood with Nancy and watched Elaine wave once before disappearing through the door, and then the other woman put a hand on my arm.

"Let's go and show you your apartment now," she said, gesturing to the lefthand stairway. "You'll have a private parlor and a bedroom, but most people use the common room over there for entertaining or sitting around in. Meals are served in the dining room at six-thirty in the morning, noon, and six-thirty at night. If you want something to eat in between those hours the kitchen is always open, but you'll have to cook for yourself. If you do cook you also have to clean up afterward, but that goes without saying, doesn't it?"

She flashed me another smile and led the way to the third floor, which we walked to because the house had no elevator. When I asked about an apartment on the floor below, I was told that I'd be put in line for one. When someone on the second floor moved out a third-floor resident was moved down, and it went strictly on a first-come, first-served basis. She acted as if there wasn't any shmear involved, but I knew better. In set-ups like that there was always shmear, and the sooner you paid it the sooner you got taken care of.

The "apartment" was a lot smaller than I'd expected it to be, and I'd expected a place two steps above a box. Nancy said something about the apartments being small on purpose, an extra incentive for their residents to straighten up so they could move out, but that was jive crap. I was *entitled* to something better, and I'd see that they gave it to me.

After telling me that just about everyone else was out working or studying, Nancy left me alone in the box. I was one of those paying rent there so I didn't have to do jobs around the place to earn my way, but I was told that if I got bored I could come down to the kitchen and offer them a hand. I sat down in an old, stuffed chair in my parlor, hating how little they'd given me, burning for the time when I would have exactly what I deserved. They owed it to me, owed me for what I'd gone through, and one way or another I'd see they paid off.

It took a few days to get the lay of the land, and most of it was so whacked-up it made me sick. Like the fact that Elaine came by with the credit line that had been set up for me, but except for a few lousy bucks a week I couldn't get my hands on any real money. They wanted to make sure I knew what I was doing before giving me access to all of it, and it would be another three months before that time came, unless I got a job first. After the three months I would get the access no matter what, but before then only a job would shake me free.

I wasn't interested in one of their stupid jobs, so I

started rapping with some of the others in the house. I was looking for the users and through them would have found a supplier I could deal with and front for, but all those suckers turned out to be clean. Some of them used booze and most of them smoked—with the internal combustion engine and just about all dirty industry gone, people discovered they'd been handed a lot of bull about cigarettes—but none of them even had any grass.

It turned out drugs had been legalized, and anybody who wanted to use it could get it cheap and pure with no questions asked. Some of the kids laughed when they said business had been brisk right after legalization—but then it had died and had never come back again. Heavy users, those who would never stop, used themselves into the next life, and those who wanted to stop got the help to do it. The ones who started just because it was illegal had to find a different way to give the finger to those they didn't get along with, and that pretty much ended it. There were still a few around who used, but they were all losers who wouldn't have been able to hack it even if they'd been born into millions.

I tried to find somebody in that group to stooge for me, but even the real quiet ones weren't right. If I made a roundabout suggestion to one of them that I would let her hang with me if she ran errands and bought things I would like, the wimp would consider it for a minute, then smile and refuse. They couldn't seem to see that they needed me to think for them, to get them out of that set-up without either of us breaking our backsides for it. Wimps are wimps so what can you expect, but it sure annoyed the hell out of me.

Almost as much as the males in that place did. I found out from Elaine that the hospital had taken care of the infertility bit for me, so I had my certificate and could do whatever I damned well pleased. I gave all the jerks in that place the go-sign, waiting for them to figure out how much they wanted it, and most of them did. They took turns coming over to me, but when I told them how much it would cost them they laughed and walked away. One of them told me no one charged for it any more, not after it stopped being illegal and a big deal, and I really ought to start getting with it. If I didn't want to do it, all I had to do was say so; the choice was mine, and I didn't need any excuses to keep the choice mine.

I think that was the point I decided not to mess around any more. I wanted what I wanted, and if nobody was willing to give it to me, I'd just go ahead and take it. My mother and father had always treated me better than they had my brothers, and everything I got was given to me because I was special. Just because they got cheap and stingy when I started high school, trying to tell me I *couldn't* have everything I wanted, didn't mean anything had really changed. I was still as special as I had always been, and the proof of it was how long it had taken my mother to tell my father I was helping myself to the money in her purse. It had taken her a very long time, and then she'd made sure my father didn't do anything but yell. I *was* special, and it was about time everyone in that place found it out.

I got Elaine to wait another week before setting up all those appointments she wanted to make for me, and then I began going through the other apartments while the house was empty. Most things involved credit cards and computer credit in those days, but people still carried cash when they went out during their free time. Small things were cheaper when you paid for them with cash, and I intended taking every buck I could get my hands on. Once I had enough I'd take off for three months, and then I'd come back for the big credit line that would be waiting for me. I'd spend it on whatever I liked, and then I'd tell them they owed me more. They *owed* me, and if they didn't pay I'd find a shyster and sue them for all they had.

I'd worked my way through most of the apartments and had almost enough to take me out of that dump, when Elaine showed up with somebody male. I was using the fone then, speaking into the air like they used to do with speakerphones, only I hadn't had to punch up the number. My compufone was voice activated, and all I had to do was say I wanted to call somebody, and then tell the computer who it was. *It* looked up the number and then put the call through, and when I was finished all I had to do was say "off." I was checking on flights to some of the newest resorts, so as soon as my visitors showed up I quickly said, "Off." The man had cold eyes, like some of the cops I'd had brushes with, but I wasn't worried even when Elaine shook her head at me.

"You should have talked to someone first, Angie," she said, her fat face looking even sillier without the smile she usually wore. "Even if you haven't been able to make friends among any of the kids here, you should have talked to Nancy or me."

"Talked to you about what?" I asked, giving her a faintly puzzled look before going over to my stuffed chair and sitting down. "The fact that you didn't even knock before walking into my apartment? Other than that, I don't know what you mean, Elaine."

"I'm sure you don't," she answered, a hint of sadness showing briefly in her eyes. "You've been stealing money out of the other apartments in this house, and you haven't *any* idea what that means."

"I do know what false accusation means, though," I said, staring straight at her as I made myself more comfortable in the chair. "I may be new around here, but that doesn't mean you can say anything you like to me. I want the name of a good lawyer, and if you can't come up with one, I'll check the listings for myself."

I was looking forward to having fun with that, demanding a lawyer that she would *have* to give me according to her own rules and then using him to make trouble for her, but all she did was shake her head again.

"I know what kind of lawyer you're talking about, but our society doesn't have that kind any more," she said, now looking even less friendly. "I've studied the time you come from, it's one of the requirements of my job, but even so I find it hard to believe. People who work to weaken the foundations of their own civilization just for the sake of money or power are sick, no matter how hard they protest and orate about being on the side of equal rights. Using tricks to get someone out of what's due them has nothing to do with equal rights."

"But you won't get out of what's due *you*, young woman," the man said, finally speaking up. "First you'll tell us where you put the money, and then you'll come with me."

"What I'm telling you is that I don't know what you're talking about," I repeated, shifting my stare and a small smile to the man. "Do you have an arrest warrant for me? A search warrant to toss this place? If you do you'd better show them to me, and then we'll get me a lawyer. If you don't, what you two can get is out."

"You're so sure you have it all covered, aren't you, Angie," Elaine said, a statement instead of a question. "We all told you things were different now, but you couldn't be bothered with hearing us. Just the way the misery you caused among the people you stole from didn't touch you in the least. We watched you watching how upset they were, and you didn't show the slightest trace of remorse. We have videos of you going into the last three apartments, so an arrest warrant isn't necessary. Tell the officer what he wants to know, and then go with him."

"You're a real headcase, aren't you, Elaine?" I asked with a snort, happy that I could finally tell her what I thought of her. "I don't have anything to tell that geek cop because I didn't do anything, and any tape you think you have on me will be thrown out when I scream entrapment. You'll tell the court *your* softheaded side and I'll cry a little when I tell *my* side of the truth, and we'll see which one of us they'd rather believe. After I win I'll sue for false arrest, but I don't believe in holding grudges. After the settlement if you need to borrow money until you find a new job, just let me know. After all, you *were* my first—*friend*—here."

I laughed at her then, hoping she'd be stupid enough to try jumping me, but she didn't seem to be in the mood to help me with my case. She just stared at me with the weirdest expression I ever saw, and the man took one step forward.

"You said 'cop,'" he pointed out with real brilliance, the look on his face almost as spaced out as the one on Elaine. "I know from the historicals that that means police officer, but that's not what I am. I'm an officer of the *court*, in point of fact a judge's aide, and everything I hear and see will be reported to the judge assigned to handle your case."

"What are you trying to pull?" I snapped, leaning forward to glare at the jerk. "You think I don't know you can't testify against me? Anything you try to spill will be hearsay, and that doesn't happen to be admissible. You have no witnesses against me, and my word is just as good as yours is according to your own law. You say I did it, and I say I didn't; no proof equals no conviction, so go play with your fingers."

"Young woman, it's too bad you're not even half as smart as you think you are," the jerk said, and I swear he was almost sneering at me. "What you're feeling so smug about is the way your people did things; we've made some progress since then, and it's at least as important as the colony we've put on the moon. We don't play games with the law, we use it the way it's supposed to be used."

"The way your people didn't," Elaine said, suddenly waking up again. "They were so worried about convicting the innocent, they turned terror loose on all the rest of the populace. It was the stupidest thing they could have done, because it was totally unnecessary. If they'd bothered looking around themselves and thinking, they could have protected everybody with very little effort. It was possible even in your day, but they were too blind to see it."

"They spent weeks and months questioning droves of people, and then their judges had to decide who to believe," the man said, still sounding scornful. "It was stupid because they were supposed to be after the truth, but how could you get the truth when the one person who had it was never made to tell it? Why bother with others, when the only person you have to ask is the accused?"

"Didn't you flakes ever hear about the law against self-incrimination?" I countered, taking my own turn at sneering. "If all you have is a confession, you can forget about having a case. Confessions are famous for being beaten out of people, which makes it too easy an out for the heavies. You can't make people testify against themselves, so you have to keep the case open until you can *prove* what you think you know. Which you two can't."

"How do you manage to keep being that thick-headed?" Elaine had the nerve to ask very mildly, then cut me off when I started to tell her what to do with herself. "Never mind, I think I already know the answer to that. What he's trying to tell you, little girl, is that people finally had enough. When that law against self-incrimination was made, there was no way of knowing whether or not the accused *was* forced into confessing, but even by your day that hadn't been true for quite a long time. We'll forget about those lie detectors they used, because they were all but worthless. What we *will* remember about, though, is the variety of truth drugs developed by the military to use on spies."

"Meaning that once again the civilian population got a benefit from the military spending they usually complained about," the man said with a faint smile while I felt a cold, unexpected chill. "All of those complex, useless laws were scrapped, and the jury system was done away with. You still have twelve people and a judge in a court of law, but the twelve people are now witnesses, there to make sure that the accused really does get a fair deal. The judge doesn't have to guess about who's telling the truth, he or she knows beyond all doubt, and all they're there to do is give you what society owes you."

"But nobody warned me!" I shouted, jumping out of the chair to look wildly at both of them. "Nobody told me things had changed *that* much, so you people weren't telling me the truth! That's what I'll say to that judge, that you didn't tell me the truth!"

"I never thought I'd find myself feeling so sorry for another human being," Elaine whispered, staring at me with sickness peering out of her eyes, and then her voice strengthened. "But sorry doesn't mean I want to keep you from getting what you're due. That's not a very original claim, Angie, and it simply won't do it for you. The truth was something you would have gotten if you'd asked, but you thought you already knew it so you didn't bother asking. The choice was yours and you made it, freely and without pressure from anybody. And if you think you'll be able to say you didn't know stealing is wrong, think again. Once you're under the influence of the drug you'll tell nothing but the real truth, because that's the choice the drug will help you to make."

"And I'll be there to describe what I've observed of you once you knew you were caught," the man said, what might have been pity showing on his face as well. "How you behaved is all part of it, but the judge will decide what to do with you from what *you* say, the only witness really qualified to give him the entire truth. At that point *he'll* be the one with no choice, but that doesn't count. He chose a job where his choices would be limited, but you'll never have that complaint. You were given all the choices there were, and were left free to make them. The only thing you have to do now is live with the results."

I started to scream then, but it didn't do me any good. The man called for help and they all took me away, and now I'm here just talking and talking and telling you everything. They say I can't make any deals, especially not considering the kind of person I am, a very special kind of person. I don't think they mean it in the right way, the way my parents meant it, but I can't do anything to correct any of you or even argue effectively. Whatever I say has to be the truth, the whole truth, nothing but the . . .

ISLANDS IN THE SEA

Harry Turtledove

Introduction

Islam exploded out of Arabia in the seventh century. The triumphant armies of the caliphs overthrew the Persian Empire and took Syria, Palestine, Egypt, and North Africa from the East Roman or Byzantine Empire. Muslim forces twice besieged Constantinople, in 674-78 and 717-18. In our history, the Byzantine capital held and the Byzantine Empire survived as Christianity's eastern bulwark, holding Islam out of Anatolia and the Balkans for centuries to come and converting the Bulgars and Russians to faith in Christ. But what if the Empire had fallen in the eighth century instead of the fifteenth? The still-pagan folk to the north of Constantinople would have had new choices to make. . . .

A.H. 152 (A.D. 769)

The Bulgar border guards had arrows nocked and
ready as the Arab horsemen rode up from the south.
Jalal ad-Din as-Stambuli, the leader of the Arab delegation, raised his right hand to show it was empty. "In
the name of Allah, the Compassionate, the Merciful,
I and my men come in peace," he called in Arabic.
To be sure the guards understood, he repeated himself in Greek.

The precaution paid off. The guards lowered their
bows. In Greek much worse than Jalal ad-Din's, one
of them asked, "Why for you come in peace, white-
beard?"

Jalal ad-Din stroked his whiskers. Even without
the Bulgar's mockery, he knew they were white. Not
many men who had the right to style themselves
as-Stambuli, the Constantinopolitan, still lived. More
than fifty years had passed since the army of Suleiman
and Maslama had taken Constantinople and put an
end to the Roman Empire. Then Jalal ad-Din's beard
had not been white. Then he could hardly raise a
beard at all.

He spoke in Greek again: "My master the caliph
Abd ar-Rahman asked last year if your khan Telerikh
would care to learn more of Islam, of submission to
the one God. This past spring Telerikh sent word that
he would. We are the embassy sent to instruct him."

The Bulgar who had talked with him now used
his own hissing language, Jalal ad-Din supposed to

translate for his comrades. They answered back, some of them anything but happily. Content in their paganism, Jalal ad-Din guessed—content to burn in hell forever. He did not wish that fate on anyone, even a Bulgar.

The guard who knew Greek confirmed his thought, saying, "Why for we want your god? Gods, spirits, ghosts good to us now."

Jalal ad-Din shrugged. "Your khan asked to hear more of Allah and Islam. That is why we are here." He could have said much more, but deliberately spoke in terms a soldier would understand.

"Telerikh want, Telerikh get," the guard agreed. He spoke again with his countrymen, at length pointed at two of them. "This Iskur. This Omurtag. They take you to Pliska, to where Telerikh is. Iskur, him know Greek a little, not so good like me."

"Know little your tongue too," Iskur said in halting Arabic, which surprised Jalal ad-Din and, evidently, the Bulgar who had been doing all the talking till now. The prospective guide glanced at the sun, which was a couple of hours from setting. "We ride," he declared, and started off with no more fanfare than that. The Bulgar called Omurtag followed.

So, more slowly, did Jalal ad-Din and his companions. By the time Iskur called a halt in deepening twilight, the mountains that made the northern horizon jagged were visibly closer.

"Those little ponies the Bulgars ride are ugly as mules, but they go and go and go," said Da'ud ibn Zubayr, who was a veteran of many skirmishes on the border between the caliph's land and Bulgaria. He stroked the mane of his elegant, Arab-bred mare.

"Sadly, my old bones do not." Jalal ad-Din groaned with relief as he slid off his own horse, a soft-gaited gelding. Once he had delighted in fiery stallions, but he knew that if he took a fall now he would shatter like glass.

The Bulgars stalked into the brush to hunt. Da'ud bent to the laborious business of getting a fire going. The other two Arabs, Malik ibn Anas and Salman al-Tabari, stood guard, one with a bow, the other

with a spear. Iskur and Omurtag emerged into fire-
light carrying partridges and rabbits. Jalal ad-Din
took hard unleavened bread from a saddlebag: no
feast tonight, he thought, but not the worst of fare
either.

Iskur also had a skin of wine. He offered it to the
Arabs, grinned when they declined. "More for me,
Omurtag," he said, The two Bulgars drank the skin
dry, and soon lay snoring by the fire.

Da'ud ibn Zubayr scowled at them. "The only use
they have for wits is losing them," he sneered. "How
can such folk ever come to acknowledge Allah and
his Prophet?"

"We Arabs were wine-bibbers too, before Muhammad forbad it to us," Jalal ad-Din said. "My worry is
that the Bulgars' passion for such drink will make
khan Telerikh less inclined to accept our faith."

Da'ud dipped his head to the older man. "Truly it
it just that you lead us, sir. Like a falcon, you keep
your eye ever on our quarry."

"Like a falcon, I sleep in the evening," Jalal ad-
Din said, yawning. "And like an old falcon, I need
more sleep than I once did."

"Your years have brought you wisdom." Da'ud ibn
Zubayr hesitated, as if wondering whether to go on.
Finally he plunged: "Is it true, sir, that you once met
a man who had known the Prophet?"

"It is true," Jalal ad-Din said proudly. "It was at
Antioch, when Suleiman's army was marching to fight
the Greeks at Constantinople. The grandfather of the
innkeeper with whom I was quartered lived with
him still: he was a Medinan, far older then than I am
now, for he had soldiered with Khalid ibn al-Walid
when the city fell to us. And before that, as a youth,
he accompanied Muhammad when the Prophet returned in triumph from Medina to Mecca."

"*Allahu akbar*," Da'ud breathed: "God is great. I
am further honored to be in your presence. Tell me,
did—did the old man grant you an *hadith*, any tradition, of the Prophet that you might pass on to me for
the sake of my enlightenment?"

"Yes," Jalal ad-Din said. "I recall it as if it were

yesterday, just as the old man did when speaking of the journey to the Holy City. Abu Bakr, who was not yet caliph, of course, for Muhammad was still alive, started beating a man for letting a camel get loose. The Prophet began to smile, and said, 'See what this pilgrim is doing.' Abu Bakr was abashed, though the Prophet did not actually tell him to stop."

Da'ud bowed low. "I am in your debt." He repeated the story several times; Jalal ad-Din nodded to show him he had learned it perfectly. In the time-honored way, Da'ud went on, "I have this *hadith* from Jalal ad-Din as-Stambuli, who had it from—what was the old man's name, sir?"

"He was called Abd al-Qadir."

"—who had it from Abd al-Qadir, who had it from the Prophet. Think of it—only two men between Muhammad and me." Da'ud bowed again.

Jalal ad-Din returned the bow, then embarrassed himself by yawning once more. "Your pardon, I pray. Truly I must sleep."

"Sleep, then, and Allah keep you safe till the morning comes."

Jalal ad-Din rolled himself in his blanket. "And you, son of Zubayr."

"Those are no mean works," Da'ud said a week later, pointing ahead to the earthen rampart, tall as six men, that ringed Pliska, Telerikh's capital.

"That is a child's toy, next to the walls of Constantinople," Jalal ad-Din said. "A double wall, each one twice that height, all steep stone, well-ditched in front and between, with all the Greeks in the world, it seemed, battling from atop them." Across half a century, recalling the terror of the day of the assault, he wondered still how he had survived.

"I was born in Constantinople," Da'ud reminded him gently.

"Of course you were." Jalal ad-Din shook his head, angry at himself for letting past obscure present that way. It was something old men did, but who cares to remember he is old?

Da'ud glanced around to make sure Iskur was out

of earshot, lowered his voice. "For pagan savages, those are no mean works. And see how much land they enclose—Pliska must be a city of greater size than I had supposed."

"No." Jalal ad-Din remembered a talk with a previous envoy to Telerikh. "The town itself is tiny. This earthwork serves chiefly to mark off the grazing lands of the khan's flocks."

"His flocks? Is that all?" Da'ud threw back his head and laughed. "I feel as though I am transported to some strange new world, where nothing is as it seems."

"I have had that feeling ever since we came through the mountain passes," Jalal ad-Din said seriously. Da'ud gave him a curious look. He tried to explain: "You are from Constantinople. I was born not far from Damascus, where I dwell yet. A long journey from one to the other, much longer than from Constantinople to Pliska."

Da'ud nodded.

"And yet it is a journey through sameness," Jalal ad-Din went on. "Not much difference in weather, in crops, in people. Aye, more Greeks, more Christians in Constantinople still, for we have ruled there so much less time than in Damascus, but the difference is of degree, not of kind."

"That is all true," Da'ud said, nodding again. "Whereas here—"

"Aye, here," Jalal ad-Din said with heavy irony. "The olive will not grow here, the sun fights its way through mists that swaddle it as if it were a newborn babe, and even a Greek would be welcome, for the sake of having someone civilized to talk to. This is a different world from ours, and not one much to my liking."

"Still, we hope to wed it to ours through Islam," Da'ud said.

"So we do, so we do. Submission to the will of God makes all men one." Now Jalal ad-Din made sure Iskur was paying no attention. The nomad had ridden ahead. Jalal ad-Din went on, "Even Bulgars." Da'ud chuckled.

Iskur yelled something at the guards lounging in front of a wooden gate in Pliska's earthen outwall. The guards yelled back. Iskur shouted again, louder this time. With poor grace, the guards got up and opened the gate. They stared as they saw what sort of companions Iskur led.

Jalal ad-Din gave them a grave salute as he passed through the gate, as much to discomfit them as for any other reason. He pointed ahead to the stone wall of Pliska proper. "You see?"

"I see," Da'ud said. The rectangular wall was less than half a mile on a side. "In our lands, that would be a fortress, not a capital."

The gates of the stone wall were open. Jalal ad-Din coughed as he followed Iskur and Omurtag into the town: Pliska stank like—stank worse than—a big city. Jalal ad-Din shrugged. Sooner or later, he knew, he would stop noticing the stench.

Not far inside the gates stood a large building of intricately carven wood. "This Telerikh's palace," Iskur announced.

Tethered in front of the palace were any number of steppe ponies like the ones Iskur and Omurtag rode and also, Jalal ad-Din saw with interest, several real horses and a mule whose trappings did not look like Arab gear. "To whom do those belong?" he asked, pointing.

"Not know," Iskur said. He cupped his hands and yelled toward the palace—yelling, Jalal ad-Din thought wryly, seemed the usual Bulgar approach toward any problem. After a little while, a door opened. The Arab had not even noticed it till then, so lost was its outline among carvings.

As soon as they saw someone come out of the palace, Iskur and Omurtag wheeled their horses and rode away without a backwards glance at the ambassadors they had guided to Pliska. The man who had emerged took a moment to study the new arrivals. He bowed. "How many I help you, my masters?" he asked in Arabic fluent enough to make Jalal ad-Din sit up and take notice.

"We are envoys of the caliph Abd ar-Rahman,

come to your fine city"—Jalal ad-Din knew when to stretch a point—"at the bidding of your khan to explain to him the glories of Islam. I have the honor of addressing—?" He let the words hang.

"I am Dragomir, steward to the mighty khan Telerikh. Dismount; be welcome here." Dragomir bowed again. He was, Jalal ad-Din guessed, in his late thirties, stocky and well-made, with fair skin, a full brown beard framing rather a wide face, and gray eyes that revealed nothing whatever—a useful attribute in a steward.

Jalal ad-Din and his companions slid gratefully from their horses. As if by magic, boys appeared to hitch the Arabs' beasts to the rails in front of the palace and carry their saddlebags into it. Jalal ad-Din nodded at the other full-sized horses and the mule. "To whom do those belong, pray?" he asked Dragomir.

The steward's pale but hooded eyes swung toward the hitching rail, returned to Jalal ad-Din. "Those," he explained, "are the animals of the delegation of priests from the Pope of Rome at the bidding of my khan to expound to him the glories of Christianity. They arrived earlier today."

Late that night, Da'ud slammed a fist against a wall of the chamber the four Arabs shared. "Better they should stay pagan than turn Christian!" he shouted. Not only was he angry that Telerikh had also invited Christians to Pliska as if intending to auction his land to the faith that bid highest, he was also short-tempered from hunger. The evening's banquet had featured pork. (It had *not* featured Telerikh; some heathen bulgar law required the khan always to eat alone.)

"This is not so," Jalal ad-Din said mildly.

"And why not?" Da'ud glared at the older man.

"As Christians they would be *dhimmis*—people of the Book—and thus granted a hope of heaven. Should they cling to their pagan practices, their souls will surely belong to Satan till the end of time."

"Satan is welcome to their souls, whether pagan or Christian," Da'ud said. "But a Christian Bulgaria, allied to Rome, maybe even allied to the Franks, would block the true faith's progress northwards and could be the spearpoint of a thrust back toward Constantinople."

Jalal ad-Din sighed. "What you say is true. Still, the true faith is also true, and the truth surely will prevail against Christian falsehoods."

"May it be so," Da'ud said heavily. "But was this land not once a Christian country, back in the days before the Bulgars seized it from Constantinople? All the lands the Greeks held followed their usages. Some folk hereabouts must be Christian still, I'd wager, which might incline Telerikh toward their beliefs."

A knock on the door interrupted the argument. Da'ud kept one hand on his knife as he opened the door with the other. But no enemies stood outside, only four girls. Two were colored like Dragomir—to Jalal ad-Din's eyes, exotically fair. The other two were dark, darker than Arabs, in fact; one had eyes that seemed set at a slant. All four were pretty. They smiled and swayed their way in.

"Telerikh is no Christian," Jalal ad-Din said as he smiled back at one of the light-skinned girls. "Christians are not allowed concubines."

"The more fools they," Da'ud said. "Shall I blow out the lamps, or leave them burning?"

"Leave them," Jalal ad-Din answered. "I want to see what I am doing . . ."

Jalal ad-Din bowed low to khan Telerikh. A pace behind him, Da'ud did the same. Another pace back, Malik ibn Anas and Salman al-Tabari went to one knee, as suited their lower rank.

"Rise, all of you," Telerikh said in passable Arabic. The khan of the Bulgars was about fifty, swarthy, broad-faced, wide-nosed, with a thin beard going from black to gray. His eyes were narrow, hard, and shrewd. He looked like a man well able to rule a nation whose strength came entirely from the ferocity of its soldiers.

"Most magnificent khan, we bring the greetings of

our master the caliph Abd ar-Rahman ibn Marwan, his prayers for your health and prosperity, and gifts to show that you stand high in his esteem," Jalal ad-Din said.

He waved Salman and Malik forward to present the gifts: silver plates from Persia, Damascus-work swords, fine enamelware from Constantinople, a robe of glistening Chinese silk, and, last but not least, a *Qu'ran* bound in leather and gold, its calligraphy the finest the scribes of Alexandria could provide.

Telerikh, though, seemed most interested in the robe. He rose from his wooden throne, undid the broad bronze belt he wore, shrugged out of his knee-length fur caftan. Under it he had on a linen tunic and trousers and low boots. Dragomir came up to help him put on the robe. He smiled with pleasure as he ran a hand over the watery-smooth fabric.

"Very pretty," he crooned. For a moment, Jalal ad-Din hoped he was so taken by the presents as to be easily swayed. But Telerikh, as the Arab had guessed from his appearance, was not so simple. He went on, "The caliph gives lovely gifts. With his riches, he can afford to. Now please take your places while the envoys of the Pope of Rome present themselves."

Dragomir waved the Arab delegation off to the right of the throne, close by the turbaned boyars—the great nobles—who made up Telerikh's court. Most were of the same stock as their khan; a few looked more like Dragomir and the fair girl Jalal ad-Din had so enjoyed the night before. Fair or dark, they smelled of hard-run horses and ancient sweat.

As he had with the caliph's embassy, Dragomir announced the papal legates in the throaty Bulgarian tongue. There were three of them, as Jalal ad-Din had seen at the banquet. Two were gorgeous in robes that reminded him of the ones the Constantino-politan grandees had worn so long ago as they vainly tried to rally their troops against the Arabs. The third wore a simple brown woolen habit. Amid the Bulgar chatter, meaningless to him, Jalal ad-Din picked out three names: Niketas, Theodore, and Paul.

The Christians scowled at the Arabs as they walked past them to approach Telerikh. They bowed as Jalal ad-Din had. "Stand," Telerikh said in Greek. Jalal ad-Din was not surprised he knew that language; the Bulgars had dealt with Constantinople before the Arabs took it, and many refugees had fled to Pliska. Others had escaped to Italy, which no doubt explained why two of the papal legates bore Greek names.

"Excellent khan," said one of the envoys (Theodore, Jalal ad-Din thought it was), also in Greek, "we are saddened to see you decked in raiment given you by our foes as you greet us. Does this mean you hold us in contempt, and will give us no fair hearing? Surely you did not invite us to travel so far merely for that?"

Telerikh blinked, glanced down at the silk robe he had just put on. "No," he said. "It only means I like this present. What presents have you for me?"

Da'ud leaned forward, whispered into Jalal ad-Din's ear: "More avarice in that one than fear of hell." Jalal ad-Din nodded. That made his task harder, not easier. He would have to play politics along with expounding the truth of Islam. He sighed. Ever since he learned Telerikh had also bid the men from Rome hither, he'd expected no less.

The Christians were presenting their gifts, and making a great show of it to try to disguise their not being so fine as the ones their rivals had given—Jalal ad-Din's offerings still lay in a glittering heap beside Telerikh's throne. "Here," Theodore intoned, "is a copy of the Holy Scriptures, with a personal prayer for you inscribed therein by his holiness the Pope Constantine."

Jalal ad-Din let out a quiet but scornful snort. "The words of Allah are the ones that count," he whispered to Da'ud ibn Zubayr, "not those of any man." It was Da'ud's turn to nod.

As he had with the *Qu'ran*, Telerikh idly paged through the Bible. Perhaps halfway through, he paused, glanced up at the Christians. "You have pictures in your book." It sounded almost like an accusation; had Jalal ad-Din said it, it would have been.

But the Christian in the plain brown robe, the one called Paul, answered calmly, "Yes, excellent khan, we do, the better to instruct the many who cannot read the words beside them." He was no longer young—he might have been close to Jalal ad-Din's age—but his voice was light and clear and strong, the voice of a man sure in the path he has chosen.

"Beware of that one," Da'ud murmured. "He has more holiness in him than the other two put together." Jalal ad-Din had already reached the same conclusion, and did not like it. Enemies, he thought, ought by rights to be rogues.

He got only a moment to mull on that, for Telerikh suddenly shifted to Arabic and called to him, "Why are there no pictures in your book, to show me what you believe?"

"Because Allah the one God is infinite, far too mighty for our tiny senses to comprehend, and so cannot be depicted," he said, "and man must not be depicted, for Allah created him in his image from a clot of blood. The Christians' own scriptures say as much, but they ignore any law which does not suit them."

"Liar! Misbeliever!" Theodore shouted. Torchlight gleamed off his tonsured pate as he whirled to confront Jalal ad-Din.

"No liar I," Jalal ad-Din said; not for nothing had he studied with men once Christian before they saw the truth of Muhammad's teaching. "The verse you deny is in the book called Exodus."

"Is this true?" Telerikh rumbled, scowling at the Christians.

Theodore started to reply; Paul cut him off. "Excellent khan, the verse is as the Arab states. My colleague did not wish to deny it." Theodore looked ready to argue. Paul did not let him, continuing, "But that law was given to Moses long ago. Since then, Christ the Son of God has appeared on earth; belief in him assures one of heaven, regardless of the observance of the outdated rules of the Jews."

Telerikh grunted. "A new law may replace an old, if circumstances change. What say you to that, envoy of the caliph?"

"I will quote two verses from the *Qu'ran*, from the *sura* called The Cow," Jalal ad-Din said, smiling at the opening Paul had left him. "Allah says, 'The Jews say the Christians are astray, and the Christians say it is the Jews who are astray. Yet they both read the Scriptures.' Which is to say, magnificent khan, that they have both corrupted God's word. And again, 'They say: "Allah has begotten a son." Allah forbid!' "

When reciting from the *Qu'ran*, he had naturally fallen into Arabic. He was not surprised to see the Christians following his words without difficulty. They too would have prepared for any eventuality on this mission.

One of Telerikh's boyars called something to the khan in his own language. Malik ibn Anas, who was with Jalal ad-Din precisely because he knew a little of the Bulgar speech, translated for him: "He says that the sacred stones of their forefathers, even the pagan gods of the Slavs they rule, have served them well enough for years upon years, and calls on Telerikh not to change their usages now."

Looking around, Jalal ad-Din saw more than a few boyars nodding. "Great khan, may I speak?" he called. Telerikh nodded. Jalal ad-Din went on, "Great khan, you need but look about you to see proof of Allah's might. Is it not true that my lord the caliph Abd ar-Rahman, peace be unto him, rules from the Western Sea to India, from your borders to beyond the deserts of Egypt? Even the Christians, who know the one God imperfectly, still control many lands. Yet only you here in this small country follow your idols. Does this not show you their strength is a paltry thing?"

"There is more, excellent khan." Niketas, who had been quiet till then, unexpectedly spoke up. "Your false gods isolate Bulgaria. How, in dealing with Christians or even Muslims, can your folk swear an oath that will be trusted? How can you put the power of God behind a treaty, to ensure it will be enforced?

In what way can one of you lawfully marry a Christian? Other questions like these will surely have occurred to you, else you would not have bid us come."

"He speaks the truth, khan Telerikh," Jalal ad-Din said. He had not thought a priest would have so good a grasp of matters largely secular, but Niketas did. Since his words could not be denied, supporting them seemed better than ignoring.

Telerikh gnawed on his mustaches. He looked from one delegation to the other, back again. "Tell me," he said slowly, "is it the same god both groups of you worship, or do you follow different ones?"

"That is an excellent question," Jalal ad-Din said; no, Telerikh was no fool. "It is the same god: there is no God but God. But the Christians worship him incorrectly, saying he is Three, not One."

"It is the same God," Paul agreed, once more apparently overriding Theodore. "Muhammad is not a true prophet and many of his preachings are lies, but it is the same God, who gave his only begotten Son to save mankind."

"Stop!" Telerikh held up a hand. "If it is the same God, what difference does it make how I and my people worship him? No matter what the prayers we send up to him, surely he will know what we mean."

Jalal ad-Din glanced toward Paul. The Christian was also looking at him. Paul smiled. Jalal ad-Din found himself smiling back. He too felt the irony of the situation: he and Paul had more in common with each other than either of them did with the naive Bulgar khan. Paul raised an eyebrow. Jalal ad-Din dipped his head, granting the Christian permission to answer Telerikh's question.

"Sadly, excellent khan, it is not so simple," Paul said. "Just as there is only one true God, so there can be only one true way to worship him, for while he is merciful, he is also just, and will not tolerate errors in the reverence paid him. To use a homely example, sir, would it please you if we called you 'khan of the Avars'?"

"It would please me right well, were it true,"

Telerikh said with a grim chuckle. "Worse luck for me, though, the Avars have a khan of their own. Very well, priest, I see what you are saying."

The Bulgar ruler rubbed his chin. "This needs more thought. We will all gather here again in three days' time, to speak of it further. Go now in peace, and remember"—he looked sternly from Christians to Muslims—"you are all my guests here. No fighting between you, or you will regret it."

Thus warned, the rival embassies bowed their way out.

Jalal ad-Din spent more time before his next encounter with the priests exploring Pliska than he had hoped to. No matter how delightful he found his fair-skinned pleasure girl, he was not a young man: for him, between rounds meant between days.

After the barbarous richness of Telerikh's wooden palace, the Arab found the rest of the town surprisingly familiar. He wondered why until he realized that Pliska, like Damascus, like Constantinople, like countless other settlements through which he had passed at one time or another, had been a Roman town once. Layout and architecture lingered long after overlords changed.

Jalal ad-Din felt like shouting when he found a bath house not only still standing but still used; from what his nose had told him in the palace, he'd doubted the Bulgars even suspected cleanliness existed. When he went in, he found most of the bathers were of the lighter-colored folk from whom Dragomir and his mistress had sprung. They were, he'd gathered, peasant Slavs over whom the Bulgars proper ruled.

He also found that, being mostly unacquainted with either Christianity or Islam, they let in women along with the men. It was scandalous; it was shocking; in Damascus it would have raised riots. Jalal ad-Din wished his eyes were as sharp as they'd been when he was forty, or even fifty.

He was happily soaking in a warm pool when the three Christian envoys came in. Theodore hissed in horror when he saw the naked women, spun on his

heel, and stalked out. Niketas started to follow, but
Paul took hold of his arm and stopped him. The
older man shrugged out of his brown robe, sank with
a sigh of pleasure into the same pool Jalal ad-Din was
using. Niketas, by his expression still dubious, joined
him a moment later.

"Flesh is flesh," Paul said calmly. "By pledging
yourself to Christ, you have acknowledged that its
pleasures are not for you. No point in fleeing, then."

Jalal ad-Din nodded to the Christians. "You have
better sense, sir, than I would have looked for in a
priest," he told Paul.

"I thank you." If Paul heard the undercurrent of
irony in the Arab's voice, he did not let it affect his
own tone, which briefly shamed Jalal ad-Din. Paul
went on, "I am no priest in any case, only a humble
monk, here to advise my superiors if they care to
listen to me.

"Only!" Jalal ad-Din scoffed. But, he had to admit
to himself, the monk sounded completely sincere.
He sighed; hating his opponents would have been
much easier were they evil. "They would be wise to
listen to you," he said. "I think you are a holy man."

"You give me too much credit," Paul said.

"No, he does not," Niketas told his older colleague. "Not just by words do you instruct the barbarians hereabouts, but also through the life you
live, which by its virtues illuminates your teachings."

Paul bowed. From a man squatting naked in waist-
deep water, the gesture should have seemed ludicrous. Somehow it did not.

Niketas turned to Jalal ad-Din. "Did I hear correctly that you are styled as-Stambuli?"

"You did," the Arab answered proudly.

"How strange," Niketas murmured. "Perhaps here
God grants me the chance to avenge the fall of the
Queen of Cities."

He spoke as if the caliph's armies had taken Constantinople only yesterday, not long before he was
born. Seeing Jalal ad-Din's confusion, Paul said,
"Niketas' mother is Anna, the daughter of Leo."

"Yes?" Jalal ad-Din was polite, but that meant

nothing to him. "And my mother was Zinawb, the daughter of Mu'in ibn Abd al-Wahhab. What of it?"

"Ah, but your grandfather, however illustrious he may have been (I do not slight him, I assure you), was never *Basileus ton Rhomaion*—Emperor of the Romans."

"*That* Leo!" Jalal ad-Din thumped his forehead with the heel of his hand. He nodded to Niketas. "Your grandfather, sir, was a very devil. He fought us with all he had, and sent too many brave lads to paradise before their time."

Niketas raised a dark eyebrow. His tonsured skull went oddly with those bushy brows and the thick beard that covered his cheeks almost to the eyes. "Too many, you say; I would say, not enough."

"So you would," Jalal ad-Din agreed. "Had Leo beaten us, you might be Roman Emperor yourself now. But Abd ar-Rahman the commander of the faithful rules Constantinople, and you are a priest in a foreign land. It is as Allah wills."

"So I must believe," Niketas said. "But just as Leo fought you with every weapon he had, I shall oppose you with all my means. The Bulgars must not fall victim to your false belief. It would be too great a blow for Christendom to suffer, removing from us all hope of greater growth."

Niketas' mind worked like an emperor's, Jalal ad-Din thought—unlike many of his Christian colleagues, he understood the long view. He'd shown that in debate, too, when he pointed out the problems attendant on the Bulgars' staying pagan. A dangerous foe—Pope Constantine had sent to Pliska the best the Christians had.

Whether that would be enough . . . Jalal ad-Din shrugged. "It is as Allah wills," he repeated.

"And Telerikh," Paul said. When Jalal ad-Din looked at him in surprise, the monk went on, "Of course, Telerikh is in God's hands too. But God will not be influenced by what we do. Telerikh may."

"There is that," Jalal ad-Din admitted.

"No telling how long all this arguing will go on,"

Telerikh said when the Christian and Muslim embassies appeared before him once more. He spoke to Dragomir in his own language. The steward nodded, hurried away. A moment later, lesser servants brought in benches, which they set before Telerikh's throne. "Sit," the khan urged. "You may as well be comfortable."

"How would you have us argue?" Jalal ad-Din asked, wishing the bench had a back but too proud to ask for a chair to ease his old bones.

"Tell me of your one god," Telerikh said. "You say you and the Christians follow him. Tell me what you believe differently about him, so I may choose between your beliefs."

Jalal ad-Din carefully did not smile. He had asked his question to seize the chance to speak first. Let the Christians respond to him. He began where any Muslim would, with the *shahada*, the profession of faith: " '*La illaha ill'Allah: Muhammadun rasulu'llah*— There is no God but Allah; Muhammad is the prophet of Allah.' Believe that, magnificent khan, and you are a Muslim. There is more, of course, but that is of the essence."

"It is also a lie," Theodore broke in harshly. "Excellent khan, the books of the Old Testament, written hundreds of years before God's Son became flesh, foretold His coming. Neither Old nor New Testament speaks one word of the Arab charlatan who invented this false creed because he had failed as a camel-driver."

"There is no prophecy pertaining to Muhammad in the Christians' holy book because it was deliberately suppressed," Jalal ad-Din shot back. "That is why God gave the Prophet his gifts, as the seal of prophecy."

"The seal of trickery is nearer the truth," Theodore said. "God's only begotten Son Jesus Christ said prophecy ended with John the Baptist, but that false prophets would continue to come. Muhammad lived centuries after John and Jesus, so he must be false, a trick of the devil to send men to hell."

"Jesus is no son of God. God is one, not three, as the Christians would have it," Jalal ad-Din said. "Hear

God's own words in the *Qu'ran:* 'Say, God is one.' The Christians give the one God partners in the so-called Son and Holy Spirit. If he has two partners, why not three, or four, or more? Foolishness! And how could God fit into a woman's womb and be born like a man? More foolishness!"

Again it was Theodore who took up the challenge; he was a bad-tempered man, but capable all the same. "God is omnipotent. To deny the possibility of the Incarnation is to deny that omnipotence."

"That priest is twisty as a serpent," Da'ud ibn Zubayr whispered to Jalal ad-Din. The older man nodded, frowning. He was not quite sure how to respond to Theodore's latest sally. Who was he to say what Allah could or could not do?

Telerikh roused him from his unprofitable reverie by asking, "So you Arabs deny Jesus is the son of your one god, eh?"

"We do," Jalal ad-Din said firmly.

"What do you make of him, then?" the khan said.

"Allah commands us to worship none but himself, so how can he have a son? Jesus was a holy man and a prophet, but nothing more. Since the Christians corrupted his words, Allah inspired Muhammad to recite the truth once more."

"Could a prophet rise from the dead on the third day, as God's Son did?" Theodore snorted, clapping a dramatic hand to his forehead. "Christ's miracles are witnessed and attested in writing. What miracles did Muhammad work? None, the reason being that he could not."

"He flew to Jerusalem in the course of a night," Jalal ad-Din returned, "as the *Qu'ran* records—in writing," he added pointedly. "And the crucifixion and resurrection are fables. No man can rise from the dead, and another was set on the cross in place of Jesus."

"Satan waits for you in hell, blasphemer," Theodore hissed. "Christ healed the sick, raised the dead, stopped wind and rain in their tracks. Anyone who denies Him loses all hope of heaven, and may garner for his sin only eternal torment."

"No, that is the fate reserved for those who make One into Three," Jalal ad-Din said. "You—"

"Wait, both of you." Telerikh held up a hand. The Bulgar khan, Jalal ad-Din thought, seemed more stunned than edified by the arguments he had heard. The Arab realized he had been quarreling with Theodore rather than instructing the khan. Telerikh went on. "I cannot find the truth in what you are saying, for each of you and each of your books makes the other a liar. That helps me not at all. Tell me instead what I and my people must do, if we follow one faith or the other."

"If you choose the Arabs' false creed, you will have to abandon both wine-drinking and eating pork," Theodore said before Jalal ad-Din could reply. "Let him deny it if he may." The priest shot the Arab a triumphant look.

"It is true," Jalal ad-Din said stoutly. "Allah has ordained it."

He tried to put a bold face on it, but knew Theodore had landed a telling blow. The mutter that went up from Telerikh's boyars confirmed it. A passion for wine inflamed most non-believers, Jalal ad-Din thought; sadly, despite the good counsel of the *Qu'ran*, it could capture Muslims as well. And as for pork— judging from the meals they served at Pliska, the Bulgars found it their favorite flesh.

"That is not good," Telerikh said, and the Arab's heart sank.

A passion for wine . . . passion! "Magnificent khan, may I ask without offense how many wives you enjoy?"

Telerikh frowned. "I am not quite sure. How many is it now, Dragomir?"

"Forty-seven, mighty khan," the steward replied at once, competent as usual.

"And your boyars?" Jalal ad-Din went on. "Surely they also have more than one apiece."

"Well, what of it?" the khan said, sounding puzzled.

Now Jalal ad-Din grinned an unpleasant grin at Theodore. "If you become a Christian, magnificent khan, you will have to give up all your wives save one. You will not even be able to keep the others as concubines, for the Christians also forbid that practice."

"What?" If Telerikh had frowned before, the scowl he turned on the Christians now was thunderous. "Can this be true?"

"Of course it is true," Theodore said, scowling back. "Bigamy is a monstrous sin."

"Gently, my brother in Christ, gently," Paul said. "We do not wish to press too hard upon our Bulgar friends, who after all will be newly come to our observances."

"That one is truly a nuisance," Da'ud whispered.

"You are too right," Jalal ad-Din whispered back.

"Still, excellent khan," Paul went on, "you must not doubt that Theodore is correct. When you and your people accept Christianity, all those with more than one wife—or women with more than one husband, if any there be—will be required to repudiate all but their first marriages, and to undergo penance under the supervision of a priest."

His easy, matter-of-fact manner seemed to calm Telerikh. "I see you believe this to be necessary," the khan said. "It is so strange, though, that I do not see why. Explain further, if you will."

Jalal ad-Din made a fist. He had expected Christian ideas of marriage to appall Telerikh, not to intrigue him with their very alienness. Was a potential monk lurking under those fur robes, under that turban?

Paul said, "Celibacy, excellent khan, is the highest ideal. For those who cannot achieve it, marriage to a single partner is an acceptable alternative. Surely you must know, excellent khan, how lust can inflame men. And no sin is so intolerable to prophets and other holy men as depravity and sexual license, for the Holy Spirit will not touch the heart of a prophet while he is engaged in an erotic act. The life of the mind is nobler than that of the body; on this Holy Scripture and the wise ancient Aristotle agree."

"I never heard of this, ah, Aristotle. Was he a shaman?" Telerikh asked.

"You might say so," Paul replied, which impressed Jalal ad-Din. The Arab knew little of Aristotle, hardly more than that he had been a sage before even

Roman times. He was certain, however, that Aristotle had been a civilized man, not a barbarous pagan priest. But that was surely the closest equivalent to sage within Telerikh's mental horizon, and Paul deserved credit for recognizing it.

The Bulgar khan turned to Jalal ad-Din. "What have you to say about this?"

"The *Qu'ran* permits a man four lawful wives, for those able to treat them equally well," Jalal ad-Din said. "For those who cannot, it enjoins only one. But it does not prohibit concubines."

"That is better," the khan said. "A man would get bored, bedding the same woman night after night. But this business of no pork and no wine is almost as gloomy." He gave his attention back to the priests. "You Christians allow these things."

"Yes, excellent khan, we do," Paul said.

"Hmm." Telerikh rubbed his chin. Jalal ad-Din did his best to hide his worry. The matter still stood balanced, and he had used his strongest weapon to incline the khan to Islam. If the Christians had any good arguments left, he—and the fate of the true faith in Bulgaria—were in trouble.

Paul said, "Excellent khan, these matters of practice may seem important to you, but in fact they are superficial. Here is the key difference between the Arab's faith and ours: the religion Muhammad preached is one that loves violence, not peace. Such teaching can only come from Satan, I fear."

"That is a foul, stinking lie!" Da'ud ibn Zubayr cried. The other two Arabs behind Jalal ad-Din also shouted angrily.

"Silence!" Telerikh said, glaring at them. "Do not interrupt. I shall give you a chance to answer in due course."

"Yes, let the Christian go on," Jalal ad-Din agreed. "I am sure the khan will be fascinated by what he has to say."

Glancing back, he thought Da'ud about to burst with fury. The younger man finally forced out a strangled whisper: "Have you gone mad, to stand by while this infidel slanders the Prophet (may blessings be upon his head)?"

"I think not. Now be still, as Telerikh said. My ears are not what they once were; I cannot listen to you and Paul at once."

The monk was saying, "Muhammad's creed urges conversion by the sword, not by reason. Does not his holy book, if one may dignify it by that title, preach the holy war, the *jihad*"—he dropped the Arabic word into his polished Greek—"against all those who do not share his faith? And those who are slain in their murderous work, says the false prophet, attain to heaven straightaway." He turned to Jalal ad-Din. "Do you deny this?"

"I do not," Jalal ad-Din replied. "You paraphrase the third *sura* of the *Qu'ran*."

"There, you see?" Paul said to Telerikh. "Even the Arab himself admits the ferocity of his faith. Think also on the nature of the paradise Muhammad in his ignorance promises his followers—"

"Why do you not speak?" Da'ud ibn Zubayr demanded. "You let this man slander and distort everything in which we believe."

"Hush," Jalal ad-Din said again.

"—rivers of water and milk, honey and wine, and men reclining on silken couches and being served— served in all ways, including pandering to their fleshly lusts (as if souls could have such concerns!)—by females created especially for the purpose." Paul paused, needing a moment to draw in another indignant breath. "Such carnal indulgences—nay, excesses—have no place in heaven, excellent khan."

"No? What does, then?" Telerikh asked.

Awe transfigured the monk's thin, ascetic face as he looked within himself at the afterlife he envisioned. "Heaven, excellent khan, does not consist of banquets and wenches: those are for gluttons and sinners in this life, and lead to hell in the next. No: paradise is spiritual in nature, with the soul knowing the eternal joy of closeness and unity with God, peace of spirit and absence of all care. That is the true meaning of heaven."

"Amen," Theodore intoned piously. All three Christians made the sign of the cross over their breasts.

"That is the true meaning of heaven, you say?" Telerikh's blunt-featured face was impassive as his gaze swung toward Jalal ad-Din. "Now you may speak as you will, man of the caliph. Has this Christian told accurately of the world to come in his faith and in yours?"

"He has, magnificent khan." Jalal ad-Din spread his hands and smiled at the Bulgar lord. "I leave it to you, sir, to pick the paradise you would sooner inhabit."

Telerikh looked thoughtful. The Christian clerics' expressions went from confident to concerned to horrified as they gradually began to wonder, as Jalal ad-Din had already, just what sort of heaven a barbarian prince might enjoy.

Da'ud ibn Zubayr gently thumped Jalal ad-Din on the back. "I abase myself before you, sir," he said, flowery in apology as Arabs so often were. "You saw further than I." Jalal ad-Din bowed on his bench, warmed by the praise.

His voice urgent, the priest Niketas spoke up: "Excellent khan, you need to consider one thing more before you make your choice."

"Eh? And what might that be?" Telerikh sounded distracted. Jalal ad-Din hoped he was; the delights of the Muslim paradise were worth being distracted about. Paul's version, on the other hand, struck him as a boring way to spend eternity. But the khan, worse luck, was not altogether ready to abandon Christianity on account of that. Jalal ad-Din saw him focus his attention on Niketas. "Go on, priest."

"Thank you, excellent khan." Niketas bowed low. "Think on this, then: in Christendom the most holy Pope is the leader of all things spiritual, true, but there are many secular rulers, each to his own state: the Lombard dukes, the king of the Franks, the Saxon and Angle kings in Britain, the various Irish princes, every one a free man. But Islam knows only once prince, the caliph, who reigns over all Muslims.

If you decide to worship Muhammad, where is there room for you as ruler of your own Bulgaria?"

"No one worships Muhammad," Jalal ad-Din said tartly. "He is a prophet, not a god. Worship Allah, who alone deserves it."

His correction of the minor point did not distract Telerikh from the major one. "Is what the Christian says true?" the khan demanded. "Do you expect me to bend the knee to your khan as well as your god? Why should I freely give Abd ar-Rahman what he has never won in battle?"

Jalal ad-Din thought furiously, all the while damning Niketas. Priest, celibate the man might be, but he still thought like a Greek, like a Roman Emperor of Constantinople, sowing distrust among his foes so they defeated themselves when his own strength did not suffice to beat them.

"Well, Arab, what have you to say?" Telerikh asked again.

Jalal ad-Din felt sweat trickle into his beard. He knew he had let silence stretch too long. At last, picking his words carefully, he answered, "Magnificent khan, what Niketas says is not true. Aye, the caliph Abd ar-Rahman, peace be unto him, rules all the land of Islam. But he does so by right of conquest and right of descent, just as you rule the Bulgars. Were you, were your people, to become Muslim without warfare, he would have no more claim on you than any brother in Islam has on another."

He hoped he was right, and that the jurists would not make a liar of him once he got back to Damascus. All the ground here was uncharted: no nation had ever accepted Islam without first coming under the control of the caliphate. Well, he thought, if Telerikh and the Bulgars did convert, that success in itself would ratify anything he did to accomplish it.

If . . . Telerikh showed no signs of having made up his mind. "I will meet with all of you in four days," the khan said. He rose, signifying the end of the audience. The rival embassies rose too, and bowed deeply as he stumped between them out of the hall of audience.

"If only it were easy," Jalal ad-Din sighed.

The leather purse was small but heavy. It hardly clinked as Jalal ad-Din pressed it into Dragomir's hand. The steward made it disappear. "Tell me, if you would," Jalal ad-Din said, as casually as if the purse had never existed at all, "how your master is inclined toward the two faiths about which he has been learning."

"You are not the first person to ask me that question," Dragomir remarked. He sounded the tiniest bit smug: *I've been bribed twice*, Jalal ad-Din translated mentally.

"Was the other person who inquired by any chance Niketas?" the Arab asked.

Telerikh's steward dipped his head. "Why, yes, now that you mention it." His ice-blue eyes gave Jalal ad-Din a careful once-over: men who could see past their noses deserved watching.

Smiling, Jalal ad-Din said, "And did you give him the same answer you will give me?"

"Why, certainly, noble sir." Dragomir sounded as though the idea of doing anything else had never entered his mind. Perhaps it had not: "I told him, as I tell you now, that the mighty khan keeps his own counsel well, and has not revealed to me which faith—if either—he will choose."

"You are an honest man." Jalal ad-Din sighed. "Not as helpful as I would have hoped, but honest nonetheless."

Dragomir bowed. "And you, noble sir, are most generous. Be assured that if I knew more, I would pass it on to you." Jalal ad-Din nodded, thinking it would be a sorry spectacle indeed if one who served the caliph, the richest, mightiest lord in the world, could not afford a more lavish bribe than a miserable Christian priest.

However lavish the payment, though, it had not bought him what he wanted. He bowed his way out of Telerikh's palace, spent the morning wandering through Pliska in search of trinkets for his fair-skinned bedmate. Here too he was spending Abd ar-Rahman's money, so only the finest goldwork interested him.

He went from shop to shop, sometimes pausing to dicker, sometimes not. The rings and necklaces the Bulgar craftsmen displayed were less intricate, less ornate than those that would have fetched highest prices in Damascus, but had a rough vigor of their own. Jalal ad-Din finally chose a thick chain studded with fat garnets and pieces of polished jet.

He tucked the necklace into his robe, sat down to rest outside the jeweler's shop. The sun blazed down. It was not as high in the sky, not as hot, really, as it would have been in Damascus at the same season, but this was muggy heat, not dry, and seemed worse. Jalal ad-Din felt like a boiled fish. He started to doze.

"*Assalamu aleykum*—peace to you," someone said. Jalal ad-Din jerked awake, looked up. Niketas stood in front of him. Well, he'd long since gathered that the priest spoke Arabic, though they'd only used Greek between themselves till now.

"*Aleykum assalamu*—and to you, peace," he replied. He yawned and stretched and started to get to his feet. Niketas took him by the elbow, helped him rise. "Ah, thank you. You are generous to an old man, and one who is no friend of yours."

"Christ teaches us to love our enemies," Niketas shrugged. "I try to obey His teachings, as best I can."

Jalal ad-Din thought that teaching a stupid one— the thing to do with an enemy was to get rid of him. The Christians did not really believe what they said, either; he remembered how they'd fought at Constantinople, even after the walls were breached. But the priest had just been kind—no point in churlishly arguing with him.

Instead, the Arab said, "Allah be praised, day after tomorrow the khan will make his choice known." He cocked an eyebrow at Niketas. "Dragomir tells me you tried to learn his answer in advance."

"Which can only mean you did the same." Niketas

laughed drily. "I suspect you learned no more than I did."

"Only that Dragomir is fond of gold," Jalal ad-Din admitted.

Niketas laughed again, then grew serious. "How strange, is it not, that the souls of a nation ride on the whim of a man both ignorant and barbarous. God grant that he choose wisely."

"From God comes all things," Jalal ad-Din said. The Christian nodded; that much they believed in common. Jalal ad-Din went on, "That shows, I believe, why Telerikh will decide for Islam."

"No, you are wrong there," Niketas answered. "He must choose Christ. Surely God will not allow those who worship Him correctly to be penned up in one far corner of the world, and bar them forever from access to whatever folk may lie north and east of Bulgaria."

Jalal ad-Din started to answer, then stopped and gave his rival a respectful look. As he had already noticed, Niketas' thought had formidable depth to it. However clever he was, though, the priest who might have been Emperor had to deal with his weakness in the real world. Jalal ad-Din drove that weakness home: "If God loves you so well, why has he permitted us Muslims dominion over so many of you, and why has he let us drive you back and back, even giving over Constantinople, your imperial city, into our hands?"

"Not for your own sake, I'm certain," Niketas snapped.

"No? Why then?" Jalal ad-Din refused to be nettled by the priest's tone.

"Because of the multitude of our own sins, I'm sure. Not only was—*is*—Christendom sadly riddled with heresies and false beliefs, even those who believe what is true all too often lead sinful lives. Thus your eruption from the desert, to serve as God's flail and as punishment for our errors."

"You have answers to everything—everything but God's true will. He will show that day after tomorrow, through Telerikh."

"That He will." With a stiff little bow, Niketas took his leave. Jalal ad-Din watched him go, wondering if hiring a knifeman would be worthwhile in spite of Telerikh's warnings. Reluctantly, he decided against it; not here in Pliska, he thought. In Damascus he could have arranged it and never been traced, but he lacked that sort of connections here. Too bad.

Only when he was almost back to the khan's palace to give the pleasure girl the trinket did he stop to wonder whether Niketas was thinking about sticking a knife in *him*. Christian priests were supposed to be above such things, but Niketas himself had pointed out what sinners Christians were these days.

Telerikh's servants summoned Jalal ad-Din and the other Arabs to the audience chamber just before the time for mid-afternoon prayers. Jalal ad-Din did not like having to put off the ritual; it struck him as a bad omen. He tried to stay serene. Voicing the inauspicious thought aloud would only give it power.

The Christians were already in the chamber when the Arabs entered. Jalal ad-Din did not like that either. Catching his eye, Niketas sent him a chilly nod. Theodore only scowled, as he did whenever he had anything to do with Muslims. The monk Paul, though, smiled at Jalal ad-Din as if at a dear friend. That only made him worry more.

Telerikh waited until both delegations stood before him. "I have decided," he said abruptly. Jalal ad-Din drew in a sudden, sharp breath. From the number of boyars who echoed him, he guessed that not even the khan's nobles knew his will. Dragomir had not lied, then.

The khan rose from his carven throne, stepped down between the rival embassies. The boyars muttered among themselves; this was not common procedure. Jalal ad-Din's nails bit into his palms. His heart pounded in his chest till he wondered how long it could endure.

Telerikh turned to face southeast. For a moment, Jalal ad-Din was too keyed up to notice or care. Then the khan sank to his knees, his face turned toward

Mecca, toward the Holy City. Again Jalal ad-Din's heart threatened to burst, this time with joy.

"*La illaha ill'Allah; Muhammadun rasulu'llah,*" Telerikh said in a loud, firm voice. "There is no God but Allah; Muhammad is the prophet of Allah." He repeated the *shahada* twice more, then rose to his feet and bowed to Jalal ad-Din.

"It is accomplished," the Arab said, fighting back tears. "You are a Muslim now, a fellow in submission to the will of God."

"Not I alone. We shall all worship the one God and his prophet." Telerikh turned to his boyars, shouted in the Bulgar tongue. A couple of nobles shouted back. Telerikh jerked his arm toward the doorway, a peremptory gesture of dismissal. The stubborn boyars glumly tramped out. The rest turned toward Mecca and knelt. Telerikh led them in the *shahada*, once, twice, three times. The khan faced Jalal ad-Din once more. "Now we are all Muslims here."

"God is most great," the Arab breathed. "Soon, magnificent khan, I vow, many teachers will come from Damascus to instruct you and your people fully in all details of the faith, though what you and your nobles have proclaimed will suffice for your souls until such time as the *ulama*—those learned in religion—may arrive."

"It is very well," Telerikh said. Then he seemed to remember that Theodore, Niketas, and Paul were still standing close by him, suddenly alone in a chamber full of the enemies of their faith. He turned to them. "Go back to your Pope in peace, Christian priests. I could not choose your religion, not with heaven as you say it is—and not with the caliph's armies all along my southern border. Perhaps if Constantinople had not fallen so long ago, my folk would in the end have become Christian. Who can say? But in this world, as it is now, Muslims we must be, and Muslims we shall be."

"I will pray for you, excellent khan, and for God's forgiveness of the mistake you made this day," Paul said gently. Theodore, on the other hand, looked as if he was consigning Telerikh to the hottest pits of hell.

Niketas caught Jalal ad-Din's eye. The Arab nodded slightly to his defeated foe. More than anyone else in the chamber, the two of them understood how much bigger than Bulgaria was the issue decided here today. Islam would grow and grow, Christendom continue to shrink. Jalal ad-Din had heard that Ethiopia, far to the south of Egypt, had Christian rulers yet. What of it? Ethiopia was so far from the center of affairs as hardly to matter. And the same fate would now befall the isolated Christian countries in the far northwest of the world.

Let them be islands in the Muslim sea, he thought, if that was what their stubbornness dictated. One day, *inshallah,* that sea would wash over every island, and they would read the *Qu'ran* in Rome itself.

He had done his share and more to make that dream real, as a youth helping to capture Constantinople and now in his old age by bringing Bulgaria the true faith. He could return once more to his peaceful retirement in Damascus.

He wondered if Telerikh would let him take along that fair-skinned pleasure girl. He turned to the khan. It couldn't hurt to ask.

KALVAN KINGMAKER

John F. Carr
(with Roland J. Green)

Introduction

The saga of Lord Kalvan of Otherwhen is one of the most well-known and loved of all science fiction alternate histories. Much of the background and history of this alternate Paratime world is given in *Lord Kalvan of Otherwhen* by H. Beam Piper and its sequel *Great Kings' War* by Roland J. Green and John F. Carr. H. Beam Piper began the saga with the story of a Pennsylvania State Trooper, Calvin Morrison, and how he got picked up by a passing Paratime Transpositional conveyor and deposited on an alternate world on the Aryan-Transpacific, Styphon's House subsector.

On Aryan-Transpacific, the Indo-European migrations of about three thousand years ago did not stop in the east in India and go south into the Middle East as they did in our world. Instead the Sabines (later the name changed to Zarthani) left the eastern Mediterranean and moved through China into Siberia during the period of the Sea Peoples migrations, circa 1100 B.C. They were so far down the pecking order that they had to take the northern flank when the "Aryans" hit China, which means by happenstance they led the march around the Sea of Okhost into Alaska. When the main body arrived in the New World, all the settlements spoke Zarthani and the late-comers were absorbed into a Zarthani melting pot.

Along the Pacific Coast they started a Mediterranean-style civilization, utilizing horses, cattle, and the iron weapons which they had brought with them from the Old World. Most of them settled along the coast of Southern California, especially in the harbors of San Francisco, Long Beach, and San Diego. There the Zarthani established a series of sea-trading city-states, much along the Mycenaean model.

Later Indo-European migrations of proto-Celts and Goths followed to find the Pacific coast settled and so moved into the Great Plains and Mississippi Valley, where they formed the Middle Kingdoms. Grefftscharr, at about the site of Chicago, became the greatest of the powers using the Great Lakes basin and a flourishing iron trade with the Pacific Coast peoples.

About 1500 A.D. a series of wars collapsed the Pacific Coast city-states and there was a great migration over the Iron Trail into the Appalachians and along the Atlantic Coast. After a war of extermination with the Indian tribes, they expanded north into Canada and south as far as Florida, forming the Five Great Kingdoms.

Around 1650 A.D. a priest of a minor healing god, Styphon, discovered the formula for gunpowder. The Temple gave the gunpowder secret divine overtones and created a theocracy called Styphon's House. Styphon's House used their gunpowder monopoly to extend their political and economic influence and to keep competing states in technological stagnation. By the time of Calvin Morrison's arrival, Styphon's House had grown corrupt; they were using their great power to enrich the priesthood and enslave those who did not accept Styphon's divinity and special status of God of Gods.

Kalvan arrives when Styphon's House, desirous of the sulfur springs within Hostigos' border, uses the subject states of Nostor and Sask to annex the small princedom of Hostigos. In his attempt to save Hostigos, Kalvan breaks the gunpowder secret and fights a number of successful wars that lead to the formation of the new kingdom of Hos-Hostigos. But the war with Styphon's House has become a religious war and as Kalvan is soon to learn, they are the dirtiest wars of all . . .

1

Despite the autumn chill in the air, Grand Master Soton felt his tunic grow wet from the exertion of guiding the donkey along the series of switchbacks that cut through the cliffs leading up to Harphax City. The rock-paved road was lined with swarms of beggars and hideously scarred veterans of the war with Hos-Hostigos. The fact that last year's maimed and their poor cousins kept their curses under their breaths showed that the Order's banner—a large white flag bearing a black, broken sun-wheel with curved arms—was still feared in the Great Kingdom of Hos-Harphax, even if not respected.

Not that Soton relaxed the tight grip he held on the mace that rested against his saddle pommel in plain view. He had good reasons to be cautious; the House of Styphon and its agents, the Order of Zarthani Knights, were held responsible by many in Hos-Harphax for the beating the Harphaxi took at the hands of King Kalvan at the Battle of Cothros Heights, where the heir to the throne and half the Harphaxi nobility had been slain.

Most appeared to have forgotten that Soton himself had lost another equally disastrous battle to this self-proclaimed Great King Kalvan, who had appeared out of nowhere like a demigod, a moon later at the Battle of Phyrax.

Despite the reform within Styphon's House, led by the fanatical Archpriest Roxthar, the Temple's control over her earthly allies was in great jeopardy. The Usurper Kalvan had not only defeated every

237

army Styphon's House had thrown at him but had let loose the great miracle of fireseed—the magic powder that made muskets and bombards, such terrible weapons of destruction. Now anyone, even nonbelievers, could duplicate Styphon's Great Miracle or buy fireseed direct from Kalvan. Now even those allies who still believed in Styphon's divinity were shaken in their faith by Kalvan's otherworldly ability to shake victory from almost certain defeat.

Grand Master Soton himself, ruler of a domain equal to that of any Great King's in the Sastragath border lands, was not pleased that the fanatics within Styphon's House had taken command of the Temple—aided and abetted by Supreme Priest Sesklos' growing senility. Yet, were it not for the Temple taking him in as an orphan thirty-some winters ago, he would now be a simple farmer or blacksmith in some isolated backwater village. For that and allowing him to raise himself so high—Grand Master of the Order of Zarthani Knights and Archpriest of Styphon's House—the Temple had his undying loyalty.

Furthermore, there was no denying that Roxthar and his followers had put new mettle into Styphon's Will on Earth. They had certainly given him an unlimited draft on the Temple's earthly resources; all of which, gold and arms especially, he was going to need if he was going to turn the broken Harphaxi Royal Army into any semblance of a military power.

Soton halted his party before the next steep grade and peered down onto Port Harphax, which appeared surprisingly busy for this late in the year. Galleys, galleassas, and wide-bottomed carracks were scooting across the harbor below like water beetles. As he kneed the donkey into reluctant motion, Soton cursed the memory of Erasthames the Great, the legendary king who had conquered the Iroquois Alliance. Four hundred years ago it might have made sense to put Tarr-Harphax up at the top of these cliffs when the native Ruthani were an everyday threat.

Now it was a beastly nuisance. It made feeding Harphax City and the castle a nightmare. Since the lower Harph flooded almost every spring, cutting off

river transport, the city had to take in enough stores
to last a long winter and spring as well. Food that
arrived by sea had to be carted or packed up the
Upper Road, at great expense in time and animals,
or pulled up in great iron buckets by the rope
tramway.

During a bad year such as this one, when fields
had been trampled and burnt, most of Harphax City's
food had to be imported by seagoing merchants.
Thus the great number of boats crowding Harphax
Port's limited docking facilities. Now there was less
than a half moon before winter storms made sea
passage impossible. Most of the captains were less
than pleased by chancing the seas this late in the
year and only generous gifts of Styphon's gold kept
them at sea at all.

If all this weren't bad enough, the burnt fields and
farms had brought tens of thousands of refugees into
the already bursting-at-the-seams capital. Plus all the
war casualties who were too crippled or maimed to
work, yet had to be housed and fed. Already the
strain of short rations and over-crowding were visible
on the lean faces of the city's beggars. Only great
need could force them to take their chances on the
steep Upper Road and the occasional visitor's generosity.

At the top of the cliffs the city walls showed the
abuse of more than a hundred years' neglect and civil
complacency. Here and there teams of workmen were
shoring up walls and replacing fallen stones, but—as
far as Soton could see—it was clearly a case of too
little, too late. He guessed that Kalvan's three-and
four-pounder field guns would bring down most of
these walls. As for the old castle itself, Tarr-Harphax,
with proper siege guns, Kalvan would have a dozen
breaches in a half moon.

Soton shuddered to think of the slaughter Kalvan's
veterans would make upon the shattered remnants of
the Harphaxi Army. It was a good thing that acting
Great King Lysandros, since his brother King Kaiphranos' death two moons ago, had taken his advice
and appointed Phidestros Captain-General of the Royal

Army, rather than one of his cronies or aging mercenaries. Phidestros was young for such an appointment, but he had fought against Kalvan three times and lived to tell about it.

If anyone could turn this whipped rabble into a fighting force again, it was Phidestros. He had more ambition than an Archpriest of the Inner Circle of Styphon's House and as much gall as Kalvan himself. Even so Phidestros would need Appalon's luck and Lyklos' cunning to forge this base metal into good fighting steel.

For all that, Phidestros was still a mercenary and owed his allegiance to the highest paymaster—gold before god. Therefore, he would have to make sure that the pupil did not come to best his master in the art of war.

The cobblestone and dirt streets of Harphax City were lined with makeshift tents and temporary housing. The stink alone was enough to bring tears even to the eyes of a seasoned soldier. Twice Soton had been forced to use his mace to beat off attempts by thieves to steal the trappings off his horse right under the noses of his guards. It took a full sandglass to navigate through the narrow city streets to Tarr-Harphax where Captain-General Phidestros had his headquarters.

Soton was pleased to note the severe appearance of Phidestros' audience room; the only adornments were a pair of crossed muskets, a well-used sword, and a large deerskin map of Hos-Harphax, which included the new Great Kingdom of Hos-Hostigos outlined in red ink within its borders.

"Please take a seat, Grand Master."

"Thank you, Captain-General. My men will bring it in." This time he'd had his own seat brought with him from Balph and when he sat down on his elevated chair, he was eye-to-eye with Phidestros. The long-boned Captain-General looked thinner than he had last spring and the lines of his face were etched bolder and deeper. Soton sighed; at least, it showed that Phidestros had no illusions about the near-impossible task set before him.

When Phidestros' aide had filled their wine goblets, Soton asked, "How does your command look these days?"

Phidestros frowned. "Not so good. They were not much of a fighting force before Kalvan ground them up. Now they're little better than a rabble."

"That bad?"

"Many of the units are at half strength—probably more due to desertions and the flux than Kalvan's lead. Some, like the Royal Lancers, were almost annihilated. That might have been a blessing, though. I would like to disband the entire unit if Lysandros would let me—or the nobles let him! The Lancers are more worried about gaining honor than winning battles, I fear."

"You might think that Kalvan's artillery would have taught them a thing or two."

"Those iron hats! No such luck. They see Kalvan's style of fighting as unjust and dishonorable. With the Succession Crisis, Prince Lysandros doesn't dare dismiss them. But, with Kalvan's help, I've reduced their number by almost half. I'm also turning them into more of a Household Guard than a line unit. I've also recruited about two thousand more mercenaries and brought the Royal Pistoleers back up to full strength. The Foot Guard is still seriously undermanned."

"How many troops could you muster if Kalvan were at the city walls tomorrow morning?"

"A little over four thousand Royal troops and another five thousand mercenaries. I am supposed to have about twelve thousand city militia, but they are next to worthless—even though I've made them spend at least one day a quarter moon in training. Most of them would take off, as they did at Cothros Heights, at the first sound of cannon fire. At least, I've managed to get them uniforms and guns that fire without exploding. You wouldn't believe the ordnance I had to replace—musket locks that were rusted shut, stocks half-rotted away, and barrels fouled beyond belief."

"I believe it," Soton said. "Kaiphranos the Timid

was more a tightpurse than a coward. I was aghast when his son asked to meet Kalvan on the field man to man; well, he paid for his impertinence. What you're telling me is that I'd better not depend upon the Harphaxi Royal Army for any duty more pressing than staying inside the City walls."

Phidestros looked crestfallen. "If Kalvan invades Hos-Harphax next spring, only the gods will be able to stop him from taking the entire Kingdom, Tarr-Harphax included. The only bright news is that I don't believe Kalvan has any idea just *how* desperate our situation really is."

"I take it you have told no one else this."

"Only First Prince Lysandros and yourself, Grand Master. Kalvan has his intelligencers everywhere, even here in Harphax City. We almost caught a big one a moon ago. I've made a big show of parading the militia up and down the city streets in their new uniforms and arms. They look all right, but those whoresons couldn't be counted upon to stand before a good sneeze!"

"You've done well," Soton replied. "Now it is up to the gods and I believe they have done well by us. I have come up with a plan that will keep Kalvan busy all next year. And, with Galzar's Grace, it may even cost him his throne."

"By the Wargod's Beard, tell me! What miracle is this?"

"I plan to let the nomads fight the war against Kalvan for us. The Mexicotl in their war against Xiphlon have driven the fierce southern pony warriors into the Sea of Grass, driving the nomads from their traditional hunting grounds into the Middle Kingdoms and over the Great River in their desire to find a safe haven. Only a few thousand have crossed the Great River thus far, but already the entire Lower Sastragath is aboil as new tribes move in and others use the disorder to settle old scores or build great clans. Three times this year the Order has had to fight battles against barbarians trying to move into Hos-Ktemnos and Hos-Bletha.

"Now things are beginning to settle down as the

tribes search for shelter and forage for the cold months. The Order has seen these migrations from the Plains many times before and events should come to a head next year. The nomads are caught between an anvil, the Middle Kingdoms, and the Ruthani hammer from the south. The only place they have to go is across the Great River and into the Sastragath. Next year will see ten times as many tribes fording the river, which will kick loose all the tribes and clans of the Lower Sastragath and push them either east into our forts or north into the Upper Sastragath.

"Instead of fortifying the border and holding our forts, my plan is to move half our Lances into the Lower Sastragath and drive the nomads up the Pathagaros Valley into the Lydistros Valley and from there into Kalvan's backyard. With a nomad invasion threatening the Trygath and Kalvan's own westernmost princedoms, Kalvan will be forced to go on the offensive and call back his own troops on the Hostigos/Harphaxi border."

"It is a brilliant plan, Grand Master. But surely things are not so bad that our only choice is to allow the barbarians to enter the Five Kingdoms through our own backdoor?"

"In words for your ears only, our situation *is* that desperate. If Kalvan invades Hos-Harphax, he will conquer it before the first moon of summer. With Hos-Harphax defeated, Great King Demistophon of Hos-Agrys will quickly sue for terms; especially after the beating he took with his army from Prince Ptosphes last summer. Great King Cleitharses of Hos-Ktemnos is still in shock over the losses his Sacred Squares took at the Battle of Phyrax; he won't go to battle again unless ordered to by the assembled Inner Council to Styphon's House. Hos-Beltha is too far away to be of any consequence and Great King Sopharar of Hos-Zygros is flirting with the League of Dralm. So, without the Great Kingdom of Hos-Harphax as an anchor, the war against Kalvan is doomed."

Phidestros massaged his temples as if he had the grandfather of all headaches. "Things wouldn't be so bad, Soton, if I could hire some mercenaries. They are nowhere to be found. I know it's winter and that a lot of them died at Fyk, Tenabra, Cothros Heights, and Phyrax . . . but still?"

"In Balph I learned that Kalvan has been offering mercenaries bonuses and *year*-round pay for signing up in his Royal Army of Hos-Hostigos. That is where many of them have gone."

Phidestros groaned. "Why didn't I think of that?"

"More mercenaries have been hired by barons and princes for protection from the nomads. In all of Hos-Ktemnos there are no mercenaries to be hired at any price; I understand that things are likewise in Hos-Agrys. Even if Kalvan defeats the nomads, he will do more than just give us breathing space."

"How so, Grand Master?"

"He will give us the greatest gift of all—time. Time for you to train the Harphaxi rabble. Empty the prisons and the gaols. Take the strongest and the toughest and forge them into an army."

"By what magic will I turn riffraff into a real army?"

"By the magic of Styphon's gold and your own will. I will go to Prince Lysandros and tell him that you will build an army twenty thousand men strong. Styphon's House will supply the gold and victuals."

"It could be done—the Royal Foot Guard can be my petty-captains. I can train them night and day until they drop. It doesn't take great marksmanship to make a musketeer. It will take a lot of work . . ."

"Good, Captain-General, you are already thinking along the right lines. Kalvan will think twice about invading Hos-Harphax—*if* he defeats the nomads—and hears tell of a great army here."

Phidestros smiled for the first time. "I say a toast to Grand Master Soton and the *new* Royal Army of Hos-Harphax!"

Soton downed his goblet in a single gulp. When it was filled again, he made his own toast. "TO VICTORY! TO THE USURPER KALVAN'S DEATH! TO STYPHON'S HOUSE!"

2

Ranjar Sargos leaped out of the tree, flapped his wings, and caught an updraft which propelled him high into the sky. It was dawn and the sun was rising above the distant horizon, bathing the world in red flames. Looking down he saw a great herd of beasts flooding the Pathagaros Valley.

As he glided closer to the earth, he was able to discern the true nature of the teeming animals—only they weren't animals but thousands upon thousands of men—the two-legged beast. They were painted in war colors and carrying bows, spears, axes, and all the weapons of war.

He glided above their heads and they looked up at him. Suddenly they began to beat their weapons against their shields. It was as if he was the sign they had been waiting for and it came to him that it was his destiny to lead this sea of warriors.

At the other end of the valley there was a rumble like thunder; he flew closer to see another great clan of men wearing the metal skin of the dirtmen.

He shrieked a warning to his followers and raised his talons. The roar of war cries smashed against his ears like clubs—

"Ranjar, wake up! Wake up!"

Ranjar Sargos, Warlord of the Tymannes, removed his hands from his ears and slowly raised up on the cot he had been sleeping on. *Where am I?* The open door let in enough moonlight that he could see that he was inside the tribal longhouse where he had been sleeping during the clan gathering.

245

"What is it?" Ranjar asked.

"Ikkos has returned."

"Where are the others?" By the others, of course, he meant his eldest son, Bargoth, who against his private words had ridden off with the scouting party.

"I do not know, Chief. Only Ikkos has returned and he was on foot with many wounds."

Sargos brushed the sleep out of his eyes. "Take me to him."

"Follow me."

Sargos, who still had enough wits about him to tuck his pistol into his belt, followed the sentry into the night. The tribe's longhouses and sweathuts filled most of the small upper valley and he could just make out another score of men gathered near the palisade's gateway. *If none of the sentries have stayed at their posts, there will be blood spilled this night!*

The Tymannes had come to this gathering, not as in the past to settle tribal boundaries or exchange furs before the coming cold, but to talk about the great movement of peoples that was taking place in the lowland valleys and along the Great River. Never in living memory had so many tribes and clans been uprooted from their traditional lands; already his tribe had been forced to defend their valley from invaders.

Interrogation of the prisoners had told them little, only that many tribes and bands were being forced to flee their homes by other tribes and the Black Knights. Sargos had never fought against the Black Knights, but he had heard stories of their war prowess from those who had and in old tales passed down by the clan fathers. Yet, in times past the Black Knights had not burned villages and slain whole tribes without provocation. So a gathering of all the Tymannes had been called at a time when men should be setting traps, hunting, and fishing.

I wonder if this has anything to do with my vision? Before he could mull this over, they had arrived at the circle of men surrounding Ikkos. A few held torches and he could see that Ikkos was bruised and shirtless. Several tribesmen were trying to question

Ikkos all at the same time; Sargos stilled their voices with a clap of his hands.

"Where is Bargoth?"

Ikkos shook his head as if dazed. "I left him with all the others when we were ambushed. He may be behind me, I don't know. The last I saw him, he was shooting his bow and telling me to escape."

Sargos mentally steeled himself for the worst. Bargoth had never been one to turn away from a fight, no matter what the odds. He was big for eighteen winters and could run, chase, and fight as good as any man in the tribe; yet, Sargos had often wondered if he had the cunning necessary to make a good chief or lead his people. Tomorrow, at first light, he would send out a party to find out what had happened and if anyone else in the scouting party had survived.

"Did you recognize the tribe that set the ambush?"

"No, Chief Sargos. But one of them wore the blue tattoos of the Great River tribes . . ." Ikkos began to shake with fatigue and cold. Someone passed him a blanket and he curled up into a ball.

"We will get little more out of him tonight. Let him get a good rest so that he can talk to the Council tomorrow. You others, get back to your posts before our foes walk in through the gate!" The men trotted off as if stung by bees. When everyone had left, Sargos squatted down in the grass and clenched his hands over his chest until tears streamed out of his eyes.

All the chiefs of the Tymannes sat in the clan's Council Hut. Only Old Daron—who every winter survived his half-moon winter trail—had his son with him, a middle-aged man with too much belly and watery eyes. *Why, if the gods had to take a son, couldn't they have taken one such as this?* Sargos shook his head to help clear his thoughts; then he rose to make the opening prayers so the gods might bless the Folk in this year of trial.

When the rituals were complete, Sargos had Ikkos called into the hut.

"We traveled five days until we reached the banks of the Great River. Many times we had to hide from strange tribes and war parties. Many of the camps we passed were burned out or deserted. At the camp of the Lyssos we discovered only the dead; the entire tribe had been massacred—even the women and children."

There was a collective shriek at this news. The Lyssos had long been allies of the Tymannes and all had lost friends in their unclean passing. To kill unarmed women and children was usually a sign of madness or great drunkenness . . .

"At the banks of the Great River we saw many grass people cross the ford on rafts so large they could hold the entire clan! We saw little fighting there, but the river was clogged with the bodies of the dead. Whether from some earlier battle, or one upstream, we never did learn.

"Downstream we came upon a great battle. The Black Knights were attacking a large village, ten times the size of our own camp. They burned the palisades and used great fire tubes to knock them down. When the walls collapsed they stormed the village, killing everyone who did not flee and burning everything left behind. We ran too for fear they might attack us as well!

"Later we talked to some of the villagers who escaped and they told us the Knights were burning and destroying every village and camp in the Sastragath. They claimed the end of the world had come. They left us to flee north where they hope to join up with others of their people. After that we left to return, when three days later we were ambushed by the grass people."

Hearing about the ambush brought the pain back again, but Sargos pushed it aside. Little new was told during the questioning so Sargos pondered over the death of his son and the vision he had been gifted with last night. *Was his son the gods' price for leadership over all the clans, or was it all some jest of Lyklos, the Trickster?*

Before he could make sense of all this, his other

son Larkander entered the hut. The boy's eyes were red and Sargos felt his stomach drop like a stone.

"Father, the riders have returned . . . They brought Bargoth's body back with them. They say he died with honor, surrounded by dead foes. Why, Father, why?"

Before this son embarrassed them both, he ordered, "Sit down. The time has come for *you* to prepare for your place in the tribe."

Larkander stifled his emotions and sat down with all the dignity his fourteen winters could muster. Not for the first time, Sargos was proud of his young boy—no, man now. His voice had already broken and he was halfway through his last growth. The time had come for him to learn a man's duty and responsibility.

Sargos rose to speak. "Where there is one army of Black Knights, there are more. Either they or the grass people will soon come to drive us from our lands. We have two choices: we can stay and fight— and die, since our foes are in number like the summer grass. Or we can join the other tribes and clans and move up the Pathagaros Valley. How do you vote?"

There was little discussion. The clan leaders agreed to move north as their Warlord had suggested. The women and children would go into the hills with the warriors of Old Daron's tribe to protect them.

As they left the Clan Hut, Larkander moved close to his father and asked, "Father, may I come along with the rest of the warriors?"

Ranjar Sargos looked down at this youngest son— now his only son. *Was this to be the price of his visions? Both sons dead?* He shook his head.

"But Father, I can ride a horse and shoot a bow as good as any man in this camp."

Sargos knew this was no boast. "Larkander, you are my only son now. I need you safe."

"Will it be safe in the hills with the women and children? If it is my time, I can die anywhere. I am only a few moons from my manhood rites. It is time I learned how to lead our people; where better than at my father's side?"

Sargos clenched his hands until his palms bled. "If it is your wish, you can go. Tell your mother now."

Larkander let out a loud whoop and took off at a run. At another time it might have lightened Sargos' spirits, but at the moment all he could see in his mind were the hundreds of bodies drifting down the Great River. The gods were capricious: Sometimes they gave a man great gifts, but often they took much in return.

3

Colonel Kronos nodded to his sovereign to signify that everyone was seated. Great King Kalvan banged his pistol on the table for silence. "Princes, lords and generals, we have very little time and a lot of items to cover. Please keep your questions to a minimum. General Baldour, would you bring us up-to-date on the nomad invasion."

General Baldour was a former mercenary Grand Captain in the Army of Hos-Ktemnos and thus more familiar with the western territories than any of the Hostigi generals. He walked over to the deerskin map of the Middle Kingdoms and pointed to a spot just north of the Middle Kingdom city of Kythar (Louisville, Kentucky) with his sword point.

"Yesterday, I talked to a merchant just returned from Kyblos City; the word there is the northern-most horde is just outside Kythar Town. In years past, the nomads would have stopped there to sack Kythar Town, but not this year with Grand Master Soton's army less than five days behind.

"We must, however, remember that this informa-tion was a quarter moon old when it reached Kyblos City and it took another half moon to reach us here in Hostigos Town. We can expect the nomads to follow the trade routes along the Lydistros River so that by now they should be less than half a moon from the Trygath border."

There was a collective sigh from around the plank table.

Queen Rylla asked, "Do you think the nomads

might possibly move into Hos-Ktemnos or will they travel through the Trygath until they reach Kyblos and then invade Hos-Hostigos?"

"I believe the nomads would be going right into Hos-Ktemnos, as these migrations have done in the past, were they not being chased by the Zarthani Knights. The plunder is much richer in the Great Kingdom of Hos-Ktemnos. Yet, if they travel east they are going to run straight into Tarr-Lydra, where they'd be caught between Soton's army and the Knights' garrison in Tarr-Lydra—which would be suicidal.

"Prince Tythanes of Kyblos and Prince Kestophes of Ulthor are right to believe the nomads will soon be invading their realms and thereby have a legitimate claim to their overlord's protection. There is no way to avoid supporting them without our Great King acquiring the name of a king who advances himself at his princes' expense."

"That was my own analysis," Kalvan said.

Chancellor Chartiphon rose to speak. "Then it looks like we are going to have to delay the invasion of Hos-Harphax until the nomad problem has been settled."

Which is exactly what the Styphoni want, thought Kalvan, cursing Soton and his progenitors in four languages. *Did he dare split the army into two smaller forces as he had done with such disastrous results last spring?*

"Harmakros, what do you think of splitting the army in two, sending one half after the nomads and the other to invade Hos-Harphax?"

"I don't believe it would be wise, Your Majesty. We have reports that the nomad hordes number anywhere from one hundred thousand to just under a million—and that depends upon whether you're talking about the advance horde, the main horde, and all the divisions. Nor do we know the proportion of fighting men to women, children, and old men. We do not have enough information to judge what we may be up against. If we don't take at least thirty thousand troops we may be overwhelmed by sheer weight of numbers. In a situation this fluid I don't believe we can risk fighting a two-front war."

"On the other hand," Prince Ptosphes added, "we can be certain that the Army of Hos-Harphax is going to stay inside its borders and not be on campaign unless we attack first. If we do that now we may find ourselves fighting the Harphaxi in the east, the Ktemnoi in the south, and the nomads everywhere else. As our Great King has told us repeatedly, the only thing worse than fighting a two front war is fighting one on three or four fronts. Which is exactly what we will have if we undertake the invasion of Hos-Harphax."

Kalvan sighed and decided that in future he was going to have to be more careful about throwing out military maxims in front of his General Staff. Although he had to admit that his own advice struck him as frightfully sound. Here he was not only caught on the horns of a dilemma, but on the prongs and antlers as well!

At times like this he sometimes wondered if his friends and family might have been better off had he never been dropped off here-and-now by that cross-time flying saucer. It was when he landed that things began to get complicated. Here-and-now was still Pennsylvania, but nothing like the one he had known as a Pennsylvania State Policeman.

Here-and-now was an alternate world where the Indo-Aryan invasions had not stopped in India, but continued east across China, then by ships along the Aleutians until they reached the Pacific Coast as far down as Baja California. Later waves of related peoples had settled the Great Plains and the Mississippi River valley. They had brought with them horses, cattle, and iron. A new civilization, five or six centuries old, had settled in the Appalachians and along the Atlantic Coast.

The new civilization, which called itself the Five Kingdoms, was the most advanced; they alone had discovered the secret of gunpowder. A theocracy called Styphon's House had grown up around the gunpowder miracle, dispensing the sacred fireseed

to allies and subject states. Over the centuries they
had used their monopoly of gunpowder to maintain
their political status quo and enrich the priesthood.
They almost matched the ancient Aztec priesthood of
his own world for sheer bloody-mindedness.

It was a late-medieval to early Renaissance culture, with gunpowder and good hand weapons, including a modified flintlock. When Corporal Calvin
Morrison, forcibly retired from the Pennsylvania State
Police, had landed in the small Princedom of Hostigos,
he had found himself in the midst of a war between
Hostigos and Styphon's House—who wanted to annex the Princedom for its sulfur springs. After helping rout an enemy raid, he was accidentally shot by
Prince Ptosphes' daughter, Rylla. He'd spent his con-
valescence in Tarr-Hostigos as a guest of the Prince.

Then he had fallen in love with lovely Rylla and
decided to stay and help them in their fight against
Styphon's House. First, he had shown them how to
make their own gunpowder; not only freeing them
from Styphon's House but involving them in a war to
the death with the gunpowder theocracy. After that
Kalvan had been like a man hanging onto a runaway
horse. There had been battles against Styphon's
allies—the Battle of Listra-Mouth against Prince
Gormoth of Nostor and the Battle of Fyk against
Sask—both of which Kalvan had won.

Kalvan's knowledge of military history and stupid
generalship by Kalvan's opponents had helped. So
had new field artillery, with trunnions and proper
field carriages, able to outshoot anything else in this
world. A superior grade of gunpowder had helped
too. Soon Hostigos was a major power, whether it
wanted to be or not. There was nothing else, really,
but to proclaim it the Great Kingdom of Hos-Hostigos.
And Kalvan had become Great King and Rylla his
Great Queen.

Then there had been the year of war, with attacks
coming from Hos-Ktemnos to the south, Hos-Harphax
to the east, and Hos-Agrys to the north. Kalvan had
won three Great Murthering Battles and only lost
one—the ill-fated Battle of Tenabra, where Prince

Ptosphes had been given a good licking by Grand Master Soton. But three out of four wasn't bad odds anywhere, even here-and-now, so Kalvan still held his throne—for now.

Kalvan rose to his feet. "I agree with Harmakros and First Prince Ptosphes. We must abandon our plans for the invasion of Hos-Harphax and draw up new ones for the defense of Kyblos."

All the assembled Princes and generals nodded their accord. Prince Sarrask of Sask stood up and said, "A cheer for Great King Kalvan, who has brought us several seasons of good fighting and now promises us more!"

There was a collective cheer and a chorus of 'Down Styphon!' "

Sarrask added, "Aye, and when we've finished giving the barbarians a good arse-kickin' let's come back and finish the job we started last year in Hos-Harphax!"

There were more cheers and Sarrask sat back down.

"Thank you, for the vote of confidence. Now, let's get down and work out the details of how we're going to get there and which soldiers we're going to take. First, General Hestophes is going to need reinforcements for his Army of Observation at Tarr-Lorca in Beshta. We don't want to give the Harphaxi any cute ideas while we're away. What's Hestophes' army look like right now, Captain-General Harmakros?"

"Hestophes has four regiments of Royal Horse and one of infantry, plus about another two thousand Beshtan cavalry."

"That's only five thousand men," Kalvan said. "Let's send him the Second Musketeers, and the King's Heavy Horse and the Heavy Cavalry—they won't be of much use where we're going." Since so many of his cavalrymen, even the former mercenaries, were titled or the younger sons of the nobility, Kalvan had been forced to create three regiments of old-style fully armored cavalry. He had thought them almost useless until they had proved their mettle against the Zarthani Knights at the Battle of Phyrax.

Their real value now lay in the east where they

could help shore up his defenses against the Harphaxi. In the Trygath they would be a liability in the broken terrain and matched against the much lighter nomad cavalry.

"That will give Hestophes about seven thousand seasoned troops. Prince Phrames, do you think you can spare any men?"

"Some, Your Majesty. I can send a thousand musketeers and pikemen. But no cavalry, since I need all I have in order to train my recruits. I don't have to tell Your Majesty the shape I found the Beshtan Army in."

Prince Sarrask made a loud hoot. "Half-dead, half-starved, and half-armed. Old Balthames was a choke-purse, he was."

No one bothered to mention that Kalvan had taken the cream of the captured mercenaries—forty acres and a mule for each recruit—into the Royal Army, leaving only those free companions too infirm or too old to fight for Prince Phrames and the other princes. Still, all in all, Phrames had done wonders with the remnants of the old Army of Beshta and had managed to retake a border castle that had renounced fealty during the war with Beshta in the dead of winter.

"We'll leave Queen Rylla"—Kalvan ignored Rylla's grimace as she realized she wasn't going to be invited to the party—"four infantry regiments, including the Hostigos Rifles." That got a smile out of Rylla. "And a regiment of horse. The rest will form the nucleus of the Army of the Trygath."

"That will give us better than eleven thousand men for a start, not including the Royal Artillery," Harmakros said. "Are we going to take any of the field guns?"

"A battery at most," Kalvan answered. "The guns will only slow us down. We are going to be crossing countryside that's a nightmare—everything from ravines to swamps. Mobility is going to be all in this war against the nomads. If I can—and I'm going to try—I'll mount every infantryman in the Army of the

Trygath. We'll be taking the entire Mobile Force, which will give us another five thousand men."

"You're not leaving me with much of anything," Rylla complained.

"That's right. Because you're not going to be needing anything more than glorified garrison troops while I'm gone. I want you to stay right here at Tarr-Hostigos the entire time I'm gone. Unless Prince Lysandros is crazier than a rat in a drainpipe, he's going to be holding firm in Tarr-Harphax. Grand Master Soton is busy stirring up the Sastragath, while Great King Cleitharses of Hos-Ktemnos is back to counting scrolls in the Royal Library. You, my love, are staying here to keep everyone else honest. If it makes you feel better, I'll leave the Army of Hostigos and the Army of Sask here under the command of Prince Sarrask."

Sarrask rose to his feet sputtering, dropping half a cup of dark wine down his robes. "But Your Majesty, I'm not one to set watch over the Royal Nursery—Excuse me, Great Queen Rylla, no offense meant. But I'm a man of plain-spoken words."

Rylla was up and fumbling for her dagger as if she meant to beard Sarrask or cut off his tongue.

"Order, please!" Kalvan shouted. "Prince Sarrask, you are a valiant warrior and one of my best commanders. I would prefer to have you at my side fighting the nomads, but I need someone here I can trust to guard my home and household. I can think of no one better able to protect my throne in my absence." Actually Kalvan could think of half a dozen in a moment, but all of those he needed by his side and those he didn't, like Prince Ptosphes, would take it as a personal slight if he left them home.

Sarrask swelled up like a peacock on display and made a courtly bow. Rylla, who sat at Kalvan's right, turned so that no one else could see the horrible grimace she made at her husband.

"I will ask Prince Pheblon of Noster to support the Army of the Trygath with three thousand of his troops, Prince Balthames of Sashta with another two thousand, three thousand from Nyklos, and I'm sure we can depend upon Ulthor and Kyblos for an additional eight to ten thousand men—since they will be defending their own lands and can call upon their lordly levies."

Harmakros grinned. "That should give us more than thirty thousand men for the Army of the Trygath. Enough teeth to grind the nomads' bones to dust."

Everyone smiled at that thought and there was another chorus of "Down Styphon!" followed by an equally loud one of "Death to All Barbarians!"

"Harmakros and Chartiphon, I want you two to get together with General Baldour and decide which passage we take, the northern Nyklos Road or the Akyros Trail through Sask. Then I want you to go over possible foraging areas, ambush sites, and where to set depots in case we have to make a hasty retreat. Also consider we might want to link up with some of the more civilized kings and princes once we reach the Trygath. Duke Skranga and General Klestreus, I want you both to make a list of every Trygathi king, prince, baron and everything we know about them, from their fighting ability to whether they are pro-Styphoni or anti-Styphoni. I'd like it by tomorrow at the latest."

Skranga nodded and smiled as if he'd just been thrown a tasty morsel. His other intelligence officer, General Klestreus, looked like a fish that had just been hooked.

"Now, one last thing before I let you all get back to work. The Pony Express route we've set up between Hostigos Town and the Army of Observation at Tarr-Lorca has given us a quarter-moon jump in our border communications. I'd like to run a similar route into Ulthor, and possibly Kyblos, so we can obtain adequate intelligence rather than having to depend upon itinerant peddlers and vagabonds. Colonel Kronos, I'd like for you to attend to that. Don't hesitate to pull as many of the experienced riders as you need off the Great King's Highway.

"That's it for now, gentlemen. This meeting is dismissed." Actually, Kalvan would have preferred a working semaphore system to the Pony Express, but he'd decided that building the Great King's Highway was more important.

He didn't have enough trained manpower to do both. By Father Dralm's Beard, he didn't have a tenth the trained manpower to do any of the things he wanted done, but give the new University of Hostigos a few years . . . Then he would not only have good interior communications and roads, but he could start working on some more reliable vehicles, like a Butterworth stagecoach. Anything would be an improvement over the Conestoga-style wagons the Zarthani used for everything from overland transportation to mobile homes.

Note: After road is finished start stagecoach line. With leaf-springs, too!

4

Thunder roared and shook the rooftree of Ranjar Sargos' temporary longhouse. For a few moments it drowned out the squeal of horses and the babble of more tongues than he had heard in all his days. Not since the time of his grandfather twice removed had such a great wave of humanity flooded over the Great River and spilled its way into the Sastragath. Like flotsam tossed by the Great River, Sargos and his tribe had been picked up and pushed into the Lydistros Valley.

Yet, like a flood which replenishes the land it destroys, there was good which came with this river of humanity. Since few of the chiefs knew these lands, they had been forced to rely upon the knowledge of those who did. Ranjar Sargos, having spent four years of his youth as a mercenary in the Trygath, knew more about this land than all but a few of the headmen in this great war band. This, along with Sargos' renown as a warrior, had placed him at the forefront of this human wave.

Now only the constant pressure of the Black Knights gave the wave its form and kept it from dispersing into hundreds of separate war bands. Once that drive was gone the horde would break up and lose its cohesion, whereupon each tribe and clan would be destroyed piecemeal by the Trygathi iron men and their allies. The time had come for a great warlord to guide the horde and Ranjar Sargos knew that this was his destiny—for had not his own vision foretold of such triumphs?

Sargos took several deep breaths, held them, and waited for Thanor's banging on his sky anvil to cease. When the air was still, he spoke again to the assembled Plains headmen and Sastragathi chiefs. "The gods have allowed the Black Knights to take the field. They have allowed the demigod Kalvan of Hostigos to bring his army into the Trygath—"

"Demigod or demon, this Kalvan is no friend to the Trygathi, less so to the Black Knights," Chief Alfgar interrupted. "Let all three of them fight one another, I say. *This* is what the gods intend. Then let us pick the bones of the survivors!"

"Or Nestros and Kalvan swear brotherhood and pick *our* bones," Sargos replied, his voice growing in volume. He had never been even-tempered and knew it. He also knew that since the Tymannes had left their ancestral hunting grounds he had grown even sharper of tongue.

"By Galzar's Mace, this is as the gods will—" Chief Alfgar began.

A wordless muttering stopped him, as Headman Jardar Hyphos once more tried to form words with a jaw yet unhealed from the blow of a Knight's mace. His son held his ear against Hyphos' mouth for a time, then nodded.

"My father says he doubts the gods have willed it that we come so far only to fall to our pride as well as our enemies."

"You yapping puppy! Your father is a man. You are—"

"Silence," Sargos bellowed. He did not know what this would do, except perhaps make all the chiefs angry at him rather than at one another. That could be a gain, if he were able to do something with their attention.

"To be proud is the mark of a warrior, as all here are," he began. "To let everything yield to that pride is the mark of a fool. More than four hands worth of tribes in this great war band have set aside their pride and sworn to follow me. The gods have not punished them. Why should you fare otherwise?"

"Witlings and women," Alfgar muttered just loud

enough that Sargos alone could hear. Sargos decided for the moment to ignore him.

"How many of these tribes are fighting as they please?" Chief Rostino asked. Of all those present, he appeared to have the most Ruthani blood as well as the most dignity.

Sargos chose an equally dignified answer. "I am not a Great King, with a host of armed slaves to punish disobedient warriors as if they were children. I am chief over the Tymannes, and those who swear to follow me as Warlord do so by choice."

"Then it is my choice," Chief Alfgar said, "not to swear any oaths to Ranjar Sargos or any other sachem or chieftan. We of the Sea of Grass have fought each chief his own master since the Great Mountains rose from the earth. Maybe the dirt scrapers and log builders of the Sastragath are more accustomed to following at the heels of their masters like curs!" Alfgar slammed his fist against his bone vest, making a sound like that of a gunshot.

The hands of about half the chieftans in the longhouse streaked for their knives, the only weapons allowed inside during the parlay.

Sargos signaled for attention. "This is not the time to hurl baseless insults nor fight among each other. There is great booty to be won and much glory to be gained in fighting our real enemies."

Most of the chiefs sat back down and nodded their agreement to this sage advice.

But Hyphos' son stood his ground. "You have not fought Kalvan, Alfgar. We have fought others like him and know that to win we must stand as one, like wolves not dogs."

"Nor have you," Alfgar replied, his face twisted into an angry leer. "What has Sargos given you, that you take his word about Kalvan?"

Hyphos' son would have drawn his knife if his father's arm had not been sounder than his jaw—a bronzed arm gripped the young man's wrist and twisted. He gasped and dropped his knife.

"See! How the Sastragathi lick their master's hand.

When Sargos nods his head, the old rein in the young. This is not the way of the plains!"

Rage flowed into Sargos, lifting him like a giant's hands—or perhaps the hands of the gods. Certainly he had never felt their presence more strongly, even in the steamhouse of his manhood rites.

"Let us submit this matter to the judgment of the gods." Sargos drew from the hides of his chieftan's chair the sacred ax of the chiefs of the Tymannes. "With this ax and no other weapon I will fight Chief Alfgar, this day, in this place. He may use any weapon his honor allows him."

"No!" Chief Ulldar exclaimed. Next to Sargos, Ulldar Zodan was the wisest man in the room in the new ways of warfare. Two of his sons had served Chief Harmakros in Kalvan's wars and told him much. They had also brought him a tooled and engraved horsepistol that was the envy of every chief in the longhouse. "The gods have taken away Alfgar's wits. What if they have taken away his honor as well?"

Several of Alfgar's fellow chiefs had to restrain him from trying to kill Ulldar with his bare hands. When the uproar had subsided, Alfgar had found his voice again. "I will fight with the hand spear against your ax, godless son-of-a-bitch who weaned you on stinkcat piss!"

"Let it be done, then," Sargos commanded. His rage was already fading, and in its place were doubts that he was really in the hands of the gods after all. If he fell—and Alfgar promised to be a formidable foe—his son would do well to see the Tymannes great longhouse again.

Why not be hopeful? he thought. *If you win, it will prove the gods' favor, and your own prowess as well. Then all the chiefs and clan headmen assembled here will proclaim you Warlord, and those lesser chiefs who were not here will quickly follow. Cast the bones and let the fates see to where they fall. By Galzar's mace and Thanor's Hammer!*

Sargos led the chiefs and headmen out to the square in the middle of the chiefs' longhouses. The rain was still falling and what had already fallen made the square a sea of foul-smelling mud. Sargos judged this would be to his advantage: Alfgar could seldom have fought on foot, on a slope, in mud up to his ankles.

So it went for a half-score of passes. Sargos quickly realized he had but one advantage. Alfgar was so confident of his greater youth and strength that he was careless of what fighting in mud would do to them. If the time ever came when Alfgar could not dance away in time—

As if to warn Sargos against hopefulness, on the next exchange Alfgar drew first blood. It was barely more than a thorn prick and on Sargos' left arm, but it held an arrogant message: "I can do this at will. The next time, who knows where my spear will land?"

Both men's friends were shouting threats and promises. If Alfgar won, there would be a permanent broach between the plains and Sastragath chiefs. At first blood, all fell silent and remained so.

Sargos said nothing at all. He had better uses for his breath.

In time the rain stopped. Both men now bled in a hand of places, though nowhere seriously. Sargos began to wonder if he would have breath for any use at all before long. Beyond any doubt Alfgar was spending his strength freely. But he'd had rather more to begin with. The mud, it seemed, might not be the gods' way of saving Ranjar Sargos.

Alfgar made a thrust that would have disembow-eled him had he not jumped in time, slipping in the mud. Sargos had to use all his arts in war while he still had the strength and speed to use them.

Silently he prayed to the gods: *Guard my Folk and my son. Send them wisdom and courage, if there is justice in you. But if you sent Kalvan to be as a wolf to the flocks, then you are not the gods and my spirit will tell my son to worship something else!*

"Pray for an honorable home for your spirit, old man," Alfgar said with a sneer. "It will soon need one."

Then he sprang forward so fast that if Sargos had

not been prepared, both in mind and body, for the final grapple he would have been doomed. As it was he had already begun to turn, presenting his left thigh when Alfgar closed.

Offered a target, Alfgar thrust hard with his spear, forgetting that his target was mostly bone. As the spear point grated on that bone, Sargos' long arms whirled. His left gripped the spear, jerking it from Alfgar's hand.

His right arm brought the ax down hard on Alfgar's knife hand, as it leaped toward Sargos' groin. For an instant the gods might have turned both men into stone. Then the knife splashed into the mud.

The spear whirled in Sargos' hand, then seemed to sprout a red bloom in Alfgar's belly. The knowledge of what had happened was just dawning in his eyes when Sargos' ax came down on his head.

"The gods have spoken," Sargos cried. He hoped if more needed to be said, the gods would say it themselves. Neither Sargos' wits nor his wind seemed to be fit for the task, and as for his legs, he prayed they would not tumble him into the mud beside his foe.

Ranjar, son of Cedrak, you are too old for this and so you will learn the next time you confuse the voice of the gods with the memories of your own youth.

Egthar and Pydox, chiefs of his own clan, ran forward to aid him. "Stop treating me as if this was my first wound! It's more like my tenth, and one of the least." In truth it would need some care, and he would be riding more than walking in the coming battles. But only the flesh hurt.

Meanwhile the crowd around him had grown and was beginning to chant, "Sargos! Sargos! Warlord Sargos!" He wasn't sure if his own men had begun the chant or if it was a spontaneous outburst; regardless, he knew how to grasp the moment and squeeze it with both hands. He stepped back and raised his arms.

Together, Headman Jardar Hyphos and his son stepped forward and lifted Alfgar's motionless body.

Behind them came Chief Rostino. He knelt before Sargos and pressed his forehead against Sargos' hands.

"The gods have truly spoken. What do they wish that we swear to you?"

Had it been a Sastragathi chieftan making this pronouncement rather than a plainsman, there might have been jeers and catcalls—as it was there was naught but silence.

"They ask little," Sargos said. He took several deep breaths and found that he could hope to speak instead of gasp. *At least, I will ask little. The gods will not help a man who asks more than those who follow him are willing to give.*

"Little indeed," Sargos repeated. "Only that you follow me in war and peace, save when I ask for war against blood-brothers or peace with blood-enemies. And that you bind yourselves by this oath until I release you or death take you."

"I swear—" Chief Rostino began, but Sargos stopped him. "Rise, I will have no brave warriors swearing anything to me on their knees. That is more pride than the gods allow."

There was a boisterous round of oath-taking as all the assembled chiefs who had not already done so swore their allegiance to Ranjar Sargos as Warlord.

After all the oaths had been given, Sargos said, "Let us take a visit to the bathhouse, and heat us some beer. Or there is wine if any of you wish it."

Sargos could not tell what drew more enthusiasm, the gods' judgment, the baths, or the prospect of a good drinking party.

5

"Present—aaarrrmmmss!"

Forty bayoneted muskets snapped into position across forty Hostigi breastplates. A hundred sabers leaped to the vertical. Even in the watery spring sunlight, the reflection from all the steel made Kalvan blink.

The herald of Nestros, King of Rathon and self-proclaimed High King of the Trygath, rode forward. His mounted escort rode up on either side, fifty big men on beer-wagon-sized horses. By the customs of the Trygath, heralds went guarded until they were actually in the presence of the men they were sent to parlay with. Also by custom, the horsemen rode with their visors up and their swords held upright by the blades, as proof of peaceful intent.

Kalvan studied the guards as they rode up the slope toward him. They reminded him more than a little of the late—R.I.P.—Harphaxi Royal Lancers, swathed head to toe in armor about as useful as cheesecloth in keeping out a musket bullet or a piece of case shot.

Except that this was the Trygath, a frontier area where in nine years out of ten the only fireseed available was what neighboring Eastern Princes were willing to sell illegally, risking both shortages and Styphon's Ban. Against other armored men-at-arms or lightly armored nomads, riding around looking like a blacksmith's version of a lobster made a certain amount of sense.

This had already begun to change, with the

emerging trade of Hostigos fireseed for horses, ale, and furs. It was about to change even more, but not quickly or easily. Military technology was generally about as slow to change as priestly ritual. So for now, the Trygathi iron men had a few remaining days in the sun.

The herald signaled; the Rathoni guardsmen reined in, leaving him to mount the slope alone. At a nod from Captain-General Harmakros, Aspasthar rode out, his first sword reversed in his hand and the sun shining on his first suit of armor.

"Who has come to the host of the Great King Kalvan of Hos-Hostigos?" Aspasthar's voice was high-pitched but steady.

"Baron Thestros of Rathon, herald and envoy of High King Nestros." The herald took another look at the Royal Page. "Does the Great King lack men, that he has me greeted by a beardless boy?"

"Had he thought you saw wisdom in a beard, my lord, the Great King would have sent you a he-goat!"

In the ensuing silence, Kalvan and Harmakros exchanged eloquent looks. Kalvan's said, *If the boy's tongue has run away with him and we have a fight, he is going to get the flat of my saber across his arse.*

Harmakros' reply was, *Don't worry. The boy knows what he is doing.*

The herald was the first to break the silence, with a roar of laughter. Seeing themselves given permission, the Rathoni Royal Guard also broke into laughter. Then everyone was hooting and guffawing, and Harmakros was riding forward to clap Aspasthar on the shoulder so hard the boy nearly fell out of his saddle.

At last silence returned, except for the distant rumble of thunder. Baron Thestros wiped his face with a yellow-gloved hand.

"Well-spoken, lad. You do honor to your sire, your King, and your realm. But I think there must be a person of more rank than you in a host as large as this. Might I seek the honor of speech with he who holds the most rank among you? Captain-General Harmakros, I believe?"

Harmakros nodded. "At your service. But I am not the highest among those present." He turned in the saddle. "Your Majesty?"

Kalvan urged his horse forward, letting his cloak flow back from his shoulders. The herald did a good imitation of a man whose eyes are about to pop from his head. Then he swung himself swiftly, if not gracefully, from the saddle and went down on one knee.

"Your Majesty! In the name of High King Nestros, greetings!"

"Surely you have more than greetings to bring, Baron Thestros, since you have four thousand cavalry at your summons. Your King has a name for wisdom, and would not send such a host with a message a beardless boy could bring."

The imitation of eye-popping was even better this time. Kalvan let it go on until he was sure the herald needed reassurance.

"No. I have no demonic arts, only good scouts. They saw your men two days ago and rode swiftly to bring word to me. I came up to the van, so that there might be no misunderstandings about why the men of Hos-Hostigos and its allies have come to the Trygath."

"I believe Your Majesty. But then, pray tell me what *is* the reason for such a host being upon the domain of High King Nestros? He wishes peace with all who wish it with him, but those who wish peace seldom come with twenty thousand armed retainers!"

"Your scouts are not inferior to mine," Kalvan said with a grin. That was a remarkably accurate count of the Hostigi who'd crossed into the Trygath. Another ten to twelve thousand were strung out all the way across Kyblos, ready to either join the main body or cover its withdrawal. Kalvan had hoped for a larger levy from Kyblos, but many of the southern barons had not responded to Prince Kestophes' requests for men and probably wouldn't at anything less than sword point.

"I thank Your Majesty. But—forgive me for being inopportune, but I have only the cause of peace at heart. I ask once more, why are you in my King's realm?"

To call the Trygath King Nestros' realm was more than just an exaggeration, thought Kalvan, since Nestros' sovereignty was only recognized by four of the Trygath's nine legitimate kings and princes. Two of whom, in fact, Ragnar and Thul, were subjects of King Theovacar of Grefftscharr. Diplomacy, however, was the order of the day. "We do not come in search of peace."

Kalvan would have sworn he heard the thud of the baron's jaw hitting the ground. Quickly he added, "We have come to wage war on the nomads, enemies common to all of us."

The herald shook his head. "High King Nestros has taken counsel with his princes and kings, and he has devised ways of meeting the nomad host. It insults him to think that he must wait upon an Eastern realm for the defense of his own."

"I am sure the true gods fight for your King, and his princes and people likewise. Yet is it not true that the nomad horde counts more fighting men than the Trygath and the Great Kingdom of Hos-Hostigos combined?" Three times, if the estimate of a hundred and fifty thousand on the way northeast was correct.

"It is also true that during the last moon riders of the horde reached the Lower Saltless Sea, sowing death with every step their horses took. They did not return, but would it not have been better that they not even start?"

Kalvan wanted to meet the local magnate who'd caught the raiders on their way back from the shores of Lake Erie. King Crython of Ragnar had outthought as well as outfought the nomad raiders. By all reports that kind of ruler would make almost as good an ally as King Nestros. But it was King Nestros who controlled the back entrance to Hos-Hostigos, not King Crython.

"Indeed," the herald said, "and no such raids will come again."

"Is this certain? Certainly they will cease after the valiant men-at-arms and footmen of King Nestros have broken the strength of the horde. But Nestros will do this only if he gathers all his strength under his own hand. Then who will be left to defend the lands of those who march against the horde, against raiders and outlaws? Or those nomads who break away from the main body?"

Kalvan had pitched his voice loud enough to be heard by the Royal Guardsmen. All of them would be nobles or sons of nobles; all must share the fear of what would happen to their lands at the hands of nomad outriders and bandits. None of them dared think of the consequences of a nomad victory over their King.

"Your Majesty, do you swear you can prevent this if King Nestros and you become friends?"

"We are not enemies even now, nor shall we be. What you mean is, if we become *allies*. I only say this: If we become allies, there will be thirty thousand Hostigi to strengthen your King."

"And if there is no alliance, there will be thirty thousand fewer?"

"The host of the Great King of Hos-Hostigos will fight the horde wherever we find it. But is it not better that we fight it together? Sticks separated are easily broken. Tied into a bundle, they defy the strength of a giant."

"Your Majesty speaks eloquently. I think, perhaps, it would be wiser if you spoke thus to High King Nestros."

"Nothing would give me more pleasure, if I knew where to find your High King."

"Let Your Majesty ride to Rathon City, and I believe he will find no obstacles in his path."

Rathon City was the here-and-now equivalent of Akron, Ohio. About fifty miles away—two days' easy riding.

"The High King will see me in Rathon City before the horde can wreak any more harm upon his vassals. Now, I see that the sky promises rain. Would you and your guard commander care to accept the hospitality of my tent, which I believe is closer than your own?"

The herald and his guard commander exchanged

looks, then the herald nodded. "We are honored by Your Majesty's hospitality."

"Call it the first repayment of the hospitality we have received from Nestros' subjects." The herald frowned, and still looked puzzled as he led his guards off behind Aspasthar.

When the Trygathi commanders were safely on their way, Harmakros rode close to Kalvan. "Your Majesty, far be it from me to tell you how to guide the realm—"

"If you ever stop telling me, Harmakros, I'll find another Captain-General. Out with it. I don't want to get caught in the rain if I can help it. A fine spectacle for our allies, me leading a charge with sword in one hand and handkerchief in the other!"

Harmakros quickly ordered the First Royal Horse Guard into a wide circle, then put them in movement toward the tent. Riding practically boot to boot with Kalvan, he grinned.

"Your Majesty is as silver-tongued as any bard, but is this the time to be so truthful about what we want?"

"It is the best time. Any earlier would have given the Union of Styphon's Friends or the League of Dralm time to make noises. Not to mention letting the Zarthani Knights send scouts on to our line of march, and maybe more than scouts. Four thousand Trygathi could give us enough trouble. Think about four thousand Knights."

"I'd rather think about more pleasant things."

"Like that blonde at Mnebros Town?"

Harmakros flushed. "I didn't know Your Majesty noticed."

"Just because *I* slept alone doesn't mean I don't know the officers who didn't." They were silent for a moment, guiding their horses over a rough patch of ground.

"It's Mnebros Town that made me think the time was ripe to tell the truth. Those people were so Dralm-damned *glad* to see us, it was almost pathetic. We could have had anything we asked for, not just wine, women, and banquets. They were *scared* of that horde!

"What the Styphon! A horde that size scares *me!*
But our lands are farther than they're likely to reach.
Around here, nobody knows if they'll have a roof
over their heads and all their family alive come winter. Nestros will do his best, but if that isn't good
enough . . ."

"If that isn't good enough, the princes and barons
will start looking around for someone whose best
might be good enough. Which might not be so good
for us."

"Exactly, Harmakros." The gray sky was overhead
now, and to the northwest was turning black. The
royal pavillion was in sight ahead, and the herald's
party was just turning into it.

"The Trygathi nobles here," Kalvan continued,
"have always had more independence than the ones
in the east, at least since fireseed came along. Things
aren't as settled here and a good castle gives you
more bargaining power when the only way to take it
is starving it out. Nestros will be down to Prince of
Rathon if he lets too many of his nobles' lands be
overrun.

"An alliance with us is really a gift from the gods,
which Nestros will see unless he is a greater fool
than I can believe. An alliance with us would allow
him to send home, to defend their homes, all the
second-line troops he probably can't feed anyway.
We will put our men into line with his, and he'll
have twice as big an army as he would otherwise.
And a better one to boot! Nestros will keep the
loyalty of his barons, defeat the horde, and have his
title recognized all at once. How could any man—?"

At the word "resist," the skies split apart in a
thunderclap that made the horses jump. As the thunder rumbled into silence, the hiss of rain took its
place. A few drops spattered across Kalvan's hands, a
few more across his face, then the deluge struck.

He reined his horse to a walk and sneezed as
drops found their way up his nose. So much for
Royal dignity.

6

None of the forts and towns Kalvan had encountered in the Trygath had prepared Kalvan for the sight of Rathon City. Unlike the wooden stockades of most Trygathi towns, Rathon City was encircled by immense stone walls—about the size of the Great Wall of China—which dwarfed the out-buildings and storehouses that had sprung up at their base. Not even the great Eastern capitals had such massive stone bulwarks, but then they were not subject to periodic invasions and large-scale migrations.

The Great Gate was large too, wide enough that four of the Conestoga-style wagons could pass abreast. Most of the inner city's two-and three-story buildings were of the usual beam and plaster construction. At the center of the city were a score of large public buildings constructed of stone, half of which appeared to have been constructed during the past decade.

Kalvan guesstimated the population at about seventy-five thousand; smaller than a comparable Eastern Kingdom capital, but very impressive for a so-called "barbarian" kingdom. Most of the people he saw in the streets wore homespun trousers and shirts, although there was a goodly number of hunters and trappers in furs and buckskins. The men, with a few exceptions, wore full beards, rather than the trimmed beards and goatees worn in the Eastern Kingdoms.

Kalvan suspected that being in Rathon City was like visiting one of the Eastern capitals three hundred years ago.

At the center of the city was a great plaza, cover-

ing about two city blocks. Surrounded by a great
garden stood Nestros' palace, a magnificent building
that made Kalvan's own "palace" (actually Prince
Ptosphes' summer palace) look like a poor relation's
summer home. When this Great Murthering War
with Styphon's House was over, Kalvan was going to
have to build himself a palace more suitable to his
rank—maybe something along the lines of Louis XIV's
Palace of Versailles—or he was going to have problems maintaining the respect of despots like Nestros.

Half a dozen richly dressed ambassadors came to
meet the Hostigi party at the garden gates. Kalvan
noticed that all of Nestros' retainers had their beards
cut and trimmed in the Eastern fashion. To either
side of the road leading to Nestros' palace stood the
King's Guard, all over six foot, with finely engraved
ceremonial halberds and black and gold armor.

Inside the palace Nestros himself looked every
inch the warrior King, from his bright, inquisitive
eyes to his big callused hands. He had the ruddy
complexion of an outdoorsman with a face that was
dignified if not handsome. He and Kalvan locked
eyes and neither turned away until they both did in
unspoken unison.

"Welcome, Great King Kalvan, to our humble
abode. Can I offer you some refreshments? Ale or
winter wine, perhaps?"

"Winter wine would be nice," Kalvan responded.
It took at least two goblets to complete the usual
diplomatic niceties. Before starting on his third, Kalvan
said, "As I told your herald, we come in peace. I
would like to aid you in your war against the nomads."

"If this be true, then fine. Yet, I have to wonder
what brings a distant King to our land. Truly in all
our history we have found that the Eastern Kingdoms care little about our wars and struggles. Why
should this suddenly change now?"

"There are great changes afoot during these peril-
ous times."

"Change may be new to you in the Eastern Kingdoms, but here it is constant like the seasons."

"Not in all things. Since when have the Zarthani

Knights driven nomads into your lands, instead of chasing them back across the Great River?"

Nestros' forehead furrowed as he tried to puzzle out an answer. "Are you trying to say that the Knights are using the nomads as a cat's paw against Hos-Hostigos?"

Kalvan was impressed with Nestros' instinctive grasp of *Realpolitik*. "Yes, that is exactly what Grand Master Soton hopes to accomplish. And since your lands are in the middle they are going to take the brunt of the bloodletting."

There was a harsh noise as Nestros ground his teeth.

"The Grand Master may well think we are but tools to be used, but we have prepared ourselves well for this invasion. I need neither his Knights nor your help to keep my lands."

"How do you plan to keep the nomads away? They are now less than two days' ride from Rathon City itself."

"We are well provisioned here and our great walls will keep out ten times their number. All farms and gardens within a day's march of the city will be burned to the ground. All villagers and peasants will come to the City. There are royal storehouses in every large town in Rathon, Mybranos, Cyros, and Kythax. We shall feed our own while the nomads starve like wolves in the midst of winter famine. When they have grown hungry and weak, my men-at-arms will till the soil with their bones."

"That may be a good plan for normal times, but not now. You have never fought a horde as large as this one. I doubt there is a town or city in all Rathon, except for this City, which can hold back the nomad flood. But, say that you are right, and the walls of your towns and cities keep the nomads at bay. What then? In their anger they will poison your wells, burn your villages, and sow your fields with salt in retribution. What will your people have to return to then? And what will your nobles have to say about a High King who saves lives by hiding behind walls so they can starve when the wolves have fled?"

Nestros' face turned bright red and for a moment Kalvan feared he had gone too far.

"Arrrgh! As bad as they taste, there is truth in your words. The nomads are as numerous as the great herds of bison on the Sea of Grass whose numbers stretch from horizon to horizon. It is enough to make one believe in the old legends. What help do you offer?"

"My plan is simple. We join both our armies and drive the nomads back south as the Knights have driven them north. Let the nomads find *our* steel even less to their liking than that of the Zarthani Knights."

Nestros' eyes brightened at the idea of a direct attack. "Will we have enough swords even united to drive such a great horde?"

Not if we were facing the Huns or Mongols of Otherwhen, thought Kalvan. *But these nomads have fewer horse archers and fight more in the manner of Caesar's Gauls or Hadrian's Britons. And they lack a great khan like Atilla or Genghis Khan.*

"In a way their great number is to our advantage, King Nestros. With so many warriors they are pressed to fight like heavy infantry, yet wear little armor and make massed targets for our muskets and arquebuses. Also, they have many leaders instead of one chief."

"No longer, King Kalvan. We have just learned that the nomads have elected a Warlord, a Sastragathi chief named Ranjar Sargos. He is a former Cyrosi mercenary and knows our way of warfare."

"He may know Trygathi strategy, but I doubt he's ever faced a regiment of musketeers. Also, as a new leader his hold will be uncertain, and we must exploit it by moving quickly. How soon can you muster your troops?"

"Most of my army is within a day's ride of Rathon City where there are enough victuals to feed them. However, before we clasp palms on this alliance, I have a request I'd like to make."

Suddenly Kalvan feared for his good sword and his richly-chased breastplate. In another incarnation,

Nestros must have been a horsetrader like Duke Skranga. "What can I do for you?"

"I would like to change my title to Great King and claim my lands a Great Kingdom, as you have done in Hos-Hostigos. Will you recognize my claim?"

This looks too easy! There's a catch in here somewhere. If he recognized Nestros as Great King of the Trygath, it might legitimize him in the eyes of his own people, but it wouldn't mean twiddle-dee to the other Five Great Kings—none of whom had yet recognized Kalvan as Great King. Furthermore, Nestros claimed sovereignty over several princedoms that were within Grefftscharri borders. Kalvan didn't need to start another war in the west with King Theovacar just because he needed to placate Nestros now.

However, if Kalvan worked this right he could bind Nestros to Hos-Hostigos and possibly bring him into the war against Styphon's House.

"King Nestros, I will recognize you as Great King of all those princedoms and kingdoms who agree to be a part of your new Great Kingdom and who are not already under the sovereignty of King Theovacar."

From the furrowed brow on Nestros' face Kalvan knew he had safely navigated one minefield, but if he estimated Nestros correctly this would not be the last, nor the most dangerous.

"I welcome Your Majesty's support of the new Great Kingdom of Hos-Rathon. I only pray you will be equally swift in helping us to modernize our army."

This request was going to be easy to fill since Kalvan still had half the ordnance of Hos-Harphax at his disposal after last year's war—much of it dropped without even being fired. Not that he would ever let Nestros know that.

"Great King Nestros, when our armies have defeated the nomads, I will have two thousand arquebuses and five hundred muskets delivered to Hos-Rathon to finalize the alliance between our two Kingdoms. I will also send five tons of Hostigos fireseed and will train two score of apprentices in its manufacturing and curing at our new University."

This must have struck Nestros as more than satisfactory as he jumped out of his throne to give Kalvan a bear-hug that all but crushed Kalvan's ribcage.

"Truly, Great King Kalvan, you are as generous as you are wise and a master of the art of war. But enough of this, we will have plenty of time to share ale and wine when the nomads have been vanquished. Now we must plan our campaign. I have ten thousand troops billeted in and around Rathon City and two times ten thousand within a two days' ride. And another ten thousand within a five days' ride."

"Excellent. Send riders out to gather all those within a two days' march. Meanwhile, we can gather provisions and prepare our troops for the battle ahead."

Nestros rubbed his big hands together. "You speak my language, Great King Kalvan. The time has come to teach the nomads that it is safer in Regwarn, the Caverns of the Dead, than it is here."

7

Great King Kalvan dismounted at the top of Gyrax
Hill. While his dignity might require meeting King
Nestros on horseback, his horse required a rest. The
retreat of the Hostigi royal party from the left flank
had been more speedy than dignified, over rough,
muddy ground. A few of the Royal Horse Guard
were still fishing themselves out from under bushes
and rounding up their horses.

From the hilltop, Kalvan had his first good view of
the battle in more than an hour. The nomad horde
was large, maybe seventy-five to a hundred thousand
warriors, a flood of men as hard for Ranjar Sargos to
direct as for Kalvan to stop. Not much had changed,
and that little for the better. The enemy's right and
center, under Sargos, still overlapped the allied left.
They had even advanced all the way to the redoubt
on the banks of the Lydistros, then stopped among
the caltrops and pitfalls, under the fire of the one
four-pounder Kalvan could spare for fixed defenses.

As far as Kalvan was concerned, Sargos could take
his men halfway to the border.

On the allied right, masses of horsemen, light
infantry (the only kind the horde had), and an occasional chariot surged back and forth. Each chief was
giving his own orders to his followers and taking
none from anyone else, including Sargos. They were
the less dangerous but more numerous part of the
enemy army, fifty thousand against Sargos' forty thousand, give or take a few boys.

They faced mostly Nestros' Trygathi, eight or nine

thousand heavy horse, with twice that number of supporting infantry, spearmen, gallowglasses, and missile troops: crossbowmen, archers, and some arquebusiers. They were stiffened by three Ulthori pike regiments, two regiments of Royal Musketeers, a battalion of riflemen, and two four-pounders. Not that the Trygathi needed much stiffening; they were fighting with the knowledge that they had a chance of victory and that meanwhile their homes were safe. The alliance with Hostigos had let Nestros leave a third of his army home to make raiders a poor insurance risk. The twenty-five thousand he had on the field were his best.

"Alkides," Kalvan called downhill. "Is the Flying Battery ready to move?"

"With Galzar's favor, yes," the smoke-blackened artillery general replied. "I wish the guns really did have wings. This cursed mud's going to butcher the horses!"

"Not half as fast as the guns will butcher Sargos' warriors," Kalvan called back. The gun crews cheered their Great King's words. There were only eight guns for the Flying Battery; three were in emplacements and one had been lost in a swamp on the Nyklos Trail. As much as he wished for another battery or two, with maybe some six-or eight-pounders, the Flying Battery was a far cry from the half-a-dozen catapults the enemy was using.

Kalvan walked over to General Alkides and asked quietly, "How is Great Captain Mylissos doing?" Nestros' chief of artillery had started the day a bit peevish over the council of war. It had been agreed that his ancient bombards would remain with the reserves, and not try to advance with the major attacks. Kalvan could even sympathize with him; after all, it was the first time in memory Mylissos actually had enough fireseed to fire his massive hooped-iron pipes more than once or twice without exhausting his magazines.

"A sight happier than he was, now that he's got targets and fireseed to burn on them. I think he shifted a couple of those twenty-pounders without orders, but I'm not complaining. A twenty-pounder loaded with rocks and old nails isn't something I would care to face!"

Kalvan would have said more, mostly to Aspasthar. The boy was fighting his first battle away from his father, riding with Alkides as one of his messengers. But the boy looked as if he would take the encouragement as an insult, and by Dralm, there were Nestros and his guards in their red and white colors coming up the other side of the hill!

By abandoning royal dignity and running back to his horse, Kalvan was mounted by the time Nestros reined in and hailed him.

"Greetings, friend and ally! We are smiting the horde as if the gods themselves fought for us!"

So we are. Maybe too hard. Corpses can't fight the Zarthani Knights. Thank somebody for Ranjar Sargos. He made the horde more dangerous, but if we had to take the surrender of every petty chief one at a time we'd be here until winter!

A Hostigi messenger rode up and saluted both kings. "The lookouts in the Willow Spirit Grove report that Warlord Sargos is advancing on them."

"Tell them to wait as long as they can, and imitate a strong force meanwhile," Nestros said. "Then they can withdraw. Meanwhile, Sargos will be drawn forward. Perhaps we can meet him hand-to-hand!"

Kalvan and Captain-General Harmakros exchanged amused looks. Nestros was no fool; he was learning such Kalvan-style tricks as feints and deceptions almost hourly. He was also an old-style Trygathi warrior, whose highest ambition had to be meeting the opposing leader hand-to-hand and defeating him.

"As the gods will it," Harmakros said. Kalvan decided to let his Captain-General speak, even if protocol said he should be talking King-to-King. Even four-star generals needed something to take their minds off their sons' winning their spurs—or their shrouds.

"The gods willed that Sargos should be a fool," Nestros said cheerfully. "They also willed that Kalvan should come and bring his fireseed and strength to join ours. I think they will give us this one more small favor."

Kalvan doubted the accuracy of Nestros' description of his opponent. The Warlord had pulled his chariots back the moment he realized the ground was too muddy to let them get up speed. He still had his in reserve, while the other chiefs had mostly lost chariots, riders, and teams together.

"Let the gods will that all our men hold their fire until they have a clear target, and that be an enemy," Kalvan said. "We have more fireseed than any army ever seen in the Trygath, but not yet enough to waste!"

"My men are not children," Nestros said with offended dignity.

"Then let the heralds sound for the advance," Kalvan said. Both kings looked at Harmakros; he signaled the trumpeter. The brazen voice sounded, was picked up and relayed, triggering the launching of two signal rockets.

When the green rockets rose into the sky over Gyrax Hill, six thousand reserve cavalry would be launched at the heart of Sargos' army.

Sargos flung a light lance high into the willow branches. A scream rewarded him; an enemy lookout toppled from his perch and lay writhing until an archer dispatched him with a knife.

The heavy thud of many horses on the move reached the Warlord over the noise of his warriors clearing the willow grove of enemies. Sargos jerked his horse around and drew his last lance from its leather bucket next to his right stirrup. His tribal guards followed suit, and the whole band streamed at a canter around the left side of the grove.

Ah, would that I had men to be my eyes and ears on parts of the field I cannot reach myself! Such is Kalvan's way, or so the prisoners have told us. Yet how could they reach me, in the midst of my foes, to bear their messages? To remain in the rear merely so that I may know more—that is a coward's way and no warrior would follow me.

A contrary voice in Sargos' mind muttered, *Kalvan leads that way, as often as not, and who says that those who follow him are not warriors? Enough of yours are with the spirits after meeting them!*

Clear of the willows, Sargos reined in and stared in disbelief. Down the hill in the enemy's center moved two mighty bands of armored horsemen, like vast steel-scaled serpents. At the head of each band floated banners, the red and white colors of King Nestros and the red and blue of King Kalvan.

So Kalvan will take his chance of joining the spirits today? Well and good.

Warlord Ranjar Sargos stood tall in his stirrups. "Meet them at that hedge. Cydrak and Trancyles, ride like the wind and bring all the warriors Chiefs Hyphos and Ruflos can spare!"

The two were young men on fresh horses; they vanished in a spray of clods. Sargos drew his sword and adjusted his throat guard, his one piece of armor that was metal all through instead of metal over leather.

The sword hummed over his head as he whirled it. The day was too overcast for sunlight to shine on it, but those close by saw it and heard it humming. Their shouts told others what was happening, and the war cries rose until they seemed a solid wall across the front of the advancing foe.

Then Sargos lowered his sword and spurred his horse toward the hedge.

Only one of the green rockets flew high enough to be seen. That was enough. The cheers from both armies drowned out the trumpeters and captains like a hurricane drowning out a mouse's squeak.

Nestros was pointing frantically downhill. "There! Behind that hedge. Sargos forms his battle line. We must reach it before he brings up reinforcements."

Nestros couldn't have been in more of a hurry if he'd read Napoleon's maxim, "Ask me for anything but time." Once again he was doing the tactically sound things, out of a desire to cross swords with an enemy chief.

On his head be it.

No, wait a minute. If Nestros gets too far ahead of you, the Trygathi will say their Great King was braver than the Great King of Hos-Hostigos.

"Harmakros!" What would have been a shout under other circumstances was about as audible as a whisper.

The Captain-General reined in beside Kalvan. "Yes, Your Majesty?"

"You stay back here with the mobile command post. I have to charge with Nestros."

"That—" began Harmakros, who apparently thought better of using his trooper's vocabulary about an allied King, then mock-saluted. "As Your Majesty wishes."

Kalvan started to count off guards to ride with him, then saw Nestros and his heavies digging in their own spurs. This time Kalvan had to restrain his curses. Instead he signaled his own bannerbearer and dug in his spurs.

The bannerbearer took the reins in his teeth and drew his sword. Bearing the Great King's banner had been a much safer job than fighting in the front ranks—at least until today!

Sargos jumped his horse over a ditch and turned it, meanwhile drawing his last lance. To retreat was cowardly more often than not, but to stand with the men he had would not even slow the enemy. Like the Great River flooding, the enemy horse flowed on as if only the gods could stop them.

Archers were running up, but the range was still long. Against armored men they would waste most of their arrows. Against the enemy's horses, perhaps—

"Look, my chief!" Chief Ruflos was pointing. He had just arrived with a hundred and fifty men not six deep breaths ago. "My chief, the Kings offer themselves to the gods!"

It was true. The two royal banners were forging steadily toward the head of the enemy horsemen. Under those banners, Sargos could now see tight bands of splendidly-armored men.

"They offer themselves to us!" Sargos snapped. He tried to quiet his own doubts. *Have the Kings had an omen, that the gods will give victory if they offer themselves as a sacrifice?*

"Then let us take what is offered," Chief Ruflos said. He also sounded as if he wished to quiet inward fears.

Sargos patted his horse's neck and looked about him. The warriors he'd summoned were streaming toward him from all sides. Not all would be with him before he had to face the Kings, but the rest would know enough to fling themselves upon the foe.

"Hoaa! Tonight we offer two Kings' heads, to the gods of our land and the spirits of our dead!"

8

The advance of the Kings was turning into a race.
Nestros reached the hedge first. Kalvan swerved without slowing, nearly colliding with his bannerbearer.
The trooper's sword pricked Kalvan's horse, who
protested by nearly bucking his rider into a ditch.

By the time Kalvan had sorted himself out, Nestros
was crossing swords with everyone in reach on the
far side of the hedge. Nestros had won the race but
not by enough to dishonor his ally.

In fact, his ally was going to have a busy time in
about two minutes, keeping this from being Nestros'
first and last battle as Great-King-Elect. On both
right and left, warriors were streaming toward the
battle of the leaders.

"Stands the standard of Great King Kalvan!" the
bannerbearer shouted. He thrust the butt end of the
staff into the muddy ground and drew a pistol. The
bannerbearer pistoled the first warrior to come within
lance-range, but the nomad stayed in the saddle.
Kalvan shot him with his last loaded horsepistol,
then drew his own sword and cut a second opponent
across the face, a third in the arm.

After that Kalvan lost count of his opponents and
all track of what he was doing to them. Somewhere
in the next five minutes he managed one coherent
thought that was not concerned with his own survival.

*If I was fighting armored opponents, I'd be dead
by now.*

Then about five minutes after that, it struck him
that armor might not make all that much difference.

287

These nomads were damned hard to kill, like the Moro *juramentados* he had heard an Old Army veteran describe. *Come on, Alkides! Are you the Flying Battery or the Flighty Battery?*

A moment later, Alkides' octet of four-pounders signaled their arrival with a blast of case shot that tore into the ranks of friends and foe with awful impartiality. A chunk of lead snapped the banner staff; the bannerbearer dove to keep it from hitting the ground and sprawled with his nose digging up the mud. He held the banner clear of the ground, though.

Kalvan leaned down to pick up the banner, then found his horse sagging to one side. As the horse toppled, Kalvan leaped clear, the weight of his armor driving him to his knees. The horse fell on its side, blew blood from his nostrils, and died.

Kalvan waved his sword at the enemy and cursed Alkides' gunners, both emotionally satisfying if not very useful. At least the litter of dead men and horses and around him included more enemies than friends.

Let's hope to Galzar we didn't wing Nestros!

More cavalry were riding up, a second troops of Nestros' Bodyguard. Their captain reined in, shouting a request for orders.

"Look to your King!" Kalvan shouted back. "He's beyond the hedge. If you get no orders from him, advance cautiously five hundred paces."

"As Your Majesty commands," the colonel called. "Will you be here?"

"Here or in Hadron's Realm!" was Kalvan's parting shot. The regiment cheered as their colonel maneuvered his horse through the hedge.

Kalvan mentally crossed his fingers, hoping he had not sent away men he would need for his own protection. But no live enemies were within pistol shot that he could see, and Alkides' guns were now firing steadily. That meant Harmakros and the reserves had to be closer than any organized enemies.

He was safe enough, from his enemies. He wished he could say the same about Rylla's tongue.

When my lovely wife hears that I raced a Trygathi king into the enemy lines, the first thing she'll do is laugh herself silly. The second is remind me never to complain about her leading from in front again as long as I live!

Ranjar Sargos awoke with the sense that a blacksmith was driving a chisel into the side of his head. He stifled a groan and tried to reach the pain.

It was then Sargos discovered his hands were bound.

Outrage gave him a voice he would not have found otherwise. "Is this honor—to treat a warrior like a rebellious slave?"

At least that was what he had intended to say. From the blank looks on the faces around him, he suspected he had croaked like a frog.

A face Sargos remembered thrust itself forward, and the others gave way to either side. It was the last face he had seen before what appeared to be a thunderbolt crashed into the side of his head and flung him from his saddle.

"Ranjar Sargos! Who has bound you?"

"No one, Your Grace," a gray-bearded man said.

"Captain-General Mylissos, he did not bind his own hands!" snarled the man, who must be King Nestros. Nestros drew a fine, if somewhat mud-specked, dagger from his riding boots, knelt, and cut Sargos' bonds with his own hands.

"I trust your honor as I would my own or Great King Kalvan's," Nestros said. "You led your men most valiantly to the end, but the gods' favor was not with you. Yet if you are willing, you may win more in defeat than you could have gained by victory."

It seemed to Sargos that King Nestros was talking in riddles. Beyond him a tall man in fine armor stood, smoking a pipe and nodding slowly.

"Kalvan?" Sargos asked, pointing.

Nestros nodded.

So they have both come to gloat. No, that is not true. Nestros was truly angry with those who dishonored me.

"I have fallen, and doubtless those around me,"

Sargos said. "That does not mean victory for you or defeat for me."

"Your men from here to the redoubt are trapped against the Lydistros River," Nestros said. "The rest are fleeing. We are pursuing them, as wolves pursue rabbits. If you will sit down with us and discuss peace, we shall call off our pursuers and spare your trapped men. Otherwise, the Sastragath and the Sea of Grass alike will be lands of widows and orphans."

If he lies, he does so well. If he is telling the truth . . . But I must see for myself.

Sargos tried to rise. He not only failed, but would have fallen if Nestros and Kalvan both had not aided him.

To take healing from one's enemies is a sign of submission. Yet, if submitting will save those who swore to follow me . . .? Sargos knew from his days as a mercenary and as Warlord of the Great Horde that most casualties came not in battle, but in the headlong flight that followed defeat. Already too many of his people had died between the grindstones of the Black Knights and the two kings.

"Can you summon a healer and a horse? If I see with my own eyes what you have told me, then we shall talk."

The two kings nodded as if their heads were on a single neck.

Kalvan stepped out of the royal tent and nearly stumbled over Aspasthar. The boy woke up with a squeak of panic.

"Your Majesty!"

"Aspasthar, sleeping on watch is still a serious offense. Even after doing so well in your first battle."

"Your Majesty, I beg forgiveness. But my father came by and said he would watch in my place. He—" A rumbling snore interrupted the page.

Kalvan looked into the shadows on the other side of the tent door and saw Captain-General Harmakros curled up under a blanket, even more soundly asleep than his son. Making sure that the armed sentries were all in place, Kalvan ducked back into his tent, burrowed into his piled baggage, and came out with a jug of Ermut's Best.

By the time he came out of the tent, both his unofficial "sentries" were rubbing their eyes and yawning. Harmakros did a double-take upon seeing his Great King. "Your Majesty, it is not the boy's fault. I relieved him of his duty and then fell asleep myself—"

"Don't berate yourself, Harmakros. There are other sentries, some of whom actually have slept within the past quarter moon. Think no more of it. I feel like celebrating, but I didn't want to drink alone."

"What about our friend and ally, Great King Nestros?" Harmakros asked.

"Please," Kalvan said. "Remember when I said it was all over but the shouting? I didn't know what I was saying. A discreet whisper for both Nestros and Sargos is what you would use for drilling a whole regiment! I'd be as deaf as a gunner if we had any more private sessions. But, Dralm be blessed, that was the last one!"

"Then we have an alliance?"

"Signed, sealed, and about to be delivered to Grand Master Soton. Sargos is no fool. The Zarthani Knights are the hereditary enemies of the Sastragathi. He'll fight them rather than anyone else if he has half a chance of victory. We are giving him much more than that."

"And the rest of the nomads?"

"Those sworn to Warlord Ranjar Sargos will follow us. The rest have half a moon to either join us or leave the Great Kingdom of Hos-Rathon. Nestros would like to make it a quarter moon, but he'll swallow this."

"I imagine most men would swallow a lot more, to be a Great King."

"Likely enough." *Being a Great King must be the dream of everyone who doesn't know what a headache it is!* Not to mention aches in other places. Kalvan couldn't recall having been out of the saddle for more than twenty minutes at a time from dawn until dusk. He could recall the fields three-deep in dead men and horses, and worse, those who weren't yet dead. He didn't want to recall them, but they had glued themselves to his memory.

Kalvan uncorked the jug and passed it to Harmakros. As the brandy gurgled, Kalvan added, "Even with what we have in hand now, we'll be leading a hundred thousand men south. That should be a real headache for our friend Soton—and no aspirin for it either!"

"*Aspirin?*"

"An alchemy potion from my homeland. Good for the headaches we'll surely have if we finish this jug."

"I'll gladly take the burden on myself, Your—"

"Hand that jug over, Harmakros, if you don't want to be charged with treason!"

9

"How many men does Kalvan now lead?" Grand Master Soton asked. He knew his voice was as high-pitched as the squeak of a new-hatched quail chick. He did not care. The number he thought he heard could not be what Knight Commander Aristocles had actually said.

"More than a hundred thousand men," Aristocles repeated. He sounded like a messenger bringing news so bad that he hardly cared if he was punished for bringing it.

Any gods worthy of the name know that the news is that bad. There is no fault in Aristocles for being unmanned by it. Forgive me, old friend.

"A hundred thousand," Soton repeated meditatively. "Is that the grand sum, or only those bound by oath to one of the three supreme leaders?"

"The second, Grand Master. The number of those who will march against us without being oathbound is not small. It may exceed twenty-five thousand."

"That is very nearly all the rest of the great horde," Soton said. "Also, if the subjects of"—he could not shape his tongue to Nestros' presumptuous new title —"the Pretender Nestros need not fear the nomads, all their garrisons will march south. Everyone will wish to be in at the death of the Zarthani Knights."

"Then they shall be disappointed, Grand Master. The audience may gather, but the players in the pageant are going to slip out the back door."

"Leaving all their tavern bills unpaid, of course. Are you thinking as I am?"

"What else makes any sense? We face odds of perhaps five to one. Two of those five are civilized soldiers under captains not to be despised, with more guns than have been seen west of the Pyromanes since fireseed was sent by Styphon! Half our strength are light troops or half-trained, or both."

This bald statement of the truth made it neither less nor more endurable. In the end, that did not matter, if one was the Grand Master and sworn to bear any burden in the name of the Order.

Soton mentally ran over his mental army table of organization: fifteen Lances, comprised of nine thousand Order Brethren and two thousand auxiliaries; seven thousand levy, mostly Sastragathi mounted archers and lancers; and three to four thousand unreliable nomad light cavalry—who in a pinch might change sides or run off the field.

To stand and fight the great horde would be suicide. Yet it still seemed to Soton that his own death by Kalvan's hand would be easier to face than the orders he knew he would have to give before this campaign was done. Nor could he hope to find peace by seeking that or any other death.

To do that would be to cast the Order into the hands of Archpriest Roxthar, who in the name of Styphon would surely finish the work of destruction Kalvan had begun.

"We must be across the Lydistros within five days. Organize messengers and escorts to ride with word to Tarr-Ceros. The bridge of boats is to be ready within three days, or I personally will decorate the battlements of Tarr-Ceros with the heads of those who have delayed it."

"At once, Grand Master," Aristocles said. No one hearing him could have imagined this was one friend carrying out the wishes of another. "Ho, Heron! Summon Knight Commander Cyblon to the Grand Master's tent—at once!"

When he had heard the order repeated by his messenger, Aristocles turned back to Soton, hand on his sword hilt. Soton wondered if the tales of wizardry in Aristocles' sword had any truth to them.

Certainly the sword was the better part of two centuries old. By grasping it in times of trouble, Aristocles appeared to soothe himself and sharpen his wits. Also, he had never suffered a sword wound on the battlefield. A half-score of weapons had left scars, but never a sword . . .

"Grand Master, what about sending some of our boats up the Lydistros to strike at Kalvan's barges?"

"With the river running as it must, after this rain? They would never be able to reach Kalvan's fleet and return in time."

Aristocles wished shameful and wasting diseases upon those who had sent the rains, finishing with some choice comments on the uselessness of Styphon's Archpriests and priests in general.

Soton shook his head. "Guard your tongue, for even I cannot save you from Archpriest Roxthar."

"Roxthar—" Aristocles began, in the same tone he would have used to speak of a pile of dung on his tent floor. Then he took a deep breath. "Roxthar serves Styphon with holy zeal. Doubtless he has done all that mortal men could do even with Styphon's favor.

"Yet, I could still wish the rains had not come."

"The gods give with one hand, and take away with the other," Soton replied, glad for the opportunity to change the subject from priestly politics to other less dangerous topics—like war. "The wet ground and flooding will slow pursuit.

"Also, we know the Lydistros River. Kalvan does not. It will take much luck and more boats than he is likely to have just to cross the river. While he is trying to cross, *then* we can attack his fleet."

Conversation died for a while as the messengers rode up to receive their orders. Soton's servants took the opportunity to light the lamps in the tent, sweep the latest coat of dried mud from the floor, and ask the Grand Master what he wished for dinner.

"Kalvan's heart," Soton said sharply. "If you cannot produce that, whatever is ready to hand."

The servants departed; Aristocles poured the last wine from a jug into the two least dirty cups in the tent.

"Another message, I think," Soton said after the first swallow. "To the Commander of Tarr-Ceros, to prepare it in all respects for a siege."

"Holding our whole host?"

"Hardly. We will send within the walls as many as Knight Commander Democles thinks he needs and can feed for a moon or two. The rest will fall back on Tarr-Lydra and Tarr-Tyros.

"Then we can pray that Kalvan will cross the Lydistros. Once his men have dug themselves into the hills around Tarr-Ceros, they will be like bears tethered in a pit. We will be the dogs, free to move where we will and strike when we think wise. Oh, the bear will take a lot to kill, but we will have him in the end."

It was an improbable vision, unless Kalvan lost his wits, but for a moment it warmed Soton more than the wine. Then he sobered.

"We must keep well ahead of Kalvan. That means lightening ourselves as much as possible. All the artillery, all the spare armor, all the horse bardings—"

"That makes Kalvan a free gift, Soton."

"But a lesser gift than the whole Order! Besides, the gold of Balph can buy blacksmiths to make new armor, saddlers to fit our horses, iron and bronze to recast the cannon. It cannot buy good men. If we save the men, nothing else matters. Nothing!"

Aristocles' eyes over the rim of his wine cup made all the answer Soton needed. He lifted his own cup and drank again.

Summer heat had come as the united host moved south toward the Lydistros River. The rain had not stopped completely, but it had diminished. So had the depth of the streams and the mud. While saddling up that morning, Kalvan had received a message from General Alkides, who had ridden ahead to the banks of the Lydistros (what Kalvan had once known as the Ohio) to meet the boats coming downriver from Kyblos.

"The high water has left no shallows and few rapids. It has also left less dry ground than one could wish. However, we may thank the gods for this, too. Prisoners say that the Zarthani Knights have withdrawn most of their river galleys and other vessels to Tarr-Ceros."

Thank the gods indeed. Counting bottoms, the Zarthani Knights had the second-largest navy here-and-now. Few of their ships could navigate beyond the mouths of the Great River, but they didn't need to. The rivers of the Sastragath, the Dellos (Tennessee) and Ellystros (Alabama) systems, were their domain.

Harmakros was less grateful for what he saw as dubious favors. "His Grand Craftiness Soton may just be planning to lure us across the river. Then he can strike with us bogged down before the great fortress of Tarr-Ceros with the river at our backs."

"We'll play that one by ear when we reach the Lydistros," Kalvan said. "Meanwhile, I won't have to answer to the Ulthori and Kyblosi for wrecked boats and drowned subjects."

"Your Majesty, with all due respect," Captain-General Harmakros said, "I suggest we decide beforehand. Right now the Sastragathi see us as a gift from the gods. We give them hope of final vengeance on their ancient foes. If we don't cross the Lydistros and besiege Tarr-Ceros, the alliance may wash away down the river with the snags and dead pigs."

"We shall see," Kalvan remembered replying. Now he wished he'd delayed his mounting-up to question Harmakros more closely. He should have remembered that Harmakros had commanded Sastragathi irregulars in the original Army of Observation, during the Year of the Wolf. The Captain-General knew more about handling them than his Great King, who was so damned tired he forgot to listen to advice even when he had it ready to hand.

Now sheet lightning played along the darkening sparks of light from the mountain of armor and equipment left by the fleeing Knights. There was enough here to equip an army, and that fact hadn't escaped the nomad warriors. They were swarming over the pile like ants on a heap of sugar.

Shouts of anger joined the shouts of triumph. Kalvan recognized Trygathi accents. He signaled to Colonel Kronos, his aide-de-camp. "Take a troop of the Horse Guard and find out what's happening down there!"

Kronos took sixty men, leaving the rest around Kalvan. The Great King dismounted to spare his horse. If the united host didn't end its campaign with everybody walking and half of them barefoot (half of those who'd had shoes to being with, that is), it would be Galzar's miracle.

Harmakros and Aspasthar rode up as the shouts reached a climax, then faded. A messenger breasted the hill, flinging himself out of his saddle as he reached Kalvan.

"Your Majesty. The Sastragathi wish to claim all the Knights' gear, against your orders. They say they're under orders from Warlord Sargos, and you had promised them first choice."

"Dralm-damnit!" Kalvan growled. "First choice" was a fair offer to the unarmored, sometimes unclothed nomads. It wasn't same as "everything," but try to tell that to a Sastragathi warrior! It was like telling a wolf to take only one bite.

Captain-General Harmakros was carefully avoiding looking at his Great King. Then he turned in the saddle, and Kalvan saw his I-told-you-so expression, quickly replaced by surprise. A moment later Kalvan knew he must be matching expressions with Harmakros.

The Warlord rode at the head of a gaggle of his guards and subchiefs. Maybe they thought they were keeping a precise formation, but when Kalvan couldn't tell which was the main body and which were the stragglers—

"Great King Kalvan! Is this the way you keep your promise to the clans? Your men have laid hands on mine, to keep them from their due. A treasure lies down there! Will you have us put it to use, or have a blood-feud with the tribes and clans?"

"I might ask you the same question," Kalvan replied, more patiently than he felt. Not all of the impatience was with Sargos either. "If blood has been shed, it was without my orders or consent. And against my will. Those who shed the blood of tribesmen will be punished (*tough luck, Kronos, but you were sent to find out what the trouble was, not make it worse*) and a blood-price will be paid."

"Will blood money guard the backs of men from the Knights' swords?" someone cried in a high-pitched voice. Kalvan saw that Sargos' teenage son Larkander was riding with his father tonight.

"No," Kalvan answered, raising his voice to keep the argument from turning into a mob scene. There was too much steel and firepower to make this safe; one hothead could blow the alliance sky high.

"No," he repeated, when Kalvan saw the nomads were giving him at least half the attention a Great King deserved. "Yet not all the bare backs are tribesmen. Will not the men of the Trygath fight better against our common foe with armor and weapons from the pile down there?"

"We of the tribes have fought the Black Knights longer," someone said.

"This is well known. Yet if the Zarthani Knights are cast down from their castles and the land cleansed of Styphon's minions, who loses? If they survive to fight us again, who wins? Let us join together and fight as one man."

Kalvan rested his hand on the butt of his pistol. It was a presentation weapon from the Gunsmith's Guild, an unsuccessful effort to prove they could produce elegant weapons quickly. It was a weapon Kalvan carried only when he wasn't riding with the vanguard.

"Let us divide the loot into two piles, one for the clansmen and one for the Trygathi. Then let each chief judge those most in need and give them their pick." This would cost them more than a day's travel time (he could almost hear Soton's chuckle) but if it would keep his so-called allies from each other's throats it would be worth the delay.

"I will begin the first pile with this pistol of mine. Whoever carries it, Trygathi or clansmen, he will carry it with my blessing. So speaks—"

"He seeks our Warlord's life!" somebody shouted. Kalvan's hand completed the drawing of the pistol

before his ears could signal his mind to stop the
motion. Then the sky appeared to fall upon him, a
sky consisting of armored bodies.

Two shots crashed overhead, followed by a scream,
a babble of curses and warcries, and Harmakros roar-
ing above everything, "Take the bastard alive!"

The weight lifted from Kalvan, enough to let him
draw breath for cursing. There was an audible sigh of
relief from his Horse Guard. He spat out mud and
grass, then rose to his knees. A Sastragathi subchief
was lying on his back, with Aspasthar kneeling on
one arm and several hefty Sastragathi warriors holding other portions of the chief's anatomy—none too
gently.

"What the Styphon—?"

Warlord Sargos answered. "This fool thought you
sought my life. He drew a pistol. Your war leader's
son seized his arm so that his shot went wide of you.
It struck my son in the arm. Yet with his other hand
he joined—Aspasthar—in dragging the fool from his
saddle."

"There is more, Father," Larkander said. "Aspasthar
shed blood too in the fight, and it mingled with
mine."

"You are blood-brothers?" Both fathers seemed to
speak at once, then looked at each other. Kalvan
swallowed a laugh; he knew just enough about the
Sastragathi to know that blood-brotherhood was a
deadly serious business among them.

"It is an omen," cried one of the chiefs.

"This seems to be so," Larkander said. His voice
was no longer high-pitched, but he was holding his
arm against his side. His father's face was as white as
if he'd seen a premonition of his own death.

Since nobody else seemed to have the wits to do
so, it fell for Kalvan to call an Uncle Wolf to tend the
wound. The question of dividing the booty dropped
from everyone's mind until both Larkander's arm
and the subchief's were tightly bound.

"Question him rigorously," Sargos ordered. "It must
be known, whether he was only a witling or a tool of
Styphon's House."

Kalvan relaxed. If Sargos was ready to torture one of his own captains to help the alliance, the worst danger of the split was already past. *Note: Have to give Aspasthar something really impressive as a reward—consulting with his father and blood-brother first, of course.*

As the subchief was carried off, Sargos dismounted. He almost stumbled as he touched the ground. Kalvan realized that the Sastragathi Warlord had driven himself to the edge of exhaustion.

"I don't think our dignity will suffer if we sit down and share some wine." Kalvan wanted to wash the grit and grass out from between his teeth. Sargos looked ready to lie down and sleep for a week.

Well, the man's in his forties. He'd probably be just as happy if being Warlord of the Sastragathi was a headquarters job, in a headquarters equipped with cool ale and warm women.

That brought to Kalvan's mind a picture of his own warm woman. He wondered what Rylla was doing. Her last letter had promised to take no drastic action against the Harphaxi unless provoked, but to patrol the borders heavily and keep the Army of Hostigos ready to move swiftly.

Knowing Rylla, Kalvan knew far too well how "border patrols" could be turned into scouts, and they into an invasion. From five hundred miles away, however, he couldn't do much but hope and consider learning how to pray.

10

From the grim look on Knight Commander Aristocles' face, Soton knew he was the bearer of more bad news. The Great Master's first thought was that it was too early in the morning to hear any more.

When he had heard Aristocles out, Soton realized there was no time of the day or night fit for the hearing of such a tale. Kalvan was driving his host on as though he truly had demons at his command to put them in fear. The vanguard was already past Xenos, two whole days before Soton had expected them.

"That means they will be up with us in their full strength before we reach Tryphlon."

Aristocles nodded. "Unless they can be delayed."

"By whom?"

The two men looked at each other. The both knew the answer. The rearmost four Lances would have to stand, fight, and most probably die to the last man—like the three Lances at Cothros Heights.

"Who is senior Commander among of the rear?"

"Drakmos, of the Sixteenth Lance."

"May Kalvan's own demons flay him alive!"

Aristocles looked startled. Soton knew that some of the agony he felt must have showed in his voice. "No, it's just that I am growing weary of sending friends to die."

"We could send another—"

"That would take time, which we do not have. His learning the land where he must stand would take

302

more time. Besides, Drakmos would never abandon the Sixteenth."

You are doomed, old friend. All I can do is let you die with honor, as you have lived.

Soton looked at Aristocles. The hardbitten Knight Commander was a trusty right arm, a fine captain, and more often than not a wise counselor. Yet he had not been among the company of youths to whose ranks had come one day a peasant boy, small of stature but with an ambition to be a knight burning bright enough for six giants.

Some of the boys had bullied Soton in practice bouts, with wooden weapons or unarmed. Others had held back, out of pity for so small an opponent with such a large and clearly foredoomed ambition. Only Drakmos had done neither, giving Soton his best and taking Soton's best in return. Since Drakmos had been the best fighter among the youths, Soton learned more from the bouts with him than from all the others put together. It would not be too much to say that Soton's own prowess on the battlefield, which had saved his life a dozen times over, was in large measure Drakmos' gift.

And now Soton was repaying the gift of life with one of death. An honorable death, to be sure, but there was something to be said for an honorable life.

"Summon a messenger," Soton growled, to hide his urge to scream curses to Kalvan, the gods, and anyone else who had brought this about. Himself included, since it was his plan that Kalvan had turned so neatly and dropped upon his head! "Drakmos is to attack Kalvan's main body and keep on attacking until he has drawn that main body onto himself. We need not fear barbarians or light-cavalry scouts sent on ahead."

It hardly needed saying that the barbarians and scouts in advance of Kalvan's great host would cut off what little chance of retreat Drakmos and his Lances had. To balance the odds, Soton added, "We will leave a thousand of our Auxiliary light horses and all our Sastragathi irregulars."

The Sastragathi would probably all desert before

Kalvan was within a day's ride, but the Auxiliaries would keep Drakmos from being stung to death by the light nomad cavalry. It was the least he could do.

"More orders," Soton snapped. "All the baggage, everything except a man's weapons and what he wears on his back, is to be left for Drakmos."

Aristocles' eyes were eloquent. Soton shrugged. "Drakmos will need what supplies we have left. For the rest of us, it is as true now as when I said it before. Styphon's gold can buy new armor, new tents, new fireseed, before the snow falls. If we lose the seasoned Knights, not all the gold of Balph will be able to rebuild the Order before Kalvan has crushed and cast down Styphon's House on Earth. If we do not think to the future, there will be none."

But there will be a large debt to pay, Kalvan Servant of Demons. A very large debt indeed.

"Toss oars!"

The cry floated up from the boat on the muddy Dellos River, to the hill where Kalvan stood gazing at Tarr-Ceros. The great fortress of the Order of the Zarthani Knights marched across nearly a mile of hills on the far side of the river. Some of those hills had clearly been flattened, others carved into the fortress's outworks. Kalvan counted three concentric layers of trenches and wooden palisades, each furnished with artillery positions and covered ways to let ammunition and reinforcements come up.

The stone walls only began beyond the trenches, rising like seats in a theater up the central hill to the massive keep in the middle. Two, maybe three, concentric circles of walls, each with its own moat and array of towers. Armor and guns glinted from the towers and the walls alike.

In the center the keep rose a good hundred feet above the highest tower. And were Kalvan's eyes playing tricks on him, or was the keep faced with something shiny? Marble? There were marble quarries up near the head of the Tennessee River in his own world; why not here? Certainly water transporta-

tion for the marble wouldn't have given the Knights
any problem, not with their river fleet.

Marble was not the stone Kalvan would have chosen for a fortress. Under artillery fire, it would splin-
ter and the splinters scatter like shell fragments.

But then, Tarr-Ceros had been built when the
Zarthani Knights had no enemies who could bring
artillery against their citadel. Until recently, neither
the tribes nor the Trygathi had much to bring against
Tarr-Ceros except numbers, archery, and a few arquebuses, and the odd wrought-iron four-pounder.

Kalvan signaled to the horseholders, who led
Harmakros' mount and those of his aides down to the
bank. So far the Tarr-Ceros garrison had paid their
visitors less attention than cockroaches. If they changed
their mind, some of the guns in the outer fortifica-
tions could certainly reach across the river.

Harmakros held his horse to a walk as he led his
party up the muddy hillside, then reined in and
saluted his Great King. The Captain-General's face
was grimmer then ever, and far more than could be
blamed on fatigue and the strain of a long campaign.

"Your Majesty, that floating barrier of spiked logs
is no tale. There's no way through to the quay until
the logs are removed."

"How long would that take?"

"With a few tarred barrels of fireseed and no enemy fire, an hour of any night. But they've got
tarpots and what looks like bundles of arrows all laid
out in the trenches right behind the quay. They
could light up the engineers and pick them off like
rats in a kitchen corner. Even if the barrier went,
the trenches would be manned and ready for the
landing party."

"So going for the quay would be a waste, even as a
feint?"

"The Knights would get a good laugh and we
would get a bloody nose," Harmakros said morosely.
He did not put into words what his tone added.
"And there was no need to send anyone up under
the guns of the fortress to learn this. Once Your
Majesty decided it had to be done, it became my

duty. But if I don't have any more such duties for a while, it won't break my heart."

"Harmakros, for at least the hundredth time—well done. If we find ourselves with a vacant Princedom, would you consider taking it?"

"Once Your Majesty doesn't need my services in the field, I won't say no. But I have a bad feeling that it's going to take a long time. We've driven the badger into his lair. Do we have any way of getting him out and taking his hide home?"

Again, tone spoke volumes. "Galzar Wolfshead might knock down those walls with his mace, but nothing we have will even come close. As for a siege, unless you have figured a way out to feed any army on air, forget it."

Harmakros was right. Kalvan had known as much the moment he'd laid eyes on Tarr-Ceros. It reminded him of one of the great Crusader castles in the Holy Land—but an aerial photo of a ruin didn't give the full picture. You had to see one of those stone monsters armed and garrisoned and intact, looming over you, ready to defy the worst you could do. And when that worst wasn't enough to do more than give the garrison a few sleepless weeks . . .

There wasn't a gun in the whole Hostigi artillery that could both be moved here and make an impression on the walls. There wasn't enough food to keep a third of the allied host alive long enough to make the Knights tighten their belts. A simple attempt to storm the place would kill half the attackers and demoralize the rest.

Summon Soton to negotiate? That at least would waste only breath, not blood. Grand Master Soton knew the strength of his walls and the men who manned them. Probably less than half his garrison were seasoned fighters, but behind those walls children with croquet mallets could be deadly foes.

"Well, then, we can't do much at their front door," Kalvan said. "Let's wait until the scouts to the east and south return with their reports. If it's good cavalry country, maybe we can do something at the back door."

That something was likely to be expensive in time, treasure, fireseed, horses, and blood—but it had to be discussed. The rest of the allies had very little notion of what a hollow victory they had won. They only knew that they'd seen the Knights in retreat for the better part of a moon. The final battle against the four Lances of the rearguard had given them a taste for Knights' blood; they wanted more.

Kalvan remembered Napoleon's dictum about the advantages of making war against allies. Soton could wield his Knights as a single weapon, like his famous warhammer. Kalvan had to be chairman of a committee as much as a commander-in-chief.

One would think that the last battle would have made even a Sastragathi chief realize that the Knights' blood didn't come cheap. The four Lances and their allies had numbered perhaps four to five thousand men at the outset; perhaps one hundred and fifty wounded prisoners survived. The allies lost more than eight thousand men, not counting the wounded, and that was with the advantage of artillery.

At least General Alkides had all the horse artillery ready to move. Where cavalry could go, the guns could follow. Something might be made of this—not much, but enough to keep the alliance from falling apart because the Great King of Hos-Hostigos abandoned his allies!

Something else that might help, even more than artillery, at least right now—

"Harmakros, I forgot. Did we save any of that wine we picked up with the first batch of loot?"

"I had one of the barrels drawn off into flasks and loaded on pack mules under a trusted Petty Captain. I reckoned we might have a use for it."

"Another well done. I think we're going to call a Council of War. Just a small one, so I think one barrel should be enough to keep even Sargos happy."

At least until he finds out that he's still going to have the Knights on his borders, almost as strong as ever and out for vengeance.

"Then there is *nothing* more we can do against

those fatherless Knights?" Sargos glared around Kalvan's tent as if ready to challenge any King or captain present to personal combat.

Maybe he was. Kalvan began to think that breaking out the best wine hadn't been the best idea. Sargos had grown increasingly belligerent instead of mellow.

"Not *nothing*," Harmakros said, with the air of a man trying for the twentieth time to persuade a stubborn child to go to bed. "But we can't knock down the walls of Tarr-Ceros or besiege it for long enough to do any good. What else is there is what we need to ask."

Sargos emptied the last of a jug into his cup and looked into the ruddy depths. He seemed to find wisdom or at least a better-guarded tongue there.

"Nothing that will end the Knights for all time, I suppose. But is there anything else worth doing?"

"Yes," Great King Nestros said. Nestros wore a gold circled crown set with turquoise picked up from the Knights' baggage and hastily set into place by an armorer. "Anything that will keep the Knights quiet for a year or two will be almost as good. United, with no enemies at our backs, we're their match. We know it, they know it, and neither of us is going to forget it soon. Let us do something to make them remember it as long as possible."

Several faces around the tent wore, "Yes, but what?" expressions. It was time for the god-sent Great King Kalvan to take a hand. The rest had finally wrangled themselves into being ready to listen.

"Now a lot of what we can do depends on how long we can keep the boats and barges in range of Tarr-Ceros—"

"Oh, demons fly away with those boats and barges!" Sargos growled. "If they won't let us destroy the Knights, what good are they?"

"If we have half a moon, we can destroy the Knights' lands," Kalvan answered. "Alkides, do you think we have that much time?"

The grizzled artillery officer sucked in on his pipe and released a small cloud of smoke. "Your Majesty, with guns mounted in the right places, I suspect we can keep off anything short of all the galleys at once. That's using mostly the Trygathi bombards, which wouldn't be much good in the field anyway."

Sargos looked ready to curse the boats and barges again, but Kalvan fixed him with a sharp look. "War-lord Sargos, those watercraft are like herds or chosen warriors to the Princes of Kyblos and Ulthor. Would one of your chiefs thank you if you lost all his horses or two score of his best warriors?"

Sargos appeared to ponder the question and came up with an answer that at least kept him quiet. Kalvan signaled to Harmakros, who handed him a map of the area around Tarr-Ceros. It was a rough map, but it was a historical document—the first here-and-now map ever drawn on paper. (There was also a second copy, on the more usual, not to say durable, deerskin.)

"The Knights have left a belt of forest around their fortress, between them and the lands that raise their food and horses. They've always relied on the forest to let their light-armed troops delay an enemy while the heavies moved out.

"Now suppose we throw two forces across the river. One is infantry, with light artillery support. They'll hold the forest belt, keeping the Knights *in* instead of enemies *out*. I'll wager half the Treasury of Balph it will take even Soton a while to figure out what to do about that."

"Yes, yes!" Sargos cried. Eagerness crackled in his voice. "Our archers are without peer. Given time to hide themselves, they can hold the forest—"

"Boast about your archers when they've proved themselves!" Nestros snapped. "We of the Trygath are no children with the bow, as you yourself—"

"Hold!" Kalvan shouted. "There will be enough Knights to go around, I am sure. To the archer who takes the most, I will personally give ten Hostigos gold Crowns and a weapon of his choice. Alkides, can you move your four-pounders in that kind of wooded country?"

"With a little help from Galzar and a lot of help from men who aren't afraid to drag a gun—"

The two allied rulers couldn't promise their help fast enough.

"The second force will be cavalry. It isn't intended to stand and fight. It's going to burn out every farm and village, run off every head of livestock, terrorize every peasant it can reach. If the Knights come out, they will have to fight their way through their own forest belt. If they stay in Tarr-Ceros, they will have to watch their peasants, crops, and herds ruined.

"They can get some supplies from upriver, but not all. It will be a lean winter and a lean couple of years for the Knights. Soton will gladly march the Knights out in their breechcloths with clubs if all else fails, but they won't be nearly so formidable."

The picture made the others in the tent smile. Harmakros produced another jug and began to pass it around. When the jug reached Sargos, he held it high in the air. "To the best ally a man could have in this lifetime—Great King Kalvan!"

11

Grand Master Soton of the Order of Zarthani Knights sat in his private audience chamber at the heart of the great fortress of Tarr-Ceros and stared at the stone walls. Too many good men dead, he thought, and four more banners to hang in the Hall of Heroes. During his term as Grand Master he had now hung a total of seven banners, representing seven decommissioned Lances; more than any Grand Master in the past two hundred years. Those seven Lances also accounted for almost a quarter of the Order's strength. . .

Am I destroying the Order to salve my own pride?

No, damnit! I am trying to save the Temple, and part of the Temple is the Order of Zarthani Knights —my part. Kalvan means to destroy the Temple and to do this he must destroy me and the Order. Kalvan is the enemy and must be stopped at any cost!

A gentle knocking at the plank door took his mind off Kalvan and these all too familiar thoughts. "Come in."

Knight Commander Aristocles entered the chamber. "Good news, Soton. Kalvan and his allies are leaving—at last!"

"Ahh. Finally. They must be growing short of rations. Either that, or they have run out of farms and barns to burn."

"True. There will be little produce left to harvest this fall, but we can bring in victuals by boat. The real cost has been time—there we have cost Kalvan dearly. Just as you planned. It is already the middle

311

of summer and by the time Kalvan's tired army marches back to his not-so-grand kingdom, it will be too late in the year to mount a successful attack on Hos-Harphax, or any of our other allies."

Soton paused to strike a flame with his tinderbox and relight his pipe. Suddenly his mood seemed to lift with the fresh smoke rising from his pipe. "Yes, there will be no war this year in Hos-Harphax—our friends there owe us much. I hope they have used this gift of time wisely."

"They have. A messenger from Balph just arrived. Lysandros has used Kalvan's attack on us to persuade the Harphaxi Electors to crown him Great King of Hos-Harphax. Now Captain-General Phidestros will have the full might of a Great Kingdom behind his rebuilding of the Harphaxi Army."

"Good news on an auspicious day. I must go to Balph and take council with the Inner Circle. It is time to make further preparations for the war against the Usurper Kalvan. I will need the Archpriest's help to convince Great King Clietharses to mobilize the Ktemnoi Army for next spring. There are many things to be done and already the summer is half gone.

"Call my oath-brother, we have a trunk to pack. And a debt to settle with Kalvan—on a bill that is long overdue."

WILL *YOU* SURVIVE?

In addition to Dean Ing's powerful science fiction novels—
Systemic Shock, Wild Country, Blood of Eagles and
others—he has written cogently and inventively about the
art of survival. **The Chernobyl Syndrome** is the result of
his research into life after a possible nuclear exchange . . .
because as our civilization gets bigger and better, we
become more and more dependent on its products. What
would *you* do if the machine stops—or blows up?

Some of the topics Dean Ing covers:
* How to *make* a getaway airplane
* Honing your "crisis skills"
* Fleeing the firestorm: escape tactics for city-dwellers
* How to build a homemade fallout meter
* Civil defense, American style
* "Microfarming"—survival in five acres
  And much, much more.

Also by Dean Ing, available through Baen Books:

ANASAZI
Why did the long-vanished Anasazi Indians retreat from
their homes and gardens on the green mesa top to
precarious cliffside cities? Were they afraid of someone—or
some*thing*? "There's no evidence of warfare in the ruins
of their earlier homes . . . but maybe the marauders they
feared didn't wage war in the usual way," says Dean Ing.
Anasazi postulates a race of alien beings who needed
human bodies in order to survive on Earth—a race of
aliens that *still* exists.

FIREFIGHT 2000
How do you integrate armies supplied with bayonets and
ballistic missiles; citizens enjoying Volkswagens and
Ferraris; cities drawing power from windmills and nuclear
powerplants? Ing takes a look at these dichotomies, and
more. This collection of fact and fiction serves as a
metaphor for tomorrow: covering terror and hope, right
guesses and wrong, high tech and thatched cottages.
